THE DRAGON FAVORITE

BEGINNINGS DUOLOGY
BOOK 1

ONIKA HOWDYN

ISBN: 979-8-9918749-0-8

Editor: Erin Larson-Bernett & Anna Moss

Formatting + Section Images: Onika Howdyn

Cover Design: Nox Benedicta

Cartographer: Danny Ride

listen to the playlist on spotify

listen to the EP on YouTube

For every mother.

CONTENT WARNING

This book contains subjects that some readers may find triggering. Please read with caution if you are sensitive to content surrounding the following:

- Symptoms surrounding women's health (including postpartum health, depression, nutritional wellness, and psychosis)
- The trials of motherhood
- Frail marital relationships
- Infidelity & sexual conduct

If you are struggling with or know someone who is, know that you are not alone. There is help out there. Below are a list of supports that could provide the answer:

Postpartum Support Intl
 1-800-944-4774 or text "HELP" to 800-944-4773

National Alliance on Mental Illness
1-800-950-6264 or text 988

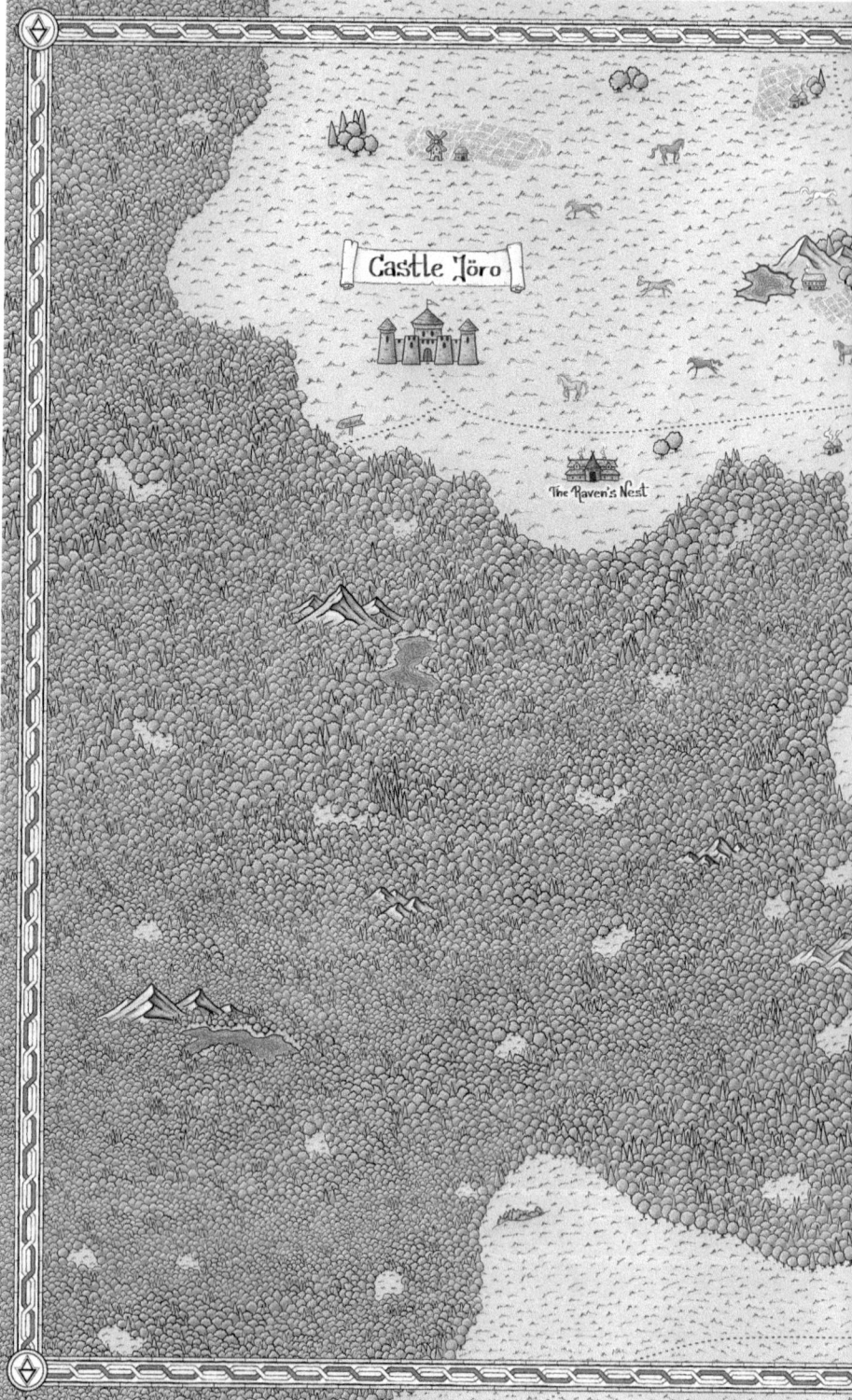

Castle Jöro

The Raven's Nest

2,195 SÓL SETT | THIRD SEASON

SÓLSUN

ONE

"In the beginning there was only fire. At first it was small, a tiny flame adrift amongst the vast darkness of the unknown. It traveled without direction, before time began."
- Excerpt from *Sól; The First Life*

Amalya awoke from her dreams. She looked around, trying to focus on the sound that had stirred her. A small pebble bounced to the floor as she sat up, bringing her to more awareness. Another flew into her room from the small open window beside the bed.

Gathering her blankets, her wheaten locks swayed as she balanced on her tiptoes to venture a peek into the glow of Dag Light. Wesley stood in the still-lingering fog of the night, wearing nothing but his shabby brown trousers and a white undershirt. His dark red hair was unkempt, outlining the maturing stubble along his jawline.

Sól was about to crest the hills of Rau's countryside.

"Wesley?" Amalya rubbed the sleep from her sea-cast eyes. "What in Marin's name are you doing?"

"Come with me!" He gestured, whispering, "I have to show you something."

"At this hour? Surely it can wait."

"No, it cannot."

She studied his eagerness, almost like a child about to receive a present or something sweet for the palate.

"Come. I promise you won't regret it."

She sighed and leaned against the window. "It had better be worth it."

She tied her green apron around her pale nightdress, her once-straight, girlish figure now embellished with supple breasts, curving down to her waist. She never left without dried medicinal herbs, terry cloth wrappings, and her trusty collection of needles and thread. Living on a farm raising livestock as her father did, she could never be too prepared.

Amalya drew a dark cloak around her shoulders. Quickly releasing a ribbon from her apron pocket, she tied her hair loosely over her right shoulder. Slipping on her loafers, she jumped up onto a small night table and climbed out of her window. Wesley reached for her, holding her by the waist as she descended.

"Follow me."

He took her hand and led her through the wet grass and past the barn. Only a few choice sounds could be heard from within. The hogs and ox were surely beginning to stir. Soon they would grow anxious for their morning feed. Wesley did not seem concerned about overlooking his daily chores. He was in quite a hurry, too quick for her liking at this hour. She just wanted to be back in her comfortable bed and lost in her dreams.

They descended a small hill and entered the underlying trees. The land was flat and level here. Fallen leaves lent a crisp scent to the air. Their decaying bodies slid and crunched at their feet, a sign that Nótt Wind was nipping at the heels of Sólsun. Soon the warm days would welcome the arrival of the cold winds to breathe their last goodbyes before the eve of Sól Sett.

Amalya could feel her toes grow colder as her loafers were not fit for traipsing through such terrain. A small stream ran beside them into a larger body of water just below. They moved down into the grove, passing a few fir and birch trees, delving further from the comforts of home.

Wesley was only a hand taller than her, but his legs were strong from working on the farm, matching his eager ambition to lead her to wherever he meant to take her.

Amalya huffed as she tried to keep up with his pace. "If Father finds out we've gone. . . "

"He won't."

"He will kick you out on the spot, I have no doubt. Right onto the road. I hope you know that."

They dipped over a hill decorated with small shrubs and flowers, standing still and glistening with morning dew. He was taking her to Willow's Lake, just as she thought. A large weeping willow hung over the flat water like a mother drowning in her own tears. The small stream that trickled into it kept the water in motion. She had built a small house there as a child, out of branches and mud. It was still there, as far as she could recall, though her excursions to the lake had become fewer and fewer as of late.

Just as they were about to crest the top of the hill to look down into the water below, Amalya slipped on the wet grass. Falling forward, she extended her hands, catching herself on her knees.

"You all right?" Wesley asked as he bent down to help her up.

"I'm fine."

This was turning into quite a morning. If all this was for nothing, she would never let him forget it.

Amalya wiped any sign of dirt and disarray from her damp clothes. "Wesley, if this turns out to be nothing but a silly little joke you've played on me, I will not. . . "

He placed a hand over her mouth, which she pushed away.

"How dare—"

Her eyes traveled down his pointed finger. At that moment, her heart stopped. She could not breathe or move, as if time had entombed her to remain in this very spot for all eternity. Just below them, underneath the willow trees' outstretched branches, lay a dragon.

Its dark, ashen scales shimmered with their own light. Two massive horns protruded from its magnificent head. A fine array of rounded plating ran down its back to its pointed tail. Its wings tucked against its body, limbs drawn, eyes closed as if in a deep slumber. It was the most beautiful thing she had ever seen.

Wesley took her hand as they slowly descended for a closer look. They settled behind two large bustles of pine, both staring at the beast in wonder. The dragon stirred, perhaps aware of their presence, grunting uncomfortably and moving its massive talons closer to the water.

"A Draughtrìnd." Wesley looked quite pleased with himself.

Amalya had not heard them called as such since she was a child. "Dragon" was the name men bestowed upon them during the first gift of fire, when language had yet to blossom and minds wandered in naivety. But they were Draughtrìnd. The gods of man's beginning.

There had not been a dragon sighting in almost ten Sól Setts. So rare they were to venture outside the safety of their mountain dwellings, Amalya could not fathom why this one was left so vulnerable. Perhaps it landed here from somewhere else deep in the kingdom. Or from the mountains just beyond the rolling countryside.

But why? Something was wrong. There had to be.

"A God of Old," she whispered. "Why is he just lying there?"

"Perhaps it is sick."

She leaned forward as the beast shifted closer toward the water's edge. It was struggling. Her eyes traveled up its massive hide. As its leg met the water, a dull redness leaked into the clarity of the pool.

"He's wounded."

Without thinking, Amalya broke away from their hiding place and flocked toward the creature.

Wesley sprang forward to grab her. "Don't!"

The brush of his hand did not stop her, but she did not get very far before the dragon reared its head, weakly but still unwavering. Opening its eyes, it was as if Sól himself lived within its orbs. It bared its sharp, pointed fangs at her, a warning to not approach any further. A low, powerful quake rattled from the beast's stomach, rippling the water, stopping her approach.

She waited, strands of her hair waving against her cheek as its golden eyes bore into her very being. With another cautious step, its angry fangs drew nearer, threatening her life if she dared to take another. She felt its warm, ashy breath consume her entire body. Her instincts screamed for her to run for her life or she would die. It was her good nature that forced her to stay.

"I want to help you." Her voice shook as she spoke.

The dragon only growled, its tail twisting beside it.

"Please," she raised her hands out in front of her, "let me help."

Her stillness continued, and so did the dragon's. It did not move, nor brandish another warning through its fangs. She inched forward again, her hands reaching out as she drew closer to its strength. The beast's eye did not leave her, but it did not show any sign of stopping her.

Amalya took another step and then another. The dragon did nothing but watch, its teeth still bared as its nostrils breathed in the air surrounding her. She kept her eyes on the injured leg until her fingers graced its warm, darkened hide.

Every scale of its flesh only seemed to deepen its magnificence. They were not rough as she had imagined, but smooth as glass. The intensity of the heat escaping from its body was overwhelming, as fierce and blistering as a forest dancing with flame. It was also comforting, like a steaming bath on a Nótt Wind night.

She lowered her body into the water to examine the wound. Her hands ran down the smoothness of the dragon's hide to the inside of the leg. The skin felt more like flesh here, but thick like leather. A large, glistening spear, smooth and pointed, punctured deep into the beast's body. It did not look fresh, judging by how the blood had dried around the swelling. But its positioning must have made it impossible for the dragon to reach if attempting to release it.

She studied the wound, trying to find the best way to extract it. To cut at the dying hide and gently ease the spear out seemed to be the only viable solution. It would take all her strength for her to do this, but she could not let it stay or it would fester and eventually lead to the dragon's death.

"Amalya, don't. . . "

She looked up at the dragon, ignoring Wesley's weak attempt to draw her away. "I will need to cut it out. Do you understand?"

The dragon only grunted as steam leaked from its nostrils.

Amalya raised her hand to where Wesley was watching. "I need help."

Wesley did not move from just atop the hill when she motioned for him to come nearer.

"Give me your knife."

He shook his head. "Are you mad?"

"Please, Wesley." She was desperate to get this done as quickly as possible. Even though the dragon was permitting her to be so close, there was no telling how much longer it would allow.

Wesley took a step back, his arms tight against his sides, mimicking the tension leaking from his soft brown eyes. "It'll kill us."

She extended her hand farther toward him in insistence. "The longer we wait, the more keen it will be to do so."

Holding his breath, Wesley took a hesitant step. The dragon looked at him with fire in its eyes. It pushed its arms forward, extending its neck to its fullest length. A low, effective roar brought Wesley to a standstill, like he had been caught with a pocketful of sweets.

Amalya stood, asserting herself to grab the dragon's attention. "I need his help!"

The dragon stared Wesley down a moment longer before lowering its body again, its eyes still keen and watching. Wesley released a rattled breath, continuing forward before falling in next to Amalya, sweat dripping from his forehead. He fumbled a large knife from his belt and handed it to her.

Amalya grasped his hand, drawing his focus to her. "You have this. I know you do."

Her encouragement at the quality of his character eased his shoulders down from the tips of his ears. Amalya gave him a weak smile before slipping the knife from his hand, taking its edge, and prying it into the dragon's wound.

The dragon's muscles tensed, but it remained still. There was only a little she needed to cut to ease the spear out, but she was unsure if she could do it. Looking up, she motioned for Wesley to join her. "I need you to cut this free."

Taking a deep breath to settle his nerves, he nodded his head. "All right."

They switched positions, Amalya taking a steady hold of the long, cool body of the spear in her hands. On careful knees, Wesley bent down and inserted the tip of the knife on par with the spear's steel. He looked up at her nervously and, without taking another moment to think, pressed the blade through the thick, fleshy skin. The dragon flinched and exuded a grunt of discomfort, but otherwise remained calm.

Wesley was getting through, but not fast enough. Expelling the blade repeatedly only to reinsert it to cut away the infected flesh was only irritating the dragon. Its massive leg began to fight against them, twitching and stirring the water into a frenzy. Lifting its head, smoke emitted from its mouth, encasing its already glistening eyes.

"Calm him down somehow," Wesley breathed to her.

"How?"

"I don't know, but I cannot do this if he doesn't stop moving. He needs to be still!"

Amalya struggled to hold the spear steady. Only one thought came to mind to soothe the creature's anguish. Clearing her throat, she sang.

"The wind, the Nótt Wind,
It carries all in sway.
Into unknown skies,
To lands far away.
Across the seas of green,
Through stretching lands of blue.
It carries through time,
Ever silent, ever new.
Oh, forbidden Nótt Wind,
Cold and dark are my days.
Cast away all my burden,
Or forever I will fade."

The dragon's horned head rested across its body, watching her serenely. The more she sang, the more its eyes seemed to focus on her. They were no longer tormented, but calm, swimming in their brilliant hues of gold and yellow. They haunted her, transfixed, as if in a dream.

"Amalya," Wesley's voice refocused her, "I need you to be ready." The knife sawed a few meager inches more before he pressed the blade firmly against the dragon's skin. "Now!"

With all her strength, she pulled the object free. As quickly as they expelled it, Wesley moved over so she could sew up the wound. She fished through her apron and pulled out her largest needle and thread, passing the end through the eye three times over. With determined effort, she pierced through the newly cut flesh to tie it closed. The skin was thick, but not impenetrable, even for her needle to pass.

Every so often, she took a few dried herbal leaves from her apron and placed them in the folds. She did not know if they would help, but there was no time to find the proper herbs that would. It would at least keep any infection from spreading, giving the skin a chance to close before letting anything else pass through.

She could hear Wesley breathing heavily behind her as she continued to stitch up the beast with intense precision.

"*Hurry,*" Wesley coaxed her.

As she drew the last of the thread through, the dragon stirred. A deep rumble passed through her hands as she broke the string with her teeth. The dragon lifted itself up. They fell backward, Wesley grasping her around the waist as they slid into the shallow water. Moving its head, the beast inhaled where the wound had been, sending ripples pulsing along the lake's surface.

Quick as a hare, Wesley helped Amalya to her feet. "Come on, let's go before he eats us."

They backed away, keeping a watchful gaze as the

dragon shifted its front legs in the water, dragging its long, sharp talons against the rocky lakebed.

At first, it did not seem the Draughtrìnd noticed they were retreating. It shook its massive head as if trying to stay awake. Upon opening its eyes, it turned toward them, stretching its neck to its farthest reach. Both of them remained still. Amalya could feel Wesley's arms tighten around her, slightly shaking with anxious fear. The beast's nostrils flared, pulling in the air surrounding them as if trying to remember every inch of what they were. Amalya's heart was pounding, threatening to burst from her chest—not out of fear, but from pure exhilaration. She had never felt so alive.

The dragon's wings freed themselves from its body, stretching out on either side, their size large enough to block out the slow rise of Sól. Seeing it standing in fullness only made its presence that much more brilliant. Amalya found it hard to breathe beneath the heaviness of her soaked clothes.

The dragon focused on Wesley for mere moments before turning its full attention to her. Drawing in close, its face inches from her frozen body, she did not know what compelled her—maybe a need to discover if this was indeed a dream conjured up from a deep slumber—but she reached out her hand. The dragon remained still as she placed her palm on the crest of its nose. That comforting warmth flooded her fingers yet again. She smiled, seeing her reflection in his golden orbs. A gentle rumble escaped from within this dark God of Old, watching her in a moment that seemed to last an eternity.

It stood firm in all its splendor, wings extending to their fullest reach as it drew away, Amalya's subtle fingers falling from its darkened flesh. With a thrust of its powerful limbs, it lifted into the sky in a torrent of wind. Its wings reached far beyond the span of her vision, coating her and Wesley and all that surrounded them in ominous shadow.

Amalya held her arms over her face as it ascended, the storm it created shaping the air around them with deafening grace. Peeking through the cracks of her fingers, she watched its armored flesh glint in Sól's light like a precious jewel. Its tail wrapped under its powerful frame, bending like a ship's rudder so that it moved like a feather across the sky until it was too high to bear witness to its splendor.

This was a sign; a gift from Marin herself. This Draughtrìnd, though cautious at first, showed no signs of wanting to harm them. It was so trusting, nothing resembling the stories skalds continued to weave of their terrible vex against the kingdom.

"Come on." Wesley grabbed her arm, pulling her out of her rambling mind.

They climbed back up the hill toward home in silence. Sól's light was almost upon them. Amalya could not focus on her surroundings as she tried to hold on to the last few inches of warmth the dragon had gifted her. She hoped to hold the memory of her hand on its flesh for as long as Sól deemed her worthy of life.

They retraced their steps until the house was in sight. With a sudden stop, a warning transpired that she had not thought of before. "We cannot tell anyone."

Wesley turned to look at her. "Of course not—they'd have our heads if they knew what we did." He breathed a relieved sigh, arching his brow playfully. "You are. . . unbelievably brave. And stupid."

14

Amalya cut across his hand with her own, letting the slight brevity release some fear from her mind. "And you were so frightened. I did not think I could pull you from it."

"I did not think you could either. But far more extraordinary things have happened here that not even that dragon's dripping fangs could dissuade me." He held out his hand, his callused fingers extended. "Let's promise right now, this is our secret. Swear it?"

Reaching for him, she entwined her hand with his own. "I swear it."

TWO

"Out of this light arose two magnificent winged creatures. Sól
bestowed upon them his knowledge and his strength. He
gifted Dag as the bearer of light and Nótt with the darkness."
- Excerpt from *Sól; The First Life*

"The Draughtrìnd gave us fire," a little girl said.

"That's right." Amalya smiled, pushing her long blonde hair away from her face. "That was the first gift they gave us. Then the knowledge to grow food, create tools to build. They gave us the gift of language and taught us how to be good. Through all they have given us, we created this vast and majestic kingdom that is Jöro, which they continued to protect for thousands of Sól Setts. The Draughtrìnd are our protectors, our teachers, our gods."

The circle of children surrounded her where she sat on the outskirts of Rau's bustling market. Watching her intently, they caught the light of Sól in their eyes. It was midday, and the dirt-covered streets were packed from the surplus of visitors. Being on the largest river in the kingdom made Rau perfect for trading. Merchants from offshore kingdoms, with their vibrant colors and peculiar wares, sailed from the south of the Safír Sea. Quarried rocks and gems came from the northern city of Jar and sea stones from the western tip of Berge.

Skalds from all walks came and went, weaving tales into song for those who cared to listen. Amalya loved sitting by the fires of the inn, drinking a cup of hot cider as a skald pinched his fingers on his lyre and sang about distant lands, brave heroes, and the might of the Draughtrìnd in the days of old.

So much to learn and see; the perfect place for a girl who fancied herself a storyteller. She did hope to find some of her own stories one day, amongst the magnificent lands of Jöro. To live out her own story was the one thing she longed for above all else.

"The Mad King did not think so," a boy with dark hair exclaimed. "He didn't like the dragons very much."

Amalya shook her head. "No, he did not. He was greedy and wanted more than what the Draughtrìnd would give. He wanted to become a god himself."

Another voice rang from the small group. "Tell us about the Dragon Wars next!" Mouths curled with excitement.

With a smirk of her very own, Amalya leaned closer toward the eager faces of youth. "King Aethelwulf persuaded all the cities of Jöro to aid him in bringing an end to the Draughtrìnd gods. The war waged against man and dragon for nearly a hundred Sól Setts. Many men lost their lives to the deadly power of the Draughtrìnd. The city of Enda burned and fell in the wake of this war, only adding to the ferocity that festered in the king's stomach. The need to conquer the Draughtrìnd grew behind his terrible eyes.

"When Aethelwulf slew the fourth of the first Draughtrìnd, they deemed it necessary to obliterate all mankind once and for all. They staged the final battle in the Southern Plains of Jöro."

"But they didn't destroy us!" another girl with short brown hair voiced joyously.

"If they did, you would not be sitting here, listening to me tell you the tale." Amalya raised her hands to the sky. "Just as the battle had reached its breaking point, and thousands of men lay dead in its wake, Sól broke free from the harrowing darkness above to shine down on the one who would save them.

"Lady Marin stepped out onto the battlefield. Her words spread over the land like swift running water, extinguishing the fires of war that brewed in the bellies of both man and dragon. But one man did not heed Lady Marin's words."

Amalya moved her hands forward, clenching her fingers into fists and sharpening her voice. "Aethelwulf sought to end all chances of peace and drove his blade through Lady Marin, swiftly ending her life. Dag and Nótt ascended from the skies to deliver her to our creator, into the warm fires of their embrace. Seeing a chance to end that which sparked this terrible war, General Earfinn cut down his king, ending the tyranny once and for all. The land then became good for both man and Draughtrìnd to live in peace. Together."

"Have you ever seen a dragon, Amalya?" a small redhaired girl asked.

Amalya's lips tightened. She wanted nothing more than to share her encounter with the Draughtrìnd by the lake, just ten days before. The vision of its splendor had infiltrated her dreams every night since. But she dared not breathe a word of it. Not even to one so young, whose mind still flowed with wonder and the magic of childhood.

"I have not," Amalya finally answered, leaning down on her lap to bring herself closer to the girl. "But I dream of them."

"My father said they are monsters," a boy exclaimed. "Corrupted by their own power!"

A tall, rather thin waif of a girl stood up, her light dress wrinkled against her chest. "My father's in the Dragon Guard. He killed a dragon already!"

"You're lying!" Another boy stood up in protest. "No one's seen a dragon in forever!"

"He did too!" the waif shouted. "He brought me home a tooth, see!" She then presented a rather large, pointed object from around her neck.

"That's not a tooth!"

"Is so!"

"Is not!"

"Is so!"

"Children!" Amalya raised her voice to silence the bickering. "You must remember, if it weren't for the Draughtrìnd, we would not have become what we are today. They protected us for thousands of Sól Setts. We should honor them, not belittle and slander them."

"Amalya is right," the first little girl proclaimed, holding her hands close together in uncertainty.

"Stop being a girl!"

"I am a girl!"

"That's enough now!" Horace, a large, burly man with

graying hair, approached them. He waved his arms about for the children to scatter. "That's enough fer that. Go back to yer homes!"

Their little voices arose in cautious protest. "One more story!"

"My father is right." Amalya smiled at them. "Your parents will worry. I will return in a few days for another adventure." She stood up and placed a hand on her heart before extending her palm to face them. "Marin bless you and keep you all."

The children stood and gestured in the same fashion as they dispersed. Some gave her a hug before disappearing into the streets in search of their families. The little red-haired girl approached her, pulling at Amalya's cotton dress for her to bend down to her.

"I dream of dragons too, Miss Amalya," she whispered.

Amalya smiled and brought her closer. "Keep dreaming of them. And maybe one day, you will see one for yourself."

The girl hid her smile in her little hands before scurrying away through the streets of Rau to her home.

Horace stepped in next to Amalya, looking a bit disappointed. "You shouldn't be fillin' their young minds with Draughtrìnd sympathy."

"They are children, Father. Did it sound like they agreed with me?"

"One did—that's all ya need ta be made suspect."

"You worry too much." She rested a hand on his shoulder. "I can take care of myself."

"That's what I'm worried about." He scratched his head. "Come on then, Wesley'll be waitin' for us."

They walked through the marketplace together. Stalls

sat against brown-slated homes, their curtains tied to resting posts on either side. People slowly shuffled by, moving from station to station. Many greeted them warmly, saying their goodbyes until they would return. Amalya enjoyed their trips to Rau's marketplace. The city was always bustling with interesting people from all over the kingdom.

The life of a farmer was rather mundane. One day she would find her adventure, but for now, she had to help her father. It was not always easy after her mother died, but they made do. Today, their farm was very successful, producing the most sought-after hogs in the east. Her father was very proud of its success, but he was a man who doted on simple pleasures. And Amalya wanted her life to be anything but simple.

A high-pitched voice rang out from the crowd. "Amalya!"

Long, slender arms wrapped around her simple dress before she had the chance to face who had called for her.

"Mira!" Amalya exclaimed, returning the warm greeting.

Mira's bright hazel eyes illuminated her soft, amber skin. Her dark hair sat atop her head, loose strands dangling against the low-cut back of her crimson dress. "I'm getting married!"

"Married! Marin's blessing, that's wonderful, Mira!"

"Oy, congratulations, m'dear," Horace added with a smile. "Who's the lucky man?"

"Laird, Blacksmith Lorrigan's apprentice."

"A fine man, indeed." Horace nodded his head. "He will make a good husband."

"Laird?" Amalya raised a brow. "What happened to Baldir, the guardsman?"

"Oh, he was a brute of a man! Such a mouth on him, but Laird. . . " Mira crossed her hands over her chest. "So kind and gentle, even with those leathered hands of his."

"Come now, Mira." Amalya shook her head with a smile. "I thought you were waiting for your knight to come and sweep you off your feet."

"Oh, that's childish! I have to stop dreaming if I want to have a family before I become old and enfeebled." Mira looked at Horace, who seemed more bemused than offended by her words. "I mean no offense to you, of course."

With a hearty chuckle, Horace ran his hand down his rough beard. "Ya always could give me a good laugh there, Mira."

"Well, I am glad to have never abandoned that skill of mine."

Horace took a deep breath and patted Amalya on the shoulder. "We better get a move on if we're ta make it home before Sól Sleep." He gestured warmly to Mira. "Good day to ya now, Mira."

"You as well, Mr. Horace. You'll both come to the wedding." Mira looked back to Amalya. "I will not take no for an answer."

"Of course we'll come."

"Good!" Mira gave Amalya another enthusiastic hug before slipping away giddily. "Say hello to Wesley for me!"

Following the trail of Mira's dress into the crowd, Amalya glimpsed a reflective gleam from the corner of her eye. She turned swiftly, her heart forgetting to beat in her chest for the briefest of moments. The familiar flash of gold fell into her vision, only for her to find a man holding a shimmering gem by its chain, hoping to entice a curious buyer.

Despite its origins, it stirred the same tingling feeling of warmth that she felt when she touched the ashen scales of the dragon.

The image of the beast's powerful yet comforting orbs stayed with her as she continued toward the gates of the city with her father. Nearing the passage, two guards stood ready at their posts. Copper-plated armor, with the body of the river Vandermarchen winding across its face, sparkled in the waning light of Sól. The guards' eyes did not stir as Amalya and her father walked past them, remaining alert to any potential threats that may linger just before Nótt coated the sky with her ominous wings.

Wesley's muddied red hair came into view, looking up from an ox-drawn cart as they approached. He was an orphan when her father first brought him home, a wandering boy Horace had picked up off the streets of the capital. Despite his past, he was a hard worker and proved himself a capable farmhand.

"That Wesley," Horace leaned in toward her, "I reckon he's sweet on you."

Amalya scoffed. "Even if he was, and even if I cared to notice, you would never let me marry a farmhand."

"Who says I wouldn't? He works hard. I think it would be a nice reward fer all the Setts he's been with us."

"A reward?" Amalya objected, tossing her hair back over her shoulder. "I am not a trinket to be given away to whomever you please!" She shoved him away with a smile. "Besides, I have no interest in marrying Wesley."

"Yer waitin' for yer hero, come to sweep you off yer feet and carry ya into Sól light." Horace shook his head. "Yer just like yer mother, rest her soul. Always dreamin'."

Before the other day, she would have believed him, but she had seen a dream. To not only witness a true Draughtrìnd God of Old, let alone grace her fingers against its flesh, was more than a dream. It was life; something forever locked away in the confines of her memory, which she could remember and relish in the brief moments they had shared. She could feel her face glow just from the thought of the dragon's heated wind caressing her face. "It's not a dream."

Horace grunted. "Best focus on what's real."

They reached the cart. Wesley extended his hand to help Amalya up to the rein bench.

"Get to the back, boy!" Horace shouted, his nostrils flaring.

Jolting his hand back, the corners of Wesley's lips curled into his lightly speckled cheeks. "Why can't I ride up here?"

"I need someone ta ride with them hogs. You work fer me, not the other way 'round. Now get back there!"

Wesley rolled his eyes and hopped in the back with the pigs. Amalya smirked at her father as he climbed up to his post, pulling her up with him.

"What?"

She shook her head as her father took the reins and ushered the ox forward through the gate and onward, away from the city and into the dotted countryside surrounding it, the sky painted a beautiful silky rose as the light crept beneath the plains.

The land was flat and rolling as they traveled north. To the west across the Vandermarchen River lay the Southern Plains of Jöro. And to the east, the long line of the East Eldur Mountains rested against the sky like a faded memory. A land with so many possibilities. That was the beauty of it;

the reason Amalya could stare out into its endlessness day after day. Maybe one day they would build more farms, or perhaps a castle or dark fortress ruled by exiled witches. Maybe the land would open up for a river to flow and trees to grow along its edge. There was nothing it could not hold. It was all left to the mysteries of fate.

The tall grass swayed in the tickling breeze. It rippled across the land like water, traveling down the straightened road. They passed by another farm from time to time. The countryside of Rau was the most prosperous farmland in all of Jöro. Most of the kingdom's food was grown here, just a few days' ride from the capital.

Amalya found her dragon again, painted in the distance through her eyes. Memories placed its dark shadow swiftly flowing from one mountain crest to the next, the wind wrapping around its body as its large, elegant wings carried it through the sky.

She reached into her belt pouch and pulled out a small leather-bound book. It fell open against her pale blue dress to a long-wilted flower and a half-blank page. Taking a piece of charcoal from her pouch, she scratched lines on the page.

Horace leaned against the edge of the cart as he noticed her. "What are ya doin'?"

"I have an idea for a story."

"Humph," Horace scoffed. "The day I find the skald that taught ya to read an' write, I'll kick them crooked teeth in."

"What's wrong with me learning how to read and write? If I hope to be a skald one day—"

"No woman's ever been a skald."

"Maybe not here, but I am sure women skalds are fruitful in other parts of the kingdom."

25

With a dull, crooked eye, Horace snorted to himself. "Well, then, why don't ya write somethin' real, like our journey to trade in the city and back?"

"Because it would bore the children to tears, myself included."

"Well, stop writin' them silly little tales. They'll do ya no good."

"I'll stop when no one wishes to hear them. Until then, I will write."

"I like your stories," Wesley interjected, leaning his arms on the wood behind their seats.

"No one asked you!" Horace grunted.

With a swift flick, Amalya hit her father across the arm with her book. "Stop badgering him!" She turned to Wesley. "Thank you, Wesley; and you know he does not mean what he says. He just enjoys yelling at someone."

"If I took his criticism to heart, I would have left on the first day I started working for him."

Muffled laughter escaped them, causing Horace to squint with distaste. "Best keep yer comments to yerself, boy."

"You are quite irritable today," Amalya said. "A nice cup of tea by the fire will do you good."

Horace shifted in his seat, grunting as his hand moved to his back in agonizing support. "I still got them hogs to unload."

"Nonsense. I am more than capable of assisting Wesley in doing that. You just head straight inside the moment we reach home." Horace looked ready to protest, but Amalya lifted her hand in insistence. "I will not take no for an answer."

"She's more like your mother than your daughter, isn't she?" Wesley said with a smile. Horace shot a threatening glare at him, which caused Wesley to recoil. "I'll keep quiet now."

Wesley sat back down against the snorting sows. Amalya shook her head at her little put-together family. They were small and loved to bicker, but they were all she had.

THEY SOON REACHED THE FARM, nestled just below the rolling hills that stretched toward the eastern stretch of the Eldur Mountains. It was quite a large piece of land her father inherited. It had been in their family for generations, passed on from father to son. Amalya would be the first daughter to inherit it from her father, which was probably why he was so keen on her marrying Wesley. It was difficult to trust strangers, and Wesley was already a part of the family. It would be an uncomfortable transition for him, but Amalya did not intend to be comfortable here for the rest of her life.

They rode up to the barn, where the ox drew to a halt. Amalya slid down from the cart, taking the reins from her father's hand. Jumping down from the back, Wesley soon joined her. She unhooked the ox from the cart as Wesley drew the barn doors open. Her horse, Bard, rested sleepily inside his stall, and a black barn cat whisked its tail in the air just above them in the rafters.

Slipping the bit from the ox's mouth, Amalya fashioned a rope to the wooden collar of his neck to lead him to his stall. The ox followed her calmly, nudging her into his hay-laden home. She hung the reins on the wall as her father approached.

"Now make sure them stalls are locked tight," Horace said. "Boris fancies himself a thief and looks to pilfer through the feed when no one's lookin'."

"I will. Now get inside and start that fire. We can handle this ourselves."

With a grunt and a scowl to hide his smile, Horace lumbered from the barn toward the house. Both Amalya and Wesley unloaded the hogs into their pen. Wesley lowered the cart ramp with a stick in hand as Amalya laid a gentle hand on one hog.

"Is that really necessary?" she asked him, nodding to the stick.

"You try chasing an irritable hog down without it."

He dropped the gate, and the livestock made their way down the ramp one by one. They seemed as relieved to be home as she was. After a long day of being carted around the city for trade, a nice quiet night in their pen seemed like a welcome comfort, even for them. Wesley slowly led them on and they filed into the pen with little fuss.

Amalya fell in behind them, closing the gate behind her. They drew out straw to refresh the bedding and refilled the empty troughs with fresh water. The hogs agreeably ate whatever slop remained, muddying their snouts in leftovers before settling down comfortably in their straw beds. Amalya watched as they nuzzled comfortably and shut their eyes for the night.

"I wonder," she mused aloud. "If they know what their purpose is, would they be happy with this life?"

"All living things have a purpose." Wesley looked on with her at the now-sleeping pen. "Do you pity them?"

"No. How could I pity them? They are so content and I know when death takes them, they will not suffer needlessly. Truly, who could ask for a better life?"

They exited the pen together, quietly leaving the barn to rest. Wesley shut the doors and slid a heavy piece of wood across them to secure the barn.

"I envy them," Amalya continued. "I wish I could be as content as they are."

"What life would you have?" Wesley asked. "One filled with adventure and danger? To see the unseen and do things you never thought you ever would?"

She smiled. "You know me too well, Wesley. I do not find that fitting for a boy in your position."

"So you think chopping wood is not adventurous enough?" A knowing smirk drew charm into his face. "Or digging an irrigation trench for the corn? Or perhaps breaking a gelding only to have it kick you to the dirt?"

Amalya shook her head, unable to hide her amusement. "My father does keep you on your toes."

"I believe your father is still trying to break me, as it were. The work is harder, yes, but I do not see it as mundane." He squinted one eye as they walked to the house together, keeping a comfortable distance apart. "More like a new mountain to climb or tree to rip free from the root. He longs for me to give in, but I myself refuse to fail. As long as it doesn't kill me, that is."

"I do not think he would go so far."

"Oh, I wouldn't be surprised if one day he did." He leaned toward her. "If only to prove his assumptions of me."

Amalya shook her head as Wesley drew back to walk beside her. She found her eyes wandering to the diminishing colors of the sky. Sól's dim form was already breaking up the light cast upon the day. She could feel Wesley looking at her but took no notice, or at least tried not to.

"Was the dragon not enough adventure for you? You wish for me to show you more?" Wesley glanced at her.

She turned to meet his hopeful gaze. He wasn't a knight in shining armor by any means, but he had a good heart. His bravery shone through at the water's edge that day, right alongside her as they faced her dragon together. Despite his hesitation, there was kindness in how he tended to the dragon—care for a creature deemed unworthy of anything but malice and scrutiny.

But she thought him too comfortable with the life of a farmer. He had purpose in his work, and she saw how much it satisfied him to be useful. To be needed.

"I think you are too comfortable as you are to want in any adventure."

"There is more I wish for. I will bring you before a hundred dragons if I must. If that is what it takes for you to believe me."

"Until that day comes, farm boy."

They reached the house. It was small but comfortable. A few windows lay shuttered closed against the darkened wood of its face. A stone-laid chimney stood erect toward the front of the weathered red door, plumes of smoke escaping into the night sky. Flowers just about to bloom lined the sides, leading up to a small, roped line attached to two posts for the linen to dry in the sun.

The gentle lick of flickering light escaped from under the

door. Horace would never allow Wesley inside unless instructed to. He would retreat to his small little room in the barn shed and be happy with it. Wesley opened the door for her.

Stepping in, Amalya saw her father sitting comfortably by the fire, taking a long drag on his rustic pipe. The house was filled with the harsh scent of weed and burning wood. He looked up at them. "Yer not comin' in here, are ya?"

"I wouldn't think of it, sir." Wesley turned to Amalya and offered her a gracious bow. "Sleep well, Amalya. Until our next adventure." He turned into the house once more. "Good night, sir!"

"I expect ya to be up befer I am tomorrow to get that field ready! Ya better be halfway done by the time I get to it!"

"Of course, sir!" Wesley smiled jovially and left Amalya at the door.

Amalya watched him briefly, admiring his stature. For an orphan-turned-farm boy, he was never far from her thoughts. He had a charming way about him that always left a smile on her face. That, and he could handle her brashness, as well as her father's. Not many could tolerate such a trait.

She closed the door behind her, locking the latch and breathing in the home's fiery scent. "You are despicable." Her words gave way to a slight smile.

"Does that mean no tea, then?"

A sly turn of Horace's mouth sent her straight to the kitchen.

"It's a good thing you're my father."

THREE

"Dag and Nótt were good to the land. Through the wisdom and power granted to them by Sól, they began to breathe into the soil, giving life to all."
- Excerpt from *Sól; The First Life*

The candlelight flickered in the quiet of the barn. The air was crisper now that the leaves were beginning to fall from the branches of the trees. Soon, Nótt Wind would carry the snow on her back and blanket the land in a sea of white. It was Amalya's favorite time of the Sól Setts—still warm enough to not rely on heavy cloaks and boots, but just enough chill that a warm cup of tea made all the difference to one's comfort.

She lay on her belly in the loft, hay scattered across the wood as she let the sleeping light of Sól creep through the crack in the door. A heavily knit wool blanket kept the cold off her skin. She leaned on her elbows, hovering over a cloth-bound book she had acquired on their last visit to Rau.

Amalya turned the page gingerly, taking the words into her mind. The season of Sólsun was nearly over. It had been many a day since she first laid eyes on her dragon, the memory of it leaving her wanting to hold all there was to know about them.

"The magic created by Marin and the White Dragon was passed on during the peace that followed King Aethelwulf's demise. Known as Skuldabréf, it was a rite granted to the lords of the Draughtrind, allowing them to court and, if accepted by the courtess, bond with a woman.

"Dragon lords would disguise themselves as men, though their features were highly distinguishable and not easily hidden. A village that a Draughtrind lord had frequented was said to be blessed by Marin herself and, if a partner was found, granted great favor."

Amalya turned the page, drawing her candle closer as she continued reading.

"A woman could not be taken against her will. Only if they consented to the union would they leave their homes and live out their days with their chosen lord, bestowing upon them the title of Mother of the Draughtrind. *From this rite came the first of the* Draudkin, *born from this chosen union.*

"The Draudkin acted as the keepers of the kingdom, protecting the peace Marin had given her life for."

The wood of the ladder behind her creaked, causing Amalya to turn abruptly onto her side as she stared into the sleeping sounds of the barn. A tuft of dark red hair eased her nerves as Wesley climbed up to the loft. He was loosely dressed in a pair of trousers and a pale work shirt, a candle balanced carefully in his hands.

"You're lucky I didn't wake your father," he said as he approached her. "I thought you might have been a squatter."

Amalya turned back around and closed the book softly, keeping a strand of hay between the pages she had not yet finished. Wesley glanced over her shoulder as she shielded the book with her arm.

"What have you got there?"

"It's nothing." Amalya whipped her braided hair across her shoulders, giving Wesley a hard glare.

Not fooled by her attempt to thwart him, Wesley presented that boyish smile of his before slipping his hand underneath her arm, grabbing the book, and relinquishing it from its hiding place.

Amalya reached to grab it from him, but to no avail. "Wesley."

Wesley looked the book over, fumbling it around in his hands as it fell open to the front page. "Where in Marin's name did you get this?"

With a huff, she sat up on her knees, crossing her arms across her nightdress in distaste. "I. . . borrowed it from the apothecary. Whilst Father was making a delivery."

"Borrowed." There was that smile again that was beginning to shift the beating of her heart. "I get the feeling that term is used loosely."

Tightening her lip, Amalya stood and hurried over to him, taking the book without protest.

Wesley dropped his hands to his sides as she moved from him. "You can get into a lot of trouble for that."

"You needn't worry. I'll return it." She sat back on the floor, returning to the last page she had read.

Wesley moved in beside her, settling his hands on his

knees. The warmth of his exhale sent tingles across her skin, momentarily shifting her focus.

She glanced at him. "Are you not the least bit curious to learn all that there is to know about them? Why did the dragon not end us at first sight if they are as terrible as King Ulfrick claims them to be?"

Wesley leaned back ever so slightly. "Attacking our cities and villages after over a hundred Setts of peace is all the reason the king needs to want to rid them from these lands. And using the Draudkin to enact their will goes against everything Marin had done to usher peace between us." He gestured toward the book. "I don't need a book to tell me that."

"But they have not done so in many Setts," Amalya said, "yet they hide away in their mountain fortresses. Watching their kind flee like moths seeking the sleeping light of Sól."

Her attention returned to the book, unable to discover the answer to questions one would never dare ask. "Why do they no longer protect the witches who still call them their gods? Why have they abandoned everything?"

Wesley shrugged. "Perhaps they have given up. Or—" Amalya looked to him once more, "perhaps they are planning to retaliate somehow. They waited many Setts to enact violence on the king during the Dragon Wars." He moved to the book, softly pressing against Amalya's fingers to hide its contents. "Whatever the reason, it is not something we need to concern ourselves with."

Amalya let him linger on her hands for a moment before she tucked the book against her chest.

"You are making me regret my decisions," Wesley said, drawing her attention again.

Amalya pushed him gingerly on the arm, allowing a brief smirk to pass across her lips before she stood. "If I found out you discovered a dragon and did not inform me about it, you would be far worse off than this."

She walked over to the loft doors, easing them open to let the sleeping light of Sól flood her entire being. Clouds rolled quickly across their resting form, which hung like a jewel over the peaks of the East Eldur Mountains.

"Seeing him. . . the magnificence of a dragon. . . " She turned as Wesley came to join her. "Does it not give you hope?"

"What hope are you speaking of?"

"That perhaps there are still songs left to be sung of man and Draughtrìnd. Songs of peace."

Wesley smiled, looking to the sky. "Songs you wish to sing for yourself, I imagine." He moved closer to her, his arm pressing gently against hers. "Perhaps you will pen them on our own adventures. One day."

Amalya glanced at him, finding the cotton threads of his shirt against her bare skin somewhat comforting. "You entertain yourself with what you think me to be."

"And what is that?"

"A foolish girl with foolish dreams."

Amalya leaned against the frame of the door as Wesley did the same across from her. She could not help but enjoy their little games, as if toying with each other was just a form of flattery. He could not match the grandness of her dragon, but he was slowly becoming more than just a farm boy in her sea-cast eyes. Perhaps she was afraid of what would happen if she continued to indulge him. But there was a yearning as well—though she would never admit it, if only to keep him at arm's length for a little while longer.

Wesley placed his hands in his trouser pockets and turned to face the light once more. It caressed him like a kiss, falling over his charming smile and adding brightness to his eyes. "If that were true, then I too would be foolish," he came away from the frame, taking a few slow steps across the wood and coming to rest before her, "for feeding those dreams and wishing you would make me a part of them."

They remained there, never moving to be taken from the other's sight. Amalya could feel the rosying of her cheeks despite the chill that still hung in the air. With a careful step, she placed a hand on the buttons of his shirt, grasping it firmly in her fingers.

"We best return, farm boy. Before my father discovers I am gone and draws unfavorable conclusions as to why we are up here."

"Unfavorable?" He turned as Amalya drew them both away from the door, toward the ladder leading down into the barn. "What sort of unfavorable things could a foolish girl and an equally foolish farm boy possibly get up to?"

She let him go as she reached the ladder. "Things unfavorable enough for him to dismiss you from this farm for good."

"Oh, well then I better not." He watched her descent, bending down onto his knees to follow her. "For being away from you is a punishment I never wish to endure."

FOUR

"Keep sacred the gifts I have given you. Care and nurture this land as I have cared and nurtured you. Do as I wish and the fire will always burn within you."
                                    - Excerpt from *Sól; The First Life*

I t was fitting for the passing of one season to conclude with such joyous festivities. The evening danced on in the lights of the flickering firelight. Mira looked stunning in her lace white dress, pale flowers dotting her flowing dark hair like the stars during Sól Sleep. Her eyes beamed with love and elation in the arms of Laird, her strong and gentle husband. His bearded face would not break from the smile that was painted across his rich russet skin. He looked at her as if she was all there was and all there ever would be.

Amalya sat quietly toward the edge of the elation. Guests scattered everywhere in the grass. Small round tables and wooden benches created an oval pattern, surrounding the dancers as musicians played their pipes, strings, and other instruments to help move the patrons' feet. Most of the food had already come away, with only a few pies and pastries left for guests to pick at in between dances.

Adjusting her soft green dress, Amalya pulled small strands of curled hair away from her sea-gray eyes as she watched her friends bask in the joy of their union. Wesley slid in beside her. He cleaned up well, wearing a dark lavender tunic and earth-toned trousers. His hair was combed to one side, truly bringing out the freckles beneath his soft brown eyes.

"Taking a rest?" he asked her as she turned to look at him.

"You know I dislike dancing." She smiled, looking back at the happy newlyweds as the music wound down to finish its song. "They look so happy."

"They do," Wesley muttered. "Very much so."

Bows and curtsies ended the dance and a few couples removed themselves from the cool grass to partake in refreshments. Mira and Laird strode over to them, arm in arm, each possessing an airiness Amalya could not help but match.

Standing up, Amalya hugged her friend joyfully. "You are stunning tonight, Mira."

"There's something in the air; do you not feel it as I do?" Mira practically fell into Amalya's arms with a swoon.

A light smile graced Amalya's lips, followed by a sullen thought that she did not wish to bear, but had the urge to deliver. "I know your mother and father would have loved to see you so happy."

Mira slid from Amalya's grasp. "Yes," she said, "perhaps one of the few times they would have been."

Amalya squeezed her friend's bare shoulders. "Forgive

me. I was hopeful it would have brought some comfort to you."

Mira caressed her cheek. "Good intentions are never unappreciated, dear. Despite the shadows cast by memories."

Wesley stood to join them, extending his hand to Laird, who took it graciously. "You are a lucky man, Laird."

"Luck has nothing to do with it." Laird smiled and looked at Amalya. "Though I cannot bear to see a lovely lady sitting quietly as the rest of us enjoy this night." He extended his hand to her. "It would compliment me if you joined me in a dance, Amalya."

With an upturned grin, Amalya raised a brow to the groom. "Compliment you more than your lovely Mira? Surely you have done well for yourself already."

"You cannot talk yourself out of this one," Mira laughed as she grabbed Wesley by the arm, "and neither can you. Now come on, both of you!"

Mira dragged Wesley into the oval as the minstrels tickled their instruments, the chords weaving another song. Finding an adequate space, Laird placed a hand on Amalya's waist, lacing his fingers through hers as the music flowed into the night air. Amalya rested her palm on his upper back, feeling the softness of his dress coat beneath her fingertips. Laird was quite a stunning specimen of a man. Strength could be felt in the muscles that lined his back. His deep black hair shone even in Sól Sleep, complimenting his dark complexion. His smile was the grandest she had ever seen, stretching across his entire face, framed perfectly by his well-groomed beard.

He led her in time with the other dancers. Amalya kept herself fluid, letting her feet move with his.

"For someone who claims they cannot dance, you are doing rather well," Laird said with a smile.

"You give me too much admiration where none is due."

They twirled and spun across the field in unison with the others. Amalya glanced to where Mira and Wesley were also partaking in equal steps, the elation prominent through the whites of their teeth.

"Something is different about you, Amalya," Laird spoke. "You seem less yourself tonight."

"I do not know what you mean."

She was herself, and yet nothing of who she was before experiencing the dragon at the bloom of Sólsun. It had haunted her dreams almost every night since, its golden orbs completely consuming her in a comforting blanket of understanding and love. Most days, she touched everything she could place her hands on, trying to replicate the feel of its skin against her fingertips. But nothing could compare to how much the Draughtrìnd had possessed her.

"You know," Laird continued, "Wesley and I have been friends since the orphanage. The past does not define us."

"I never said it did." Amalya smiled. "You have both become honorable men. I am glad you have found a purpose in your work and your life."

"He's found purpose as well."

"As a farmer, yes."

"There is more to purpose than what you can shape with one's hands." Laird smiled as he led them into a full circle. "He has found purpose in you."

She shook her head. "I do not care for the life he is destined for."

"Destiny is not set in stone. Like the iron of a sword, it is shaped through discipline."

The music wavered as a slow breath on the verge of extinguishing. Amalya studied Laird's light brown glance as their feet steadied themselves. "We must not let others shape what we become."

"No," he replied, "but it is far more enjoyable to share in the creation of it with someone beside you."

As the melody wilted into the air, they fell from each other with gracious appreciation.

"You always were one to keep me on my toes." He bowed to her. "Thank you for the dance, my lady Amalya."

She could not help but smile as she curtsied. "It was my pleasure, good sir."

Mira and Wesley joined them before Amalya could fully rise from her curtsy. Grabbing Laird's arm, Mira smiled into his hopeful face. "You're mine yet again. Care for another dance?"

"It is impossible to deny you." Laird looked to Amalya and Wesley. "Will you have another as well?"

"I think not," Wesley said. "One is enough for me."

"Suit yourself." Mira tugged on Laird's sleeve. "Don't keep me waiting, my love."

Amalya and Wesley made their way from the sounds of music and dancing. As they passed a table full of crisp pastries that filled the air with tempting sweetness, Wesley unexpectedly took her hand. "Will you walk with me?"

Looking at him, she searched his hopeful eyes for a reason to deny him, but there was nothing keeping her from his presence. She enjoyed Wesley's company, perhaps more than she would confess. "Of course."

They strode into the night without straying too far from the firelight of the celebration. The wide stretch of the East Eldur Mountains sat quietly against the sky like shadows in the dark.

Amalya let her fingers drift from Wesley's hand, taking a few hesitant steps toward the mountains as her slippered feet graced the crease of the hill. "Do you think it was from there?" She pointed outward.

"The dragon?" Wesley came next to her. "It's possible. Dragons have not been seen this far south in many Setts."

"That does not mean they are not there." She looked at him. "We have seen proof of that."

"I have a feeling you wish to find more proof."

She hid her eyes from him, looking down at her hands momentarily. "And what of your dreams, Wesley?"

"My dreams? I'm surprised you care to know what my dreams are."

She looked up, seeing that he could not keep his smile from her. "You jest—or am I really that unaware of my selfishness?"

A chortle passed between them. Wesley drew his hands to rest on his hips, leaning into their innocent banter as Amalya moved to collect herself.

"But I am curious, if you trust me to know."

He breathed a hearty sigh before casting his gaze to the mountains left sleeping in the blanket of Nótt's tail. "I have no memory of my mother. Only that she died when I was a child. Growing up in the home for lost children wasn't really a home. Though I knew nothing better at the time."

His attention shifted down to the bed of grass at their feet. "But I did envy the ones I saw walking the capital, other children hand in hand with their mothers and fathers. A circle unbroken. Probably taking for granted what they had without awareness of how rare it was."

The warm hue of his eyes met hers, a wave kissing the shore. "For as long as I can remember, I've only dreamed of having one thing." He paused for a moment. "A family."

Amalya's heart ached, for such a simple dream seemed so attainable to someone as privileged as she had been. Though to a boy who lost everything before he was even given the chance to feel such unbreakable love, it was as precious as her dragon.

"I know I berate you for what you are, but. . . " she inched a step closer to him, "I could not fathom a life without my father. I'm certain I would feel the same about my mother, were she still alive."

She came to rest beside him, a soft gesture bringing their hands together between them. "I am sorry for the misfortune that befell you. No child deserves such a sentence. To be as you were, without anyone to give you love."

He smiled weakly as he pressed his thumb into her palm. "You're lucky your father did not give up on you as mine did. And me, he did not have to take me in. He could have left me on the road, begging for a coin to spit shine his muddied boots." He looked to the lines that tethered them. "It took tremendous courage. I'll be forever grateful to him."

Ripples disturbed the clear depths of her essence as they remained together. Amalya could sense the stir that had shifted her that night in the barn. Tonight it seemed clearer, as if there was nothing left to keep her from stepping into the depths of what he would offer her.

Though she did not want to, she began to slip away. Wesley did not keep her, letting her fingers slide down the tips of his own.

"So, when you finally have your dream," she ceased her retreat, "what then?"

Wesley ran his hands over the sleeves of his tunic before letting them fall to his sides. "I haven't given it much thought. I do not think anything would dissuade me from accomplishing more, as long as I had hold of it. I would treasure it and keep it close to my heart 'til Sól beckoned me to the skies."

She smiled. "I do believe you would be the most doting and loving husband."

"Perhaps you will see for yourself." A hopeful glint reflected in her sea-cast eyes as he murmured, "One day."

Amalya served her attention to the curve of her slippered feet. A warmth spread over her cheeks that she wished to keep from him. For if he knew that her heart had begun to patter when he spoke of such things, she would be trapped by it for all time.

A breeze carried the time between them until she had the courage to face him again. When she did look up, Wesley had moved closer to her. That maturing face, the cut of his dark red hair, even the faded marks that lived beneath his eyes were all the more compelling each time he came into view.

She pushed a stray hair from his forehead, tucking it back in the smooth comb of his reddish crown. "I do like you,

Wesley." She spoke boldly. "But we do not want the same things."

He took her hand, holding it to his chest like a precious gift. "I would follow you across the Safír Sea. Past the Eldur Mountains into the Sea of Sands, if that is where your life called you to be." He reached for her and touched her rounded cheeks, letting her fall into the warmth of his palm.

"I do not know if I believe you, farm boy."

He smirked. "I say I will abandon our home to chart a course into unknown lands and expectations, and you say you do not believe me?"

"Actions do speak more than words."

His brow arched into his forehead. "You think me to be a simple man doting on simple pleasures."

"It is all you have shown me to aspire for."

A peal of joviality escaped the slight spacing between his lips. "You are trying to fool me, for I know far better than anyone how much you observe and allow wonder to possess you. But perhaps I must think more like you. Perhaps a promise will persuade you."

"A promise." She let a breath slip through her parted lips. "You have given me so many in the past."

"Childish promises." Charm leaked from the corners of his widespread lips as he tempted her. "None compare to this."

Amalya felt herself become trapped in the lure of his possession. She had been caught in it before, perhaps for only the briefest of moments. But curiosity as to the promise he wished to give her loosened the need to deny him.

"You do enjoy this little game of ours, don't you?"

His fingers pressed firmly behind her ear as he drew himself toward her. "It is a game we've been playing for far too long without victory."

Amalya did not break or push him away. Her eyes closed as she allowed him to draw her lips to his own, tasting the sweetness of his affections. It was gentle and yet sent her senses tingling just as they did when she laid her palm on the Draughtrìnd's thick, scaled flesh. Perhaps it was love, true and pure. Love for an orphan farm boy whose dreams of happiness lay bare in her sea-cast eyes.

As he drew away from her, Amalya reached for his tunic, balling it up in her palm to keep him close to her. "You wish to cast a spell over me?"

He shook his head. "'Tis you who have cast a spell on me."

"You are accusing me of witchcraft?"

His smile made her heart flutter. "If you were a witch, I would let no one take you from me."

She fought to keep the smile from spreading across her face, but soon surrendered to it gladly. Pulling him to her, Amalya kissed Wesley again, letting her hands remain pressed against his chest, his heart beating beneath her fingers. His arms came around her, holding her to him as his succulent lips moved to her cheek before coming to rest against her neck.

Amalya nuzzled into him, drawing her eyes to crest over his shoulder's horizon. In the distance, she watched the ghostly mountains stand tall and ominous over the rolling landscapes beyond. The smoked scent of her dark Draughtrìnd's fire reached her nostrils as if drawn from memory.

She wondered if it saw her there, standing in the embrace of another, one whom she could come to love as much as the dragon.

2,200 SÓL SETT | SECOND SEASON

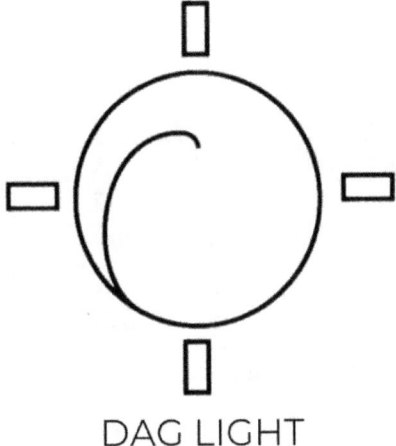

DAG LIGHT

FIVE

*"Sorrow washed over the panic brought forth by a thousand
fleeing souls as they flooded toward the plains. Each step
taken raised a hammer to her heart, now scarred by rage and
hatred."*

\- Excerpt from *The Tale of Marin and the White Dragon*

"**P**ush, Amalya, you must push!"

It had been many an hour since she last saw
Wesley and Elra, being resigned to a room with
midwives and housemaids as they hurried around her with
wet cloths and water to quell the strain running down her
face.

Leaning back on the sweat-ridden pillow of the bed,
Amalya stared up at the bare wooden ceiling above her. This
was too much; much worse than bringing Elra into the light.

"Do not rest!" the midwife urged. "You must push!"

Another constricting pull caused her to bear down,
driving her chin into her chest. Bated breath leaked through

her teeth like a whistling teapot as the pressure grew almost unbearable. Drawing back, she collapsed onto the bed.

"Marin, help me," she begged aloud. "Let this be the last of it!"

Another constricting pressure in her loins forced her to push. Unable to hold her breath, she screamed as the child passed from her into the arms of the midwife.

Immediate cries broke out as they wiped down and cleansed the child against her skin. Amalya was too weak to look up, feeling the wriggling form against her deflated stomach.

She heard the midwife speak. "You have a son."

A son. It is what Wesley had asked Sól to deliver to them, and so they had listened. A gift from the creator himself.

Smiling softly, Amalya looked up as they brought the tiny babe to her. She was ready to love him, ready to feel that instant bond that every mother felt—what she had with Elra when she was the one wriggling in Amalya's arms at her first drawn breath.

Her fingers touched his skin, still wet from the comforts of her womb. Her son looked at her with dark, confused eyes, holding her there, unable to move. The midwife laid another cloth down upon him, wrapping him up to hold in the warmth of his body, though his discomfort seemed prominent in his cries. Amalya brought him to her arms and watched him, unblinking.

"He is beautiful," the midwife said. "I will inform Wesley."

As she left the room, the sounds of those remaining became muffled and undefined. Amalya's vision began to blur.

He was beautiful, perfect in every way. A child for whom any mother would swell with overwhelming joy. But she felt no elation. She felt nothing. Only staleness and a deep, sullen agony, like a stone wet and heavy sinking into her bones, straining against the beating of her heart.

The crying continued, shutting out all her ability to think. She could no longer feel him in her arms; only the sounds of his desperate longing for love seemed to cave in her mind. It grew louder, causing tremendous strain behind her pulsing ears.

Fear festered from the panic that surged into her gut. Her eyes clamped shut, the darkness bringing no comfort. The crying suffocated her, crushing her body down into the cold stiffness of the bed until it eradicated all possibilities of love.

AMALYA'S EYELIDS fluttered to let in the dull light streaming through the window. Dust hung motionless in its wake as quiet tears fell down her face into the dampness of the pale sheets beneath her. She lay paralyzed in the bed, shutting out the stifling cries of a child resting in a small cradle on the floor.

"Amalya," a faint voice called.

She did nothing. She did not want to get up. Not today or any other day that came after. Nothing ceased the need to retreat and be left to drown in the darkness for all time. Why had it never grown tired of tormenting her? Why had it become so enamored with watching her sink deeper into the tragedy of her own mind? She never believed something so cruel could exist, but it had found her and crawled into her womb as all the joy that remained of her escaped to lay in her arms.

Footsteps approached and the door to the room creaked open. Wesley looked around, his eyes falling upon his son crying and kicking at his blanket.

"How long has he been crying?" He bent down and picked the babe up. "Amalya—"

"I don't know," she whispered.

Wesley held their son to calm him, cradling him against his chest. "Elra's already made herself breakfast. You have to get up now."

His words only knocked at the heavy iron doors of her mind. Amalya closed her eyes again, trying to listen to only the silence.

"Arthur needs to eat. He needs you." Wesley walked out of the room with the baby in his arms.

As his cries dwindled, peace found her again. It was these rare moments of peace she treasured the most. She took a deep breath, knowing she would have to leave the safety of her resting place. Her legs carefully breached the blankets to fall over the edge of the bed. She attempted to push herself up, but either her arms were weaker or her body heavier. Sitting on the edge, she looked at the dust still clinging to the light. The room was as simple and charming as she remembered from her youth, only now she haunted it.

"Amalya!" Wesley called again.

She turned her head, looking toward the floor. "I'm awake!"

Standing, Amalya pulled her hair back from her face, not even bothering to brush it. Her hand reached frantically toward the light, feeling a small twinge of warmth from Sól's rays. If she could still feel it, she was not hopeless.

Quickly, she sifted through her large standing armoire and took out a dull brown dress, pulling it over her nightgown so she would at least be presentable. It would be another busy day on the farm. So much had to be done. The days never seemed long enough anymore.

She stepped out into the kitchen. Elra, who had dressed herself in a small flowery dress and mismatched stockings, a ribbon adorning her dark hair, beamed at the sight of her.

"Good morning, Mama!" She smiled happily as she ran to Amalya, wrapping her arms around her legs.

Amalya managed a weak smile and touched her daughter's head as Elra pointed to the small table sitting just beyond the washbasin. "I made you breakfast!"

A bowl full of messy oatmeal was left waiting for her next to a steaming cup of tea. Some blueberries adorned the top and spilled over the side of the bowl. "That looks delicious. You must be an exceptional cook."

"It was easy." Elra's little hands pulled at her mother's dress. "Eat!"

Memories of who she was were the only things Amalya could draw strength from to hide herself from her daughter, though they were fading, becoming unrecognizable as each day bled into the next. "I need to feed your brother first."

Wesley brought Arthur to her and gently placed him in her arms. Amalya reluctantly took a seat by the empty fireplace, positioning Arthur at her chest as he latched on to her breast, taking in the delicious milk she carried.

Elra leaned over the arm of the chair and watched. "Did you feed me like that too?"

"I did, which is why you're so big and strong."

"Arthur will be big and strong, just like me!"

"One day, perhaps." Amalya could feel herself drifting away. There were moments when she just couldn't catch herself anymore. She stared at the desolate fireplace, so cold and lifeless.

"Mama?"

That little voice pulled her back for the moment, and she adjusted her focus onto her charming daughter. "Are you helping Papa today?"

"Yep! He said I could, right, Papa?"

Wesley walked over to them, scratching his beard as he knelt to face Elra's wondrous gaze. "We better get a move on, then. Get on your boots."

With a nod, Elra raced away toward the door. To be young and so carefree—how Amalya missed it so.

Wesley looked at her. "Your father's coming today."

"Did you ask him to?"

"He insisted." He placed a comforting hand on her shoulder and stroked her back. "Are you all right?"

"I'm trying to be."

"Come outside when you're ready. And please eat." He leaned over and kissed her cheek. "You look beautiful."

With a scoff, Amalya shook her head. "You jest. I know how I look and it is anything but beautiful."

"How could you possibly know what I see?"

She had become useless as far as helping him with the farm. The farm she never wanted. It was the beginning of her descent into this dark abyss, though she remained blissfully blind to it until she pushed the last of her happiness out into the world.

"Come on, Papa! I'm ready!" Elra pulled at his pant leg, eager to go outside and help.

"All right then."

Wesley stood and father and daughter made for the door. Amalya watched them go, leaving her alone with her thoughts. Despite Arthur's calm suckling, she welcomed the silence. She lay back in the chair and closed her eyes. The only time she ever felt alive was in solitude.

Between the realms of consciousness and dreams, the vision was waiting for her. Eyes still ablaze inside her mind, that golden hue only matched by Sól himself. She wrote about her dragon countless times and dreamed in countless ways. It was her only escape, proof that she had been able to live once upon a time.

Arthur stirred at her breast, having had his fill. Amalya lifted him over her shoulder to pat his back. A few hearty burps escaped him and she drew him away to wipe his mouth. "All finished then?"

He gurgled and cooed, his round, scrunched face bubbling with an innocent grin. Such a little thing, so pure. Arthur was all the joy she had left, given to her to hold on to for a little while but never to truly possess.

Reaching next to the chair, she gathered up a thick, brown blanket and tied it around her chest. She placed Arthur in the safe folds of the sling and pulled him to her shoulders. He rested comfortably, his little head poking out to observe the world. Taking a deep breath, she pushed herself up toward the door. Just before opening it, she looked back at the table. Her oatmeal was untouched.

Though her stomach did not yearn for food, she gathered it in her hand before stepping out the door into the new day.

It was warm despite the dullness presented by clouds overhead. They hung like tufts of cotton in the sky, suffocating the breath of Dag's first light. Amalya looked out from the house. Wesley and Elra were in the fields, pulling healthy ears of corn from their stalks. They seemed happy, Elra especially.

Amalya walked to the barn and stopped just outside the hog pen. Holding the bowl out over the fence, she poured the contents of her breakfast into the feeding trough. The hogs made quick work of it, not leaving a single scrap uneaten. Perhaps it was cruel of her, but it would have been worse if she just left it untouched. At least now Elra would believe she enjoyed it.

SIX

"If the Draughtrind hope to rule over man, they can no longer
be privy to the secrets of this world. Once I slay one of the
final four and partake in his blood, all will be known to me."
- King Aethelwulf letters, 1,802 Sól Sett, First Season,
Rókkur

Horace arrived late in the day to help around the
farm. Amalya greeted him as warmly as she
could, but there had been a secret in his weathered eyes that followed her whenever he looked at his
only daughter. He went to the fields to help Wesley and Elra
with the crop. Simple things he could manage, but not for
very long. He was here more often than not since Arthur was
born just last Sett. They were always grateful for the help he
could give, but it still was not enough.

Amalya kept to herself, if only to avoid having to be

pitied, taking the morning to finish the laundry. She hung the freshly washed clothes from the line while Arthur slept in a small basket nearby.

The day continued to loom over her like a terrible predator. It was taking everything she had to not give up on her responsibilities. Lifting the clothes to the line felt like rolling boulders up a steep hill. Her fingers rubbed against the wooden pins as she secured each article in place. She had been out here the entire morning and yet it felt as if she had only started. The pile in her basket never seemed to lessen, and the line seemed longer and longer with each pin she put into place.

Arthur stirred. She looked over at him reluctantly and, with a deep, sorrowful sigh, bent down to pick him up. He squirmed in her arms, looking rather disgruntled, his dark eyes folding into his round cheeks. Amalya tucked him in the crook of her arm for closeness as she turned back to the laundry.

Through the gently wafting blankets, she noticed movement crossing along the road past the farm. Pulling the clothes aside to get a better look, she saw a small caravan of merchants moving south toward Rau. This was not odd. Plenty of travelers used the road to get from the capital to the river city.

However, she felt drawn to one particular man walking behind the final cart, for reasons unknown to her. A large cask was strapped to his back, yet he walked as if nothing hindered him. He looked out of place amongst this party. Despite his common garb, he appeared cleaner and well-kept, as if he had never worked a day in his life. His hair was long and dark, left to flow down his shoulders. Some strands hung loosely over his face, concealing his true self.

As he walked past the path leading up the hill to the farm, he stopped. He turned with the smoothest motion. Through his curtain of coal-swept hair, his eyes fell on her. He was so far and yet felt so close. His stare was fixating, haunting almost. The air tangled like a ball of cotton stuck in Amalya's throat. She held Arthur closer to her as the caravan moved on without him, his eyes still trained on her.

The details of his person remained out of focus, but his skin was copper-toned, glinting as if from the very metal it portrayed. Dread began to fester and claw at her insides. Though it would have shattered any other, it sent her heart into a frenzy. Exhilaration was lost to her and yet here it was, locked in this man's mysterious attention.

"Amalya?" Wesley touched her arm. "Are you all right?"

"I. . . " She turned abruptly, but when she returned her attention to the caravan, it was fading down the road. The man was gone, the cask he was carrying peeking out from behind one of the carts as if he had never stopped to admire her.

"What is it?" Wesley followed her gaze toward the road.

"Nothing." She managed a smile before turning away.

Wesley lingered longer to watch the party fade from view. He moved over to her as she tucked Arthur in his sling. "We should finish up in a few hours. We'll head into Rau tomorrow with what we can sell."

Visiting Rau had become such a strain as of late. Before Arthur, they would make for the city often, but with Amalya offering little help, it had become strenuous for Wesley to recover on his own. Customers were not always keen to travel for their promised wares, and passing traders wanted payment if they were asked to transport for them, something they did not have to spare. It was too much to do for just one man. And Wesley's incredulous need to be ever-present in case something happened made it even more difficult.

"I would like to stay here."

He shook his head. "I cannot leave you alone. Not after the last time."

She sighed and looked away. "I'm. . . more myself now."

Reluctance cast a shadow over him. As much hope as he carried for her to be well, there was also a layer of truth he could not ignore. The first season had not been kind to them. It was the season of her descent from who she was before becoming a mother for the second time. The season fitting the name of Rókkur, cast in snow and blistering cold before the bloom. Only now the ground was forever frozen, even in Sòl's warming embrace.

"No, you're not."

Amalya closed her eyes as the memory surfaced, permanently staining her mind.

Kneeling by the fire, Amalya could not hear Arthur crying as she held him just above the licking tongues of death. Sweat dripped from her forehead—or perhaps tears. There was no time to comprehend nor control the shaking in her bones. No sound could match the sullen clamoring of her heart as it suffocated her ears and attacked her entire being.
It would be so easy to drop him, let him burn. She would no longer have to suffer his stifling neediness. Perhaps as his flesh peeled away, his essence would come back to her. She would

obtain the joy he had selfishly stolen as she cared for and nour-
ished him in her womb.
Her fingers twitched at the thought tempting her to release her
infant child. The fire itself seemed to beckon her to do what
she must to escape the turbulence of her own mind. It wanted
to grant her relief from this insufferable pit she had been cast
into, where no light could touch and nothing was given.

Amalya's eyes glazed over in shame as she looked away from her husband. She could not deny her ineptitude. How could he trust her to be alone ever again?

"You think I want to be like this?" How could he understand her plight, when he had never been where she was now? He had never been lost to the light.

"Of course not," he sighed, stepping closer to rub her arms before resting his hands on her shoulders. "A trip into the city will do you good. You haven't been there in a while. Maybe it will help."

"I don't know."

"Elra can stay with me. Besides, there are some who are eager to see you both." Amalya recognized his attempt to comfort her into obeying his request. "They ask about you."

"They shouldn't."

"But they do, because they care."

She didn't want to talk about this anymore. A chance to avoid the constant conversation around her state of being only worsened the pain she harbored from it. Amalya tried to smile, observing the remnants of hard labor across Wesley's eager face. "You must be famished."

"We all are."

Horace lumbered up to them with Elra in tow. She was

covered in dirt, her dress speckled with brown spots. A few strands of green sinew from the corn stuck out of her long brown hair. She would need to be washed tonight if they were to go into the city. Just one more thing she would have to perform against her will.

Wesley drew away from Amalya, reluctance and disappointment deepening the light pattern that hung from his eyes. "Come on, you." He guided Elra to the side of the house. "Let's get you washed up."

Amalya watched them hurry away together. Elra adored her father, as she should. He was filling Amalya's role as much as his own. How they would be much better off if she just disappeared. Wesley, the doting father that he was, playing in the fields with Elra. Maybe he'd find another wife. Someone who would love Arthur like a proper mother should. Equally as lovely but with an essence uncorrupted. Pure and colorless.

"Don't forget about 'em."

She looked up at her father's words. His eyes were grave, deepening the cracks of his face.

"Don't let it take ya."

Shaking her head, she gathered up the basket in which Arthur had been resting. "I do not wish to speak on this."

Horace approached her. "Yer stronger—stronger than even yer mother was."

Amalya stopped in her haste, her back trained toward Horace's plea as he spoke of her mother.

"I wasn't strong. I could have helped her, but I wasn't strong enough."

Glancing over her shoulder, Amalya watched as he attempted to keep the glisten of sadness from escaping his eyes. The secret still lingered there, only now it had shifted slightly from behind the door. To siphon through her memories was no simple task, especially when it came to the tragedy of her mother's demise.

"Mother died in childbirth," she said rather bluntly. "What could you have done?"

Fear gripped her as she saw him catch words he did not wish to fall from his mouth, replacing them with assured haste. "You got Elra an' Arthur. I never thought Wesley would amount to anythin', but he's a far better man than me."

"What are you saying?" She could hear Elra's frantic feet thumping through the grass toward them from the house.

Horace clenched his lips tight against his weathered gray beard. "I haven't been honest. . . about yer mother. I know this—this terrible magic that's takin' hold of ya."

She narrowed her eyes. How cruel for him to think he knew anything of what she needlessly suffered day after day. Men always claimed to understand a woman's strife, but they were not the bearers of life. Becoming a father was a privilege that cost them nothing but a few moments of pleasure. No seasons of discomfort or restless nights. No endless pain that drained the very wells of one's essence. There was nothing that could be taken from them other than their lives. And that seemed far more reasonable than the days she was left to wake in this.

"You cannot know."

"I do." He reached for her desperately, then caught himself, as if trying to keep the true meaning of his words from revealing themselves.

"No." Her voice grew heavy. "You do not."

"Mama!" Elra grasped onto the curtain of her dress. "Come!" She looked at Amalya expectantly.

Touching the top of Elra's head, Amalya kept her eyes locked on her father, his confession settling over her like oil on water. He had lied, and he did not warn her. As much as she wanted to know the secret still lingering in his words, it would have to wait.

SEVEN

"The Draughtrind were not seeking to exterminate man or they would have done so, swiftly and without hesitation. They were merely playing with us. Entertained by the trick man had played on himself."
- Excerpt from *The Tale of Marin and the White Dragon*

Amalya sat at the candlelit table in her room as the stranger lingered in her mind like a blur buried in the darkness. The charcoal scratched along the blank parchment, filling the space with her lines. It had been so long since she had written anything, but she could not erase the image of the dark-haired man from her mind.

He did not seem real, despite the simplicity of it. He was just a man who looked at her whilst traveling down a road walked by many. Writing it down somehow convinced her of something. Perhaps a small something that did not really matter to anyone but her. Despair or fear? It could not be fear. Fear had abandoned her long ago. This had pried her eyes open. Whatever it was, it wanted her to see, not remain hanging like a half-broken branch waiting to fall.

Footsteps sounded softly as Wesley's shadow slanted across her. "You're writing again."

Her attention did not stray from the page. "Only a little."

He sat on the bed, glancing at Arthur silently slumbering beside him. Though he remained quiet, the knowledge of him being there distracted her. She could tell there was something on his mind.

Placing her instrument atop the pages, she turned in her chair to face him. "What do you wish to tell me?"

He breathed a sigh. "We need help on the farm."

"I know that."

"Your father is appreciated but I need more than what he can willingly give."

Amalya wiped a stray hair from her cheek. "We cannot afford it."

"We have little choice. If we don't want the farm to fail." He ran a steady hand through his beard. "We'll just have to make do."

His confession deepened the chasm that kept her split in two. "I am sorry," she breathed, "I cannot do more."

Wesley looked at her, his eyes spilling truth without words. She didn't need him to pretend anymore. That she was not broken. That she would heal as time continued to drag on through the murk. But she knew he would never say it, for he did not wish for her to carry the burden of guilt on her shoulders.

"You have nothing to apologize for."

She slammed her fist on the desk and stood. "I am tired of being pitied. I caused all of this. It's all over your face, my father's face. . . riddled in your words and your sorrow-filled glances! Stop pretending it is not because you think it will hurt me if I hear you say it."

He stood to join her, taking her fragile arms into his callus-worked hands, pulling against her stoic form. "I don't know what to do, Amalya. I have no direction. I am. . . as lost as you claim to be."

She sank down in her chair. "We are both lost."

His hand folded into hers as he came with her on bended knee. Gripping his fingers, she wished she could feel strength or strain, but there was nothing.

"We aren't meant for this. You promised me this would never happen to us."

"We will not be lost forever. We will find a way." His gentle touch caressed her face. "Were we not happy before all this? Happy with our lives and the path we had chosen? To start a family before we set off on our adventures across the kingdom?"

Amalya dragged her gaze to meet the empty hopefulness plaguing his eyes. They were happy then. She could not deny that they were anything less. The flame of their promise burning strong in the heart of their home as if nothing could silence it. How naive she had been in thinking nothing could break the spirit of that promise.

"We were happy," she said as he kissed her on the forehead.

Not even the lips she once relished could pull her from the depths. Unwelcome resentment now burned in the ashes of that promise. It had mattered little to her after they were married and Elra was born. Her life was full then. Now, it was so empty, even though she was not physically alone. The only chance to dream of anything other than her confinement was remembering what could have been. What had been taken from her without protest.

IN THE EARLY MORNING, they arrived at the city. Amalya stepped off the cart into the crowd, Rau already flowing with city-goers and tradesmen from Jöro and beyond the Safír Sea. Arthur was already resting in his sling across her back, sleeping soundly. It was early yet, but many of the merchants and traders were already up and about to set up shop for the day's customers.

The city was just as she remembered it. Streets lined with dark, sanded carts and clamoring voices. The wood of the stalls stuffed with the wares laid bare to purchase. Some stalls were accompanied by homesteads, lines of brownstone buildings with clay roofs bleached from the creator's light. Mixed aromas of cured meats, decadent steaming pies, and intoxicating perfumes either burned the tips of noses or hypnotized them.

Nothing had changed in the last few seasons of her absence. Many of the same faces, doing the same things each day. It left a stale taste in her mouth now more than ever before. Once, she had looked forward to this—the energy, the friendly conversations and warm embraces. Now it seemed so mundane. The same meticulous wheel with no indication of amending how fast it spun.

Wesley dismounted, lifting Elra to the ground. They did not have their own shop in the city; instead, they sold their crop and livestock to established merchants. Wesley would make the rounds to each one before the market grew too busy. The merchants would sell most of their wares, and whatever was left they could sell themselves. In the past, they had come to the city twice a week to sell and trade. Now they were lucky if they made one trip.

Taking a deep breath, Amalya could feel herself wanting to hide as Wesley approached her.

"We'll make a few stops before heading to your father's."

"I think I'd like to go it alone."

His brow furrowed at the notion of her alone in this lively place. "I don't think. . . I do not wish to bar you, Amalya, but—"

"Whether you are with me or not, I am barred." She could see her words pierce through his eye like a thread. Perhaps she was being too honest, but honesty was all she had left to offer. The only thing that did not breathe the stale stench of deceit.

Amalya swallowed, pressing her hands to the wall of her stomach. "I am sorry," she swallowed, "perhaps it is best if we stay together. For a little while."

Wesley folded his lips together, shifting his jaw to lessen his discomfort at her words. "I am doing my best." He took hold of the bridle of their ox and pushed forward. "I expect nothing from you but a little understanding."

He nudged the ox onward, Elra close beside him. Amalya watched as they began to disappear into the crowd, bodies flowing around them before swallowing them whole.

She could remain where she was. A blur in a sea of faces. Perhaps she would become as lost as she felt. But she did not let herself remain, her duties as a wife and mother forcing her feet to follow. She could not pretend to be vacant here.

Not here when so many eyes were waiting for a chance to pry into others' lives despite them having no significance on their own.

Even though she was amongst so many, she remained isolated. It was the closeness that wore on her as she pushed through the masses carefully. Her focus remained on her steps, counting them steadily in her mind as her skin began to lose all sense of feeling, tingling with every movement.

The point of her boot nudged into the cart's wheel. Amalya looked up, seeing Wesley had stopped to converse with a vendor. Amalya leaned on the cart, closing her eyes, waiting for the uneasiness to pass.

Arthur wriggled uncomfortably for a moment before settling back down. What a talent to delve into dreams amongst so much noise. Concentrating on his body, she wondered where his life would lead him, though nothing hopeful could be conjured by such a hopeless mind. A thought festered and grew each time she harped on it. How could she draw hate from a child's innocence? Her child? He never asked to be born or become the harbinger of her joy. If only she had not fallen so far from herself.

Her eyes closed briefly as she faced the street. Each day, it was becoming more difficult to remember who she was before. If she, by chance, could find that girl again, would she even recognize her?

As the wilted blue of her eyes caved to the morning air, her body tensed. He was there—the man from the road. Hair pulled away from his face, clothes unchanged. He did not seem to notice her as he roamed from stall to stall without direction. When he finally did turn, his curiosity locked onto her. He did not stop walking, and he did not draw his gaze.

His eyes were strange but familiar. She still could not tell of their hue, but they were bright, standing out against the copper tone of his skin.

The cold chill returned and trickled down her spine. It seemed fated that he remained in the background of her sad life. As he crossed her path, an unexpected smile graced his lips. Amalya did not know why, but it shifted her heart into naive elation, like an innocent, happy child.

Something pulled her from the cart, yanking the strings of her feet to draw nearer and discover if he was a man or just something she had conjured from nothing.

"Amalya." Wesley's voice tickled her ears as she passed but did not deter her.

The stranger's ebony crown glinted amongst the common rabble that graced the market. He moved like a serpent, maneuvering so seamlessly he never once touched another. Amalya bumped and shoved her way forward. But every shoulder, hand, and ill voice that chided her to watch her step sank her deeper into the stagnant waters of her essence. Her lungs tightened as she caged her head between the bars of her fingers. She could not focus on anything but the blurred lines and disembodied colors that shadowed her every move.

Arthur stirred at her back, exacerbating the need to crumble to the ground. She clamped her teeth so tightly together she thought they might break. She heard something coming toward her, but she dared not see. She would let it charge her, let it stamp her into the dirt, and she would become nothing but pieces of someone who was once whole.

Strong hands grasped her shoulders, pulling her to the left and wrapping her in the safety of their arms.

"Amalya." The sound of Wesley's voice stirred her gaze.

"Oi," a harsh yell directed his focus to the street, "watch it, ya cloth-eared fool!"

"People are walking here! Or are you as blind as you are thick?" Wesley's retort garnered no response as the carter went on, perhaps too pressed for time to squabble.

Amalya tightened her arms against her body as Wesley looked to her again.

"Are you all right?"

"I. . . " The gentle pressure of his hands on her shoulders slowly eased the tension from her bones. She looked into his bearded face, the sweet, boyish charm he had possessed in their youth bending his lips into a weak smile.

Elra pressed against Amalya's leg, capturing her attention. "You need to go home, Mama?"

"No, I. . . " She forced the last of the uneasiness from her lungs. "I'll be fine. I just. . . I thought I saw some—"

"Wesley! Amalya!"

The voice startled them. It was Mira, still as beautiful as ever. Her dark hair lay braided against her forest-green dress, coming off of her round, tanned shoulders. A woven basket hung in the crux of her arm and her welcoming hazel eyes beamed at the sight of her friend.

Wesley dropped his arms as Mira squeezed Elra's little frame before gathering Amalya into a tight hug. She pulled away as she noticed the small child sleeping soundly across Amalya's back. "Oh, he is precious!" Mira raised her hands to him. "May I?"

With Amalya's nod of approval, Mira gently pried the sleepy Arthur from his warm sling, holding him up as his eyes adjusted to the newness of this place. He did not seem at all disturbed by this stranger holding him for the first time, merely curious as he gurgled and stuck his tongue out.

Mira could not be more pleased, her face brimming with excitement. "He's the spitting image of you, Wesley, isn't he?"

Pulling at his belt, Wesley sighed. "You would know, with your keen eye for details, Mira."

"Always with your compliments, Wesley." Mira looked at Amalya. "I have missed you, my dear. You'll have to let us visit you soon. Poll would love to see the farm; it's been so long. She and Elra get along almost as well as we did growing up." She hesitated, looking at Wesley. "Laird has a good reference for someone looking for work. Real hard-working fellow, he's been a big help to us over the last few seasons."

Wesley nodded with an appreciative smile. "That is very kind of him."

"Go and see him. You can do all your trading after."

"Running me off already?" Wesley shook his head. "Fine then. Come on, Elra."

"Can I stay with Mama?" Elra pouted, giving Wesley her big, round eyes to contend with.

"Polli's at home." Mira smiled, bending down to brush Elra's hair behind her ears. "She'll be so excited to see you if you go with your father."

"Polli's there?" She grabbed Wesley's hand and tried to pull him back toward the cart. "Hurry, Papa! Hurry!"

Wesley wasted little time and heeded his daughter's request. To Amalya, he said, "I'll see you at your father's."

Amalya nodded and watched them depart from sight. The two friends stood in silence before Mira's hand on her arm drew her attention.

"Perhaps we'll walk a bit. Before heading there?"

Amalya did not wish to dismiss her friend, whom she had not seen for over a season, nor did she think Mira would leave her alone to wander the city. "I suppose so."

"Good."

They continued down the road together. Mira took every moment they had to fill Amalya in on everything that had been happening in her life—how well Laird was doing with the blacksmith shop, her daughter Polliann, and so on. Amalya listened obediently, making small remarks from time to time just to let her know she was listening. The focus did not last very long. Her thoughts wandered to the mysterious man. She felt as if he was there still, his face lost amongst the crowd, safely hidden from sight.

Sól sat highest in the sky when they arrived at Amalya's father's home, just east of the market district. Wesley and Elra were already there, eating a well-deserved lunch. Elra stood up as they entered the small rustic cottage, very excited to see them. She ran to Mira, wrapping her little arms around her legs.

Mira laughed. "What a greeting! Did you see Polli?"

Amalya took Arthur from Mira to allow her friend to greet her eldest child. The cottage was small, perfect for one man to dwell. The kitchen had but a washbasin and a few shelves for cutlery and utensils. A large barrel sat in the corner and drying meat hung just outside the small window, facing the squared patch of land her father owned.

Wesley stood from the table, which spilled into the cozy

living space, to greet them warmly. "Will you be joining us?" he asked.

"No, I cannot stay long," Mira said, "I was just curious how it went with Laird."

"Wonderfully. He introduced me to Tristan, and it seems we've come to an agreement. He starts tomorrow."

She breathed a sigh. "I'm so happy to hear it. He will be pleased to have some steady work."

Amalya's eyes trailed across the lifeless details of the dwelling. Crates and a pair of workman's boots sat in the corner next to a basket of quilted blankets and wood for the fire. An empty rocking chair rested beside a lifeless brick fireplace. Her gaze continued down the small passageway to the left, leading down a narrow hall to two more rooms, both closed by simple wooden doors. Light streamed through a window at the end of the hall, breathing life into the entire home.

"Be sure to pass on my gratitude again." Wesley came beside Amalya, distracting her from her quiet observations. "We can't thank him enough."

"Of course, of course. I was just telling Amalya Polli misses Elra so. If it's all right with you, we'd love to come visit the farm soon. Get away from all this business the city provides."

"I want Polli to come!" Elra pleaded. "Please! Please!"

Wesley placed a hand on Amalya's shoulder. "Sometime soon. We will have to arrange it."

Amalya looked at him, her brow slightly furrowed, as if he was seeking her approval for the suggestion to come to fruition. She was not his keeper, nor did she feel her opinion would hold sway over the final decision. Wesley would never admit how much he needed to distract himself from the cloud that hung over her each passing day. She welcomed it if it meant she could spend most of the day alone and unjudged.

"Well, I must be off." Mira gave Elra a hug before walking over to Amalya. She kissed her on the cheek. "It was so good to see you, my dear. We'll be seeing you soon, I hope."

Amalya smiled as Mira left, stepping cheerfully out the door.

Everyone settled back down at the table. Wesley took Arthur without protest as Amalya picked at some bread from the large wooden bowl.

"You hired someone, then?"

"Yes; the man seemed hard-working and Laird recommended him."

"What were the terms?"

"For now, just a roof over his head and food in his belly is all he needs. Once we can get the farm back to where it was, payment will be discussed." He chewed down a mouthful of food. "We got lucky—Laird really pulled through for us."

The lump of bread struggled to pass down her throat. "What was his name again?"

"Tristan. He'll arrive in the morning. I'll probably be busy working, if you don't mind greeting him when he arrives."

She nodded her head as she took another bite of food. It was soft against her palate, but no taste would escape it as it passed down her gullet.

EIGHT

"When dawn comes, we will see the signs. We will hear its whispers. We will feel the chill of death."
- King Aethelwulf letters, 1,804 Sól Sett, Third Season, Sólsun

There was a knock on the door.
"I'll get it!" Elra sprang to her feet and skipped toward the door.

"Stay here and mind your brother." Amalya wiped her hands on her apron as she ceased Elra's stride, watching her closely until she went back to where Arthur sat safely on the floor.

Amalya grasped the handle to open the door. The light of day carried warmth to the shadows as a man, standing with his gaze adrift to the sky, turned slowly to meet her.

He was tall, taller than Wesley by at least a hand, his coal-black hair pulled back and left to lie across his shoulders. When he turned to gaze upon her, his hooded golden eyes drew up in a smile.

Amalya's breath caught in her throat. It was him—the man she had seen following the caravan and in the market. Her entire body went numb. Only the reflection of Sól's light in his beautifully brilliant orbs kept her from falling.

He wore a plain tunic, untied at the nape, his copper-toned skin peeking out into the morning, smooth and toned. Brown trousers and weathered boots covered the remainder of his frame. They seemed haphazardly placed, as if he had pulled them from the line of a common farmer in an attempt to hide his true self. They hid the remainder of his physique well, but Amalya did not need proof that he was strong. It carried in his face, with brows ridged and cheekbones high, pulling away from his proud nose.

He bowed to her courteously. "Good day, my lady." His voice was low, as if guarded or unsure of its purpose.

Forcing down the stone lodged in her throat, Amalya stepped just outside the door, keeping one foot behind the threshold. "Good day to you, sir. You must be Tristan."

He was silent, looking at her as if he was unsure himself. "If that is what you say."

His response pinched her ears like a subtle sting. "Either you are or you are not." She kept her hand on the edge of the door. "So which are you?"

"I am." He spoke confidently now, his tone more robust as his head raised slightly. "May I ask your name?"

She hesitated, almost afraid to answer. "I am Amalya."

"It is an honor to meet you." He bowed to her again.

"My husband is in the barn. He will be expecting you."

"Thank you." His prominent cheekbones pressed against

his hooded eyes. "Good day to you, my lady." He walked toward the barn like leaves in the wind.

Rushing back into the house, Amalya closed the door, her folded hands falling against it. Fingers steadily shaking against the wood, Amalya could not expand her lungs as her heart raced like a broken steed.

What a peculiar man. He was elegant in his mannerisms, but also clumsy, as if he had never interacted with a person before. He was certainly built for labor, but he seemed so out of place. He didn't belong here; his hair was too clean, his face too perfect, and his voice. . .

"Who was that?"

Amalya turned with a start to face her daughter's curiosity. "Tristan."

"He's here to help us, right?"

"He is." A deep breath helped steady her heart as she returned to the kitchen with Elra.

Wiping down the table and stacking dishes could not take her mind off of the strangeness that still lingered in the air. It was something new—not tense or light or even dreary like a heavy rain. Nothing that her thoughts raced through could accurately compare. She would be sure to ask Wesley about it.

She glanced out the window to try and catch a glimpse of them. They were talking just outside the barn, though Tristan was hidden behind the crudely painted door. Her husband seemed quite jovial in his responses, giving her reason to believe they were getting along rather well. Wesley extended his hand and Amalya saw Tristan come forth to grasp it. After their friendly exchange, Wesley headed back toward the house.

Amalya quickly busied herself, trying to appear productive as he entered the home. Every moment that passed sent her stomach fluttering. She did not know why. Perhaps it was in response to the uncertainty that followed that man on his arrival.

Wesley came through the door. "Did you meet him?"

"I did." She looked up at her husband.

"He's more than happy to take up my old sleeping quarters in the storeroom. Could you make sure that is taken care of so he's more comfortable?"

"Of course."

He smiled. "Good."

"Can I come help you?" Elra asked, tugging on Wesley's work pants.

"You stay with your mother for now."

"Wesley." Amalya approached him, pressing her lips together but forcing herself to speak. "Does Tristan seem a bit odd to you?"

"Odd? In what way?"

"He seems misplaced."

Wesley lifted his brow. "He did say he is not used to farm work, but I'm sure he will be quick to pick it up."

"It doesn't seem that simple."

Wesley placed his fingers in the loose strands of her hair, tucking them behind her ear. "The thought of an unfamiliar face making you a bit nervous?"

She nodded her head, even though it was not nerves that had stirred this inside her. "I suppose you could be right."

He smiled again, touching his finger to her chin. "You'll get used to him being here." Kissing her on the cheek, Wesley returned outside to resume the day's work.

His conclusions were not unfounded, but he was wrong. Tristan did not seem unfamiliar at all.

Securing Arthur to her person, Amalya grabbed some blankets and fresh linen to bring to the storeroom. Elra took an empty bucket as they exited the house. The day did not seem as dull as it normally did—not dull in the sense of its overall nature, but in the sense that she did not feel so averse to being a part of it.

There was a gentle wind casting through the hills, which brought a peculiar feeling across her face, like soft, lapping water upon a dry shore. The warm scent of baking corn husks was almost new to her. New in a way she could not entirely explain.

They rounded the house toward the storeroom. The chicken coop lay just outside. Fat brown and white fluffs of feathers meandered from side to side, plucking at the ground for sustenance.

"Can I feed the chickens, Mama?" Elra jumped up and down in her speckled blue dress, eager to spend some time with the feathered fowl.

Amalya nodded. "Run along now, but stay in sight of the storeroom. Don't wander off on your own."

"I won't!"

They entered the storeroom together. Elra immediately filled her bucket full of feed. She carried it clumsily, letting a few crumbs spill to the floor. Amalya kept the door open as she watched her daughter make for the coop.

The storeroom was very large and housed most of the products they were preparing to sell. Cracks let in streams of light between the planked walls. Barrels of feed, wooden gardening tools, and the like sat neatly to one side. Shelves decorated the walls, storing canned peaches, onions, cucumbers, and other preserved food for harder times. There was a loft where extra equipment and feed were kept. Another entrance was located in the back, next to a small workbench. The room where Tristan would be staying lay just beyond it, tucked away with a separating wall and opened frame.

The space was large enough that a hay-stuffed bed and wooden drawers were kept there. A single window hung just above the bed, though she was not sure how recently it had been opened. There was another door from the room that led outside, slightly ajar, letting in the crisp morning air.

This room had been Wesley's for many Setts before they were married. It was never anything more than that, though sometimes it harbored secrets only privy to them. The meeting place for mischief-planning and escaping the safety of her father's watch. There were so many nights when they would escape somewhere, always returning here to rest and reflect before she climbed back through her window to her bed. How distant those memories seemed now.

Setting Arthur down gently on the floor with some hay to play with, Amalya set about placing the linens on top of the weary drawers. The hay smelled fresh. Wesley must have stuffed the bed before Tristan arrived. She pulled the linens apart and shook them free from their fold. As she looked up from her work, she noticed Tristan walking up to the back door.

He looked at her, surprised. "Excuse me, I did not mean to..."

"I was just bringing some blankets for you." She went back to dressing the bed. "Wesley already filled the bed."

"Thank you, my lady." He had nothing with him, no

extra clothes or personal effects. Perhaps he left them behind, though she couldn't imagine why. He knew he would be arriving today. Perhaps given less than a day to prepare was too short notice.

"You have nothing with you?" she asked as she glanced at him.

"I do not require much." His eyes wandered to Arthur, who was now gumming a piece of hay. He bent down gingerly and looked at her son with curious wonder, his brow flexing as if observing a rare creature for the first time.

Arthur was too young to pay Tristan's attention much mind. He continued to drool as he stuffed the hay deeper into his mouth. Amalya moved to free him of it, but Tristan reached forward, hooking his finger in the strand and pulling it free from Arthur's moist trap.

Tristan then reached into a pocket of his trousers, pulling a rounded piece of what appeared to be darkened wood into the light. He presented it to Arthur. Amalya could see markings on it before Arthur shoved it in his mouth. Two triangles atop each other, their points to the north and south. Arthur gummed it too deeply for her to make out anything else. It was too big for him to swallow, so there was no harm in him possessing it.

Her eyes did not leave him as Tristan rose to his feet. He shifted his stance, almost relaxing as a slight smirk tickled the corner of his lips.

"Thank you," she stated as she concentrated on his fluid movements. "You're not from around here."

He took a step further inside the room. "Why would you think that?"

"You act differently. You seem out of place." She took

another blanket from atop the dresser and fanned it over the bed. "And I've never seen you before the other day."

Tristan proceeded forward, taking the edge of the linen in his hand, assisting her in guiding it to flow over the bed almost perfectly. As it came down to drape along the sides, he let go, allowing it to fall naturally into place. "Perhaps you just do not recognize me."

Amalya dropped her edge of the blanket, studying him with a newfound curiosity. "I think I would have remembered seeing you." She tucked the folds into the bed without his assistance. "May I ask where you're from?"

His fingers pressed against each other as he held them in front of him. "Far from here—farther than you've seen."

She found herself smirking as she rose. "So you are *not* from here, just as I imagined."

His eyes gleamed as if Sól's light had somehow lent them its brilliance. "Right now I am, but then I was not. I am not from anywhere. I am from everywhere."

A slight tingle left her unable to swallow the unusual taste of his response. She wanted to know more about this man, this mysterious stranger who had forgotten his own name when he had first spoken to her.

"You're rather peculiar." She was not afraid to speak boldly on her observations and he did not seem to mind her truthfulness.

Careful steps brought him to stand on the opposite side of the dresser. A strong scent of ash and winded leaves tickled her senses as he leaned against it, his hair falling from his shoulder. "Is that to your displeasure?"

Amalya adjusted her posture, pressing her booted feet

together tightly so her knees touched underneath her dress. "If that is how you are, it does not matter what I think."

She turned away from him, hastily gathering Arthur in her arms. This man's scent was intoxicating, leaving her mind fuzzy and disoriented. Rich pine and dampened leaves after a Sólsun rain filled her lungs with every breath. Arthur still possessed the trinket Tristan had given him. She moved to expel it from his mouth, but Tristan raised a hand as if he knew her intentions.

"It is a gift," he said, lowering his hand again.

She straightened to adjust her balance, leaning against the doorframe just across from him. Arthur was steady in her arms, so transfixed on making a meal of his new toy, nothing else seemed to deter him. "Will you be joining us for dinner this evening?" Her words were shaken, steady with the pacing of her frantic heart.

"I do not think that would be appropriate, don't you agree?"

"I do." She did not know what compelled her to say such a thing. It was rude and not becoming of the wife of his employer. Perhaps it was the darkness inside of her that did not want him around her family or the undeniable effect his mere presence was having on her. Whatever it was, it must have been prominent in her eyes for him to know he would be unwelcome at their table.

"I hope the rest of the day treats you well."

Rising from the dresser, Tristan bowed his head to her. "And you, my lady."

She turned and made for the front entrance. She could have easily slipped out the back door but she did not want to take one more step closer to him. As she breathed the fresh air, her mind began to clear. The flurry of disorientation dissipated back to blandness.

Elra was running about the yard, followed by an entourage of chickens as she leaked feed from her tiny hands. She giggled at their immediate need for sustenance, their pestering clucks amusing her greatly. The innocence of it would have made any doting mother swell with joy, but it only managed to crack Amalya's heart just a little bit more.

Every passing moment sank her closer to the ground until she was there again, facing only the walls of her dark prison. The sudden lift that arose in her when she was in the storeroom was unwanted, but strangely tantalizing. She had gotten so comfortable being this way, cold and immovable, part of her did not want it to be anything but what she was. As much as Wesley and her father wanted her to find herself again, she was afraid to.

"Come on, Elra."

They hurried along to attend to whatever chores the day brought.

SÓL BEGAN to fall as Nótt slowly painted the sky in darkness. Amalya finished up in the kitchen, a warm meal of roast pig, bread, and fresh vegetables. The symphony of smells rose from the warm, smoking food, rich and welcoming the call of hungry stomachs, though only twisting hers into an agonizing knot.

Elra grabbed a plate and took a seat at the table.

Wesley began to dress another plate with plentiful helpings of food. "Would you mind bringing this out to Tristan for me? I invited him to eat with us but he did not want to."

Tensing her shoulders, Amalya gave him an unwelcome glance. "Can't you bring it yourself? After all, you're the one who hired him."

"Aren't we hospitable this evening?" He pulled the plate back with a subtle sneer at her disagreement. "Still unsure of our new worker?"

"So what if I am?"

"He is here now. The more effort you give, the less uncomfortable you will be."

Amalya sensed the abrupt haste his words carried. Perhaps it had begun to chip away at him too.

"I can bring it to him!" Elra raised her hand to volunteer for the duty.

Amalya raised her voice slightly. "You will do no such thing! Now sit down and eat."

Elra settled back in her chair with an unpleasant look.

Wesley finished gathering food and headed for the door. "I don't plan on getting rid of him after the good day's work he's put in." He left the house to deliver the food to their worker.

Carrying a plate of meager rations, Amalya sank into a seat at the table and sat quietly while Elra ate, spooning juicy helpings of pork into her mouth.

"He was nice to me. You should be nice too!"

"Ladies do not talk with full mouths."

"I'm not a lady, I'm a girl!"

Amalya gave her daughter a look and the two resumed their meal in silence. Throughout the night, the memory of her uneasiness when faced with Tristan lapped behind her eyelids. His rich aroma both cooled and set her heart ablaze. Perhaps she was coming down with something. That moment was foreign to her and yet wanting in a way she could not fully understand.

After Wesley returned and they finished eating, she cleaned the kitchen, put the children to bed, and retreated to her writing. Every moment of the day flowed out upon the blank pages of her parchment. It was so freeing to see the words form so seamlessly. She did not need to think at all; they were waiting at her fingertips, wanting to be written.

Wesley did not disturb her. Seeing her writing was surely encouraging to him, as it was something she had rarely done in many seasons. Or he still carried unwanted distaste for her from her actions at dinner. Whatever the reason, she was glad of it.

She wrote until night had consumed all of Dag's light and everyone was asleep except for her. The light of her candle dipped in all directions as she drew the last of her letters.

Waning eyes commanded her to sleep. She blew the candle free of fire and crawled into bed. The window was closed but let the sleeping light of Sól trickle to the floor. Even as her eyes grew heavy from weariness and her mind more at ease, something still lingered, like fingers touching her skin ever so gently. It was enough to keep her attention, but comforting, lulling her into a deep, restful sleep.

NINE

"Men fall so easily. There may have been the need for vengeance in their hearts, but whether vengeance or fear, they fall just the same."
- Excerpt from *The Tale of Marin and the White Dragon*

Amalya stared out over the open landscape. The wind tossed the tall grass from side to side as the trees joined in the dance, their leaves outstretched. Clouds rolled by as peaceful birdsong trickled through the branches. Small creatures roamed without worry or fear of death. Sól sat silently above it all, admiring all he had created.

Amalya took a deep, soulful breath. Her hair sailed against her face and down her back, blending into her pale nightdress, which hugged her legs as it folded in the wind. Erratic as it was, it did not bother her. The air filled her, invigorated her essence, casting away all the dust and decay left clouding her existence. She fell into the grass, looking up toward the sky. The sound of grass strings performed beautifully all around her. Wind lent itself well to the music of the landscape. This was what peace was like. Free, unattainable peace.

Turning her head to one side, she saw Tristan sitting beside her, looking down with a calm smile. He wore dusty work pants and a cotton white shirt, sullied from a day of heavy labor. His hair was tied back, revealing the firm lines of his jaw. His copper skin captured the rays of Sól's brilliance, reflecting into his gold, hooded eyes.

His presence did not shock or surprise her. He joined in her peace because it was he who had brought her here. The why and the how remained unanswered and unneeded. She stared back into the blue sky as faint white clouds rolled into view.

"I do not deserve to be here," she thought aloud, so swiftly and without consideration that Amalya only knew it was her who spoke because it is what she truly believed.

"But you are here." Tristan's voice was deep and calm, as if he held all the knowledge anyone would hope to seek.

Amalya rolled over on her side to face him, resting her cheek in the palm of her hand. "You brought me here."

She watched him gaze into the openness, at peace, eyes not wandering but merely accepting all that surrounded them. He did not seem to carry any burden or suffer from any wrongdoing. It was beautiful to see a man in such a state of being. It made it possible for all who hoped to achieve such a way, even herself.

"Why?" she asked him.

"This is your dream, inside your own mind," he said, unmoving. "It is you who have brought me here."

She sat up in the grass, pressing her hands across her knees to iron the folds of her nightdress. A sense of insecurity fumbled her fingers and held her tongue inside her mouth. A dream that was not diluted with darkness was strange. She had almost forgotten everything that came before this, and how it changed her. But this man, even without words or proximity—the thought of him stirred her gut and left her lightheaded. "I do not know why you have affected me so. I do not know you."

"Are you sure you do not know me?"

His question drew her gaze to his. Amidst all the misguided currents he had cultivated, there was something familiar about him. A warmth she had thought would never again be present. "What is the truth behind all of this?"

Tristan remained calm. As he turned to look at her, she saw herself present in his eyes. So much beauty in her own reflection, now unrecognizable even to herself. Tears streamed down her face, falling into the vibrant grass below.

"Truth is a fickle thing," Tristan said. "Sometimes we are blind to it and only see what we do not wish to see." He reached for her face and wiped away a tear. "We must learn to seek answers elsewhere. Everything we need is within ourselves. Our very bodies are vessels to the only understanding we need to discover."

He pulled his hand away and held it close to his chest. A faint glowing mist surrounded his fingertips. It pulsed with its own breath, casting and receding through the fabric of his shirt. When it dissipated, he held his palm outstretched to her. A single white rose without imperfections lay in his hand, waiting for her to reach for it.

The flower was so perfect, so pure, Amalya was almost

afraid to touch it. As she grasped its stem, being careful not to prick her fingers on the thorns, she held it up to gaze upon its undeniable beauty.

"There is beauty in all of us, just waiting to be found." He moved closer to her, cradling her cheek in his hand. "The darkness only hides it from sight. Search amongst the shadows. In the deepest corners. It is there. Waiting."

The scent of ash and winded leaves enveloped the space surrounding them. A deep yearning erupted within her, begging her to be closer to him. The desire was sudden and powerful—so powerful she did not think she possessed the strength to wield it. Holding the rose close, Amalya stared at the small gap of grass between them. "You have awakened something within me."

He came closer to her, sending her heart fluttering into her throat. "Then why are you afraid?" She looked up to find his face hovering mere inches from her own. "Do you fear me?"

The answer was uncertain. She did not know what it was that had taken control of her. It could indeed be fear—a deep, longing fear that she would welcome. She would welcome anything other than the sense of loss that had cast her into this unforgiving darkness. "I only wish to see."

"Then open your eyes."

A fierce wind pulled him from her as it tossed the surrounding grass. Sól shone with a blinding light, hiding everything there was. Amalya folded her arms around her face, trying to block the rays from clouding her vision. She could not see where he had gone nor hear anything but the chattering grass pulled by the wind.

The sound grew deafening as she closed her eyes from

the force of it, her hair whipping against her body and pulling her like winding yarn. Just as her arms came undone, her eyes opened.

———

AIR RUSHED into her lungs as she rose from the bed. She clutched her chest, feeling her heart beat with a renewed vigor that cleared the cobwebs encumbering her veins. Sól's light crept in from the window, casting calm upon her skin. She was in her room in the house she knew so well. Arthur was still asleep in the small cradle next to the bed. Noises shifted from beyond the closed door, and for a rare moment, a sense of wonder swung her legs from the blankets as she stepped onto the floor.

Something fell from the bed as she stood, coming to rest at her feet. Amalya looked down, not believing what she saw. It was the rose, as pure and unblemished as it was in her dream. She bent down to pick it up. Rolling the stem between her fingers, she raised it to her nose to inhale its potent aroma. As she closed her eyes, the scene of the rolling hills kissed by the wind returned. Tristan's stoic frame, looking down at her with his glowing skin and Sól-kissed eyes.

"Amalya!" Wesley's voice rose from beyond the door.

"I'll be right there!"

Cradling the rose, she carried it over to her books and parchment, sliding it between the pages of her writing to keep it out of sight. Before she could leave it, she lifted the pages to be sure she was not imagining things. It sat serenely, lying still between the spaces of her words.

TEN

"Dag so coveted the night Nótt did bring. She was a flower petal, sailing above the flickering outstretched fingers of the flame. Each kiss that fell upon her singed her skin and darkened her soul, like velvet, beautiful and soft."
- Excerpt from *The Song of Dag and Nótt*

Amalya was actually looking forward to her friend coming to the farm. It had been three weeks since she saw Mira in the city and the airy freshness from the dream her mind had conjured had seeped deep within her bones, carrying her into the day.

Amalya fished through her small wardrobe of dresses until her fingers finally touched the one she had been looking for. Pulling it out, she held it against her body. She had not worn this since before she and Wesley married. It was long and flowing, a delicate shade of emerald-green. Light ribbons of lace frilled from the waist and scooped collar. The sleeves were long but cut off just below the elbow. It was perfect;

long to keep the cool draft at bay, but leaving just enough exposed to refresh her skin.

Pulling her long blonde hair back with a ribbon, she tied it at the back of her head, letting a few strands frame her face. For a moment, she wondered what she looked like. Her hands pushed away the remaining clothes in her wardrobe to reveal the mirror at its back. The edges were tarnished and spotted from lack of care, but the image it projected was clear.

The woman staring back at her—though she looked just as Amalya did—seemed like a stranger. Her face was thinner, eyes drawn and casting shadows on her once-full cheeks. More gray than blue swirled around the black stone of her iris. Her mouth still carried that bow shape and her skin was the same creamy hue. Pulling the loose hangings of her hair over her shoulders, Amalya glanced at its reflection. She'd forgotten how much she loved its shade, like wheat encapsulated in Sól's light.

Arthur cooed, eager to rise from his slumber. Moving away from the wardrobe, she picked him up, holding him straight out in front of her. He was growing into that always lovable roundness all babies had. His eyes were just like his father's and a few small tufts of dark hair had sprouted atop his otherwise peach-fuzzed head. He had mastered steadying his head and looked at her, his mouth puckered outward in disgrace as if she had done something terribly wrong to offend him.

Amalya tilted her head. "Why so serious, little man?"

She could not help but smile. It came so naturally; she had forgotten what it felt like. Arthur wiggled in her hands, demanding to be catered to.

Placing a hand underneath his bottom, Amalya laid him over her shoulder. As she moved to leave the room, she noticed the small, rounded trinket Tristan had given her son lying amongst his blankets. Bending down slowly, she took it into her hand. It was smooth, like a pebble found at the bottom of a riverbed. The surface appeared to be wood, but carried more weight than a small piece of cut wood usually would. The markings on its surface were foreign to her, yet they enticed her wonder as to their meaning and reasons for being placed on such an object. Voices rose again from the kitchen. Amalya quickly pocketed the piece and made her way out of the room with Arthur on her shoulder.

Elra was already up and quite eager to start the day. She was wearing a long, plain sandstone-colored dress and her best blue slippers. Considering all the dirt and mud she would accumulate today, Amalya did not think those were the best choice, but she would not reprimand her. If Elra wanted to get her best shoes muddied, that was perfectly acceptable.

Both Wesley and Elra looked up upon her arrival.

"Mama looks pretty today!" Elra ran over to her and hugged her legs.

Another smile crept upon Amalya's face as she rubbed her daughter's back. "That is so kind of you, though you look far prettier than me."

"Will you braid my hair?"

"I will after you eat your breakfast."

"I already ate, Mama!"

There was an empty plate with nothing but crumbs decorating its surface sitting on the table. "So you have! You are an early bird after all."

"When will Polli be here?"

"She'll be along soon." Amalya tilted her head. "Clean up your place, Elra."

Elra hurried along and grabbed her dishes from the table, taking them over to the washbasin and throwing them in haphazardly. Dipping her little hands down into the soapy water, she pushed them toward the bottom of the basin before wiping the soap off her arms.

Amalya could not help but turn to spy Wesley still looking at her, his dark eyes glowing as if he was seeing her for the first time. She moved around the table to stand near him. "Anything wrong?"

He shook his head, still caught in whatever trance entrapped him. "No. Nothing at all."

Elra tucked her lip under her teeth eagerly. "Papa thinks you look pretty too."

Amalya brushed away something on his brown tunic before gently combing through his dark red hair with her fingers. "You could use a good trim, Wesley. When's the last time I cut your hair?"

"I can't recall."

"Well, looks like you're due for some pampering." She begrudgingly put Arthur into his hands. "Take him for a moment, will you? Let me braid Elra's hair first."

Ushering Elra to sit down, Amalya came to stand behind her in the chair and sectioned out her wavy brown hair. She pulled it apart to sit between her fingers as she wound each section into the other. Despite her many months of inactivity, she always remembered how to braid. Elra swung her feet in excitement at this most unexpected treat. Amalya pulled the last section over, tying the bottom off with some ribbon, and then proceeded to the other side. It was just an insignificant gesture of good mothering on her part, though she did not know how long it would last. The only thing that mattered was that it was here now, and she would not squander it.

A knock came at the door, none too soon. Before either of them could fetch it, Mira pushed herself in with Polli prancing about behind her. Amalya finished up tying the last braid before Elra sprang from her seat. The two girls ran to give each other the warmest hug.

Mira smiled. "You look in the right spirits today." She walked over to Amalya and gave her a gentle hug. She was wearing a pale dress, with a braided leather belt tied around her waist.

"Look, Mira, look! Mama did my hair!" Elra jumped happily around like a rabbit.

"And it looks beautiful, doesn't it, Poll?"

Polli shook her head in agreement. She was smaller than Elra, with soft, dark curls tied back from her ashen skin. She wore a sweet green dress that complimented her complexion almost too well. A beauty just like her mother.

The energy of the room simply lifted the roof from the house. Everyone was in such good spirits; it was infectious and a little overwhelming. Amalya could feel the joy closing in around her, though she dared not show it.

"Laird should be along for dinner tonight." Mira homed in on Wesley. "Shouldn't you be getting to work?" She took Arthur from him and shooed him off. "Go on now. I can handle this lot."

Taking one more look at Amalya, Wesley ventured out to begin the day's chores.

"What are we going to do today?" Elra asked. Both she and Polli seemed eager to start their adventures together.

"Well, I'm sure there are a few things we can help with around this place," Mira replied. "Let's see what we can do to move things along. . . We can go feed the chickens!"

Both girls agreed with that proposal.

Amalya shook her head. "Mira, you are a guest. You do not need to busy yourself with farm work."

"My dear, please. Take your time and catch up with us when you can. I do not mind." Mira breathed a sigh as she settled Arthur against her hip. "You do seem different today. Not so. . . lost."

Amalya took Arthur from Mira, keeping her mouth flexed with gratitude. "I had the most unusual dream."

"A dream?" Mira's brow arched. "It seems to have stirred you."

"It stirred something. Though I am not quite sure what." She had forgotten how easy it was to be open with Mira. She had been her dearest friend since childhood and they had shared many secrets between themselves over the Setts.

In her isolation, Amalya had spoken very little to anyone. Being so open now felt foreign, raising the hairs of her neck and prickling down her spine. Amalya glanced at Arthur, eager to quiet their tongues so he may quench his.

"I'll be along." She stepped away from her friend toward the fireplace. "He's waited long enough to eat."

"Of course." Mira smiled. "We'll see you out there."

The girls hurried out the door, not wanting to waste another minute. Then all was silent.

Amalya took a relieved breath, closing her eyes. The tension lifted, for now. It was wonderful for her family and friends to see her in such a positive mood, she was sure. But perhaps too much too soon. She had let the aroma of the dream get the better of her. Not being accustomed to such jovialness, perhaps it would have been better if she never found it at all.

Arthur burbled hungrily against her chest. She settled down in the chair and moved him to feed, which he did with vigor.

Tiny steps; that was how she must progress. Just tiny steps. It was all right if she needed to retreat. Luckily for her, she had Arthur to take care of. It would be the first time since he was born that she was grateful to have him.

SHE FINALLY MADE it outside into the Sól-lit day. Bundling Arthur close to her chest, she walked toward the barn to start whatever duties she could attend to. Mira and the girls were still over with the chickens. Elra and Polli were chasing them around, having a grand time together. Mira was not too far from them, enjoying seeing their fun. She noticed Amalya and waved to her, but did not usher her over. Amalya was glad of it. She still needed some time to herself before joining them.

The barn reeked of old hay and stale manure. It was early yet, but all the animals were up and about. The hogs were stuffing their faces in their troughs, brimming with food. The oxen munched on hay, licking their nostrils clean.

Coming up to the last stall, Bard, the family's only horse, was impatiently waiting to be let out into the paddock. Amalya ran her hand along the old horse's pelt before grabbing a rope to tether to his bridle. Bard had been a member of her family since Amalya was a little girl. A gift to her mother, given to her after she died unceremoniously.

A flash of her father's recent words distracted her momentarily—words of her mother's untimely death left shrouded in mystery. But she would not let it dampen the light cast this day.

Bard would let no one handle him but Amalya. She would have given anything to have seen him when he was just a young stallion. His rich mahogany pelt must have been breathtaking, now graying and slightly coarse. Bard was too old to do much of anything but enjoy his last days here on the farm.

She opened the stable door and led him out of the barn, toward the paddock. The gate swung open with ease as she untied him from the rope. Bard gingerly trotted out into the bright new day. His tail whisked across his back as he lowered his head to graze in the dew-covered grass. The paddock overlooked their only field of wheat. Most of the stalks were not yet ripe for harvest. There was hardly any wind, so their long, whimsical tails stood perfectly still, like proud and vigilant soldiers.

Amalya watched Bard eating contentedly, not having a care in the world aside from what he was putting in his stomach. Some slight movement distracted her from across the paddock. Tristan emerged from the wheat field, picking gingerly at the stalks. There was a mess of harvesting tools sitting against the fence that she had over-looked upon first glance. Perhaps he was using them. It wasn't time to harvest just yet. Wheat was usually gath-ered when it came closer to the colder season of Nótt

Wind. The fresher the wheat, the fresher the food and ale made from it would be.

She sauntered around the paddock fence toward him. He seemed lost in his own mind. She believed him when he told her he was a man who needed very little. A lover of wisdom and truth, wanting to know more than what others knew. That is what she saw in him.

She thought herself foolish for thinking such things. She knew nothing about him, but that was what she wanted. She did not want to know the answers to all her questions because then her stories would not be true. Everything she had or would discover from him would be broken, scattered to the wind. She had quite enough of broken things. Let this be the one that remained whole.

Amalya stopped herself before reaching him, her approach garnering his attention. He looked over, standing a fair distance away. "What is the occasion?" He stepped out from the wheat to stand in the cut pathway before the paddock fence. "You, dressed as you are."

Amalya looked down at her dress. "No occasion. Garments need to breathe, same as I. And this one surely needed to taste the fresh air again."

He walked to the fence. Each step he took sent her heart racing. If it were not for the steady rise and fall of Arthur's little chest against hers, she may have succumbed to his intoxication once again.

"What does Wesley have you doing today?"

"Little things here and there." He leaned his arms against the top of the fence post. "I do what is needed."

"You have done much for us already."

"If you say so."

"I do not just say." Her chin dipped closer toward her chest, eyes unmoving from his gaze. "I know."

Finding words to give him proved difficult. All she wanted to do was tell him of her dream—to see if he had shared in her experience, even just a little. It would be rude to bring it up, inappropriate even.

Tristan seemed to notice her inner conflict and moved his head curiously, releasing a strand of hair across his forehead. "There is something else, isn't there? A reason."

She cocked her head curiously. "A reason?"

"Why Sól seems to shine ever brighter as you stand before me. Why you are so eager yet hesitant to speak, which only enhances the brightness of your sea-touched eyes."

Amalya turned away, taken aback by his words. She could feel her cheeks glow. No stranger had spoken so boldly to her before. He knew she was married and yet he did not care to suppress his words. She felt a rush of wind emerge from the darkness, stirring her essence as if caught in the rain.

"I apologize." His voice softened. "I have spoken too boldly."

She took a deep breath before facing him again. "Yes, you have. That was completely uncalled for." A coolness tickled the hairs on her arm, sending a refreshing chill pillaging across her skin. "But you are right. There is a reason."

She tried to swallow the sinking feeling in her stomach warning her not to speak. All of this should stand as a caution, deterring her from drawing another step forward. But she could not help it. The chance to catch a dream and hold it close, to feel its breath against her cheek and follow the curves of its form with her fingers. Why would one think to suppress such a chance? This man, whoever he truly was, had offered her something when all others pulled away. Perhaps not intentionally, but Amalya was beginning to understand that his presence here was not by chance.

Arthur stirred at her chest, erasing the need to say what threatened to be revealed to Tristan. Cupping his small head, Amalya brought her mouth to his ear. "Shh, little one."

"May I see your son?"

Amalya watched Tristan carefully, but no fear or uncertainty surfaced as she waited for her instincts to take hold. "If you wish."

Tristan passed between the fence posts and walked over to her. He settled his gaze on her child, who was growing ever more disgruntled. Gathering him up, Tristan held Arthur upright to face him, supporting his bottom in one hand and his upper shoulders and neck in another. Arthur went completely still, staring at the man who he now faced. Tristan's thumb rubbed against his tiny ear, feeling the small plumes of brown hair springing from the back of Arthur's head.

Amalya watched, her heart beating ever strongly in her chest. Her hand moved to her pocket, where the trinket still lay. She grasped it inside her dress, feeling an urge to present it to him along with her question. But she waited, more interested in what was transpiring before her.

Carefully, Tristan brought Arthur closer to him. His wide nostrils took in the scent of the babe, pressing Arthur's forehead to his unopened lips. It was an unusual moment, but Arthur never stirred nor cried out in distress. As Tristan moved him away, Arthur blew a gurgle from his rounded cheeks, causing the corner of Tristan's mouth to curl into a soft smile.

"He will grow to be a fine man." With steady hands, he presented her son back to her.

Amalya took Arthur from him, looking down at her child, whose calm expression both quieted and confused her. "What did you do?"

"You saw it with your own eyes."

"Yes, but—" She stopped, not wishing to delve into it any further. He was not harmed, nor did he seem to be in any distress. Some things were better left unexplained, if for nothing else than to keep this dream alive. "Thank you."

He nodded his head.

"Do you have any children?"

Brushing his hand through his dark hair, Tristan began to gather the tools propped against the fence posts. "No, but I hope to. One day."

"Is there someone special you have in mind?" She leaned against the weathered wood as Tristan picked up the tools, slinging them onto his back.

"There is," he looked at her, "but she does not know of me yet."

Amalya's lower lip began to tremble. She quickly tucked it between her teeth, tightening her muscles to straighten her stance. "What are you waiting for?"

"For her to see." He bowed to her again, his grin spreading closely into his almond-shaped eyes. "Good day, my lady."

Cutting across the paddock, Tristan walked toward the barn. Bard approached him suddenly, his tail flicking behind him and ears erect. A grunt escaped him, his square teeth still grinding away at the feed in his mouth. When Tristan extended his hand, it quieted the stallion. His nostrils flared as he took in Tristan's scent before pushing his nose into his hand without precedence. Bard nudged into his palm and Tristan remained poised and unstirring, as if speaking through his eyes.

Amalya could not find the will to breathe. Bard would not even let Wesley touch him and yet here was Tristan, reaching out to him as if they were old friends. She could not understand who this man was. She could associate nothing he did with hard work and lofty expectations.

This was a man with a broad understanding of life, someone of ambition. He was intelligent and in tune with Sól's creations. One could almost think he was that of a magical sort, but no man had the power to wield magic. He did not need to infringe on other moral standings.

The more she discovered, the fewer answers she needed. Only one remained vigilant in her mind, and that was why he had come here. Though the answer seemed almost too obvious, without his say as to the validity of her thoughts, they were nothing but dust in the wind.

As Tristan disappeared into the barn, Amalya made her way back to where Mira and the girls were still tending to the hens. The girls were so preoccupied with their fun, they did not seem to notice her arrival.

Mira smiled at her before noticing the troubled state of her mind. "Are you all right, my dear?"

Amalya felt almost embarrassed about bringing up such a thing. It was not a very appropriate conversation for two married women to share, but Laird recommended Tristan before he ever stepped foot on the farm, having hired him himself. He had spent time with them, and perhaps Mira had her own interpretation of his peculiarity. If anyone could shed some light on all Amalya was thinking, it was Mira.

"I just ran into Tristan."

"I thought he was working with Wesley today, in the field? I pay little attention." Mira leaned to one side. "Did he speak with you?"

"He did."

"I assume it was a rather strange conversation."

Amalya was both surprised and relieved at her words. "You know, then?"

Mira nodded. "When he first came to work for Laird, he barely even looked at me, let alone spoke. Unless we were alone, he said nothing in the presence of Laird. He would talk my ear off about, well, anything really. He's a storyteller like you, only without an audience. I would try to avoid him most days. If he wasn't such a dedicated worker, I would have made Laird get rid of him far sooner."

"Has he been forward with you?"

"Blatantly so, to the point of discomfort."

Relief took hold of Amalya's mind for a brief moment, followed quickly by an unfounded jealousy that burned her cheeks and tensed the muscles in her arm. To hear that Tristan may not be treating her any differently than any other lady diminished the uniqueness of their time together. It was unsettling to hear that she may not be the only one taken by his poetic prowess and strangeness, though she did not want Mira to know what truth harbored in her heart for this farmhand.

"I suppose that attempts some relief."

Mira laughed heartily, placing a hand on Amalya's arm.

"What in Marin's name did he say to you? All this has gotten me quite curious." She faced her fully, awaiting more details about their encounter.

Amalya understood the need for gossip, but she did not want to tell Mira. His words were for her and her alone. No one needed to know of what passed between them, not yet.

"It is odd that it seems he does not want to disappoint me. He carries this almost magical nature."

"Magical? Amalya, you've always been one to exaggerate."

Looking out back toward the barn, she took a step in its direction without making it noticeable to anyone but her. "I suppose so."

"I am sure he does not mean what he says."

Both Elra and Polli looked as if they were ready to find something else more exciting to do.

"Tristan is a good man, despite his tendencies. You're less inclined to judge and more inclined to ignore him in no time." Mira ushered the girls on. "Where to next?"

Mira could be right. Perhaps overlooking was the best course of action for Amalya, but something was still amiss. Maybe she had felt so dull to all the pity, and now that there was a new face with unfamiliar words, it thoroughly distracted her. That would be something to hope for, not deter. Maybe the distraction was helping her see past all that had buried her to this depth. But she could not help but feel there was something remaining that she did not understand and, apparently, no one else did either.

Hope that something would arise overtook her. It would be so obvious; she would believe it had always been there.

ELEVEN

*"When she gazed upon him, all sense of malice had
dissipated, like a flame drenched by frozen water. His blue
gaze captured her in their tides, gently lapping at her heart,
making it pliable and willing to fall into the waves that he
unknowingly offered her."*
- Excerpt from *The Tale of Marin and the White Dragon*

"Long ago, during the lull of the Great Dragon Wars, there was a girl. She was not a beautiful girl. In fact, she was quite plain and lived a plain life in a city by the Safir Sea. She came from a family of fishermen, so fishing was all she knew. This plain girl who came from a plain family and who had seen very little of the world wanted nothing more than to remain in her plain life as the land breathed chaos, painting the world red with blood.

"This girl, who we know as Marin, was thrown into the bowels of war, stoking an angry fire in her heart when her home was destroyed, leaving her plain life smoldering with the ashes. But one day, as she found herself lost among Skarpur's Teeth, she encountered the unexpected. Large pale wings, claws of ivory, and deep blue eyes that glistened like Sól over the sea.

"His name was impossible to pronounce, but beautiful to hear. Love grew between them, a love so great and powerful it never aged with time. No one knew how or why, only that it was.

"This love was so precious that Marin bottled it up in a small vial around her neck to keep it close to her heart. But the tyranny of war breached to find them. Not wanting her to come to harm, the White Dragon faced death and convinced it to take him so that Marin could live. And so, death took the White Dragon."

"Oh, no!" Polli cupped her hand over her mouth.

"What did Marin do?" Elra asked, her eyes wide with wonder.

Amalya leaned in toward them, casting a shadow over them where they sat beside the house, the storeroom at their backs.

"It plunged Marin into despair. For many long days and nights, she hid away from the world, lost in her grief. Why had she found something so pure, only to have it ripped away? Through her sullen eyes, she soon realized the answer. The vial she wore around her neck possessed the magic of this truth, the essence of pure, untainted love that would end the terrible war befalling the land of Jöro."

Raising her hands, Amalya spread her fingers out in front of her, moving them slowly through the air. "So she set out and told others of what she had discovered and shared with them the magic she'd created with the White Dragon.

Each one who heard her words was granted a single drop from her magic vial and each one, whether man, witch, or Draughtrìnd, spread Marin's teachings to others."

Polli and Elra kept their gazes on her as Amalya brought her hands close to her chest. "She had given to so many that soon the magic was widespread throughout the warring lands. Despite all this, it did not spread fast enough. King Aethelwulf and the Draughtrìnd were ready to face the end in a battle that would lead to inevitable death.

"All eyes drew toward the heartland. In the endless smoldering ash of the city of Enda, they made their final stand. Before the first blade struck, Marin appeared before them, standing between man and dragon with her words of peace for all to hear. They resonated like water over a parched land. She had lifted the veil of hatred so that all could feel the warming light of Sól once again. Her speech calmed both the Draughtrìnd and men, but there was one man who would not hear her."

Elra brought her hands to her mouth, leaning in toward Polli and saying in a whisper, "The king."

A faint smile breached Amalya's face as she glanced at Mira, who sat quietly behind the girls, matching the children's elation. "King Aethelwulf wanted the land to be soaked with the blood of the Draughtrìnd, spoiled so that no good could ever grow from it again. He moved to strike down his enemy, with an army at his back and fear to lead them."

"What about now, Miss Amalya?" Polli's soft voice reached her ears. "Why does the king hate the Draughtrìnd now?"

She looked down at Polli's hopeful and curious eyes. Elra sat next to her, clutching her dress, eagerly awaiting her answer. Tristan stood not too far from where they sat, watching Amalya from the safety of the storeroom door, though no one else seemed to notice his presence.

Amalya returned her focus to the children. "None truly know the answer, my dear. Young King Ulfrick tells us the Draughtrìnd have become dangerous, falling into their old, selfish ways. They have attacked us without reason, which has forced his hand. Many dragons have since abandoned the four Draughtrìnd lords that remain, each locked away in the safety of their hidden fortresses."

"They won't ever come out and hurt us, right, Mama?" Elra's eyes were wide with subtle fear.

"No, but if they do, the king will be ready for them. He builds his Dragon Guard army day by day to be the strongest force Jöro has ever seen. If the Draughtrìnd ever decided to harm our lands, the Dragon Guard will be strong enough to protect us."

"Come along, you two." Mira stood, wiping her hands on her apron. "Wash up for supper."

"Did you like the story, Mama?" Polli asked as she and Elra stood with a bounce in their step.

"Of course! No one tells stories like Amalya." Mira smiled and looked over at her. "You'll be coming along too."

Amalya nodded. "Yes, just let me gather my things."

Mira took the girls by the hand and led them back to the house. Amalya picked up her leather-bound book. She did not need the stories that were woven onto the parchment; she had kept them stored in her mind for many Setts, ever since she was a girl. But keeping them close while she sang her tales aloud kept her firmly planted, never chancing to be lost in the words of the past. As she stood, she saw Tristan's shadow moving closer.

"Must you always sneak up on me?" Her eyes trained on him. His hair was down now, casting half his face in shadow as his piercing gold eyes narrowed in their hooded bed.

"Do you trust your king?" His words were forceful, carrying weight too heavy for her to catch.

Amalya clutched her book to her chest and turned to leave him. "He is your king too."

"One man cannot truly rule over so many."

Something escaped her grasp, falling from the closed pages of the book. The white rose from her dream fell into the rough, short grass like a gentle feather. Tristan bent down to pick it up, taking it in his hand and slowly rising again to meet her. She kept her gaze on him, her heart pounding as he observed the flower between his fingers. It looked as it did when she had awoken that morning. As if it had never been pressed against the pages.

With a choice glance, he offered the rose to her, letting it pass from his fingers as she took it from him. "Such a lovely reflection."

Amalya placed the flower back in her book. "Reflection?" She stared into his haunting golden eyes.

"The rose," he amended with quiet contentment. "It appears beautiful and pure. But along its stem it is full of peril that prevents any from truly embracing it without pain. It is how you believe others see you. Is it not? Or at the very least. . . how Wesley sees you."

Her mouth ran dry, desperate for his words to quench. He stripped her down to her very bones without needing to physically see what was festering beneath her skin. The embodiment of her essence in the mouth of a stranger. "How could you possibly know such things?"

Tristan swept his curtain of locks aside to reveal the angles of his strong face. "One only needs to open their eyes."

Amalya pressed the book against the harsh labor of her lungs as he remained stoic and forthright in his stance. He had awoken the fire; a passion she had long forgotten how to wield.

He lowered his head. "Good evening, my lady."

With that, he turned to leave, and she watched him disappear back into the storehouse. Her muscles tightened as she followed him with a heavy stride. As she came to the doorway, she drew to a halt. "Why must you do this?"

Tristan stopped, turning to face her slowly. "Do what?"

"Say these things. Allow me to feel things I have forgotten how to feel."

Tristan faced her fully. So smooth were his motions, it was as if a silent wind had carried him. "Is that so troubling?"

She held her lips tauten, refusing to let air escape. Tightening her arms across her chest, Amalya felt herself waver on unsteady legs. "My mind is already troubled. You've only troubled it more."

They stood in silence, waning in Sól's retreating light. Then she felt it again, that invisible pull to be closer to him. So familiar and yet so strange. The desire for this man—this peculiar, cryptic man who only made her feel like she was nothing and yet everything at the same time. Ferociously sifting through the darkness, doing away with everything that had kept her in the shadows for far too long.

It was only then she remembered the trinket, still lonely

and awaiting freedom in her pocket. She plunged her hand within the fabric to retrieve it and held it out for him to see. A circle encompassed the triangles, each supporting the strength of the other. "What is this? What do these markings mean?"

Tristan took a step toward her, placing his hand over her fingers, which gripped his gift to her son. His touch was fire, but not one threatening to scar and maim. It surged up her arm, awakening her essence from its stagnant state.

"The markings are ancient." He spoke softly, gracing her knuckles as he traced down her palm. "In a language only known to the first men." He lingered on her skin, his eyes studying the feel of her, quickening the pace of his breath.

Amalya pressed her hand against his palm, seeing how it forced him to yield. He grasped her tighter, looking into her eyes with an intensity matched by her own. Waves of fire surged through her body, eliminating the cold, dark fortress of her prison. A blaze so intoxicating she could no longer sense the passing of time through her pale locks.

He only allowed her to entice him for a minute before removing his hand from her and slowly lowering it to his side.

"Do you speak to others like this?" Amalya asked with a quickening breath as she lowered the trinket from sight.

"I only speak to you." His words, though softly spoken, cut through her like a harsh, icy wind, sedating the fire his touch had conjured.

Amalya gave a slight shake of her head. "You must speak to others."

"Words only mean something when you want them to. They either carry it or are there to simply make noise."

She took a rigid step toward him, dropping her fist to her chest. "Who are you?"

"You do not know who I am—"

"I know you only by what you say and what you say is everything! You see me more than I could ever hope to see. Peeling the layers that have tightly bound me in this life with little effort." Her words caught in her throat. "How is this possible?"

"I see and I listen."

"You have not been here more than a season. Am I truly laid out so bare?"

His eyes captured her, resting quietly against the falling light of Sól. "If you were, do you think others would still be blind to what you truly need?"

Amalya was so fixated on his gaze that when his hand cupped her fragile cheek, her breath fell short. "I see your eyes. They are the keepers of your essence. A tormented whirlpool, sucking you down to the cold absence of its depths. One must slow the tide if you ever hope to find the strength to fight against the current."

Moving toward her, Tristan came a mere hair's breadth from her face. His earthen scent quickened her pulse, each attempt to fill her lungs clinging to the back of her throat.

The golden hue, twisting and swirling inside their marble shells, was like nothing she had ever seen before. So full that they may burst. She longed to find solace in them; to discover the pieces he was hoping she'd find.

Her head began to spin like spooling wool. She drew in, the tip of his nose gracing her own, spreading a warmth through her face that flushed her cheeks and silenced the chaos of her mind.

A familiar dream came into focus. A yearning to reach when she could not touch. It was there, behind his eyes.

"I know you."

The words escaped from her as she placed a weary hand on his face. His skin was like fire, spreading into her fingers and down her arm, igniting her heart and tossing her mind into a turbulent sea—just as it did when she placed her hand on the surface of the Draughtrìnd's scales. Entrapped by the same eyes of the God of Old.

Tristan relinquished her touch, pulling from her with haste. He seemed distressed, confused by what had transpired between them almost as much as she was. They stood together, lost in how to speak or act. Amalya knew she could not linger much longer if only to keep the suspicions of her family and friends at bay. No words were worth muttering as she did not wish to be parted from him. Not for a single instant.

"Good evening, my lady." He moved abruptly from her sight.

She did not follow, petrified in the mixings of all he had stirred. She placed her hand, with the trinket still clutched inside, to her cheek. She savored any warmth captured by his touch before it melted away in the cooling air.

Looking into the sky, she saw Sól retreating into the darkness of Nótt's blooming night. She'd been gone too long. Turning on the balls of her feet, she scurried toward the house, hoping the dizziness that lingered did not show in her stride.

TWELVE

"Each day bled into the next. The mountain refused to break from its unyielding haze. The ground on which they settled along the skin of Skarpur remained dead and lifeless, just as the tree that hung above them."
- Excerpt from *The Tale of Marin and the White Dragon*

Mira and the girls were already settled down at the table. Wesley and Laird laughed by the fire, smoking pipes with an herbal scent. All noticed Amalya's entry and greeted her with warm smiles. Amalya was no longer accustomed to having so many people in the home.

Remnants of heat still lingered on her cheeks. The last thing she wanted was to draw attention to herself. She headed to her room to put down her work. Drawing her hands through her hair down to her bodice, she pressed the folds of her dress as she breathed deeply to collect herself. As the experience faded into memory, she placed the rounded stone trinket on her desk and entered the kitchen once again.

Mira was getting everything ready for their first meal together since Arthur was born.

Amalya headed over to her. "Let me help you, Mira."

"I'm almost done." Mira smiled and gestured to the table. "I can manage."

Amalya did not insist any further and took the seat across from Wesley. Polli and Elra sat next to one another, giggling and fussing as little girls do. The food looked delicious, roasted chicken with fresh greens and potatoes, spiced rum, milk for the children, and, of course, two freshly baked pies left cooling by the window.

This was more than Amalya expected—something she did not deserve. But she would keep her thoughts to herself. Mira had worked so hard; she would be appreciative. Though she could not help but feel the need to run back into her room and lock the door.

"You're looking well this evening," Laird commented as he smiled across from her.

Wesley placed an unwanted hand on Amalya's, forcing her gaze to fall upon him. "One of the best days she's had, I would say."

Amalya pulled from him, genuinely startled by his touch. Wesley looked injured by her reaction, but shielded it well.

"Yes." She forced a weak smile and looked at Laird. "Though I must say I am feeling its effects. I am not used to all this attention."

"Understandable." He glanced at Wesley before resuming his meal.

The conversation quickly diverted from her to more menial things that carried little weight. She could not get Tristan out of her mind. The familiarity of his touch, how it engulfed her. Cleansed her. Eradicated all the frigid emptiness within her. Though it did not carry to her where she sat at the table, the memory was enough to keep her locked within its delicate clutches.

She smiled when appropriate and agreed when her voice needed to be heard, but nothing could keep her from what had been kindled by the presence of their hired help. No one cared to notice, only grateful that she seemed more herself. But that was so far from the truth.

It was foolish to think things could ever go back to how they were, no matter how hard they wished it to be. Becoming a mother had changed her, and it could not be undone. She might enjoy life again, but there would always be a small part of her that remained in despair. It would come up for air before descending back into the depths, so she would never forget its presence.

When the meal was over and the night settled in the sky, their guests prepared to leave.

Elra pulled at Amalya's dress. "Can I go with them, Mama? Can I please?"

"If it is all right with your father and Mira, of course."

Elra turned to Wesley with puppy dog eyes.

He gave her a look like he would deny her the opportunity. "I don't know, Elra. . . ."

"Oh, stop teasing her," Mira interrupted. "Of course you can, my dear. We would love to have you."

Both girls jumped up and down in delight.

Amalya placed her hand on Elra's head. "Let's go get you ready, then."

They got a small satchel of essentials ready for her stay. Elra bounced around her room, clearly excited to be spending some time away from home. She handed Amalya a few of her favorite effects before closing up the pack tightly.

"Mama."

Amalya looked down at her daughter.

"I had a good day today."

"I'm glad."

"Did you have a good day?"

Amalya touched Elra's hair and drew her fingers to her chin. "Of course, dear." She smiled at her. "Come on, before they leave without you."

Elra wrapped her arms around her mother. "I love you."

Amalya sank down to the floor to meet her soft brown eyes. "I love you too."

Elra's little arms squeezed around her neck. Amalya held her with eyes closed. If there was any love that would come without consequence or burden, it was the love of a child. She tried so hard to feel it as she once did, but it was so far away, so blurred inside her very being. It was impossible to know if it was still there or just a memory.

Mira peered into the room. "We're about ready to go."

Elra let go of Amalya and kissed her cheek. She grabbed her pack and bounded out of the room.

Mira smiled as Amalya stood up to meet her. "She's a darling girl."

"She is."

"Now," Mira approached her and gathered Amalya up

in her arms, "Wesley will come fetch her tomorrow. Sleep well."

SITTING QUIETLY IN THEIR ROOM, Amalya brushed her long, blonde hair methodically. Her mind had wrapped around itself. The day drew to a close. Some would say it was a day of progress, but it only seemed to raise more questions for Amalya. Curiosity seemed to be the only distraction.

Wesley shuffled back and forth behind her. Arthur was sleeping soundly in his arms, his round face peacefully dreaming up at him.

"Wesley," she whispered as he laid Arthur down to rest in his cradle.

"Yes?"

She waited for him to tuck their little one away. "What do you see when you look in my eyes?"

He crouched down next to her and pulled her hair from her face so there were no obstructions. Now that he was here, facing her, she could not remember the last time they had a moment alone together.

"I see you as you are now."

"You see nothing?"

A slow release of breath passed through his nostrils. "What do you want me to say?"

She shook her head, looking away from him. "I don't know."

He drew back from her, his face flexing as he tightened his jaw. Amalya could see how unsettled he was. There were many things that had transpired today that drew him toward hope. But hope was fickle.

Amalya felt his rough farmer's hands rub against her pale skin. "You seemed. . . well today."

Leaning back, Amalya slipped her hand from him, shaking her head. "What meaning does that word carry now, Wesley?"

"I don't know." Wesley recoiled, drawing his gaze to the wrinkled wood beneath their feet. "So much seems to change. Day by day."

He was being honest with her, something rare but welcomed, even if it meant hearing the truth of how she had damaged them.

"Ever changing."

He only allowed himself a moment of hesitation, shaking the doubt from his mind. Moving closer to her, he captured her hands with his own, settling his gaze upon her face. "Remember that day we stole the cart to go to the capital in the middle of the night?"

A flash of the memory caused her to smile. "I remember."

"It was so dark that we ended up crashing into a ditch and losing your father's best ox. I was in pretty awful shape."

"Your head was bleeding."

"Blood was all over your dress, if I remember correctly." He leaned in closer, the faint smell of hay and dirt tickling her senses. "I remember waking up in your lap. You looked down at me with Sól's sleeping light touching your face. You smiled at me and said, 'You''e awake. Are you ready for what today will bring?'"

The innocence of their youth tickled the corners of her mouth. "I remember."

"That was it. The moment I knew I had fallen in love with you."

Biting her lip, Amalya fought the urge to move away. "Love is such a fragile thing."

Wesley cautiously settled his palm against her cheek. "Fickle and ever so hopeless."

She shook her head in his hand. As cold as she had been in her disparity, there was a part of her that yearned for the boy who worked her father's farm; whose youthful charms held sway over all the wonder and magic that lapped at the edges of her life. "You dare try and make light of this, farm boy?"

"Farm boy." That boyish smirk peeled away the weathered look in his soft brown eyes. "You have not called me that since—"

Her motions did not feel like her own as she leaned in, his soft beard brushing against her chin. She had not kissed him in such a way since before Arthur was born. His tender lips on her own, relishing the airiness of the moment. Weightless and free of all things.

When he drew away from her, she pulled him close. "Will you stay with me tonight?"

Hesitation flashed in his eyes. As confident as he was that they would overcome, Amalya could see just how fragile that confidence was.

"I. . . " He pressed his lips together, reaching to pass his fingers through the blonde tendrils tucked behind her ear. "I am unsure if that is what you truly want. You have not—"

"Can we forget, just for tonight? I want to be how we

were when you found me in the barn loft. Do you remember? How I wished we could have but I dared not?" Her fingers graced his temple, drawing him in. "I want to feel you —all that there is of you."

She saw her words swimming alongside caution in his dark brown eyes. It had been many seasons since Amalya found herself wanting. The desire was strong, as strong as it had ever been. She knew it was not Wesley himself that had fed the flames of desire, but she did not care. He would be as gentle or as savage as she asked him to be.

To use him in such a way was not right, but he yearned to be close to her. She felt it in the gentle strokes of his fingers. The way he searched her face as she inched closer to him. He would not deny her.

Wesley's hand carefully settled on the crux of her neck. He reached up to the light flickering from the candles. With two quick fingers, he snuffed them out.

The room fell into darkness, but this time, Amalya was not alone.

THIRTEEN

"Take her to the sea and let her gaze upon the reflection of the skies. Even in the night cast by her tail, it will sparkle bright."
-Excerpt from *The Song of Dag and Nótt*

Wesley and Tristan had left in the early morning. A prominent trader from Mare, the city by the sea, was visiting Rau looking for trading opportunities.

"This would be a successful venture if I can secure a deal," Wesley said just before he departed.

It would not be as long as their usual trips to the marketplace—most likely they would return in the early evening. Being on her own with Arthur left Amalya quivering with excitement, and with excitement came fear—fear that she would find herself wanting to end the innocence she had brought into the world. But she was not the same as she was when she held Arthur over the flames of the hearth. She had not been that person since before Tristan.

After eating a small breakfast and feeding Arthur, Amalya spent most of the day cleaning the home. The unexpected lightness that had carried her throughout the previous day left a stale, horrid taste in her mouth. She had been alone in the dark for so long that it had become comforting to her. Despite the chill from the emptiness she carried, she was accustomed to it. She did not want to linger on such unfamiliarity. To become lost in it only to have it become just another dream unfulfilled.

The morning was soon drawing to a close as Sól climbed to the highest point in the sky. Amalya looked out over the land to the hills that led to the lake. She could not remember the last time she had been there. Perhaps when Elra was just a baby as Arthur was now. That place was where she had seen her dreams spread their wings and take to the sky.

The mighty Draughtrìnd had carried her dreams away and never looked back. It was foolish to dwell on those times in her life when she knew she could never return to them—though the thought of the Draughtrìnd did reflect in Tristan's touch. When she pressed her palm against its mighty skull, the same comforting fire ignited her from the inside. Though with Tristan, it burned more intensely than she could remember.

One decision could have changed so much.

Arthur popped bubbles from his drooling mouth. This was her life. That day by the lake was becoming a distant memory, one she had held on to for so long, clinging to the line as she remained adrift in a turbulent sea. The thought should have left her throat in a knot, unable to swallow. But it did not, for something else was slowly taking its place in the form of a mysterious man with raven locks and copper-toned skin. And eyes she would not soon forget, not for all the days she remained.

Her gaze traveled to the fields. They lay open and bare, the new crop still juvenile in the season. Even though it was sparse, beauty lay in the stillness. To have all that emptiness meant room for something more. It merely needed time to bloom.

The sudden shift in her thoughts sent her eyes ablaze, catching herself as if mid-fall. She was thinking as her old self did, looking toward the future to attain some form of newness.

Amalya wiped her hands on her apron and made for the house with Arthur cooing in her arms. She did not get very far when she saw a man walking up the path toward the home. She hesitated for a moment before she recognized his face.

Despite his tiredness and need for a bath, Tristan seemed rather pleased to see her. "Good afternoon, my lady."

"Back so soon?" She peered down the road, waiting for any sign of Wesley, Elra, and the ox-pulled cart. "Where is Wesley?"

"I elected to come back early." His hair was drawn back and his clothes slightly sullied with dust from the road.

"I see." It was awkward he would return without Wesley, but perhaps her husband's fear of her being on her own had gotten the better of him. He would never want her knowing how much he worried, so she was sure Tristan would not give the real reason for his return.

"I was about to prepare some food. If you are hungry, I can make you something as well."

He smiled warmly. "Thank you, my lady."

His smile only seemed to elevate his finesse. No manner of indecency could separate him from the prestige he carried, like a prince of old lost to the fires of hardship.

"Wash up first. Food should be ready by the time you return."

She quickly turned toward the house. Her stomach began to flutter, sending tingles of elation down her arms. The sensation made her eyes seem less heavy as she stepped through the door to prepare the midday meal.

She could not believe how excited the prospect of them dining together had made her. It was not very becoming, especially since she was married. It read like a skald's tale, maybe the first new adventure she'd had in a long time. Who knew what would happen? An intellectual conversation, perhaps a story or two about his travels? She could not see the harm in it when her intentions were so innocent.

She quickly placed Arthur on the floor amongst his small wooden toys as she bustled about the kitchen, taking out bread, cheese, and the always succulent basket of dried fruit. A pitcher of freshly made tea already sat on the counter. It was not immensely cold, but it would still be refreshing after a long walk back from Rau.

The thought stopped her momentarily. Rau was miles from here. If Tristan indeed walked back, it would have taken him most of the day and well into the night. Amalya looked out the window as Sól sat still in the sky. It could only have been a little past midday. He must have turned back before they reached the city. Wesley truly was that worried about her.

Peering outside, Amalya caught the scent of salt from the drying barrels just below. Dried fish would be the perfect complement to such a meal. With a quick glance to be sure Arthur would not fall under duress, she popped outside to pry open the barrel. An overwhelming scent of salt and cod burst forth as the seal was broken. Taking a cloth from her apron, she plucked two fish from the barrel before securing it shut once more.

A bounce arose in her step as she returned to the table setting, carefully placing the fish on their own serving dishes, making sure there were knives to capture a slice. Though by the looks of the tanned morsels, it would be easier to rip it apart with one's hands.

Amalya quickly visited the washbasin to remove the preparations from her hands. A slight shift in the floorboards turned her attention to the door as Tristan walked through. His hair was no longer pulled back, but down and appeared to have been combed. He seemed lost, eyes wandering until they fell upon her. This may have been the first time he had ever been inside, at least to her knowledge.

"Please sit." Amalya hurried past him as she grabbed a chunk of bread from the table and presented it to Arthur. He took it excitedly, wasting no time in placing it in his mouth to soften the bread.

Tristan gracefully slid into a chair, looking over all there was to offer. Amalya filled his flagon with refreshment and took a seat across from him. Her stomach fluttered like an ever-mounting storm. He was looking at her, calm but with so much intensity. It was pouring from his eyes like a rushing waterfall.

Reaching steadily out in front of her, she took a generous amount of soft bread and butter to occupy herself.

He sat quietly and watched, taking a meager sip of his drink. He pulled the cup back. "This is very good."

"It's my little creation, one of Wesley's favorites." She shifted in her seat as she tossed some dried fruit onto her plate. "Did Wesley send you back? I must confess, I was a little shocked he would leave me alone. I'm sure he has told you what happened."

"He has divulged nothing to me."

"Oh." She licked her lips, moving to take more bread. "I would have thought he—"

"I do not believe he needs to be concerned." He took another sip from his flagon.

Amalya watched him, unsure how to interpret his answer. Though his words seemed bold and assured, they did not fill her with concern. Perhaps she agreed with him or understood that, as long as he was here, there was nothing to fear.

"I know Wesley will pay you when he can."

"As I have said before, I have little need for coin. Besides," Tristan laced his fingers together calmly on the table in front of him, "those who have patience receive plentiful rewards."

The corner of her lip twitched up into her cheek. "I had a notion that you do not covet coin as other men do."

The fluttering in her stomach rose to her chest, intensifying with every breath she took.

What did this man who wants nothing desire most?

The thought put her on the edge of exhilaration. She dared not ask out of fear of what he might say. She did not want to know, even when it pulled at the sinews of her heart for him to reveal his intentions.

Another bite of food passed down her throat, almost tasteless. "I've heard something about you."

His eyes lit up as he flexed his brows into his dark, ashen locks. "What have you heard?"

"That you like to tell stories. I fancy myself a storyteller as well."

"As I've seen." He took a piece of dried fruit and popped it in his mouth. "You wish to become a skald?"

"I did. A long time ago." Amalya reached for her cup. "Though I have written very little in recent times."

"I've seen you writing." He leaned against the table. "What is it you write if it is not a story?"

She hesitated, finding it difficult to hide her honesty. "I write about you." Her confession surprised even her, though it carried no falsehood. Every word she had written in the weeks he had been here was indeed about him. Or the memory of the dragon he had enticed back into her mind.

Her words did not seem to surprise him. "Why do you write about me?"

A quick glance at Arthur, still gumming his bread, brought no reprieve from the growing lightness now infiltrating her mind.

"I don't really know, but since I first saw you on the road, it has awakened the words." She folded her sweaty palms into one another. Her heart was beating out of her chest, but she did not feel the need to control herself. As the words slipped out, more and more waited to be said.

Tristan did nothing but watch and wait for them to be heard.

"I do not know how or why. But you are a walking memory." She bravely lifted her head as her hands fell to the table. "Of a time when I cared to dream."

Tristan sat up stoically in his chair, his posture unwavering and his eyes calm. "That has been absent from your life."

Then, he did something she did not expect. He slid past the plates of food and drink and gently placed his hand on her own. As he grasped her wrist, he pulled her forward ever so slightly, raising her out of her place of solitude and into the strange realm that hovered around him. They came together across the table, Tristan's long, ashen hair framing his face. His eyes burning their yellowish hue.

Amalya did not pull away. His hand was comforting, a warmth daring to overtake her entire body. Every inch of her, from the top of her head to the very tips of her toes, buzzed with life. The same as she felt the day before and again so many Setts into her past, when her dreams lay wounded in Willow's Lake.

"Tell me a story," she whispered.

Tristan's eyes fluttered like a flame caught in a subtle wind. Every few moments, she witnessed shreds of uncertainty within them, as if he feared she would dismiss him without reason. "I will tell you a story. But I do not know if you are ready to hear it."

Her eyes searched his. "I'm ready now."

Without warning, he recoiled from her. He would not appease her, nor even grant her a taste of what his presence truly meant. His words and touch weaved her insides into a tight, impenetrable suit of armor, so strong and yet too heavy for her to bear without him.

"Why must you leave me to waver on the edge?" she asked.

"I do not wish to cause you duress. But there are traditions I must—" He drew away, standing firmly across from her as he cut himself off, replacing his words with an escape. "Thank you for your hospitality."

Like a swift wind, he departed, closing the door behind him. Amalya stood quiet and vulnerable. Everything left of her was bare amongst the bread, butter, fish, and dried fruit, waiting to be tasted. He knew everything she wanted to say and heard all she needed him to hear. Yet he would still keep her skirting along the edge of this unfathomable bliss, teetering between eternal night and endless day.

She could not think clearly. Her heart continued to pound in her chest. Without another moment wasted, she rushed to the door and pulled it open, stepping outside into Sól's light. "Who are you?" Her haste wafted her hair across her shoulders.

Tristan was only a few paces from her. He hesitated, then turned, giving her no reply. His silence was deafening.

"Why won't you tell me who you are?"

"Perhaps I am afraid of the consequences."

A valiant approach, one not laced with fear but determination, carried her to him. "I do not believe you. Why are you here?" She struggled against her words. "I cannot understand."

Tristan stepped toward her. His finger reached out and touched her forehead. "What does this tell you?" Then, his finger traveled to rest on her beating chest. "What does this tell you?"

It was all too obvious now as he stood in front of her, connecting the path between the mind and the heart.

Could he truly be?

It did not seem possible, but it was. It had to be. There was no other explanation.

His eyes continued to trap her. "Do you believe what you feel or what you think you feel?"

She hastened to reveal what her mind had concluded, but could not bring herself to speak it. "Are they not the same?"

"Are they?"

He drew away almost forcefully, as if he were afraid of what might happen next. She would not allow it and her hand shot out to grasp his wrist. Unblinking, Amalya took a step toward him, reaching with her other hand for his forehead. Studying his eyes, that same fire radiated into her palm and down her arm. It spread across her chest, down her back, to the very tips of her Sól-kissed locks.

The dark-coated armor surrounding his eyes as brilliant as Sól himself, watching her with acute curiosity and a hidden longing for her touch. His gnarled horns rested gallantly atop his head and his teeth glinted in the water's reflection as it lapped against his powerful legs to bear the weight of his greatness. The winged beast of fire, a Draughtrìnd in the flesh, steady beneath her shaking hand.

Part of her always knew the truth, but she had gotten too accustomed to being in the shadows to understand the light from the memories that still lingered. Her body shook with excitement or fear. The sudden realization of his identity forced her hand from him. She staggered backward toward the house, unable to breathe.

Tristan stood, unmoving. "I will do nothing to lead you astray. Nothing against your will." His eyes pulsed as if eager for her to reveal what she had finally come to know.

She opened door, stepped inside, and closed it behind her. Arthur gurgled and glanced at her, bread falling from his mouth.

Her eyes traveled to her bedroom, where her desk sat empty and waiting. She stumbled across the room to reach it. Falling into the chair, her fingers scrambled for a blank piece of parchment. Already written words fell to the floor to join the existing pile resting at the side of her desk. All her suspicions and realizations poured from her through rapidly moving fingers. The torrent of whatever this was she was feeling overhelemed her, running her cheeks hot.

If this was real, she had to remember it—hold it in her mind and feel it in her hands. That was the only way it could be. That was the only way no one could deny her the truth.

FOURTEEN

"She had never loved before, not this fiercely. A love that could not be broken by fire or death. One that would live, even when she perished and surrendered to Sól's light. Embracing him only heightened the truth of it."
Excerpt from *The Tale of Marin and the White Dragon*

Amalya stood in the kitchen, her palms gripping the washbasin for support. The children were already sleeping soundly in their beds. Wesley was sitting by the fire, enjoying a comfortable rest after another long day. She had spoken little after he returned from the city just this morning. His exhaustion left her tranquil. Too much had been spinning in her mind since her discovery. Knowing what Tristan was, she had to say something to Wesley. He would believe her. He had to. It was the only way she could believe it herself.

She stepped away from the washbasin and approached

the fire. Wesley looked up at her, immediately sensing the tension she carried.

Taking a deep breath, Amalya held her hands to her stomach and stood in front of him. "Something's happened."

He eyed her cautiously. "Is it Arthur? He seemed fine when I returned."

"No, he is good." Her thumbs rubbed across her knuckles. "Tristan, he's. . . he's not who he appears to be."

Wesley straightened in the chair and leaned closer to her. "What did he do? Did he say something to you?"

She was at a loss for words, knowing the truth would somehow scar him. How she was, what became of her after Arthur was born—how much more could he bear? Amalya loved Wesley, but it was never as love was supposed to be between a husband and wife. Maybe it was before, but not anymore.

Her silence forced him to his feet slowly. "I'll have a talk with him."

She grabbed him by the arm. "No! Not now."

"What is it?" Wesley watched her closely.

Her eyes searched his bearded face, wanting to lie but knowing she could not. Though she tried to remain in control of herself, she could not help feeling a tightness binding within her chest. "You haven't seen it?"

"Seen what?" He searched her eyes for some understanding.

Amalya must have appeared frantic. She did not want to seem so. This was not something created from the darkness that still infected her very essence. This was entirely different. Loosening her hold on him, Amalya steadied her voice.

"I knew the moment I saw him. It was there, in the far reaches of my mind."

Wesley's gaze cast down into his beard. He was already doubting her, seeing the disappointment at how she was acting. What she would say would only disappoint him more, but she could not hold it inside and keep it only for herself. "I thought we were past this uneasiness around our workhand," he said.

"Don't you see what Tristan is?"

He leaned away from her. "Amalya—"

Amalya could sense she was losing him. "The dragon, the one we saved by the lake when we—" She stopped, knowing he only heard her words and not the truth behind them. "How do you not know? You spend so much time with him and yet nothing has crossed your mind? The way he acts, his voice, his mannerisms. He's *not* a man."

"The dragon." Wesley released himself from her hold, pulling his fingers through his hair as he walked toward the table. "Why is he here?" His arms raised in tandem with his brow as he turned to her. "A Draughtrìnd working on a farm for his own amusement?"

"Isn't it obvious?" Amalya stood firm, keeping a weak hold on her wrist. "He is here for me."

"For *you?*"

There was no way in which she could explain this to him that did not make her sound mad. That was the last thing she wanted him to think, but it was too late. The moment she uttered the words, he was already accusing her of it.

A solemn sigh heaved from his chest. "This is just another one of your. . . songs? What you've been writing has.

. . gotten the better of you." Amalya shook her head furiously as he continued to speak. "You are. . . giddy, or—"

"Why are you trying to convince yourself of a lie? You must listen to me."

"You are making it *impossible*."

"It's not in my head."

"But it is. *All of this is*."

Parched air escaped from Amalya's throat. "It only seems that way because you do not trust me."

Closing his eyes, his hand reached for the bridge of his nose, pinching it between his fingers. "That is how it *has been*, Amalya. Whether you see it or not."

Amalya's hands dropped. She could feel her lips quivering from his disbelief. She would not create such a lie as this, not to amuse herself or anyone. Wesley had to believe her—if he wanted to help her, he would believe her.

Strong, determined steps brought her to him again, so he could not shy away from her confession. "He wants to take me away from here and you will do nothing?"

"Take you where exactly?"

"It doesn't matter where. Only that it will be away from here. From the farm. From our children. From you and—"

His head snapped around to look at her. "That's enough!"

They stood facing one another, blocked by a distance far greater than anything they could measure. Amalya could only look at him with hurt in her eyes, their sea-gray hue shifting and churning the waters behind them. He would not stand by her now when she needed him most. She did not want to hurt him, for he was nothing but good. A good father and a hardworking man. This confession was a test for both of them, and both of them had failed.

"You don't believe me," she whispered.

"How can you expect me to believe anything you've said? After everything that has happened."

"I'm telling you the truth!"

With a hard step forward, Wesley lowered his eyes to meet her gaze. "I have done nothing but bleed for this family. To keep you all safe. To keep Elra from seeing the shell you have become. She asks me day after day what ails you. And I cannot give her an answer. I can do nothing but watch this. . . this madness chip away at you. I can do nothing!"

Amalya bit her tongue, unsure why she was holding herself back now. Now, when so much truth was spilling from her lips that she could not keep to herself any longer. "You promised me we would not be trapped here as we are. Does that mean nothing? It was your—"

"Then go. *Leave.*" His voice was laced with hurt and anger. "Why do you remain here if you believe a Draughtrìnd waits for you outside our door?"

"He won't take me without my consent."

"And do you?"

The decision had been made long ago, before she even opened her mouth to speak. She hoped he would tell her to stay, tell her he did not want her to leave. If he did, she would stay. She would abandon this awakened dream to stay with him and their children in this life that she never wanted.

Wesley's beard trembled, chest heaving beneath his sullen tunic as his hands came up to grab the sides of her arms. *"Do you consent?"*

143

He searched her face, but she offered him nothing. She was guilty in his accusing stare. The promise already broken.

Shaking his head, Wesley bowed away from her, creating a distance too small to render relief. "I no longer recognize you, Amalya."

"Because I am not her. The Amalya you knew is lost." The warm tears that caressed her face brought little comfort. "There is nothing left."

"No." He shook his head. "You are sick."

"I am not—"

"Whatever crawled into your essence since Arthur. . . it has changed you." His dark brown eyes shifted and turned to keep his sadness at bay. Wesley clenched his teeth, dragging shaken hands down his beard. "And I am desperately trying to pull you from it. Can't you see that?"

Always for her, he would confess nothing else. But was it truly to save her or to keep him from accepting how much has changed. She must make him see, if words would not convince him. Glancing at the door to the outside, Amalya advanced toward it, her dress fluttering behind her in her desperation to reach it. "I'll bring him to you. You can see for yourself."

"You are not listening, Amalya."

As her hand touched the handle, she wheeled around, his dismissal stinging her eyes. "It is you who is not listening!"

With a deep sigh, Wesley ran his hands through his dark red hair, resting his palms on the back of his neck. His brows came down, creasing his eyes. "Perhaps I am done listening."

She had lost his trust. She knew it, of course, but it was

different when spoken aloud. Now there was no avoiding it. This darkness within her had injured them greatly, so much so that she did not have faith they could ever recover. Though they may try to pretend for a while.

Wesley knew that his words had struck deep. It was clear he was reluctant to speak it aloud. Walking up to her, he ran his hands down her stiff arms.

Amalya turned away from him, not wanting to look him in the eye.

"You should retire," he said. "We will talk tomorrow. A good night's rest will clear our minds."

"I have never seen more clearly." She pulled away from his attempted soothing.

Wesley kept his hand raised as she tightened her grip on the door handle. "Where are you going?"

Pushing her entire body against the wooden frame, Amalya burst into the night air, her feet moving into the grass.

Wesley tried to reach for her again, but she wrenched herself away, leaving him to stand just outside the house. He would not leave Elra and Arthur unattended. "Amalya!"

No amount of pleading would make her turn back. She hoped he would thwart her, but only pushed her further. If there was no hope of being happy again in this life, then why pretend? She was tired of pretending. If something real was attainable, she would grasp it. She was ready to breathe again.

She went beyond the farm, over the hill, and toward the lake just before the tree line. Wesley hadn't listened. He would only hear what he wanted to hear. She was not lost, not anymore. It pained her to know he did not believe her. They had endured so much and now, when she needed him most, he abandoned her. He would never truly see as long as she suffered; as long as he believed she was still suffering.

Rushing down the hill, the tall grass was already damp and coated the lengths of her plain dress. The night lay quiet over the lake's still water as she approached. Reaching the edge, Amalya fell to her knees, watching her reflection bend beneath her. Touching her face, her fingers traced her profile from her eyes down to her chin. She pulled her hair free to fall across her shoulders. She knew herself. This was her. Every inch of her was here.

A presence, a shadow, and then a face. Tristan appeared standing behind her, looking down at her through the mirror of water.

She stood up, staring out into the quiet movement of the unseeable darkness. "He did not believe me."

A hand fell on her shoulder and she reached to grasp it. Turning to stare into his safe, golden orbs, Amalya traced her finger from his forehead down to his chin. His skin was warm, like a warring fire. She could feel not one imperfection as she traveled along its surface. "This is you. You're as real as I am."

His breathing hitched slightly as her fingers tickled his skin. To see him so affected by her filled her with a need to be desired. To fall into his arms and for him to whisper sweet sentiments into her ear as she coaxed him with their closeness.

"Your beauty terrifies me." He spoke softly as he leaned toward her. "I long to fear it. To let it pass through my fingers and pour down my throat." His hand rose slowly to wrap around her wrist, drawing invisible lines upon her skin. "But I cannot allow myself if you do not wish it."

Amalya hesitated, his words shattering the void that had become her sanctuary. "What do you desire most?"

His fingers slipped into the cracks of her own. "I desire you."

Her blood quickened. He was the only thing that filled her tormented heart. It heaved from the weight of how full it had become and begged her to cease her longing to be consumed by him. Words had never been so bereft. Her tongue ached to part his lips and allow him to pour all he had offered her into the empty vessel she had become. How it left her quivering in its wake, willing to surrender to it.

Carefully and with silent effort, he slid his other hand along her neck and up through her blonde tendrils. They hovered a breath from one another. Her entire body felt as if a thousand bees covered it, crawling up and down while gently vibrating on her skin. The deep, burning scent of him, the whisper of his breath on her face. It was all so overwhelming. If she closed her eyes, she would see him, a Draughtrìnd, the same hue as his long, flowing locks. He lingered ever closer to her lips, inching just near enough for her to think of nothing else. She could feel his anxiousness through his fingertips. He had been waiting just as long as she had. She would look past everything she had ever known to be in this moment forever.

"Then fear me," she whispered quietly, "please."

A forcible kiss crashed upon her lips. It was the first time in her memory that she was part of something more than herself. The air surrounding them was now free. The rush of euphoria, the chill from his touch down her spine, the gentle ringing in her ears. She had never felt so invigorated. It was all happening so fast; she did not consciously know what she was doing. Pressing her body against him, he wrapped her in his arms as she ran her hands through his hair.

His taste was like a stinging rain that released into the air the moment it fell upon one's skin. She could feel herself moving as their tastes met and his arms held her tighter against him. They fell beneath the canopy of the willow tree, hidden in the curtain of pale green. The ground was still soft here, away from the dying rays of Sól's light upon Dag Break. His lips moved to just below her ear, then down her neck, sucking at her skin as if he needed her to live. Each kiss that he placed upon her left her yearning for more. She felt his hands lift her dress, felt him run his nails down her thigh. Each coarse sensation sent passion rippling through her veins.

Every inch of her he touched drove her deeper into the soft grass. Her mind was falling into the sudden ecstasy they had created. She brought herself against him as he shed his tunic, feeling the tight ripples of his copper skin on the inside of her legs. Her hands trailed down his back as Tristan overtook her, slipping into her soft, welcoming longing.

Arching her back, Amalya's mouth opened, the sensation of fire within her. It burned away the darkness, numbing her to everything else but him. She wanted more, digging her nails into the tightness of his back. He exposed her breasts with his strong, gentle hands, rolling her sensitive points between his teeth as he continued to give her everything that he was. She wanted all of him, breaking free with moans of pleasure.

The gradual build from his deep, satisfying rhythm began to overwhelm her senses. Amalya let her desires escape through her teeth, tightening her hold on him as she inched ever closer to the limits of her body. Tristan did not relent, one arm bracing the ground as he continued to escalate his desire for her. Grabbing her hips, he dug his fingers into her sides and seized her, feeling her body tremble as Amalya sang a song of pure ecstasy. In the same moment, she felt the release of his pressure within her, arching herself one final time before collapsing into the ground.

As Tristan's body relaxed, he took her arm in his hands and kissed it softly, allowing her to bask in the love they had shared. Each time he planted his tasteful lips on her skin, it came alive with the gentle humming of bees.

But the longer she lay there, the more the curse of their actions brought her thoughts to the adultery she had willingly allowed. This went against every promise she had made on the day she married. All she could see behind her closed eyes was Wesley, watching her without expression or need. Wesley loved her with all his heart, and she had willingly rebelled against him.

But it was too late. She had given herself to a Draughtrìnd. There was nothing left to do but let the guilt flood her mind.

Tristan released her arm and pulled away from her, letting her body fall away from his retreating form.

For a moment, she was alone and untouched. All was silent. Opening her eyes, Amalya stared into the willow tree. A gentle breeze swayed the hanging branches as a shadow cast itself upon their canvas. When she looked to where Tristan should have been, he was no longer there. Not as he was.

Heavy teeth and horns watched where she lay. Powerful, taloned arms rested on either side of her body as he cast the same golden gaze she could never forget upon her. Amalya pulled at her dress to cover her modesty. Despite his frightening form, he was still Tristan. Part of her wanted to run away as his massive darkness loomed over her, but she remained.

Her heart swelled with unimaginable love for him, but guilt from what they had done weighed heavily on her mind. She hesitated, like a small drop of water waiting to fall. She could not have what she wanted without someone coming to harm. It was a truth that followed her for her entire life. Everything she had done was for others and doing so pulled her so deep into despair, she did not wish to escape.

Perhaps she was waiting for him to come and pull the sheets from her eyes. To show her that everything she could ever hope for was not so far from reach. Wishing to feel as she did when she found him injured at the lake was not a dream any longer. Tristan had come for her. He had unknowingly saved her when she had resigned herself to her pitiful existence.

She reached up to rest her hand between his nostrils as he took in her scent. "You are magnificent," she uttered quietly. "My heart is full for you."

The gentle rumble he emitted became harsher as his teeth flared. His grand neck coiled toward the willows as Amalya scampered backward against the harsh bark, facing him, breath short with anticipation. His roar pierced the air surrounding them, shaking the branches so violently they cascaded down around her.

Amalya could feel her body tense with the expectation of death, but she was not afraid. Nothing in her mind questioned his motives. It didn't matter—all that mattered was that it was happening. It could not be prevented. Perhaps dying was the best way to end this ecstasy she now contained in her heart. Clasping her eyes shut, she opened her mouth to scream and welcome whatever fate had to offer.

As the intense burning from his fiery breath consumed her in unwavering numbness, her body jerked into awakening. Falling to the ground, Amalya's eyes shot open as she stared at the wooden panels of her home.

Strong arms grabbed her and hauled her to her feet, twisting her around to a blurred face. "Amalya! Amalya!"

Squinting tears from her burning eyes, Wesley's concern came into view. Her father was standing behind him, seeing her awake, bringing him to fall beside her. Sweat coated her bare arms and legs, her faded nightdress stuck to her as water clings to a rock.

"How did I get here?"

"Just try ta stay calm." Horace gently placed his hands on her shoulders.

Jerking away from him, she fell into Wesley's chest, but quickly retreated, coming to the floor against the leg of her desk. "How did I get here? Where. . . where is he?"

"We're here." Horace stepped forward and crouched down in front of her. "Nothin' to be fearful of."

"Where is he?" Her voice elevated. "Why am I here?"

There were no answers from Horace's rough, quivering lips. Amalya looked from him to Wesley and back again, seeing them before her but not believing they truly were. She was by the lake under the willow tree. She had given herself to Tristan and he had taken her with fire-blazed breath.

Why was she here?

Wesley bent down, threatening to touch her, but left his hands hovering close, uncertainty plaguing his eyes. "Look at me."

Amalya turned away from him, focusing on the small knot in the wood floor, staring down into the muddied darkness beneath their home.

With a hasty hand, Wesley took her by the chin and turned her to him. "For Marin's sake, *look at me!*"

She stopped resisting and stared harshly.

"You've been in bed for three days. You spoke with me, do you remember? Three days ago, you ran out of the house and collapsed. The healer has been here. You were burning with fever. We. . . we did not know if you would wake up."

Her lips tightened as her eyes narrowed. "You're lying." She pulled away from him. "That can't be true."

"It *is* true."

Amalya stood up, backing away from the men in her life and falling onto the bed. Grabbing her head between her hands, she pressed her ears flat against her skull.

Everything she was hearing was wrong. If she closed her eyes, he would be there. She waited in the darkness of her mind. And waited. But there was nothing but Wesley's voice pleading with her to stop. Upon opening them again, she was still in her room, surrounded by wooden walls and flickering candlelight.

Horace's hands covered his mouth as he walked back and forth like a caged animal. The sound of his footsteps suffocated her mind, growing louder with each pace. Wesley came to her again, but she pulled away from him.

"Don't touch me!"

He was only trying to help her, but she did not want help. She only wanted to understand how this came to be.

"Amalya, please."

"No." She shook her head. "Just leave me alone. Just go, please."

Wesley backed away slowly as Horace came over and placed a hand on his shoulder. "Leave her then."

She followed Wesley's drawn eyes as the men approached the door, carrying her gaze with him. When he finally broke from her, the door closed softly behind them. She could hear their whispers beyond, but they meant nothing to her. Every inch of her body fractured, the panicked beating of her heart rattling her bones to the point of breaking.

Drawing in her shaking hands, Amalya watched as the slight pulsing beneath her skin left her fingers numb and unfeeling. "I touched you," she whispered to herself. "I felt you. How could you not be here?"

There was no help in controlling the desperate flight that was coursing through her veins. Hot tears coated her cheeks and fell from the slight angle of her chin. There were so many pieces left scattered, reaching up blindly to grasp nothing. She was helpless.

This was a dream—it had to be a dream—but what was one to her was not to others. It was false. Nothing so vivid and so real could be nothing. Tristan had been with her. Confessed that she was his purpose. Watching. Always watching. Waiting to catch her again in his golden eyes.

Which direction could she turn when she did not know how she came to be here? She drew her knees to her chest, burying her sorrows against her cold skin. She was adrift, cast into the wind with no purpose.

"Marin, help me understand," she breathed. "What is happening to me?"

FIFTEEN

"The Draughtrind allowed us to hold titles and claims to lands that would never truly be ours. They mired our loyalty and fear to uphold their own precedence."
- King Aethelwulf letters, 1,806 Sól Sett, First Season, Rökkur

T ime passed like an eerie itch, scraping along the edge of Amalya's profile with its long, heavy nails. They pierced her feet, keeping her tethered, unable to move. Her body dropped against her curled-up legs. Sól was waning in the window as if trying one last time to pull her free, but not even the gift of Dag, the Light Dragon, could wrench her from what bound her.

Many days had passed and nothing had changed. No answers given. No questions resolved. But she remained. Constant and unchanging.

Wesley knew the truth and yet he hid it from her. She did not understand why she was being thwarted. No amount of contemplation could render a reasonable answer. This had to be some sort of plan to make her forget, but how could she forget? Every memory of Tristan was playing in her head as if she were reliving it again and again. She could not turn away from him. She did not want to forget him, nor the sin they had committed.

Frantic, her gaze landed on her desk, where the pages she had poured herself upon lay untouched. Stumbling from the bed, she reached for them, her hand slipping across the surface, causing the parchment to plummet onto the floor. Fingers graced each and every page. It was here. Everything she had written since the day she saw him on the road. The truth laid bare.

As she flitted from one page to the next, her focus began to waver. The words she had written began to bleed into each other, as if stumbling to become words at all. Amalya held up the last parchment she had scribed on, her eyes glistening as she traced every line with her diluted gaze. There were no words. No truths laid upon the page. Lines weaved in every direction, tangled and wound into a treacherous web of lies and deceit.

How could this be? she thought as her hand trapped the page against the floor, leaning over it as if trying to decipher the secrets it held. *It was here. It was all here.*

The panic rising within her chest soon subsided as she raised her gaze to the knotted walls that surrounded her. Wesley must have desecrated all she had confessed. Of course. He had defiled it to hide the truth from her. To keep her from believing all she had witnessed.

The sound of the door slowly opening roused her to see who had come. Mira looked in every corner of the room before finally her gaze fell on Amalya's crumpled-up form. Her eyes told Amalya everything she needed to know.

Mira stepped over to her carefully, bending down with her face full of sorrow. "Hello, dear."

Amalya did not want to look at her. She did not want to be pitied. This was all wrong, making her look like some sort of wild fool who had lost her mind.

Amalya began to collect everything that had fallen into a muddled heap. "What do you want?" she whispered as she cowered from her only friend.

"To see you."

Amalya quickly abandoned her attempt to guard her words and pushed herself across the floor to the bed.

Mira bit her lip, choosing her next words. "Elra and Arthur are doing just fine. They're staying with us until you're well again."

"Keep them. You are a better mother than I."

Her confession caught Mira off guard. She brought her hand to her lips. "Do not say such things."

Amalya pushed the stray hairs away from her face so nothing would distract her from her words. She studied her friend's tense posture, not giving her a moment to find peace. "They're lying to you, don't you see? I know what I saw, what I've done. They can't hide the truth from me." She reached, grabbing Mira by the arm to draw her close. "You believe me, don't you? I don't know why they insist on lying to me. Believe me, Mira. Everything I've said is true."

"I believe you." She took Amalya's hands in her own. "I believe you believe it is the truth."

There was a glimmer of hope that Mira would not betray her. Searching her face, Amalya drew a scant breath. "You know him! Tristan is not who he says he is! He showed me. I. . . I saw him become what he truly is!"

"I know, dear."

"Where is he?" Pulling away abruptly, Amalya made for the door. "Is he here?"

With subtle caution, Mira shook her head. "He's not here."

"Where has he gone? Has Wesley sent him away?"

Mira's bottom lip trembled as Amalya waited for an answer. She was hiding something as well. Tristan was still there, but they did not want her to see him. If they just saw how she saw him, they would know. Perhaps he only wanted her to see what he was. That must be it. He only wanted her to know. Everyone else was unworthy.

She did not wait for Mira's reply. Rushing from the floor, Amalya burst out the door into the main room of the house.

"Amalya!" Mira's voice carried behind her.

Horace and Wesley stood in the kitchen with Laird, grinding something that released a warm, deep scent from under the pestle. They all looked at her as she entered.

Amalya stood determined, pushing her hair from her face. "Where is he?"

Wesley tightened his lip before his body relented with a sigh. "Where is who?"

"You know who. Where is Tristan?"

"He's not here, Amalya."

Amalya watched Wesley coldly. His lies pooled around him like a slow-moving poison. Narrowing her eyes, she fisted her hands against her side. "I will find him myself."

Before any of them could stop her, she rushed outside. The night air was cool and fresh against her damp skin. She looked up and down the road leading from the house, and then to the barn. Wesley, Horace, and Laird came after her, with Mira not too far behind. She sprinted.

A faint light flickered from the barn. It was nearly time to turn the hay in the pens, preparing for the animals' rest. Without hesitation, she ran through the shortened grass, her determination keeping the weakness in her bones from giving way. She did not let her tired body disobey her mind. She would find Tristan and then they would all see how foolish they had been.

She reached the door and leaned against it, prying it open to let the air stream free. He was there, standing idle in the barn, busying himself with the straw and feed. His back was to her, bent over in his attempt to appear productive. She took a step toward him, her heart fluttering as she approached. "Tristan. . . "

When he turned around, she stopped. His hair was shorter, cut almost to the skull. A short, unkempt beard covered most of his face. His eyes were not their normal luminous gold, but dark and forgettable. The copper-toned skin she admired was a lackluster brown, dotted with unsavory splotches of darkness. She did not know this man. This was not him; this was someone else. He raised his hand to run his fingers through his beard nervously.

Amalya took a step back. "Who are you?"

"Tristan, ma'am." His voice was deep, but with no velvety flow.

Shaking her head wildly, her hair whipped against her face as a sudden rise of panic consumed her entire being. "You're not."

His eyes darted from her to the barn door. "Should you be out of the house, ma'am? Wesley said you've been ill."

"I don't know you. You can't be him."

He looked around, clearly at a loss for what to do or say. "I am."

As she continued to move away from him, a supportive hand turned her around, holding her steady. Wesley's eyes crinkled at the corners as he observed her stricken fear. "Who is this? Where is Tristan?"

"This is Tristan."

She shook her head violently, trying to keep the image of this stranger from replacing her Tristan. "No! It's not. You're. . . you're trying to trick me!"

"Amalya, please be still."

"This is not him!" She wrenched away from him, lifting an accusing finger to prod his dishonesty. "Don't lie to me! What have you done with him?"

A gentle hand touched her shoulder. She turned around and fell into Mira's embrace. Tears fell uncontrollably from her eyes. "It's not him." She wept into Mira's shoulder. "It's not. What did he do to him? What did he do to my Tristan?"

Mira held onto her with powerful arms. "Come back to the house. Come on."

Amalya went without a fuss, though she could not feel herself moving, only observing the changes beneath her blurry vision. There was no sense to be made from this. None to be found.

Everyone was back at the house, standing and talking amongst themselves. Amalya sat quietly in the chair next to the fire. The flickering flames helped keep her from thinking, the only comfort she could find amongst all this turmoil. She could hear them whispering about her and what to do next. How she longed to wake up from the dream of nightmares.

"She'll come with us," Mira said. "She can't stay here, Wesley."

"She's my wife! She needs to be home with me!"

"This place has done enough for her. She needs to be somewhere he never was!"

"I agree." Laird's feet shifted along the floor. "Some time away from here is the best thing for her."

"I'd take her meself, but I can't bear ta go through this again. . . not again." Horace's voice was stricken with sadness and guilt.

Glancing from the corner of her eyes, Amalya watched her father pace around the room with his face in his hands. The mystery of his association with what had stricken her was something she had not forgotten.

"What do I do?" Wesley sat down at the table, running his hands through his hair.

Coming up behind him, Laird sighed. "This dragon she speaks of, is it true?"

Wesley was silent. The truth was there, but he dared not speak it. They promised they never would.

Mira knelt beside him, placing her calm hands on his leg until Wesley gazed at her. "If so, you must say something."

Looking at Mira and then to Amalya, she saw he would tell the secret they held for so many Setts. Yet another promise he would break. Amalya did nothing but look at him, unblinking and undefined.

"It is true," he confessed. "The dragon she speaks of is real. We found it by the lake beyond the hill."

"When did this happen?" Horace moved toward the table to join the others.

"Before we married." Wesley looked at Horace. "It was injured. Amalya, she wanted to help it. So we did. It took to the sky, never to be seen again."

"Wesley. . . " Mira shook her head. "That was dangerous and foolish!"

"I know that now! It cannot be undone."

"You could have been hanged." Horace's arms flew into the air in disbelief. "Helpin' that monster, an enemy of the king!"

Laird glanced at Amalya. "The repercussions are not important. The fact is, this has manifested into something she believes."

"Some time away will do her good." Mira stood up. "All we can do is wait."

"Wait for what?" Wesley's hands fell to his lap, desperately hoping the ones in whom he confided held the answer he was seeking.

"I don't know." Mira placed a comforting hand on his shoulder. "But we will pray to Marin that she will get well."

"And if she doesn't?"

Shaking her head, Mira looked at Amalya again. Her grassy eyes swayed between worry and determination. She did not look as hopeless as the men who shared in their concern for Amalya's well-being. Mira was stronger than all of them.

"It won't come to that," Wesley exclaimed, standing up with forced hope.

"The cart is almost ready to depart. The children are already waiting. Whenever you're ready." Laird moved to the door.

"I will help you." Wesley followed his friend out into the night.

Mira approached Amalya, taking her hand slowly. "Amalya," she whispered. "You'll be staying with us for a while."

"Yes." There was no other option. She would have to go with them. She didn't want to do anything but forget the lies that breathed down her neck since waking in her bed. But to be away from here would mean to be away from the only place Tristan had come to know her. What if he returned? What if he tried to find her?

"Are you ready to go?"

Looking behind her, she saw Horace standing by the table, grasping the back of a wooden chair. "I would like a word with my father first—alone."

"Of course, dear." Mira rose and looked at Horace. "Bring her out when she's ready?"

He nodded. "Of course."

With a weak smile, Mira walked quietly from the home, the door closing gently in the silence of the room. Rising from her chair, Amalya moved toward her father like a shadow in the night. She did not take her eyes from his, the pale blue wavering at her approach.

"Now is the time to speak the truth." Amalya came to rest in front of him, concentrating so as to not sway where she stood. "About Mother."

Horace's lips trembled, seeing that there was no escaping the question she posed. Placing his palms together, he swallowed harshly, licking his lips to prepare. He was not her father, though he wore his skin and looked at her through the same weathered eyes. He seemed so small standing before her now, like a mouse facing a pack of rabid wolves. Hoping that his quiet voice would somehow subdue them.

"Yer mother." His words were affected by raspy sadness. "She did not die in childbirth."

He paused, expecting a response, but there was none Amalya would give. No reaction to show that another lie they forced her to live with had any bearing on her. But she had grown so accustomed to lies; they were ripped from her just as her children were. Each of them born to wrap around her body, pulling so tight that they cut into her flesh. Embedded so deeply that her skin healed over them. Now, she had become one herself. And hope of her to ever be rid of them fleeting. All she could do was wait in silence.

"She fell just as you 'ave. Deep, agonizing despair that I could not pull 'er from. I tried, for many seasons, I tried ta help 'er, while keepin' you from the worst o' it. But I failed."

"How did she die?" Amalya asked, sternly and with a newfound purpose.

Horace hesitated, knowing he had no choice but to reveal such a hurtful time in his life to the only life he was still trying to protect. "She drowned 'erself." His lips quivered at his confession. "Jumped in Willow's Lake an' drowned. She left in the night while you an' I slept. I found 'er there at Sólrise. I'd never seen 'er look so at peace."

Tears swam from his eyes into his rough, graying face. Amalya could feel his sorrow. It pulsed from his aging frame like a steady wind. Any other daughter would move to comfort their father, still suffering from carrying this burden for so long, but Amalya could not find sympathy for him, nor sadness over her mother's death. It was what he wanted her to feel. What they all wanted her to be. Consumed by sadness and regret. Buried beneath grief and longing to be set free. And now, she did not know who she was or what she should be. Perhaps her mother felt the same—so lost in her confusion that she needed to be rid of it. The only thing left was to beg death to take it from her.

Tristan gave Amalya clarity. After this trial was over, he would find her again. He would never allow her to be a prisoner to this. He would come for her and everyone would see him. They would face their ignorance and embrace the truth. And they would finally let her be what she was meant to be.

Moving away, Amalya made for the door, leaving Horace to catch his desperate breath. She could not help him in his grief. She did not want to. Knowing the truth now would change nothing. Perhaps it would have if she knew it before she became a mother. But her father had felt the risk was worth his only daughter's descent into madness. His wish had been granted and she would neither thank nor condemn him for it.

SIXTEEN

"She sat in the void of silence, unable to leave the graying shell of the glory he once carried, now deprived of life. The rot would not deter her. It had become part of her grief."
- Excerpt from *The Tale of Marin and the White Dragon*

A malya kept to herself. Sitting in a room, alone, as the world moved quickly around her. Mira and Laird's abode was attached to his blacksmith shop, so the smells of smelting iron and hot coals leaked into the house throughout the day and into the night. The room that was hers was small, housing only a bed and a small table with a few of her belongings. There were two windows draped by dark crimson curtains that let the sounds of the marketplace filter in. It was her only indication that others were continuing to live their lives while she was still trying to grasp a reason to continue hers.

Elra was quite at home here and brought Amalya breakfast every morning. Mira tended to Arthur day and night.

Amalya's only requirement was to nurse him, which was the only time of day she felt her presence in this place. She welcomed it, for the chaos of her thoughts was enough to render her powerless. Every so often, Mira would pop her head in to make sure she was all right or see if she needed anything.

Amalya needed nothing except an explanation that she would never get. She was waiting for a sign, any sign that she was not in disbelief of herself. She tried to pull herself away from her troubled mind, keep it from escaping into the darkness. But it was inevitable that she would find herself here again.

Her parchment and leather-cased book had stood watch over her since she came here. She dared not delve into the pages again for fear she would learn that everything she felt was real was just a shadow in her mind.

Tristan had to come back. He had to. The taste of him still lingered on her lips, even now. He would come back for her. She had to believe that or she would be lost for the remainder of her days.

"Darling." Mira sat next to her on the bed, a hopeful smile stretched across her face. "We're going into the market and I insist that you join us."

Shaking her head, Amalya averted her gaze.

"Come now, you've been sitting here for days and days. It's time to get out of here and breathe in the fresh air Sól has given us."

As she looked at Mira, Amalya saw the same eyes she beheld before coming to stay with them, that silent determination and poise that felt utterly understanding.

"How long?" Amalya asked.

"Dag Light is nearing its end," Mira replied reassuringly.

Amalya's gaze strayed back to the still floor. The season was almost at its end, just as her time with Tristan had ended so abruptly. It could not be false. She looked to her friend. Perhaps confessing what she had done would reveal what lay behind the veil of this uncertainty. "I have done something," she said without her mind allowing her to cease. "Something forbidden."

Mira waited patiently for her to continue her confession.

"Tristan," she continued in an exasperated breath. "I gave myself to him. Under the willow tree by the lake. I wanted him to. I wanted to feel everything that he was. I longed for it—the only thing I had longed for since Arthur ripped my essence from me."

Watching her with steady poise, Mira waited in silence as Amalya's words carried into the room. "What was it like?"

Amalya's mind flashed with his touch, her legs wrapped around him as he delved deeper, filling her with everything he could offer her and more.

She closed her eyes, her body tingling as the memory flooded her entire being. "He became part of me, and I him. He is the air in which I breathe. The very blood in my veins. The taste on my tongue. But he has chosen to abandon me. And I do not know why."

Stirring her fingers across her lap, Amalya could barely find the courage to face her friend again. "You think I am mad."

Mira took her hand, clenching it tightly in her fingers. "No, I do not."

Sudden tears behind Amalya's eyes dampened the corners of them, drawing down to trace the silhouette of her jaw. "Why must I be left wanting? Why can I not be satisfied?"

The noise of the children pierced the room, distracting her for a moment.

"We should leave now for the market," Mira urged. "There is someone I wish to take you to, at Sól Sleep. Will you come with me?"

"Who?"

"Someone who may help you find Tristan."

Amalya's heart leapt into her lungs, making it hard to breathe. Searching Mira's face, she tried to find a reason to doubt her—to ascertain that this was just another trick to confuse and diminish her—but there was none to be found.

"Do not let this be known to anyone." Mira tilted her chin down, keeping her gaze locked on Amalya.

"I won't."

"Good, now come on then." Mira stood up, pulling Amalya to her feet. "Let us go to the market. The children are waiting for us."

PEOPLE LITTERED THE STREETS. Polli and Elra held hands and took the lead, pointing at colorful confections, shining pieces of jewelry, and wooden men held up by strings. Mira kept Arthur on her person while Amalya stayed close by. He was sleeping comfortably in his sling, escaping the busy midday sounds of the streets.

Amalya tried to occupy her mind by reacting to the girls' observations. Whenever they saw something they wanted to touch, taste, or smell, she was right beside them, attempting to be present in the moment. But despite the heavy aromas of freshly baked goods and sweets tickling the air, or the sounds of children laughing as they played silly games in the streets, they could not distract her.

Mira's invitation stood at the forefront of her mind. Hearing her confession would cause anyone to deem her slanderous, deceitful, and unfaithful, but it did not seem to sway Mira's opinion of her. It intrigued her. It took hours spent wandering about the city for her to draw that conclusion.

When they weren't speaking about the mundane or calling for the girls to follow, Amalya cast subtle glances at her childhood friend. She did not appear to be harboring ill intent. She was Mira, her long, thick hair braided across her shoulder, bright green eyes alive, and a sweet smile painted across her delicate sandstone face.

Who was it she intended Amalya to see?

As they made their way back, Amalya spotted Laird laboring over his anvil with a hammer in hand. Arthur stirred at Mira's breast as the girls hurried to Laird, flashing the pretty red flowers they received for being so well-behaved.

"Take Arthur, will you?" Mira struggled to free him from the sling, slipping him into Amalya's arms. "Feed him and then get some rest. I will speak with Laird about tonight."

Glancing to the blacksmith and back, Amalya's chest grew tight at the thought of Laird knowing anything of what she divulged to Mira. "What will you say to him?"

"Don't fret, my dear." Mira smiled. "I will say nothing of where we will go or of what was said." Her hand cupped Amalya's cheek. "It is just for us to keep."

Mira's steady voice and calm support of her face loosened the bounds within Amalya. "Why are you doing this?" she whispered.

"Now, that's a silly thing to ask." Mira walked backward toward the blacksmith stall. "You are like a sister to me, Amalya. After losing one, I will do all that I can to keep from losing another." She waved her on. "Now go inside and do as I ask! I will be in momentarily."

Amalya nodded and hurried inside, Arthur peering over her shoulder as she held onto him. In all the Setts she had known, Amalya could not recall Mira having a sister. Ever since they were young children, it had always been just the two of them. Amalya and Mira, inseparable girls who fawned over flowers and threw rocks at silly boys they fancied for the day. Perhaps the strain of their walk caused her mind to forget such frivolous details of her youth.

As she sat down on her bed with Arthur suckling at her breast, she knew that reasoning was false. Mira never had a sister, or at least never spoke of one. Amalya looked to the window, the curtains fluttering as the faint wind of the day pushed against them. This secret Mira kept, which she was willingly allowing Amalya to glimpse, was something never to be spoken of, nor associated with, just as the Draughtrìnd were. There was only one other entity that carried the same weight as the Draughtrìnd in the mind of this kingdom.

Mira's sister had to have been a witch.

SEVENTEEN

*"Why would this bring me joy? I am greeted by them each
chance I raise the night. If you truly wish to impress me, show
me something I have yet to discover. Something I do not
possess."*
- Excerpt from *The Song of Dag and Nótt*

The night came quickly on the heels of Nótt, casting
her shadowy tail across the sky to awaken the
speckled remains of Sól's first light. Amalya
walked silently beside Mira into the flame-lit streets of the
half-slumbering city. Rau was far less alive at night, but there
were still taverns and brothels open for those who sought an
escape from their daily lives. This small strip of melodies,
laughter, and the occasional brawl was buried deep within
the belly of the city.

Amalya looked up as they passed one of the more
popular taverns, *"Stéinia's Keep"* painted in large, white
brushstrokes across the hanging sign above the entrance. The

smell of roasted boar and ale saturated the air, wafting from open windows that allowed anyone to glimpse the rabble within. Shadows of men and women danced across the street, lifting glasses and fawning over one another while others poured the contents of their pints to warm their bellies and forget whatever ailed them.

Looking away, Amalya thought it unusual for this tavern to keep such a name. Stéinia was a province of the Draughtrìnd in which Rau was built. It comprised all the land east of the Vandermarchen, the river that separated Rau from the rest of the kingdom. By association, they tied it to the old ways. Why it was not forced to change its title seemed unforgivable.

Mira took Amalya's hand, leading her down one of the muddied alleys beside the tavern. Barrels and old decaying boards littered the ground where they walked. A few ambling men passed them without even a glance. As they came through, they reached another road with no outlet. A small yet very tall establishment stood in the shadows. Amalya could see flickering candlelight from behind curtained windows, all shut to keep it from escaping. The door was painted a dark, violet hue with a long, knotted rope hanging from its center.

As Mira moved toward it, Amalya kept her feet firm before the path leading up to this haunting place. "Where are we?"

Looking at her, Mira's chest rose and fell harshly. "Somewhere we may find answers."

"We?"

"Yes, we." She pulled her arm again, but despite Amalya's fragile state, she held herself steady.

If Mira's sister had been a witch, Amalya could not fathom how that must have affected her friend. Witches were devoted to the Draughtrìnd, still recognizing them as Sól's protectors of Jöro. Magic only touched those born in women's flesh. If one was suspected of harboring the power of a Draughtrìnd, they were exiled, abandoned, or killed.

"Tell me about your sister," Amalya said sternly.

Mira tucked her lips between her teeth before uttering a sigh. "Her name was Ivy. We lost her before I knew you."

A cool wind touched her face. "How was she lost?"

"My parents." The mere mention of them tightened Mira's face with tension. "They abandoned her in the East Eldur Mountains and she never returned." Her gaze dropped for a moment before recovering. "She was a witch. And although they felt it justified, guilt riddled my parents essence until each of their hearts could bear it no more. The day they left Ivy in the mountains, all their joy died with themNothing I did could hide their sin. Nothing could shadow the pain that took root from their choice."

"I remember," Amalya said softly, "how elated you were when you came to live with your aunt. I did not understand why. . . I wish I had known."

"I am glad you didn't. You were one of the few happinesses of my life then. I did not wish to tarnish it with such an atrocity." Mira closed the gap between them, grasping Amalya's arm at the elbow. "We cannot linger. We must go in now. Amalya?"

Amalya gave a subtle nod. Any remnants of danger had dissipated upon being given this secret. Mira's intentions were good and her sympathies founded. Though she wished she had known sooner, Amalya could not help but feel closer than she had ever been to her truest friend. There were no more secrets that needed to hide between them.

They reached the door, and Mira grabbed hold of the rope and rapped it against its surface. It was not long before someone cracked it open—a haggard-looking man with a long scar cutting into his rough, speckled face. A cloth hid his left eye, wrapped haphazardly around his discolored head.

The man looked from Mira to Amalya, sniffing loudly with a sneer on his face. "What d'ya want?" he grunted, showing off his missing tooth.

"*Lykt af rósinni*," Mira uttered forcibly.

Amalya's eyes widened at the sound of the forbidden language of the Draughtrìnd. It was unrecognizable, but it could be nothing else.

The man's wrinkled forehead furrowed into his good eye, and he quickly shut the door before opening it fully to them. "This way."

Looking at Amalya, Mira offered a weak smile. "Don't be frightened."

Amalya followed her into the dimly lit hall. The air was stifling and heavy as they made their way down. She could barely focus on anything as they walked. A few rooms had no doors attached. Scattered debris and old possessions stood almost in a trance, frozen by time. The floor beneath them cracked and buckled from their weight. Amalya could feel the frailty of the boards through her slippered feet.

"In hea'." The man pointed to the only room with a door, chipped and eaten away at the corners. They could see flickering firelight casting a shadow onto the floor beneath them. The man held out his hand and grunted again. "Four coin. Not anythin' less."

Mira slipped her hand into a small pouch tied around the waist of her dress, dropping the payment into the man's grimy hands.

His eyebrow raised. "Eight if ya both go in."

"I will wait out here, if that is agreeable?" Mira did not let her eyes stray from him.

The man shrugged and stepped away from the door. "I'll be back when ya time's up." He lumbered down the hall and disappeared into one of the cluttered rooms.

With a hopeful breath, Mira turned to Amalya, clasping her hands in her own. "I'll be here. She will not hurt you."

"Who is she?"

"A friend." Mira smiled weakly and kissed her on the cheek. "Go on then."

Slipping from Mira's fingers, Amalya held her breath as she pressed against the door. It opened silently, the air moving the flickering candles that sparkled across the floor. A small circular table sat in the center of the room. Parchment lined its surface along with dried herbs and petrified appendages from creatures that inhabited Jöro.

Amalya walked to the table, lifting her dress slightly to avoid the edges being kissed by fire. As her upper thigh touched its edge, a shadow moved from the cloth-covered window into the light. It was a woman, wrapped in dull linens with long, dark hair flowing down her back. Her eyes drew upward, the sharp edges of her jaw tight. Looking down at her feet, Amalya noticed they were bare, painted with curved symbols that traced up her ankles.

As she approached, something familiar about the woman sent Amalya's skin tingling, raising the hair on her arms. Her heart raced the closer she came to the table, but she held herself firm, keeping her posture strong despite a small shaking in her knees.

The woman's thin, slanted brow raised ever so slightly as she reached out to Amalya. "Your hand."

Amalya swallowed and obeyed, touching the woman's long, slender fingers. As she grasped it, the woman turned her hand over, revealing the symbols extending from each of her digits and down her wrist.

"I am Primeveire." Her voice was as velvety as Tristan's, though lighter and feminine. Glancing down, Primeveire studied the lines of Amalya's fingers. "You are Amalya. Such a pretty name." Before she could reply, Primeveire's gaze flashed back to her own. "How long since you bled?"

Fluttering her eyelids, Amalya looked down at where the woman held her, uncertain of her meaning. "I do not understand."

"Your hand reveals to me the course of your life."

They stared at one another. The tingling across her arms only escalated as Amalya's mind raced. Primeveire's stoic poise was about to open a window, one that Amalya thought to be broken and rusted shut, never to draw breath again.

"You are with child."

Shaking her head, the shock of the woman's words cast a false grin upon Amalya's face. "You are mistaken."

Primeveire's eyes narrowed, studying her assuredly. "Do you not feel it?"

Pulling her hand down onto the table, Primeveire placed Amalya's palm on a wooden shaft, rounded and smooth to the touch. She forced her fingers to grasp it, illuminating the dark markings along its surface in a faint, pale light. The staff resembled that of the rounded trinket

Tristan had gifted Arthur the first day he had arrived on their farm.

Amalya did not have to draw her gaze from her host to feel the intense fire building beneath her fingers.

Gritting her teeth, Primeveire leaned in closer, finally allowing herself to blink. "A child." She smelled of dried rosemary and chamomile. "A gift no witch born would dare to wield."

Primeveire's long, dark hair fell to the sides of her face. The small touches of fire reflected in her coal-stained eyes, filling them with a never-ending light that only those who called the shadows their home could see. "Treasure it."

EIGHTEEN

"There is nothing left for them to teach us, nor is there any benefit of their presence. They bleed the land dry, dirt still lingering in the deepened beds of our fingertips while theirs remain untouched and unsullied."
- King Aethelwulf letters, 1,802 Sól Sett, Fourth Season, Nótt Wind

A malya was with child. Nothing else that came after believing this truth was clear.

The sound of the door opening startled her. Mira took her in her arms and Primeveire came beside her.

"Give her three drops of this under her tongue every day for a season." She slipped a vial of clouded liquid into Mira's hand. *"Hún verður að gleyma."*

Primeveire then grasped Amalya by the chin, turning her head to face her yet again. She studied her features, tilting her head as the strange utterances of her words penetrated her mind. "May Marin protect you."

Nodding, Mira slipped the vial into her pouch as she led Amalya away. Amalya could feel the heaviness lift from her as they stepped out of the room, down the hall, and out into the night air. Taking a deep breath, she said nothing as they made their way back home. She could sense Mira's eyes darting to her person every now and again, her curiosity unmistakably piqued.

As they rounded the corner, the blacksmith stall coming into view, Mira pressed her lips together, finally catching Amalya's eyes. "You do not need to reveal anything to—"

"I am with child." She stopped, the road holding Mira hostage to her words. Amalya watched her friend's eyes grow wide and her gaze dart across her face.

"How. . . how do—" Mira cut herself off, swallowing hard as she brought her hands to her sides.

Glancing up, Amalya watched as a small whiff of clouds crawled across the sky. "I do not know."

"Wesley?"

"Or it could be—" A sudden pinch of fear rose inside Amalya's stomach. Grasping Mira's arm, she pulled her toward her, the witch's words sending panic coursing through her veins. "We can tell no one."

"Amalya, we cannot hide this. We must tell Wesley."

"What if it's not? What I feel in my heart is true; it is not—"

Mira grasped her shoulders, forcing Amalya to keep her wandering eyes firmly on her. "It is." She spoke strongly enough to be convincing, even when Amalya's mind teemed with the memory of the warmth she had felt within her palm. "It must be."

"But—"

"No." She fixed the disturbed cloth of Amalya's dress. "No, I must. . . we cannot let this be. . . " A harsh sigh escaped her, the tension in her face falling victim to the calm. "We must rest. Yes. It will do us both good to rest."

"Mira, I—"

"Not another word. Not until Sólrise."

There was too much uncertainty coursing through Amalya for her to understand what was happening. She could feel herself slipping, her feet unable to grasp the dirt beneath her feet. Amalya closed her eyes, seeing the Sól-struck eyes of Tristan staring back at her. He was punishing her for her weakness. Would he let her forget? Would he allow her to fall from him despite her attempts to reach him?

Amalya nodded her head, not wanting the vision she had painted in her mind to dissipate into the shadows.

Mira took her hand, pulling her along toward the house once again. "Tomorrow will be a better day."

Amalya could feel the heaviness of her steps.

"Tomorrow you will be awake."

<hr/>

AMALYA AWOKE with a start to darkness. Shooting up from the bed, her chest was tight, unable to draw breath. Any attempt scraped against her ribs and crackled fiery sparks down her throat. She looked around the room, her gaze falling upon a darkened figure sitting on the edge of the bed in which she slumbered.

Tristan was here. Perhaps in a dream, but here none-theless. Rubbing her chest with her palm, she sat more erect, sensing the warmth emanating from this figure in the ashen darkness. As the figure glanced over its shoulder, she saw the golden orbs of Sól radiating back at her.

"Tristan." She went to approach him, but the strain in her chest would not allow her. Her hands fell to the bed. She slowed her breathing, attempting to recover from her weakened state. She could not look at him, feeling his gaze boring into her very essence, seeing her regret-ridden bones and exposing all of her faults.

"It is too late." His words were soft but harsh, stabbing her heart to match the tension in her chest.

Shaking her head, her hair fell into view as she forced herself to look at him. He did not seem like himself, his posture rigid and his eyes cold despite their brilliance. Long, dark tendrils of hair fell down his back, unaffected by the subtle breeze trickling in from the windows.

"What can I do? I will do anything if it means being with you!"

"Do you love your family?" he asked.

Amalya held the small portions of breath within her, closing her eyes as she fully digested his words.

She thought of her children, so young and innocent. How Elra looked at her, someone to be admired and loved despite the darkness she harbored within her. She never blamed her for what she had become, a shell of her former self. No more vibrance, no more hope, just a shell, empty and without purpose.

Elra deserved better. She deserved a mother who would love and care for her. Amalya could not fill her cup; she could not even fill her own.

"They deserve better than me."

"And Wesley? Does he deserve better?"

Her lips trembled as she stared into his unfeeling face. The lines of his distinguished jaw did not falter, revealing no sense of pity. Only his eyes comforted and tormented her.

"I loved Wesley once. Perhaps I still do, but—" Letting go of the tension in her lungs, Amalya closed her eyes, licking her lips delicately, feeling the cracks and crevices of her life extend into her words. "He does not see me. He only sees what I was, and I am not her anymore. Not the daughter of his employer, not the girl who kissed him under Sól's waning light so many Setts before. Not the girl he tried to impress with a dragon, injured and broken in the lake. . . "

Slowly, she opened her eyes to him. "You are the only one who sees me now. The only one who can still see what little light is left. I am not afraid to lose what I have, but I am afraid to lose you."

With a sudden swiftness, Tristan leaned closer toward her, his long hair curtaining his face before settling along his angled jaw. "What am I?"

"You. . . you are Draughtrìnd, a God of Old. A descendant of Dag and Nótt. You are. . . a dragon."

"Is that all that I am? Is that all you see when you look into my eyes?"

She shook her head lightly. "No."

"Tell me."

She felt the words tangle up in her throat. No matter how hard she tried to push them from her lips, they would not free themselves. Her chest caved, pressing against the weak beating of her heart. She could feel it drowning her, ripping away her life like a sail in a storm.

The longer she took to speak, the harsher Tristan's face became. Shadows covered his soft Sól-touched skin, eyes bearing down on her, contorting and bleeding into the darkness. His mouth expanded, stretching into patches of ash-covered scales as fire crackled deep within his throat.

He was changing into what the skald tales had taught her—a monster with nothing but ill intent chiseled into its heartless body and powerful limbs. But he was not a monster. Not to her.

Fear leaked into the small doubt of his presence. As much as she saw him, felt him, and smelled him, he would never threaten her—not her. As his teeth bared and sharpened with every inch of their expanse, she pressed her hands beneath her trembling form, afraid to move.

It was not until he lunged toward her that her body jerked, propelling her from the bed and onto the floor. Her eyes smashed closed, but when they reopened from the panic that crawled inside of her, it was a new day. Sól hid behind a vast casting of heavy gray clouds, but light still trickled to the floor.

Sweat pooled from her palms and down her neck, dripping between her breasts and saturating her nightdress. Her hands frantically grasped her neck, believing Tristan's anger had struck her, but she was untouched, unmaimed, and unharmed. Turning back toward the bed, she saw no one there.

Mira's voice forced her to turn toward the door. "Another day! Another—" She looked down at Amalya, worry shocking her face and widening her eyes. "Amalya, darling, are you all right?"

"Mira," she uttered, "he was here."

"Who was here?"

"Tristan. He was here. He. . . he was angry with me."

184

Rubbing Amalya's arms, Mira lifted her from the floor to settle her back on the bed. "My dear, it was just a dream."

"No, no, it was not a dream."

Moving from behind her, Mira wiped her hands on her dull apron. "I will fetch you some water." She left the room, returning with a bowl of cool water and a cloth. Carefully placing it on the small bedside table, she dipped the cloth in the water, squeezing the excess into the bowl before dabbing the cool cloth to Amalya's brow.

"He was here," Amalya repeated. "I. . . I felt him."

"It was just a dream."

Amalya watched her friend as she drew the cloth across her face, soaking the heated sweat from her brow with each dab. "Who was she, Mira?"

The question quelled Mira's actions, drawing her gaze to Amalya's eyes. With a nervous smile, Mira let out a quick puff of breath before continuing to cool her. "Who was who?"

"Primeveire." Amalya leaned back from her. "She was a witch. I could feel the magic within her, just as I can feel Tristan's. Why did you bring me to her?"

"I brought you to no such place." Mira shook her head subtly. "Honestly, Amalya, why would I endanger you by bringing you before a witch?"

Amalya clenched her hands into fists. "But. . . I was there! Behind Stéinia's Keep."

"We went to a midwife yesterday, darling."

"A midwife?"

"Yes, do you not remember?" Mira ceased her tending and placed her hands in her lap. "You are with child. Laird sent for Wesley; he will be here tomorrow."

Shaking her head, Amalya backed against the wall, bringing her knees to her chest. "That's not what happened. That can't be what—"

"Amalya." Mira slowly approached her, laying a hand on her knee. "It has been difficult for you, and I can only imagine it will continue to be. But you are safe here. I will take care of you and will let nothing happen to you."

"But Tristan—"

"He is false. Wesley, Elra, Arthur, the new life growing inside you—that is your truth. Please, do not stray from it."

"But—"

"Amalya." The strength in Mira's face faltered for a moment as she clasped her hands. Amalya remembered how she had been the night before, determined and unwavering. Now, as she sat before her friend, Amalya could sense something amiss. A loose strand in the heavy rope she had bound to be unbreakable. It could have been fear. Fear that Amalya would not conquer the darkness that warped her mind, or fear that she had done something she should never have done.

Amalya did not know what her truth was anymore. The uncertainty of her dreams throbbed and battered at her temples, causing her eyes to burn. The thought of Tristan and his anger rose in her memory. She knew he would never treat her in such a way. He loved her. That could not have been him; it was not him.

Nodding her head, the air lightened as it trickled down her throat. Her heart continued to pound but no longer threatened to break her.

Mira's eyes softened with a smile. Patting Amalya's

knees, she sat up from the bed. "Come on. Let's run a bath for you and get you freshened up."

Obediently, Amalya lurched from the bed and followed Mira from the room. Nothing was clear, her mind a cloud of terrible storms and turmoil, ripping her up from the roots.

Mira was her friend. She promised to never abandon her. Never to thwart her. Not like Wesley or Tristan.

Tristan. What has become of you?

NINETEEN

"If she shields her eyes, it is not there. If she forgets, then it never was. It is the only hope for her to ever draw strength enough to stand."
-Excerpt from *The Tale of Marin and the White Dragon*

P anic released Amalya from her slumber yet again. The room was still, though shrouded by an uneven fog. It weighed on her chest and filled her lungs with a subtle poison that yielded little taste. Amalya's frantic gaze came to every corner until it stopped just beyond the bed to the left. Movement restricted her. A tall figure broke from the wall, using the shadows to shield them from her sight.

Amalya willed her arms to grasp the blankets as she crawled across the bed. Beads of sweat coated her back and dripped in the cracks behind her knees. When she reached the corner, the figure dropped to the floor, hiding its face in a cascade of dark, flowing hair.

Her chest heaved to the rapid pulsing that pounded at her temples. Fear gripped her as she reached down to place her hand atop the figure's head. Just before it alit, their hand shot forth to grasp hers. His face turned toward her, crimson coating one side. His Sól-kissed eyes pierced through the veil that threatened to swallow him.

"Tristan," Amalya muttered as he lunged to grasp her. She fell in a heap against his tired, bloodied frame. The earthen scent of him lingered in his raven locks, mixed with iron and ash. "What has happened to you?"

"I will never hurt you." Despite his appearance, he seemed assured in his words. He pulled her from him, cradling her face in his blood-soaked hands. "I will never abandon you."

He kissed her so deeply it utterly shed the fear from her mind. Amalya closed her eyes as she fell into the softness of his kiss. It lowered her into the safety of the bed, its warmth falling over her tired frame, seeping comfort deep into her bones. All sense of panic dissipated as her mind relaxed, delivering her into the solace of sleep once again.

———

SITTING in the dull light of the day, Amalya let the loose strands of her hair dry in the heavy air. Mira had given her a light brown dress to wear that scooped from her neck and kissed her ankles with small triangles of knitted lace.

People walked up and down the streets of Rau, some peering into Laird's stall as he continued to work at molding iron to add to his wares. Elra and Polli giggled playfully beside Amalya on the ground, moving their hay-stuffed dolls and giving them silly voices to entertain themselves.

Amalya could not keep up with how fast her mind was spinning. What her dreams had revealed of Tristan did not soothe her. His desperate need to harm her followed by passionate despair and longing twisted her heart into knots.

Had she truly gone mad? Was he really a conjuring of her own desperate mind?

But the kiss he had offered was not foreign. She had remembered its taste and dreamed of how it beckoned her not to forget.

"Here you are, my dear." Mira came down beside her, holding a small vial in her hand. As she popped it open, Amalya could smell the deep scent of lavender and burnt oak escape from its mouth.

"What is that?" she asked as Mira brought it up to her lips.

"The midwife gave you this, to help you calm your mind."

Looking at the bottle, the clouded liquid was oddly familiar to Amalya. She recalled Primeveire slipping a bottle into Mira's hand as they left that mysterious place.

Amalya watched her friend, who seemed confident in her words. She tried to find something out of place, but she could not focus. If she was attempting to fool her, it was unnoticeable. Perhaps Primeveire was not a witch. Perhaps she was a midwife whom Amalya had imagined being something more, something that would keep the connection between her and Tristan alive in her own mind.

"Come on now." Mira placed the small glass vial against her lips. "Three drops."

Amalya opened her mouth, letting the potent liquid touch her tongue. Wincing at the strength of it, she let it flow into her throat. It left a warmth in its wake, hitting her stomach like a comforting blanket.

Placing her hand on her stomach, Amalya basked in the sudden calm it had given her. It expanded into her chest, caressing her heart and pooling into her loins. Just as it did, a light flutter brushed against her hand. She could feel it, a tiny pulse of life stirring within her. Though it was too small to kick and cause her strain, it was there. It was life.

"Oh, look who's here."

Looking up, Amalya's gaze fell upon Wesley's frantic eyes as he rushed toward them. As he reached out to her, he fell to his knees, falling into her lap like a lost child.

"I came as soon as I could," he breathed hoarsely.

"Come now, Wesley. Don't be so dramatic." Mira eyed him playfully, but Wesley only glared at her before surrendering to the anguish that was riddled within him.

"Come, girls, let us go check on Arthur." Mira smiled at Amalya before pushing the girls from their fun, ushering them into the house.

Laird glanced in their direction, raising a hand of welcome to Wesley before getting back to work.

"Amalya—" Wesley's words ceased as an unexpected shudder gripped him. Folding his hands into her dress, he sobbed in her lap.

Amalya watched him, unsure of what to do or say. She had never seen him so shattered and helpless. It stirred at her empathy, shaking the debris from the love she once possessed for him.

She placed a gentle hand on the back of his head,

stroking his dark red hair as he sullied her dress with his tears. "Do not weep for me," she whispered softly.

"I am sorry, Amalya. I should not have been so cross with you. I did not see how far you had drifted. I. . . didn't want to see it. To believe it would mean I had failed. I could not face it. . . Can you ever forgive me?" He looked up at her, grasping her hand in his own. Dark wells hung beneath his eyes, dragging his face down into his unkempt beard.

"There is nothing you did—"

"You're right. I did nothing. I did nothing meaningful and look what it has done to you. To us."

"Wesley. . ."

He scrambled onto his knees, grasping her arms. "What can I do? Tell me what I can do. I'll do anything you ask of me. *Anything.*"

He was desperate, so ready to lay down his life if she asked it of him. Amalya did not know if the trembling she felt was her own or his, but it trapped her. He loved her more than she ever deserved of him. Closing her eyes, Tristan's words resurfaced and echoed in her ears.

And Wesley? Did he deserve better?

There was nothing she could do to be what he wanted her to be. No magic, no potions, no hope. Every part of her was broken, every inch of her tainted in such an unfathomable way. She could not beg to bleed the same again.

Could she really abandon him? This man who had given her everything and yet nothing at the same time. He would never give up on her. She was so ready to cast him into the unforgiving waters of the Vandermarchen, even if it meant diminishing his very life, allowing him to sink into the chasm she had fallen into so many seasons ago. How could she want this for another—for someone who devoted so much to everyone else and nothing for himself?

Perhaps she was wrong. She was the only thing he treasured more, the only thing he hoped to carry so high that Sól himself could lap at her skin. They were both selfish and trapped by it. Two horribly entangled beings who only wanted life to grant them a single happiness, despite it being different for each of them.

Wesley made it clear as his eyes glassed over that he could not live without her presence. No matter how dead and buried she was, he would dig through the depths of fire to retrieve her, if only to hold her again. One final time.

Amalya wiped the tears from his face, urging a hopeful smile to grace her lips. "We will try again."

"We will?"

"Yes. Perhaps this is a gift. This child. . . is a chance." Taking his hand, she placed it on her belly. "Be still. You will feel it."

Wesley's expression eased as he waited patiently for the magic of life to stir beneath his hand. They waited together, siphoning out all the noise emanating from the streets of Rau. After a few patient moments, he gasped. Looking up at her, he matched the forced hope in her eyes with his own genuine joy.

"I can feel it." He waited a moment longer, basking in the chance that their lives together would one day be mended. That the fractures they had both delivered and endured may, once again, become one.

With a sigh, Amalya held the swelling doubt building up inside her. To think of this child as Wesley's only helped it grow into something heavy and unbearable. Tristan still laid himself bare to her as she closed her eyes, every dark image of him chilling her skin and waking her sorrowful bones.

Wesley brought his hands up to cup her face, shaking from her sight the image of Tristan's blurred frame. "I will make this right. I will take care of you. Elra, Arthur, and our new little one. I promise you. May Marin bear me pain for the rest of my days if I fail."

Managing a weak smile, she placed her hand on his wrist, squeezing it gently between her fingers. "You will not fail."

She would try, if for nothing else, to find some sense of peace in the chaos of her own heart. She could not decipher right from wrong, nor dreams from truth. But in this moment, she knew two things were unequivocally true: Wesley and this new life that had taken root in her womb.

Wesley sank against her, coming to rest atop her bosom. Amalya placed a hand on his head as she stared blankly at the dirt-covered road. Unfamiliar feet, hooves, and wooden wheels clouded her vision, caving in from the corners until there was nothing left to focus on.

To live a lie and to live in truth were slowly becoming one and the same. A disorienting blur that only Sól-kissed eyes could penetrate.

2,200 SÓL SETT | THIRD SEASON

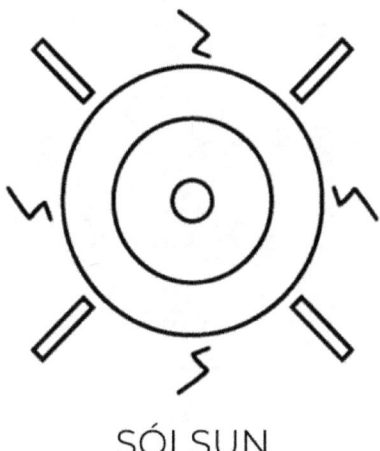

SÓLSUN

TWENTY

"I wish to have something to care for. Something to love for
eternity."
-Excerpt from *The Song of Dag and Nótt*

The days that brought forth the blossoms and harvests of Dag Light were ending. The season of Sólsun was creeping upon the city, beckoning Sól to cast his light longer in the sky, leaving Nótt, the Night Dragon, to stir and fester in aggravation before being allowed to bring forth the darkness. Soon, decay would follow. Leaving everything bare and vulnerable.

Amalya's belly was already beginning to bloom. She remembered vaguely showing earlier when she carried Arthur. This one was no different, perhaps even sooner than she had expected. Despite the evidence of her carrying, there was little else that ailed her. No sickness or swelling of her feet, as happened with both Elra and Arthur, just slight fatigue and the need to rest more frequently.

Mira doted on her each day she rose in their home, making sure she ate and took the tonic given to them by the midwife and caring for all of the children. Amalya did not deserve such treatment, but Mira would not relent in her duties. Even Laird was sure to aid when he could, giving both Mira and Amalya time to themselves. Sometimes she would catch them in secret, speaking in hushed voices but never for very long. It pulled Amalya's attention whenever she caught them, but she did not move to question them.

Wesley would come and see her whenever he visited the city on market day, spending the night if he could, if only to be with his family. Every time Amalya saw him, her heart grew a little heavier. His eyes carried a new hopefulness the moment they fell to her belly. Amalya would do her best to pretend, but it weighed on her shoulders each time he placed his hand on this new child.

Something was not right—something that drew her suspicions more each time she dreamed. Tristan was no longer there. It was only her, alone. She was always waiting for him, but he never entered her vision. She wanted to touch him, to feel that he was still there, but each night she slept, she found herself in the same position as when she was awake. Alone and lost in the confines of a troubled mind.

It was midday, and Mira insisted they take the children to the bridge overlooking the Vandermarchen River to watch the trade boats pull into the harbor. Horace lived in the area as well and would not miss the chance to see his grandchildren. Amalya had not spoken to her father since his confession of her mother's death. She did not harbor hatred toward him, just a failed sense of devotion. Fathers protected their children, and perhaps that is what he thought he was doing.

It might have changed so much, knowing the truth. Not that it mattered. Now it was too late to change.

"Grandfather!" Elra shrieked with glee as she saw the old form of Horace walking toward them from his small abode.

He smiled, bending down without a hint of discomfort to gather her up in his arms. "There's me little flower." He rested his cheek against hers.

Arthur wobbled over to him on shaky, plump legs. He had just learned to walk on his own and was still trying to manage his balance without falling. Mira was right behind him, and Polli dutifully held his hand.

"Arthur wants to say hello too!" Polli shouted with enthusiasm.

Horace looked at the toothless grin of Arthur and scooped him up in his arm, letting him bury his face against his graying chin.

"So good to see you so well, Horace." Mira took Polli's hand as they came to a stop beside him.

Amalya stood the farthest, keeping a distance between them so as to not distract her father from the little joys of his life.

"Aye, I've been better. But now that you three trouble-makers're here. . . "

"I do not cause trouble, Grandfather." Elra puffed out her lips and let her arms fall rigidly to her sides. "Arthur is the one who is always pulling my hair!"

"He's jealous," Horace said, moving some of her long brown locks from her face. "Yer hair is just so lovely."

"Mine's lovely too, right?" Polli asked with a shyness only a little girl could possess.

"Of course it is. Perhaps lovelier."

"You're supposed to think my hair is the loveliest!" Elra shouted in protest.

"Now, girls, let's behave ourselves. We don't want to miss the ships falling in, do we? Better get a move on."

Mira's mention of the trade ships shook the girls' bickering from their lips. Both their youthful faces lit up as they grabbed each other's hands and walked down the street with haste.

"Let's go!" Elra waved the rest of them on, not wanting to waste another moment comparing hair.

Horace stood up with Arthur in his arms, the weight of the boy clearly causing him to strain as he steadied himself, his hand pressing to his back.

"No, you don't," Mira protested, grabbing Arthur from him. "We can't have you falling over, now. He prefers to walk anyway."

She put Arthur gently on the ground. As soon as his little moccasins hit the dirt, he was off, trying to keep up with his sister. Mira chuckled and followed close behind.

Horace watched them before turning to Amalya, his exposed teeth disappearing behind a sullen frown. Walking over to him, Amalya watched his eyes shift as if he were afraid to speak. Taking the sleeve of his dark, weathered tunic, she yanked on it subtly, forcing a weak smile. "Come on, then."

Horace looked down with quiet relief and joined her as they traveled down the road together, keeping a small distance from each other, with Mira and the children still in their sights.

"How ya feelin'?" he asked after a few brief moments of silence.

"Fairly well." Her hand went to the small lump under her dark brown dress. "This one is being far more agreeable than the last."

"And you?" He kept his worried eyes steadily on her. "What about you?"

Pulling her lips between her teeth, Amalya inhaled the river-scented air. A tense harshness scraped at the back of her throat, threatening to stifle her lungs if she uttered a single truth of how she felt. It was wrong to lie to him, as he did to her. There had to be someone she did not have to lie to, someone who would hear her truth and not force her to forget it.

"I am fine," she heard herself say, focusing on the approaching bridge ahead, where the rest of their group had already gathered. He was not the one to hear her confession. She could not bring herself to make him suffer more than he already had.

The bridge stretched across the entire river from shore to shore, built of the darkest hardwood, overlapped and sealed with wool and tallow to keep the water from weathering its bones. It was wide enough for carts and the largest animals to cross it, with plenty of space for those choosing to make the trek on foot to have ample room without disrupting the trade route.

The incline toward the water was not too steep, with small boats and docks littered with fishing nets and traps hanging from their posts. Many small houses rested along the river's shore, mostly fishermen or ferrymen waiting to take passengers.

The girls were pressing their faces between the sturdy rails of the bridge, watching the tremendous ships from lands across the Safir Sea sail up the river to the docks of Rau. Mira gripped Arthur's hand, pointing to the multicolored flags wafting in the breeze at the masts. His little hands waved up and down in the air, catching the eyes of a few of the crewmen, who smiled and waved back in their red and purple linens and ink-dotted faces.

"They're gettin' so big now," Horace said as he looked at the children on the bridge.

"They are."

His gaze softened. "Try not to miss any of it." He fell away from her to join them on the bridge.

As he moved farther from Amalya, the hoarseness eased from her throat, making it easier for her to swallow. She knew she should be proud of her family; any woman would be. Two healthy, growing children and a loving husband, a prosperous life that gave them a home and a way of life to last them all the Setts yet to breach the horizon. Why was it so difficult for her to accept that this was how it would be? Why could it not satisfy her as it would any other?

She glanced at some of the weathered houses along the shoreline. People were going about their daily lives as normal, cutting wood, wringing out washed clothes from the river and hanging them to dry. A few men stood huddled together, laughing about this or that. Children ran down the street, holding up wooden swords as they practiced their swordsmanship against one another.

It was not until those children passed that her eyes fell on a woman scraping clothes against a washboard. The stirring along Amalya's arms permeated into a faint buzzing against her skin. She waited there, letting her heart dictate her actions as it beat against her chest. As the woman turned to where she stood, dark, angled eyes met her own.

Primeveire.

Amalya walked toward her. Dropping her clothes where she stood, Primeveire disappeared between the space of two houses. Lifting her dress so it would not drag against the ground, Amalya walked faster. She drew her hand along a house's rough, wooden surface as she turned the corner, seeing the train of Primeveire's long, dark trestle disappear to the left of another home. Slipping in slowly, Amalya hurried after her. She was still small enough to snake her way through, though every so often her swollen belly pressed against the hard surface of the mud-locked homes.

She rounded the corner to the left, following another small corridor that spilled out onto a road beside the river. Primeveire had almost reached the end. Amalya hurried with new determination, wanting to catch this woman from her memories.

As she came to the corner, Primeveire stopped and peered down the corridor. Her hand graced the wood as she watched her, dark eyes fixed on Amalya's approach. Amalya's heart leapt, believing she was waiting for her, but as she advanced, Primeveire disappeared.

Amalya stumbled into the street, looking both ways, scanning the city folk as they attended to their daily lives. A slight pain emanated from her side, causing her to buckle and shift her stance. Wincing, she leaned against the outside wall of a home, hoping the ache would cease so she could focus on finding the one she sought.

As her eyes clenched shut to hide from the light, the pain

radiated up her body, washing over her like rushing waves against a rock. It seeped into her mind as a flash of a figure cast in shadow clouded her vision, lost in the darkness except for its eyes. They bore into her own, deep, swirling torrents of orange- and red-kissed fire burning.

"Are you all right, my lady?"

Opening her eyes, she noticed one of the city guardsmen step up beside her, holding her arm to support her.

"Yes, just. . . I strained myself."

Amalya's knees buckled, forcing her to surrender to the pain those fiery eyes cast upon her. All of her weight leaned against the guard's strong, armored chest as he held her up to keep her from falling. She heard him speak, perhaps calling for aid, but his words only sounded like drowning voices in her mind.

Her eyes closed again, the figure never leaving the darkness. She could feel the seething malice pulsing in its fire-ridden stare, wanting nothing more than to destroy her.

"Let me fetch you some water, ma'am."

A woman's voice pulled her into the light again—a kind, wrinkled face, hands clasped to her chest as she left to retrieve the refreshment.

The guard lowered Amalya to a small stool. Her legs shook uncontrollably.

"No, I need to find someone," she protested.

Another stab of pain pierced her chest, forcing her lids to close once more. Amalya could not breathe as fear consumed her mind, those terrible red eyes still glaring at her from the darkness.

"Who are you looking for, my lady?" the guard asked politely. "Perhaps I can assist you?"

The voice of the guard was strong enough to pull her free from herself. A sudden lapse of coughing rattled her as the freshness of the river air seemed foreign to her lungs. For a moment, she had forgotten where she was or why she had strayed so far.

"Drink this, my dear." The friendly woman returned, placing a wooden cup of cool water in her hands.

As the refreshing water touched her lips, the memory of Primeveire drew her gaze in the direction of the woman's escape. Amalya somehow hoped that she would find her standing there, waiting for her.

But she had vanished. All that remained was the subtle shaking of Amalya's legs and that fire-ridden stare scarred behind closed eyes.

TWENTY-ONE

"Every bit of light they had shared lay collected in a vial that hung from the nape of her neck. And a talon, the only piece of him void of death, sat safely in the pocket of her dress."
-Excerpt from *The Tale of Marin and the White Dragon*

"You should not have wandered off like that, Amalya. You could have gotten hurt, or worse." Mira placed a small serving of bread and cheese on the square table overlooking the blacksmith's shop.

Amalya stared at the plate, her eyes burning for a blink of moisture. It was still unclear to her what had happened. Had Primeveire placed those images in her mind? Was it a warning? What were her reasons for running away?

Arthur was sleeping soundly in his cradle, the rune-marked trinket Tristan had given him tucked near his head. If Tristan was not real, how had they come by that trinket? Why was it here if he had never been here to give it?

Elra and Polli were playing in another room, just across

from where Mira prepared food and kept the water fresh for drinking. The days had grown hotter and longer, and fatigue more prevalent, especially in the crowded city.

It had been a long time since Amalya longed to be on the farm again. It was so open, the air free to move without boundaries or constraints. She missed the hill overlooking the descent down to the lake and the tall willow tree forever weeping its long, wispy branches onto the surface of the water.

"Amalya."

Her name refocused her gaze on Mira standing over her with a pitcher of water in her hand. The corner of her mouth turned up. "What were you doing?"

The question hung in the air like taunting prey. Pushing loose strands of blonde hair behind her ears, Amalya swallowed hard before raising her chest to straighten her slumping posture. "I saw someone."

She was unsure if she should breathe the name of the one she had seen. Mira had denied their rendezvous with Primeveire again and again. There was nothing Amalya could say that would sway her belief.

"Was it Tristan?" she asked.

Amalya shook her head, keeping a close eye on her friend's steady poise. "No, it was Primeveire."

Mira put the jug down with slight force, the impact rippling through the wood of the table. Wiping her hands on her apron, she moved toward the washbasin. "It was hot today. I'm sure you were exhausted from our walk."

Keeping her eyes fixed on Mira, Amalya laced her fingers in the small holes that cut through the back of her chair. "Did you hear what I said?"

"Of course, darling." Mira spoke without even looking at her.

"And you still do not believe that I saw her."

"Saw who?"

"*Primeveire*."

Mira shook the water free from her hands, glancing over her shoulder briefly enough for Amalya to see worry cast in her furrowed brow. "I told you before, Amalya. There is no one by that name. It is all in your head."

Amalya stood abruptly, causing the chair to drag across the floor. "I know who I saw!"

Mira turned at her assertiveness, her jaw clenched and her hands pressed at her sides. "There is no Primeveire. We never went to that place. She is not real."

They watched each other for a time before Mira broke away with a huff.

"It is just fatigue. Perhaps you should lie down. You've had a trying day." Moving toward the small cradle, she touched it as she checked on the still-sleeping form of Arthur. "There is laundry to hang. Eat and rest now. You will feel better tonight." Without a second glance, she disappeared past the girls' room and out the back door.

Amalya steadied her breath, repeating Mira's words in her mind but never believing them.

Primeveire is real.

The sharp clang of a hammer drew her attention to the window just beyond the shop. Amalya approached it, peering out to see Laird hard at work, slaving over the anvil and the hot coals of the forge. Moving her hands over her swelling belly, she took a few deep breaths as she watched him dip the blade of his work into the cool bath, the sizzle crackling in her ears and causing her courage to build.

Something was false and she would find the answers she sought, even if it meant crossing the lines of friendship.

STEPPING underneath the overhang of the forge, Laird glanced at Amalya as she entered his domain.

"Amalya," he said with a half-smile. "How was your walk?"

"Just fine." She looked around and saw a heap of wooden buckets and tools leaning on a long bench against the shop wall. "May I sit?"

"Of course." Laird hurried forward, moving the items from the bench so she would have ample space to sit.

She sat down, watching Laird return to his work.

"To what do I owe the pleasure of your company?"

Clasping her hands in her lap, Amalya pressed her lips together. "I have something to ask you."

"Well, I am all ears to your requests as I cannot deny the demands of a woman with child. That would not be very gentlemanly on my part."

She smiled, glad that Laird still had the uncanny desire to lighten the mood of any conversation. "I feel I might dampen your spirits with what you are about to hear."

"Hard to believe."

Looking down at her hands, Amalya breathed a quick sigh before meeting his gaze again. "It's about Mira. I possess a memory that she does not. She denies it ever happened, calling it a trick of the mind."

He struck the hot iron. "It very well could be. What does it involve?"

"She took me somewhere, to a place beyond Stéinia's Keep."

Laird lowered his hammer, his eyes hardening in concentration. His jaw flexed, as if he was contemplating his words carefully. Amalya had seen Laird and Mira a number of times speaking in hushed tones in the shadows of their home. Perhaps she had found the subject of their secrets.

"This is about Primeveire," he stated at last.

Amalya's heart leapt in her chest, bringing her to her feet with excitement. "Yes! Yes, it is about her! She is real?"

With careful movement, Laird drew to face her, placing his hammer atop the anvil. "She is."

"Then why does Mira deny what we did? The things she spoke of, the truth that was shared. Why does she want me to think it was false?"

Laird moved closer to her, his ebony-hued face drawn and cautious as he glanced back toward the house. "Amalya." He took her hands carefully, his fingers rough against her skin. "I promise you, it is only because she is trying to protect you."

Amalya's gaze climbed across the deep curves and bevels of his face. "Who is she? How do you know her?"

The stone of his throat rose and fell as his dark eyes searched for a reason to deny her. "You are my friend, Amalya, and as much as I wish to keep you safe, it will not do us any good if you do not stop wanting. So I will not deny you the truth."

He brought her back to the bench, lowering her down as he sat beside her. "You remember, after you gave birth to

Elra, Mira and I were trying to have our own child. We tried for so long, but it never happened."

"Yes, of course I remember." Amalya let her hands fall against his sullied leather apron.

"We heard of a witch who could help us. Help us have a child of our own. So, we found her. Primeveire. And she did.
. . she helped us."

Amalya's eyes grew wide. It was not the truth that Primeveire was indeed a witch, but the truth of her gift. She had the power to help women conceive. The power to create life.

"What did she do?"

Laird shook his head. "I could not begin to understand it. We went to see her, and she spoke in Draughtrìnd, had us speak these words and drink tasteless vials of sharp potions. Then, she told us to go home and love one another. So we did. And then. . . Polliann came to us."

Pulling away from him, Amalya could not help but look down at the life that was growing inside her. Could Primeveire have done it to her as well? It sounded impossible, but what was impossible for a witch? If she could help Mira and Laird conceive a child, why not her?

But the real question was why. She showed no signs of being with child prior to seeing Primeveire. No feeling that her body was changing. Perhaps it was her state of being—having been privy to the numbness for so long, she may not have noticed.

"What if she did the same to me?"

Immediately, Laird waved his hands in denial. "That is not possible."

"And why not? She is a witch, isn't she? There could be more ways than what you had to do."

"Amalya—"

"I need to know." She stood up, Laird following her, taking her arm as if to keep her from fleeing.

"I do not see her reasoning for doing such a thing."

She looked around frantically, feeling her heart quicken and her breath shorten. "I know what it sounds like. I know what it may seem to you, but—"

Laird placed a comforting hand on her shoulder. "Amalya, please. You must calm down."

"There is nothing left to anchor me. What is true for others is not for me. This child, I. . . I do not know where or how it came to be. My mind believes one thing while my heart another. I do not know where I stand, where to look, or if I can even trust myself." She grasped his sweaty arms. "Please. I must know."

He watched her, his eyes darting across her face, trying to decide if what she was requesting should be honored. She knew Laird did not want to betray Mira. Conspiring with witches was an offense punishable by exile or death. She knew what she was asking of him—to once again put his family in danger. Having divulged his secret to her was cause enough for unrest.

But this had only quickened the doubt that had already been coursing through Amalya's veins. Too many unknowns, too many illusions left staining her memories without truth. Even her time with Tristan was slipping away from her. Primeveire was the only connection to the magic she had felt. She needed to know, or her feet would never touch the ground again.

TWENTY-TWO

"It is the head and the heart. The heart possesses the core of their magic. And the head possesses the knowledge to wield it."
-King Aethelwulf letters, 1,809 Sól Sett, Second Season, Dag Light

"Amalya."

The gentle whisper of Laird's low voice pulled her gaze to the door. He stood against the frame, holding a cloak in his hands. With a small nod, Amalya freed herself from the bed and slipped on her shoes.

Laird wrapped her in the cloak and led her from the house with his hands grasping her shoulders. They followed the path she had taken the other day, taking a slight detour that led them to where Amalya had lost sight of Primeveire. The streets were empty. Dim firelight twitched beneath sullen lanterns, keeping their vision from delving too deeply into darkness. The occasional stray feline skulked along the outskirts of the homes, tail raised and legs bouncing as if to a melody only it could hear.

"This way." Laird led her down a small alley, keeping close to one side. As they neared the end, Amalya discovered it opened into a crossroads, five paths converging in a large, imperfect circle, filled with barrels and buckets of many wares. Some appeared as if they had been waiting in this place for ages, the faces of iron, wood, and clothing bearing the scars of time.

Laird released her from the safety of his grasp. "I will wait for you at the other end."

Amalya turned to face him. "What if she does not come?"

"She always comes." Laird did not leave her, only stood with quiet conviction as they both waited for the consequences of his actions.

Amalya placed a hand on his arm in an attempt to quiet the unrest in his eyes, knowing he was doing this for her against Mira's wishes. "Thank you, Laird."

With a single nod, Laird retreated down the alley whence they came, leaving Amalya alone in the night.

Keeping the cloak wrapped around her to shield her from the chill lingering in the air, Amalya crept closer to the haphazard piles decorating the circle. She found a rather sturdy-looking crate where she could rest until her visitor arrived. Despite her determination, her current condition had denied her the energy to proceed in haste. The child had not stirred within her the entire journey, perhaps fast asleep or sensing what was to come.

As she came down to sit upon the crate, her hands

smoothed over the roundness of the life she was forced to carry.

"If you can hear me, little one," she whispered, gently stroking the shape of her form, "I feel as though you are cursed. What will your life be in this unforgiving kingdom, with a mother such as I? You could have done so much better than me. I have done nothing to deserve this, and yet. . . " Her gaze drifted to one of the many alleys, the faded flicker of lamplight visible at its end. "I feel as though there is something more to what you will become. What you are and why I am part of it."

A faint movement entered her vision. Amalya turned to face it, seeing the pulsing eyes of Primeveire staring at her from beneath a darkened cloak. She pushed her hood away from her face, letting her hair escape across her right shoulder as her feet came to rest an arm's length from where Amalya sat.

Carefully rising to her feet, Amalya kept her hands steady, holding on to her frame as the child began to press against her sides.

"Why did you summon me?" Primeveire asked with such poise and authority that Amalya could not help but shudder.

"You are real," she replied.

Primeveire's eyebrow raised as the corner of her lip curled into her narrow cheek. "Is that why you wished to see me? To prove that I am true?"

"Yes, and no." Taking a deep breath, Amalya tightened her hold on herself, feeling the child press against her hands as if reaching for her through the walls of her womb. "I must know if you have given me this—"

"No." Primeveire took a step toward her. "That child was growing inside you before you first came to me. I did not grant you the seed that had already been planted."

A wave of sorrow filled Amalya like a sudden wind. It would have been easier to accept that magic had granted her this child. That it had been gifted to her for a chance at redemption or healing or something she did not understand.

Tristan flashed into her vision. She looked at Primeveire. "Whose child do I carry?"

The witch did not flinch or stir, only stood, stoic and poised. "It is yours."

"But who—"

Before another word could be spoken, Primeveire pushed herself forward, landing her palm on the middle of Amalya's growing form. Their eyes locked as Amalya felt a dull yet powerful warmth radiating from the witch's palm, enveloping the child's resting place. It spread as if being submerged in a warm bath, careful and all comforting.

The feeling overwhelmed her with comfort, her eyelids weighing heavy and plunging Amalya's sight into darkness. As she felt her body sway, the warmth reached her face, casting a heavy shadow upon her. The child kicked wildly, cramping her sides and causing her knees to buckle. The flash of red orbs overwhelmed her vision, delivering a quake through her bones. Each time she tried to see, the burning intensified. A frantic fire, consuming everything it touched.

She could feel their hatred, which became too much for her to bear. Bringing her hands to her face, she pressed against her temples, shaking her head wildly as the child attempted to rip from her body.

"No, NO!"

She fell against the crate, her legs shaking and her breathing short and labored. Amalya's eyes darted to each corner of the circle before falling on Primeveire once again. Her hand was still outstretched, palm facing Amalya.

"What did you see?" The witch's question came with an ounce of feeling in her words.

Amalya could do nothing as she tried to calm both her mind and body. The child was restless, but far from the frantic need to escape the safety of her womb.

Leaning forward, Primeveire's face came to rest a few finger lengths from Amalya's gaping mouth as she took in helpings of air to rid herself of the chaos.

"You are being watched."

Amalya searched for the truth in Primeveire's dark eyes. Although Primeveire exuded strength, something had caused her gaze to falter ever so slightly.

"Who?" Amalya asked. "What do they want?"

"They want your life. And your child's. . . even more."

Closing her lips, Amalya let a staggered breath escape her nostrils. "Why?"

"You are a threat." Primeveire clasped her hands around Amalya's still-wavering fingers. "But you are also the *Adgerdaleysi*."

"The what?"

Squeezing her hands tightly, Primeveire kept her gaze locked on Amalya's squinting eyes. "Do not find me again. You must stay hidden. I am a beacon, as is anyone or anything who possesses magic. The farther you are from it, the safer you will be."

Amalya leaned in, lowering her voice to a whisper. "What if this threat finds me?"

"You will know what to do."

Shaking her head, Amalya felt the witch's hands fall from hers. She moved to grasp them again, but Primeveire kept them tight against her stomach, drawing herself away, back into the darkness.

Subduing the fear from spilling out was impossible as Amalya came to stand once again. "How do you know?" she cried.

A slow, serene grin spread across the witch's face as she took her hood in her hands to shroud herself yet again. "Because it is your destiny."

TWENTY-THREE

*"A flower may not bloom in the dark. And a wave may not
catch a reflection in the sea. But if your heart is full and your
eyes are focused, you will know how love is truly meant
to be."*
-Excerpt from *The Song of Dag and Nótt*

Destiny. So much fated with a single word. If having this child was indeed Amalya's destiny, she wanted no part of it. With her eyes trained on the faded grass just beyond the shoreline, she watched the dull hue of her slippers grow hazy from the sand and rocks along the river's edge.

It had been several weeks since Primeveire spoke to her. So many questions sprang forth that Amalya felt there were no answers for. She drifted through the days as a seed on the breeze, her mind everywhere but where it should be. Primeveire had been erased from sight, even though Amalya still searched the crowds whenever left to wander the streets on her own. Amalya would abide by her words and stay away, but a part of her wanted to know more, and Primeveire was the only source she trusted.

Seeking solitude had become her only comfort. It took some convincing and Laird's support for Mira to relinquish her protective hold on her. Though she had found time with her children to be more enjoyable as each day passed, it suffocated Amalya to be confined to that house for so long, surrounded by the same voices. If she could not escape it every so often, she would surely slip back into the darkness she had not fully pulled herself from.

Wesley was coming today, and Amalya had agreed to meet him on the road just beyond the gates of Rau. He had told Laird the last time he had gone to visit the farm that he had something to tell her.

"He seemed ready to burst with his confession," Laird had said. "I have never seen him so ecstatic in such a long time."

Amalya had no inkling of what it could be, but it was enough that he wished to tell her before bringing the news to light amongst the rest of their family and friends. The river gently lapped against the small, rocky shore. A few loose stones broke free as she passed over them. She kicked them lightly, letting them skip across the ground. Some landed with a splash in the river, never too harshly as to stir the water into a frenzy.

Looking up as she walked, she breached a small hill just before the land flattened toward the gate. A girl was kneeling by the shoreline with her back to Amalya. She was wearing a cream-colored dress, layering its folds as it wafted gently in the small breeze, her hair braided and pulled back into a tight brown knot on top of her head.

Amalya moved to pass without disturbing the girl, but her presence seemed to stir her and the girl looked up just as Amalya was about to pass. Springing to her feet, the girl grabbed Amalya's arm, bringing her gaze upon her. She had brilliant eyes that, when Sól's rays reflected off the water, shimmered with a lavender hue.

The girl was just a child, though far older than Elra. Her face was sullied and her hands caked in dried mud, partially hiding the dirtied cuts and bruises across her wrists. The thickness of her eyebrows mimicked the desperate waves of her unkempt appearance. Amalya searched her face, wondering why she felt compelled to grasp onto her.

"What is your name?" She spoke softly so as not to draw attention to the rapid beating of her startled heart.

The girl did not speak, but thrust something into Amalya's chest, letting go of her hold the moment Amalya's hand caught whatever was given to her. Then the girl scurried away, her head down as her feet moved fast into the city.

The trinket pinched Amalya's fingers. As she raised her hand to look at it, she felt a tightness pinch her chest like a needle. In her hand was a white rose. It was as radiant and perfect as the one that had fallen from her bed that morning upon waking. The one Tristan had produced for her from the tears that leaked from her eyes.

Her head whipped back toward the direction in which the girl fled, but she was gone. Her heart would not cease, causing the flower to flutter against her. Bringing the rose to her nose, Amalya inhaled its deep floral scent, letting it fill her chest and seep into the cracks of her brittle essence. As she closed her eyes, memories of Tristan bloodied and weak flashed into focus. The way he moved, like a shadow, swift and seamless. The sound of his voice echoed in the chambers of her mind. The feel of his lips upon her own, his ashy hair falling into his face, brushing against her cheeks as she surrendered to his earthy taste.

"I will never hurt you." His voice broke into a delicate whisper inside her mind. "I will never abandon you."

He sounded so near, as if he were merely a hair's breadth from her ear. Her eyes fluttered open, hoping to see him standing before her. But he was not. The memory of him slowly dissipated, leaking down her legs and snaking along the rocks to the water's edge. She clutched the rose to her chest. She dared not take a step for fear that the hope his words had offered her would fade into the realms of uncertainty.

Her eyes began to wander from the shore to the north gate of the city. An ox-drawn caravan with pale cloth shielding what lay within it rolled just beyond the gate. Wesley drove it proudly, his dark red hair slicked back against his crown. The nostalgia of the rose quickly retreated into the safety of her mind, replaced by sheer curiosity.

The caravan was quite large, enough for a family to rest comfortably in. How in Marin's name was he able to afford such a thing? Amalya could feel the fluttering return, but it was scattered. With a deep sigh, she continued toward the gate, not wanting to leave Wesley to wait for her too long. Her heart matched the nerves festering within her as she stepped up toward it, leaving the rocky river shore to rest undisturbed.

She waited for him to bring the cart through. Just before

he passed under, Amalya placed the rose carefully in the belt pouch of her dark emerald dress so that it was barely visible.

Wesley drove the caravan to the side, popping off his seat with a huge smile spreading across his face. Moving her loosely woven braid from one shoulder to another, Amalya tried to appear elated. She was glad to see him in such good spirits, but Tristan's voice still plagued her mind, causing her focus to remain in constant turbulence.

"Amalya." Wesley beamed at her, taking her by the hand and planting an enthusiastic kiss on her cheek. "You look stunning."

"You always had a way of flattery, Wesley." His light-heartedness brought the corner of her lip up ever so slightly, which only lengthened his smile more. She gestured toward the wafting pale cloth of the caravan top. "What is all this?"

"I have news for you."

"So I have been told." She squeezed his hand gently. "I can only assume this new caravan has something to do with it?"

He was trying to hold in his eagerness, but the trembling hairs on his chin gave away his inability to contain himself. "I've sold the farm."

Amalya's eyes widened. "You. . . what?"

"I sold the farm. After the baby is born, we will travel by the west road from the capital to Mare."

She shook her head, her eyes wandering across his dull white shirt and tarnished brown vest. "Why would you. . . sell the farm? Does Father—"

"He helped me arrange it. He is coming with us." He tilted his head to find her gaze again. "Are you not pleased?"

Amalya could not find the words to convey what she was

feeling. Her skin prickled with sudden excitement, but her mind raced with an unquenchable panic. This is what she had always wanted. Ever since she was a child, she had dreamed of traveling to all the cities of Jöro and beyond—to see everything this endless land had to offer. Now that it was happening, she was not sure if she wanted to leave. If she left Rau, would Tristan ever find her again?

As she tried to harness any joy that had come from Wesley's confession, Amalya's eyes widened before lines of worry bore down on them. "I am. . . I just do not know if this is. . . I don't—"

"I know it's sudden, but we have at least one more season before the baby comes. And the city is allowing us to stay until we are ready to leave."

"The city?"

"Yes, they practically ripped the farm from my hands. We will have enough to travel comfortably. They offered me a job as well, so we never need to worry about coin again." Moving closer to her, Wesley sighed as he settled beside her. "It will be a big change, but we will be together, all of us."

"Wesley," she shook her head lightly, "you did this. . . just for me?"

"It's a chance. To begin again. To put what has passed to rest." He looked down at her growing belly, placing both their hands upon it. "It is our chance."

A chance. His words took root within her thoughts, bringing her back to what Primeveire had said. Rau was Tristan's hope to find her again. But that was before this looming threat of Primeveire's warnings. If whoever was behind those red eyes knew where she was, the best thing for her to do was run; to put as much distance between her and this magic that threatened her.

"Yes." The word fell from her mouth like a stone.

Wesley's face lit up as he took her in his arms, twirling her around with a hearty laugh. Wrapping her arms around his neck, she smelled the damp aroma of hay and wheat in his clothes. It tickled her nose, awakening a sudden childish innocence in her heart. As he placed her back on the ground, he leaned in and kissed her with such elated passion that Amalya lost herself in the joy cast by the moment. As their lips parted, the fear was eradicated from her mind, replaced by the sudden longing for him to never abandon her. She was young again, standing in Sól's sleeping light beneath the mountains where he first professed his love for her.

He gently pulled away, leaving remnants of him across the surface of her lips. "I love you, Amalya," he whispered. "You have made me the happiest man in Jöro this day."

Amalya beamed, sharing in his joy. She placed a hand on his chest. As fractured as she was and as hopeless as her days seemed to be, that young girl with dreams of being a skald still lingered in the essence of who she was. That girl would forever care for and love him, no matter how small she became and how silent the screams were.

"Would it be too forward of me to kiss you again?" Wesley hovered just at the cusp of her lips, tempting her to fall into the depths of his warm, full beard and give him all he desired of her.

She had not indulged in passion in so long. The need to cleanse this sudden yearning overtook her like a woman possessed. She closed her eyes, pulling him against her with a need she had not displayed since surrendering herself to Tristan under the willow tree.

Grabbing her by the waist, Wesley held her tightly against him, being mindful of what was growing between them. He carried her toward the back of the caravan, lifting her onto the step. Amalya slipped inside, seeing a few crates of corn and other vegetables pressed against the strongly built sides. The crates made a rectangular frame on the floor, covered by a cotton blanket and strands of hay.

Amalya slid down to the floor as Wesley followed her in, his arms coming around her. His mouth fell onto hers as she dragged him to the floor. He was careful not to lie on her as his hand fished under her dress. Amalya yanked the buttons free of his shirt, her hands pressing against his chest, his lean muscles tightening at her touch.

That girl who had fallen in love with a farm boy had replaced the woman who was in love with a Draughtrìnd. Pulling away from his kiss, she let him linger as she untied his belt, eager to receive his prize.

"Let me take you," she whispered to him, pushing him down onto his back, not allowing him to deny her. Pulling up her dress, she slipped her body around him, straddling him as her hands continued to explore his chest. Wesley kept his hands on her waist, guiding her to what she so desperately sought.

Amalya touched his desire as she consumed it. She moaned softly, feeling Wesley's body tense beneath her as his fingers dug into her sides. She looked down at him, bringing her lips to his chest, tasting the sweat of a hard day's work on every inch of her tongue. Wesley rocked her slowly as he peeled away the tie of her dress, letting her breasts fall free. Sitting up, he fondled them in his hands, bringing his mouth upon one tip, playing with her between his teeth.

Breathing into the air above them, Amalya ventured deeper, her mind erased of all things but the ecstasy awakening every sense in her body.

"Amalya," Wesley whispered as his teeth clenched against her neck, holding her bare underneath her dress, moving her to satisfy him.

Amalya could feel her losing herself, letting go of that which kept her barred from accepting his love for so long. Deep heaves through gritted teeth released a cry that had been yearning to escape. In that moment, her eyes fell closed as Wesley filled her, leaving him to fall into her shoulder, huffing his hot breath across her bare skin.

Amalya settled down upon him, pushing loose strands of hair from her face. As Wesley caught his breath against her collarbone, Amalya's hand traced the arch of his shoulder blades with her finger. A dullness took hold of her, bearing the weight of heavy stones as she lay across his chest. Her gaze came to rest on her belt pouch, disheveled but still clinging to her side, the soft petals of the rose peering through the gaps of its covering.

Love was never good to her. It left a stain on her essence. A mark on her heart.

TWENTY-FOUR

"But are you worthy of it? A heart so lost. A mind believing in nothing else. Eyes, who would not unsee it. Are you worthy of it?"

-Excerpt from *The Tale of Marin and the White Dragon*

Subtle movements fluttered, pulling Amalya from her slumber. Sitting up on her hands, she waited until her eyes adjusted to the darkness. A calming rain pattered against the roof, sending cool melodies echoing through the night.

She looked beside her, where Wesley was sleeping soundly. He had stayed the night with them in Rau, enjoying the rest of the day with the news of their future. His chest gently rose and fell with each deep breath taken. She could not remember the last time he slept so peacefully. It was before Arthur was born, before so much heaviness had consumed her life.

Her eyes traveled from his restful form to the dull

woolen sheets of the bed. The strain of betrayal still lingered throughout her body. After recovering from the ecstasy she shared with Wesley, the dedication and love she had for Tristan bore into her flesh, piercing her heart like a thorn. Looking to the nightstand beside her, she saw the rose that the girl had granted her, its soft, pure petals glaring as if it knew all the dishonorable things she had done.

This feeling would never cease. Love was a poison, a desire she was always willing to quench, no matter the consequences. It offered her intoxicating freedom, but also left her scattered and disjointed. Allowing the pieces of herself to fall wherever they saw fit.

Her eyes shifted to the far corner of the bed. The more she peered into the dark, the clearer her vision became. Something moved, unveiling the chiseled profile of a man with sad golden eyes.

Amalya clutched her chest, forgetting how to breathe. The intensity of her heartbeat sounded like blaring bells in her ears as Tristan turned to look at her. His back was hunched, his hands folded carelessly in his lap. His garments were indistinguishable other than the V-shaped cut of his shirt.

"Tristan," she whispered.

He said nothing, only casting his gaze upon her like a child caught in the rain. She was tempted to reach for him, but was afraid he would fade from her touch, erasing him from existence yet again.

"Your gift," he uttered, moving his lips minimally. "Is it to your liking?"

Amalya peered once again at the rose she believed he

was referring to. "Yes. It is beautiful." Her eyes returned to him. "Thank you."

He remained motionless, but Amalya could feel the blanket tighten and strain, as if it were being pulled toward him. Tristan's shoulders came up, straightening his back and allowing his head to stand erect. His sullen expression melted into stone, the golden glint of his eyes hardening as they glared into her own.

"Do you relish in unfaithfulness?"

Shaking her head, Amalya could feel her lungs tighten as she straightened her legs underneath the sheets. "No. I. . . I did not mean to—"

"Liar." Within a blink of an eye, he had moved in front of her, his face inches from hers. Heat radiated from his body like a blazing fire, his hair framing his jaw, shrouding his expression in mystifying shadow. "Everything I have done, everything I am enduring, is for you."

His voice was absent of smoothness and care, stabbing her like a fiery blade.

Licking her dry lips, Amalya clenched the blanket in her palms, unable to turn away from his unrelenting stare. "What do you expect of me?"

"I expect you to be patient. But perhaps I have misjudged your love for me."

"No. No, I. . . I love you, Tristan." Words would not leave her as she struggled to control her tongue. A sudden fear crept up her spine and came to rest in the back of her mind.

"You are incapable of love." Tristan's expression twisted as he leaned in closer, forcing her to press against the wall with the blanket still clenched in her fists. "You are deserving of the darkness. You beg for it like a wet whore with your legs spread, willing and accepting as it drains you of your life, leaving nothing but an empty shell starved of light."

Tears rolled down her face. Her chin quivered as she absorbed the hurtful words. "I am as lost as you claim me to be. Charted not in a single direction but in all. Everything is shrouded in a fog that has now settled in my lungs and calls my veins their sanctuary. Nothing. . . is. . . nothing is. . . "

She swallowed, driving her teeth into her lower lip to silence the suffering of her misguided mind. For if there was one thing she knew to be true, it was the love Tristan held for her. He would never strike her with such words to poison her already poisoned heart. Not if it meant she would be lost to him forever.

"This is not you, Tristan," she uttered. "You would never say such things."

"How do you know what I would say?" With a sudden strike, his hands crashed against the wall on either side of her head. His bared teeth lengthened into the angry fangs of the Draughtrìnd. He pressed his nose against her own, the fire steaming from his nostrils burning her skin like hot coals.

"The Tristan you know is dead. Slain by the woman he had given his heart to protect. She consumed it, blood staining her chin as she made love to a man whose only gift to her was isolation and pain."

Shutting her eyes, her entire body melted into the wall as the heat intensified around her. The child within her kicked and clawed, sending shards of numbing pain through her back and down her legs. "Stop this."

"I will never stop. Not until I *get what I want*."

231

"Stop this!" She launched herself from the bed, her side crashing against the nightstand before she fell onto the floor. The white rose skipped across the room, coming to rest behind the closed door. Amalya clutched her head between her hands, not wanting to open her eyes to the flames that were consuming every inch of her.

"Amalya?"

"No! No! Leave me alone!"

Hands grabbed for her. She tried to move away, but she could not. The pain had left her completely numb.

"Amalya. . . " The voice softened, and the care and concern forced her to surrender to the dim light of the room. Wesley was beside her, holding her by the shoulders and peering into her soaked face.

She flung her arms around him, weeping uncontrollably. Of course Tristan hated her now. Of course he wanted her to suffer. And Wesley, he would know in time that she was not worth forgiving. And he would fall victim to the pain she had willingly lashed against his heart soon enough. Barring her. Condemning her. She deserved no mercy.

Holding her close, Wesley stroked her hair to calm her. "It was just a dream," he whispered. "You're safe."

His words would bring no comfort, for she knew she would never be safe, not from him or Tristan. Not from the monster she had created; a creature more deadly and powerful than any Draughtrìnd immortalized in skald songs.

TWENTY-FIVE

"A witch can never act on impulse and desire. That is their weakness."
King Aethelwulf letters, 1,811 Sól Sett, First Season,
Rökkur

"There's been a sighting." Amalya stopped fixing Arthur's leather-padded slippers and shot a glance to where one of Laird's customers stood, conversing with him over a forged ax.

"Has there now?" Laird responded with mild surprise.

"Aye, to the east, over the mountains." The man was older, the weathered lines of his face dragging his skin to hang under his neck. "I've seen it meself." He raised his arms on either side of him. "Wings as wide as Sól himself."

"There hasn't been a sighting in many Setts." Laird handed over the ax, which the man took carefully, not even bothering to observe Laird's craftsmanship.

"Well, there's one now. And I get the feelin' it won't be the last." The customer nodded as he dropped the coin into Laird's hand. "Good day to ya now."

"Good day."

The man hobbled away, holding the newly purchased weapon against his chest. Laird lingered on his form a little longer before noticing Amalya's gaze. She drew away, resuming the adjustments on Arthur's shoes. It had been three days since Tristan came to her again. Every night since, she had been fearful of sleep, dreading the moment she surrendered to the darkness. As frightened as she was to succumb to his aggression and words, her heart ached for him, even if it meant she would be tormented by his vicious sight.

But something was not right. Tristan had hidden nothing from her, even before he came to her as a man. The morning she found him in the lake, he never moved to strike, never showed aggression, only careful curiosity and gratitude.

The one who haunted her dreams could not be Tristan. It couldn't. The Draughtrìnd sighting could not be a coincidence—it had to be connected.

Was the dragon Tristan? If so, why had he not come for her?

A sighting would raise the flag to the Dragon Guard, whose sole purpose was to rid the kingdom of them. He would not put himself in such danger, not without reason.

Tying the final strap to Arthur's leg, she straightened his clothing before looking into his round face. He chewed clumsily on his fingers, a waterfall of drool decorating the corner of his mouth and spilling onto his hand.

"So many teeth!" Amalya pinched his cheeks, causing

him to giggle. "Let's find something better for you to chew on."

"Here." Looking up, she found Laird standing beside her, holding out a thick piece of leather tied with a matching cord. "He won't chew through that."

Amalya took it with a smile, presenting it to Arthur. His little fingers wrapped around it and he immediately shoved it in his mouth, sucking and chewing like a ravenous hog.

"That will suit you." Amalya placed her hand on top of her son's head as she stood up. "Thank you," she said, looking at Laird.

The heat of the forge sprinkled light beads of sweat throughout his dark hair and beard. Adjusting his apron, he gave her a hopeful smile. "Mira took the girls?"

"Yes. I wasn't up for walking today."

"You seem better than you were since Wesley left. He is coming again tomorrow?"

She nodded. "I believe so. He doesn't want to miss a moment before the baby arrives."

"I can't blame him." He looked away momentarily, breathing a sigh before raising his brow. "Something is different between the two of you. I could tell the moment he came here a few days ago with the news of the farm."

That day carried a new fear whenever she thought about it. Amalya pressed her lips together, not wanting to confess the truth. Laird had helped her, but there was nothing more he could do. Not without putting his family at risk.

"Have you told Mira? About what you did for me?"

Laird's eyes flashed with uncertainty. "No. I cannot bring myself to disappoint her. Not with our lives changing so much this past season." He moved his hand to rest on her shoulder. "Not that you are a burden to us. We love having you. And the children."

Amalya smiled, patting his hand while adjusting her stance to support the strain from her carrying. "It would not offend me if you did or not. But I appreciate all you and Mira have done for us."

A flash of the fear she carried suddenly pierced her lungs and left her breathless, swaying on her feet as if she would fall.

Laird moved forward, grabbing her by the waist to steady her. "Are you all right?"

She closed her eyes, swallowing the sharp edges of the stone lodged in her throat. "No, I don't think I am." Opening her eyes again, she peered into his concerned face. "I am afraid."

"Afraid?"

She nodded. "Something is coming. Primeveire, she warned me to stay away. But when I sleep. . . "

She stopped, daring not to speak of her visions of Tristan, not to Laird. Laird and Wesley were like brothers. She wanted neither of them to believe she still harped on Tristan's existence. That she still felt him every day since he had come to the farm. Though now the feeling had shifted, drenched in a poisonous fume. It was foreign, but the light she had fallen in love with was still present, desperate to be seen.

"What is it?"

Suddenly, she dropped her hand from his, moving away from him to sit on a small bench while Arthur continued to chew and play on the ground. "You have patrons."

Laird turned to see two people had entered the shop. He

turned back to her swiftly, squinting as he took a reluctant step back.

"Forgive me, I will trouble you no longer." Amalya watched Arthur to distract herself from his gaze. She could still feel his eyes waiting for her to dispel more, but she would not. Her desperation had gotten the better of her. She needed to be careful not to say too much. She did not want Wesley to know.

If it happened again, she would tell someone, but not Laird. There was only one person she could trust not to repeat words spoken, despite her desire to deny everything to keep Amalya and her family safe.

AMALYA APPROACHED MIRA FROM BEHIND. She was dipping clothes in a basin, scrubbing them against the washboard with vigor. Soap foamed and spread across her wrists, her gaze focused and hardened in concentration. Her hair sat beneath a kerchief, the trials of the day laid bare on her pale, tarnished apron.

Amalya sat quietly beside her, gaining her notice. The children were already down for the night, Sól's sleeping form echoing beneath the clouded sky. A light bellow rolled through the gray plumes. A storm was near, the first one to touch down this season.

Mira raised her gaze, glancing at Amalya as she returned to her work. "You should be resting."

"I cannot rest. Not peacefully."

Mira twisted the cloth between her fists, letting the

clouded water drip back into the basin. "Perhaps some tea will soothe you."

The drops of water echoed deep within her as Amalya watched them fall, one by one. The gentle vibrations rattled the horrible image of what she had experienced that night. Terror within eyes of gold, dripping fangs hungry to rid her of her flesh.

One sudden kick from the child jarred her focus, letting Amalya break away to find Mira looking at her with quiet concern.

"What has riddled your mind, Amalya?"

Amalya grasped Mira's wrist, forcing her to drop the clothes into the soapy water. This was not the time to tread lightly. Amalya knew she could not break if there was any hope of gaining Mira's trust in what was happening to her. She would only speak the truth, and, with Marin's grace, Mira could not possibly deny it.

"I saw her again," Amalya intoned. "Primeveire."

Mira's mouth drew into a jovial smirk. "This nonsense again—"

"No." Amalya pulled at Mira's arm, forcing her hand to fall into her lap. "Laird took me to her. He told me what she had done for you."

The smirk melted from her face, Mira's eyes now wide with concentrated tension.

"Do not scold him. Please. He was only trying to help me understand. To help me find my way in the chaos that calls the shadow I cast each day home."

Turning her knees to her, Mira took a deep, sullen breath. "I'm listening."

Amalya could feel the tightness beneath her skin.

"Something is hunting me. They want to punish me. I can feel it in their eyes. Deep red pools of fire and death, setting my skin ablaze and my thoughts into a frenzy of madness. It comes not as I sleep, but in my days awake. Primeveire told me it is magic that brings the visions to me, so magic is what I must avoid."

Mira sat, listening to every word spoken. Amalya could not tell if she believed her, but it did not matter. She could not let it remain unspoken any longer. "And as I sleep, Tristan comes to me. But it is not him. Not the Tristan I know and love. . . with every strand of my heart. He is angry—jealous and menacing. He calls me the most terrible things, saying I betrayed him. There is no compassion in his eyes, just hate and the desire to rip me to shreds."

Closing her eyes, Amalya breathed slowly, taking in air like the rolling wind across the hills of Rau. It did nothing to calm the storm. The grip she had on Mira's wrist soon loosened. As her eyelids clenched with such aggression, her mind ached. It was then that the red threat revealed itself again, tossing in and out of her focus like a delighted tide.

"Amalya."

Mira pulled at her arm, forcing them both to stand in the new darkness cast by Nótt's tail across the sky. Amalya's eyes shot open, her throat once again allowing air to pass without demise. There was strength in Mira's verdant eyes, strength that Amalya had hoped to find so she had something to hold on to. To keep her feet planted on the ground beneath them.

A whisper traveling in the silent turmoil of the skies tempted them. Both Amalya and Mira turned toward the mountains that stretched beyond the city limits, now blanketed with dark, threatening clouds as the storm continued westward across the lands of Jöro.

A flash of light bared the shape of something Amalya thought she would never see again, its wings like sails to catch the wind. A long, streaming tail spread at the seams of the pressing storm, barely visible as it flickered beneath its natural shield. When it came again, this time accompanied by the deep, rumbling threat of rain, it angled down toward the mountains before disappearing into the darkness.

Pressing her palm to rest on her sleeping child, warmth pooled across Amalya's womb—the same warmth Primeveire had laid upon her in the safety of the alley. There was magic in the air, blanketing her each time the wind blew across her face, tossing strands of unkempt hair.

"Do you feel that?"

Amalya turned to Mira and met her gaze. The words she spoke sent a chill down her spine, enough to shock her into fathomable knowing that she too was affected. "You can feel it as I can?"

"Once you are touched by magic, you are a prisoner to it." A fragmented smile brushed across Mira's face. "Magic gave me a child. I cannot live without knowing of its presence." Another whisper cut away from the clouds. Mira looked back at the storm, breathing a restful sigh. "A Draughtrìnd sailing through the storm across the Eldur Mountains. It cannot be by chance. Something has lured it here, or someone."

She grasped Amalya tighter around her arm, pulling her to stand before her and harnessing her focus. "I do not understand why, nor do I wish to."

"I'm not asking you to understand it," Amalya pleaded,

"I just need someone to believe. I can no longer stand keeping this with me without someone knowing it is my truth."

"I do not know what I can do to help you."

"Believe in me. That is all I ask."

Mira lowered her head, keeping Amalya's arms steady against her. With a careful nod, she murmured, "I believe you, Amalya. I've always believed you."

TWENTY-SIX

"The light of Dag was filled with pridefulness. Could pride win the heart of one as stubborn as the dark-scaled Nótt? A creature who sought to paint the night each time her tail uncovered the stars?"
-Excerpt from *The Song of Dag and Nótt*

Days were no longer distinctive. When one waits for something to happen, it is the only thing that drives you to notice the passing of time. The Draughtrìnd sightings had become almost nightly, leading the red-eyed menace to bear fruit within Amalya's gaze. Some moments were bearable, while others left her caught in the wind, unable to stop herself from falling. It was hard to maintain the illusion that nothing was wrong.

Mira was there, using her words to weave a trap around Amalya to protect her from that which plagued her each day. She kept her well-fed and as rested as she could be. That was the one grace Marin had granted her. Wesley had been present more as the last days of her condition crept closer to finality.

Tristan had not appeared in Amalya's dreams since the day the stranger had given her the rose. It was her only escape from the deep foreboding that followed her each night the Draughtrìnd flew, poisoning the city with magic.

Holding onto Elra's hand, Amalya walked through the regional district of Rau, scanning the mortar-laden manors and clay roofs of the upper class. Wesley, carrying Arthur on his shoulders, walked proudly by their side. This was a rare place to be, commoners breaking through the line of uneven roads to walk upon the tailored streets of the well-to-do. Wesley had business to attend to here—a final signing over of the farm, sealing the fate of their future.

Elra had donned her most flowery dress, lined with knitted tassels that tickled her ankles. Braids brushed atop each of her shoulders and bounced as she moved with a skip in her step. Amalya evened out any crimps in her attire. A white bodice cascaded into the Sól-lit hue of her skirt, accentuating the perfect roundness of her belly. She had braided her hair as well, a request from her daughter she could not help but abide.

The smell of floral perfumes wafted from every open window they passed. Despite them looking their best, Amalya felt very out of place amongst the nobles and lords of Rau. Licking her lips, she looked at Wesley. He had trimmed his beard, his dark red hair resting neatly against his head. He did not own any clothes that did not require function, but the dark slacks and fitted vest buttoned against a cream-colored shirt Laird had lent him was a welcome substitute. And it suited him.

He glanced back at her, a charming smile gracing his face.

A shade of red tarnished Amalya's cheeks as she looked away briefly, before catching his eyes still upon her. "Don't look at me like that."

"Like what?"

Arthur pulled at Wesley's ears, forcing him to face forward, squinting in mild discomfort.

Elra tugged at Amalya's hand, pointing forward into the wide street before them. "Look, Mama!"

A glint from a dozen soldiers brandishing smooth silver armor marched across their path. Their greaves sounded each step as shields held firmly in their hands collided with the suited line, erect and focused; each head helmeted and straight, every stride taken in unison. The familiar image of a Draughtrìnd, speared through the tail and protruding from their fanged mouths, donned each shield that flashed before their eyes.

"The Dragon Guard in Rau," Wesley breathed. "I never thought I'd see the day."

As they moved from sight, Amalya's heart sank. The guards' purpose was to hunt and exterminate the Draughtrìnd. With so many sightings of one drifting over the East Eldur Mountains, it was not surprising they would be called into action, swarming the city in hopes of strategically trapping their prey.

She did not know if the sighted dragon was Tristan or not. It did not feel like him. The magic that bled from the east did not match what she had felt when she lay in his arms. This magic kept one erect, holding the hairs on one's arms hostage, refusing them rest. The Draughtrìnd it pooled from was doing just as the Dragon Guard was called to do. It was hunting.

Just as they were about to cross the path the guard had taken, a few more armored fellows passed them in haste. Amalya drew Elra back to keep her from crossing as they rushed by. A girl, wrapped in a dark brown cloak, did not seem to notice their approach. As she made to cross their path, one guard pushed her off her feet, sending her crashing to the ground on hands and knees. Dropping Elra's hand, Amalya lifted her skirt and rushed toward the girl, as the soldiers did not care to stop in their haste.

The poor girl did not recover herself as her unkempt locks fell to cover her face. Reaching her, Amalya bent down carefully, taking her by the arm. "Are you all right, my dear?"

With a twist of her neck, the girl looked at her. The sight of her purple-hued eyes ceased the beating of Amalya's heart. It was the girl from the shore, the same girl who gave her the white rose just before Wesley had first told her he had sold the farm. The quality of her breath shortened, taking in small bursts of panicked air as the girl stared at her.

"You. . . " Amalya's voice trailed into a whisper as the soft sounds of pattering feet shifted the purple-eyed girl's gaze.

"Is she okay, Mama?"

Before Elra could reach them, the girl pushed herself off her knees, pressing her hands to Amalya's chest as she bolted from the scene. Grasping her hand to her bodice, Amalya looked down at the offering the girl had thrust upon her. Another crisp white rose.

"Where's she going?" Elra was standing next to her now, looking in the direction the girl had fled.

The rose pulled at the fear and longing Amalya had hoped to forget. Closing her eyes, she tried to find comfort in the beauty and perfection of the gift that had carried so much meaning in every petal. Now, she did not know if this rose was a sign of hope or a threat.

"That's so pretty!" Elra jumped up and down at her side, looking at the rose with awe. "May I hold it, please, Mama?"

Amalya clutched the flower to her chest with fear that, if Elra were to touch it, she too would be tainted by whatever magic kept its purity alive. She could let no one hold it, not a single person.

"It may prick your pretty little fingers," she said as she came to her feet, even though she felt no thorns accompanying the flower's smooth stem.

Elra slumped, her arms at her sides, pursing her lips in displeasure.

"That was rather odd," Wesley said as he joined them, Arthur still observing the city from atop his shoulders. He stopped, seeing the flash of heightened concern in Amalya's wandering eyes. "Are you all right?"

"Yes." Amalya forced a smile. "I am fine. I think she was just scared. That is why she fled so quickly."

"Well, if those men just paid attention, Sól forbid. That girl is lucky she wasn't hurt." He glanced at the rose pressed between her fingers. "Where did that come from?"

"The girl, she gave it to me. Perhaps as a thank-you."

"Well, it would look lovely in your hair. Don't you think so, Elra?"

Nodding her head, Elra tugged at Amalya's dress. "Put it in, Mama! You'd look as pretty as Marin with that flower in your hair!"

"No, I don't think—"

"Please!" Elra played the pout charade with large brown eyes trained on her.

Amalya was keen to deny her daughter's request. But what excuse could she give? Swallowing her nerves, letting them flutter and stir in her belly, Amalya held her breath as she nodded in agreement. "All right then. I do not see the harm of it, I suppose."

Bringing the flower to her head, she tucked the stem between the creases of her braid, sliding it in carefully. Her hair was thick enough that the stem did not penetrate to the other side. Its head came to rest against her crown, almost as if it were made to serve this specific purpose.

Wesley's smile grew, and his dark eyes glinted in admiration. "Elra's not wrong. You look stunning."

Elra hugged her leg. "So pretty! I wish I was as pretty as you."

"One day, you will be. And I'll be beating your suitors back with a pitchfork," Wesley said as he slid his fingers into Amalya's palm. "Shall we, then?"

Clutching his hand, Amalya continued forward with her husband, Elra walking between them, her little fingers meeting their bond. Amalya could feel the rose pressed against the edges of her forehead, magic dripping from each petal as it brushed into the strands that adorned her crown. It fell like sweet honey and coated her face, a warm hand caressing her cheek.

As she tried to hold on to the comfort it gave, Amalya understood that each rose she had been given—from the very first time Tristan plucked one from her tears—had brought her hope. But perhaps that hope had become something vile, something that was being used to separate her from whom she truly loved.

TWENTY-SEVEN

*"Give me your heart and I will treasure it 'til time surrenders
to the void of death."*
-Excerpt from *The Song of Dag and Nótt*

"Y ou believe this is the catalyst?" Mira turned the
rose over in her hand, studying its perfect structure.

Amalya rifled through the drawer of her bedside
table, pulling out the leather-bound book with the inked
words she had strewn across each page of parchment. As she
opened it to a certain page, two more roses fell from the
seams, each flattened from sitting pressed in the fold. As they
fell onto the table, Amalya picked them up, holding them up
for Mira to see.

"These are all that I have been given. Each one came to
me and was meant for me."

Standing, holding the two by the stems, Mira and
Amalya watched as the petals breathed life again, extending
outward as if they were never pressed, never imprisoned in

249

the folded pages. Mira held up the third, staring in awe at how similar they were and how unsullied they remained.

"The first rose I received was from a dream I had of Tristan." Amalya gestured toward the one Mira held. "Whatever magic lies in these petals is taking me to him. To the one who is claiming to be him."

Mira swallowed hard, blinking considerably at the theory. "And you are *certain* it is not him?"

"I am. It cannot be." Amalya placed her hand over the pure white petals. "You can feel the magic. It is comforting, love seeping through every strand of beauty they portray. Yet when he comes to me, it turns into something terrible. Something to fear."

Mira dropped her hand. "We know nothing of the true power of magic. We do not carry it like a torch. How can we understand what this truly means?"

Amalya placed the flowers on the table, sitting down on the bed with her hands falling into her lap. "I know it is not him."

Her heart ached at the truth of her words. It had never betrayed her before, even when everyone told her she was mistaken. She trusted herself now more than ever. Never again did she wish to revisit those days of loneliness and despair. Tristan had opened the window that let her essence stir once again, and now someone was trying to drown her, leaving her without escape.

Mira came to sit beside her, expelling a long, concentrated breath. "If you believe it is not truly him, then show him it is what you believe."

Amalya's gaze shifted to her friend, who watched her closely.

"Tell him you know he is false. That you wish to know who he is. Do not let him feed from your fear." She took Amalya's hands in her own. "He says you are terrible, calls you weak. But he is the weak one. He hides while you lay bare. Make him feel inferior and he will tell you his true name."

"I am not strong like you."

"You are." Mira moved closer to her, keeping Amalya from abandonment. "You healed a dragon. Believed in yourself despite no one believing in you. I could not do all that you have done. You may have been afraid, but you did not let that stop you. You never have."

Amalya squeezed Mira's hand, furrowing her brow as the words filled her heart. She sat with the knowledge for a moment and they settled alongside one another, waiting in the muted silence of the waning tides of Dag Light.

"What is it like," Mira's eyes glazed momentarily, as if lost to a dream, "to love a Draughtrìnd?"

"It is all-consuming." Amalya let her hand fall into the folds of her dress, following its descent with her gaze. "The weight so heavy it hurts to carry. A burden that keeps me from drifting into the unquenchable darkness. I long to covet it." Her eyes found Mira's again. "A love that will surely end my life, and I would accept it. Without regret."

A bare truth lay between them. Magic had given them the peace to bridge the gap between ignorance and understanding. To complete the circle that had been left in pieces for so long. Each for different reasons but also for the same one: unconditional purpose. For Mira loved her daughter as Amalya loved Tristan. With unbreakable love.

Amalya blinked, her body easing to what she was left to face. "I am ready to sleep now."

AMALYA STARED at the three roses adorning the table beside the bed. She was alone, but not for long. Sitting up, she peered around the room, observing the empty corners where Sól's sleeping light dared not touch. The calm pattering of rain collided against the roof and painted the window above the bed, which had been left slightly ajar.

Letting her fingers grace the top of her swollen belly, she waited quietly for the air to drain. A slight shift of the bed turned her gaze.

Tristan sat merely a hand's reach from her, looking down at the floor at his dark boots, his hair curtaining his face. Amalya's heart leapt in her chest. Even though she knew it was not him, the first glance always tricked her into believing he was truly with her. Swallowing her hope, she waited for him to speak, but he remained silent, body barely moving, almost swaying like a hanged corpse in the trees.

Amalya licked her lips, reaching for one of the roses resting on the table. Taking it in her hand, she presented it to Tristan, holding it against the draping of his coal-streaked locks. "I received your gift."

"So you have." His head came up, straightening his posture before letting his chiseled face present itself to her. "Do you enjoy torturing yourself?"

"I wish to know who you are," Amalya said bluntly. She held the rose still, keeping it in front for her to focus on. She dared not look at his face lest she forget the strength she needed to use against him.

"You know who I am."

"No. You are not Tristan."

A faint laugh escaped from his beautiful lips. He placed two fingers around the rose's stem, just above hers, bringing himself into focus. "Look at me," he growled. "Who do I appear to be?"

Amalya tightened her muscles, keeping her ocean-swept eyes fixed on the petals of white before her. "I know who you appear to be. But you are false. Hiding within his skin like a wolf."

"A wolf? Is that what you see?"

She chanced a look into his hooded eyes as they laughed at her weak attempt to thwart him. But she would not waver.

"You are weak," she uttered. "Only cowards choose to hide themselves from that which they fear. You believe I fear you, and I do. But you fear me."

Tristan bent the flower in half before lunging at her, pushing her against the wall, pinning her between his arms as his ruthless stare cut at her eyes. Despite the pressure she felt from his body, she held his gaze. It was apparent that he wished to cause her harm, to rip her apart and perhaps even feast upon her flesh. But he was powerless.

"You cannot hurt me, can you?" she asked breathlessly, a smile tugging on the corner of her lips.

His body jerked in jest, an eerie, deep-throated chortle escaping his mouth. "You are more clever than I have given you credit for."

Pulling away, he stood and moved from the bed. Amalya

waited as he slunk into the shadows, the sound of his amusement ever-growing as it echoed against the walls.

"To think he would find such a specimen. Though I do enjoy a challenge."

Amalya removed herself from the bed, standing firm with her fists at her sides. "Who are you?"

Red eyes flared, casting her into the dark crimson of her nightmares. Amalya's heart rattled violently against her chest as the figure stepped back into focus. His hair was short and dark, crowning a strong, wide jaw and prominent cheekbones beneath rich fawn-brown skin. He was taller than Tristan, with broad shoulders sculpted against the darkness of his surcoat.

He offered her a gentle bow, waving his hands as if parting a body of water. "I commend you on your ability to see through my disguise, though I did not expect to carry his image for much longer."

"*Who are you?*" Amalya shouted.

The man's smile snapped like a whip, drawing a natural hardened gaze across his face. "That is no way to speak to your guest."

"You are no guest of mine. Now tell me who you are and what you have done with Tristan."

"Tristan. A name that can only be given by the woman he loves." He took a step toward her. "If you must know my name, I will make it simple for you. I am Fane."

Amalya's body shifted. "What do you want?"

"Is it not obvious? I want you. Or, to be more specific, I want what Tristan has given you."

She shook her head. "I. . . I do not understand."

Fane tucked his hands behind his back, craning his neck to stare at the colorless ceiling above them. "I thought as much. Tell me, Amalya, you know what Tristan is, do you not?"

She nodded. "He is a Draughtrìnd."

"Yes." Fane's blazing stare returned to her as he approached. "And what do you know of the Draughtrìnd in the custom of taking a woman as the bearer of his essence?"

Her eyes skirted the floor, trying to allow her mind to think. As he came closer to her, the weight of his power collided with hers, as if she were being pelted by stones.

The Draughtrìnd, bearing essence. . .

"It was. . . a right laid down by Marin—what she had given her life for. The White Dragon. . . gifting her his essence. The answer. That Draughtrìnd and man. . . could create peace through. . . "

"*Skuldabréf*," Fane interrupted, the offered word stirring a faint memory in her mind. "The passing of one's essence to another. Marriage, as is the custom of man. Though I hardly understand it as anything similar."

Looking up, Amalya stepped back as she realized how close Fane was to her. He reached to touch her and his fingers burned against her for an instant before surrendering to a numbness that spread over her skin like a thousand fleeing spiders.

"We are not frivolous in our ways, Amalya." His hand carefully caressed her cheek. "There are laws we must abide by. Traditions to uphold, even before man was created. Your. . . *Tristan* failed to abide by those traditions, seeking to break what we have upheld since our bearers gave us guardianship of this land. Now," his fingers moved to her growing child, "he must pay for his insubordination. And you. . . must pay as well."

Amalya could no longer quell her shaking, letting it wreak havoc throughout her body. With a sly smile, Fane stepped away from her, turning back toward the shadows of the room. Digging her nails into her palms, she rushed toward him, stopping herself to keep from falling into him.

Her voice rang through the room like a sharp-sounding bell, attempting to hide her understanding of the truth. "Only a Draughtrìnd lord may bond with a woman—"

Wheeling around, Fane came face to face with her. Seething hatred bore into her eyes, drowning the air surrounding them. "He may have eaten the heart of his predecessor, but he will *never* be a true lord of the Draughtrìnd. He will *die* a traitor, and you. . . will never see him again."

Amalya's entire body stiffened. "You cannot hurt me."

"I may not be able to harm you here, but I will find you outside the realms of your dreams. And when I do, you will thank Marin that I made it swift." Fane drew away, keeping her gaze. "Once I bring news of your death, killing him will be like drowning a helpless babe. Painful, slow, but so very satisfying."

Tristan, a lord of the Draughtrìnd, was a prisoner. Locked away by this Fane, this. . . other Draughtrìnd lord, or so she had deduced from his aggressions. All because Tristan had loved her without their consent. Without blessing. A love now forbidden by both man and Draughtrìnd alike.

"You're a *monster!*" Amalya shouted through gritted teeth.

Fane shook his head, glancing over his shoulder, expelling yet another conniving smirk. Only the fire that breathed from his eyes remained as he drew into the darkness. "I am a god."

TWENTY-EIGHT

"The heart can be perilous, but despite what it may desire,
none care to look deep into the eyes of others to know this one
truth. All hearts suffer."
-Excerpt from *The Tale of Marin and the White Dragon*

There were not many patrons in the tavern. Its wood-slatted walls were not yet flickering with light from the lanterns. The tables were strewn about, surrounding the circular bar where the innkeeper welcomed guests and distributed drinks to thirsting travelers. A heavy set of stairs led up to the handful of rooms offered for rent. Just beyond that, a skald played his lute next to a stone-laid fireplace, a large stew pot left hanging above the nonexistent flames.

Amalya sat with her feet pressed together at one of the tables overlooking the street. Leaning on her hand, she stared out of the glass as the veins of the city pulsed with life. It had been nearly a week since Fane revealed his identity to her, the threat weighing heavily on her mind. There was so much left unanswered, so much to chance.

After conversing with Mira, there was little left for them to do. Amalya wanted to find Primeveire again, but Mira did not think it wise. As much as she yearned for answers, Amalya did not want Fane to find her beyond her dreams. She would abide by Primeveire's warning and choose not to press him, no matter how anxious she was.

Two pints were placed on the rounded table, Wesley sliding into the seat across from her. He passed one to her, the scent radiating sweetness in the milky froth of the flagon.

"Honey Milk, as requested," Wesley said with a smile.

"Thank you." Amalya brought the iron cup to her lips, letting the warm liquid coat her mouth and soothe the lumps left to fester in her throat.

Taking a long gulp of his ale, Wesley licked his lips as he settled his drink back onto the table. "Any more bad dreams?"

She glanced at him briefly, shaking her head. "No. Rest has been easier."

"Good."

Taking another sip, Amalya let the soothing warmth coat the remnants of lies she had continued to weave to guard her secrets. It was not because she wished to. It was safer if Wesley was not aware of what hunted her. He would only worry, or, worse, send her away in an attempt to save her from this acute madness. She did not wish to corrupt the hope he carried for them, nor did she wish to be the one to break it.

With a deep breath, Wesley smiled. "The day is approaching. Next season, we will be parents yet again."

"I cannot believe how fast time seems to travel." Amalya placed her hands on her belly, drawing her fingers across the soft fabric of her leaf-green dress. The pregnancy had been wrought with unbridled emotion and uncertainty. Amalya was grateful that it would soon be over—or, perhaps, just beginning. Now that she knew the identity of the one fixed on ending her, the threat on her child's life would only grow by day.

This *Skuldabréf*—she could not fully grasp how Fane had drawn this conclusion. She remembered reading about it once, when she was still a girl lost in her ambitions, though the details remained unclear. Tristan was not bound to her. No ceremony was held, no vows exchanged. But Fane had said it was equal only by name to marriage. The Draughtrìnd tradition itself was unfamiliar to her. Marin. . . perhaps it was the same as this. But Tristan had given her no vial to carry, no trinket that symbolized a bond.

"Don't you think it's time?"

Wesley's words disrupted her thoughts. "Time for what?"

"For you to come home." He ran his hand through his hair, something he always did when he was unsure of his words. "We have the farm 'til next Sól Sett. And I think your time here has done you well. Mira and Laird, we are lucky to have them."

"I. . . do not know."

"We cannot expect them to keep you and the children up forever. Especially with another coming. We do not want to overstep. Besides," he reached for her hand across the table, "you have done well here. I see my Amalya again, more with each passing day."

The corner of her lip twitched into a soft smile. "I will think about it."

"Do not think too long. I am eager to have the house come alive again. Bard misses you terribly as well."

"That stubborn horse," Amalya huffed. "However do you manage him without me?"

"It has not been easy, but thankfully, his love of carrots far surpasses his distaste for me."

They laughed together, Amalya squeezing his rough hand within her own.

The urge to cast away all the trouble and strife that had befallen her grew each time Wesley had come to see her. The simple life she had despised for so long now seemed like an awakened dream she was forced to squander. It was less for her sake than for the children's. But that future was more a dream now than the one she had willingly stepped into. It was not her truth any longer.

She could not forget how much her heart pined for Tristan. To breathe in his charred scent and run her fingers through his silky black hair. To feel herself in his arms and taste the fullness of his lips. She did not know how she could hope to find him, if he was not already captured. How he corrupted her, poisoning her heart with love she could not willingly share with anyone else but him.

Wesley cared for her—so much so he would die for her happiness. Why could she not let that be enough?

She looked down into her apron pocket. The pearled rose looking up at her was a constant reminder of what she had to accept as her own. An inevitable fate, a destiny long-wished forgotten.

Glancing out the window, Wesley took another long

swig of his drink. "I must be off." He stood up, emptying the contents of his flagon before placing it back on the table. "Would you like me to walk you back?"

"No, I can find my way."

"Are you sure? You know Mira will start to worry."

"She knows where I am. I'm sure she will come to find me if I take too long."

"Fine then." Leaning down, he placed a sweet, succulent kiss against her lips. Amalya tasted the fermented sting of ale on his breath, the ends of his beard tickling her under her nose. "I will see you tomorrow."

He drew away, but before he could depart, Amalya grabbed his wrist to stop him.

"Has your dream been granted, Wesley?"

Wesley turned, lowering himself to her. "My dream?"

"Before we wed, before the song of us had been written, you told me of your dream. Of having a family."

She looked into the deep wells of his eyes, a reflection of the essence of his purpose. That dream gave him more than what he believed to be possible for an orphaned boy abandoned by love. She knew it had been given to him through her and their children. But what of it now? What had become of this dream made so many Setts ago? A dream that, as long as he held it close to his heart, would be all he ever needed to endure.

"Yes," he finally said. "It has, but—"

"It is not as you expected," she breathed with guilt-ridden eyes.

Wesley's lips parted as his tongue passed between them, holding onto her hand with a renewed vigor. "I have come to find that dreams are difficult to attain. Even more so to keep.

That is the nature of dreams, or they would not dare be dreams at all."

Amalya moved to hide her face from the wisdom he had shared, but it was impossible, just as it was to force her heart to love him as she once did. For he was right about the nature of dreams. They were a difficult path, perhaps rarely trod. And only with perseverance could one truly embrace what drove the heart to reach for it.

"But it is one worth fighting for. And I will never stop fighting for it."

With a smile, he rose from her side to kiss her yet again before drawing his hand from her lap. Amalya watched as he exited the tavern and walked past the window, bringing his hand up for one last goodbye. Clasping her cup, she stared into the milky white drink, tracing the lines around her reflection with her eyes.

The skald was plucking at his final notes, the tune traveling across the tavern to momentarily fill her mind with tales of times long since past. As the lute faded into silence, Amalya looked up to watch as the dark-skinned man paused to lift a drink from a table beside him, upon which there was a plate of bread and cheese laid out for him as well.

As he moved to garner a piece, he glanced at a young girl kneeling beside him. With a smile, he pinched a generous portion of fluffy white from the loaf's middle, handing it to the girl, who took it gingerly. Dropping the hood that sat atop her head, the girl settled down on the floor to eat her prize.

Amalya, squinting her eyes to focus, found familiar curves outlining the girl's face. As the girl sensed her attention, she glanced in Amalya's direction. The lavender hue of her eyes sent Amalya's blood coursing through her veins like a rushing tide. She did not waste time, but stood up immediately, making her way across the tavern.

The girl, stuffing the remainder of the bread in her mouth, bolted behind the stairs to reach the back door. Amalya did not slow her pace, passing the skald, who eyed them both curiously as she followed close behind.

As they breached the alley behind the tavern, Amalya reached for the girl's arm. The girl barely slipped from her grasp, falling onto the damp, muddied ground beneath her. With a single step, Amalya took hold of her, pulling her to stand against the face of the tavern. The girl flailed her arms, shaking her head violently, trying to release Amalya's hold of her.

"Please be still," Amalya said calmly. "I do not wish to hurt you."

The girl finally settled, the wild strands of her dark hair wafting from her face with her every breath. Her cautious lavender eyes trailed up to meet Amalya, unable to focus for very long.

"I am going to let go of you now." Amalya steadied her grip, slowly easing from the girl's arm. "Please, do not run away."

As her hand came free, the girl tensed, her eyes darting down the alley toward freedom, but she did not move. Amalya waited patiently for a moment as the girl's tension began to ease, seeing that she was not going to harm her.

"What is your name?" Amalya asked.

The girl glanced at her, pushing the unkempt hair from her face. Her hands were sullied, dirt caked underneath her fingernails. Even her cheeks were smeared with harsh crimson. Amalya could not tell if they were bruises.

Not rendering a response, she pulled the rose from her apron pocket. "You gave me this." She held the flower out to the girl, who looked at it with brows furrowed. "Who told you to give this to me?"

Looking around, the girl opened her mouth as if attempting to speak. She rolled her teeth across her bottom lip before bringing her hands up in front of her, crossing them and locking her thumbs together, creating what looked like wings. As her thumbs touched, she pulled her hands apart, presenting her palms to Amalya as she waved her fingers downward, fluttering in unison.

Amalya shook her head timidly, squinting. "I do not understand."

"Stéinia." The girl's accent was clearly not of Rau. She performed the motion again. This time, as her hands fluttered downward, she clutched her chest, pulling her hand free before planting it adjacent to Amalya's, where her heart lay. The girl then proceeded to point toward the East Eldur Mountains. "Stéinia."

Following her hand, Amalya started to piece together a fragile understanding of the girl's message. "You're from the mountains?"

The girl shook her head, bringing her finger around to create an invisible circle in the air. "Stéinia." She pointed to the mountains again. "Stéinia." Once more, she performed the sign, locking her thumbs together and bringing her hands down to touch Amalya's chest.

Gracing her fingers over the girl's sullied hands, Amalya looked down at their connection. "Tristan," she whispered, looking back into the girl's eyes. "A Draughtrìnd of Stéinia."

The girl nodded her head vigorously. A small smile stretched across her face.

If what Fane had told Amalya was true, that Tristan was indeed one of the Draughtrìnd lords of Jöro, then he would be responsible for overseeing his own region. Though the king did not acknowledge Draughtrìnd territories, Stéinia was the Draughtrìnd land in which Rau resided, as was all the land east of the Vandermarchen River, including the East Eldur Mountains. It was Tristan who oversaw these lands, or so she was moved to understand.

A quick rush of cold ran up Amalya's spine as she held the rose up yet again to the purple-eyed girl. "Where did you get this?"

Glancing at the flower, the girl pointed down the alley, toward the riverside road. She then angled her finger downward, thrusting it toward the ground.

"Can you show me?"

With silent hesitation, the girl drew away, her lips tightening at the request.

Bringing one hand to rest atop her womb, Amalya leaned in. "Please. If Tristan is there, I must know."

Deep, forceful breaths flared the girl's nostrils as she laced her fingers through Amalya's, grasping her hand tightly. Without a word of acknowledgment, the girl pulled Amalya toward the street.

TWENTY-NINE

"When the Draughtrind fall, I will pluck out their eyes to sit in the great hall of the castle. So that even in death, they will know who bested them and who will continue to benefit in their destruction."
-King Aethelwulf letters, 1,814 Sól Sett, Third Season, Sólsun

The girl led Amalya past the docks of fishers and trade ships, toward the rocky crags that dropped into the ocean where the Vandermarchen gained its life. Amalya looked out over the open Safír Sea, the pale light of Sól dancing in slow rhythm as the water gently rolled up toward the rough, sanded shores below. It had been so long since she traveled close to the sea. It had become lost in the city's haze. Unless one was looking for it, they did not remember it was there.

As they reached the edge of the jagged rocks, the girl looked to Amalya, the salt-kissed air brushing against their faces. Amalya watched as she pointed down toward the shoreline.

"Down there?"

The girl nodded, leading her east along the rocks. Looking down, Amalya could feel her blood race in her veins. It was a steep climb, a fall that few would survive. How this girl got down there, Marin only knew. The city was becoming one with the land's horizon the farther east they walked, and the cliff angled downward as it bent to kiss the sand.

The girl glanced back at her, gesturing toward the cliff. Amalya noticed a small footpath carved out of the rock. One could dismiss it as just a natural formation, but upon closer observation, carved steps led toward the shore.

Carefully, Amalya followed, holding on tightly to the girl's hand while pressing her body against the cliff wall. The rocks were cool to the touch as small bevels and points rolled over her back in their descent. The girl seemed to have done this many times before; she was not even trying to be cautious. The occasional glance at Amalya comforted her, aware this would be difficult for her to master.

As they reached the rocky shore below, Amalya breathed a sigh. She shook the tension from her bones, feeling the child within her stir as if it too was relieved to have both feet on the ground. Amalya looked up at from where they had come. The cliff loomed over them like a deadly shadow, its sea-swept surface reflecting off the water like an enchanted mirror.

The girl continued to pull her along the shore. There was not much space to walk. The sea lapped up as they stepped, kissing at the fabric of her dress. The water was so cold it sent shivers throughout her body. Looking up, Amalya saw they were approaching an archway that reached over the small shoreline before plunging its rocky fist back into the sea. There was a stream of water pooled beneath its arm. It sat calmly as it coated the rocks and sand of the shore.

The girl placed her bare feet into the pool, looking down at the quiet water with a hopeful smile. As Amalya approached, she looked down into the water, her eyes widening as her breath caught in her throat. The water was ankle-deep, but sitting in the middle where the water was deepest was a bed of pure white roses. Their petals ebbed and flowed in the gentle ripples of their movements, becoming almost invisible.

Bending down, Amalya reached into the refreshing water. Her fingers graced one rose, gently plucking it free, letting it draw breath for the first time. She brought it to her nose, inhaling the rich aroma of the rose's salted petals.

"Stéinia."

The girl's voice drew Amalya's attention, and she looked to find her pointing toward the arm of the archway that met the water. Standing against the dark cut of rock stood a pale statue of a dragon. Its wings clung to its body as its neck arced upward before dropping in silent surrender. Its eyes were open, though colorless and defined.

Amalya and the girl walked closer toward it. With each step that carried her, Amalya could feel the magic that pulsed from it. It was like a warm breeze cutting into the cold. A fire that blazed when one's bones could barely move.

Standing in front of it, she noticed small markings and symbols etched across its entire body. One in particular mimicked the rune etched into the round trinket Tristan had given Arthur—two triangles lying one atop the other, one pointing north, the other south, encompassed in a circle. Running her fingers over the lines, she could sense a strength omitting from every crevice her skin chanced to caress. It comforted her, melting away the uncertainty of what was to come.

With a soft gesture, the girl guided Amalya's hand atop the dragon's crested horns. She patted Amalya across the knuckles, bringing her other hand to rest against her temple. "Stéinia." The girl closed her eyes.

Holding her breath, Amalya did the same, letting her thoughts travel back to Tristan's warm touch, the soothing sound of his voice, and the strength of his arms as he held her. As the images of him intensified, she felt herself being swept up into the sea.

The water swallowed her whole, dragging her to the very depths of the ocean floor. Amalya could not breathe as she reached toward the rolling waves above her. In her struggle, her eyes glimpsed a light from below. Her dress twisted as the light reached upward. Grabbing her at the ankles, it swallowed her whole in a sea of white.

A RUSH of air forced Amalya's eyes to open. She sat up with haste, clutching her chest. Looking around, her hands sank into the dry warmth of the sand. She was on a beach, but not where she had been. It was wide and unencumbered by cliffs and broken rock. The sea that lay beyond was quiet, like a painting trapped in pristine movement. There was not a single cloud in the vast blue sky, nor was Sól there to gaze down upon her. Where the brightness that illuminated this place had come from, she did not know.

"What are you doing here?"

The voice soothed her and melted any unrest in finding herself here. Turning around, Amalya breathed quietly as she let her sea-cast eyes fall upon him.

Tristan stood a few lengths away. He was dressed in a dark tunic and long trousers, the same as what he wore the last time she saw him. The garments were sullied and frayed along their edges. His face was still marked by remnants of caked blood.

But it was Tristan. Him and no one else.

Amalya took a weary step toward him, unsure if she was truly seeing him or lost in a dream. He watched her closely, the gentle rise and fall of his chest escalating with each step she took.

"Stop." He held out his hand toward her. Amalya did as she was told, clenching her teeth together as dampness surrounded her eyes. "Do not come any closer."

"It's you. It truly is you. . . "

His golden eyes shifted and strained to look upon her, as if avoiding her would somehow erase her from his sight. "It is not safe for you to be here."

"I do not care what is safe anymore."

Lifting the hem of her dress, Amalya raced toward him. Tristan held out his arms, catching her as she fell. She came to her knees, his powerful embrace bringing her close to the comforting warmth of his chest. Breathing in deeply, Amalya closed her eyes as she took in his charred aroma, letting the woodland scent ripple across the surface of her skin.

Amalya placed her hands on his chest as she looked up

into his Sól-kissed eyes. Tristan held her to him, his body shuddering at her touch as his breath caressed her face. Not wanting to heed the warnings any longer, Amalya pressed her lips against his, falling into his strength as she kissed him with uninterrupted passion. Tristan did not resist, drawing her in to risk a taste of her.

For the briefest of moments, Amalya's chest swelled full to bursting. Every inch of skin laid bare yearned to be one with him. To feel his flesh on her own. To never let herself relinquish his taste or move to break from him. His firm hand held the back of her neck, deepening the kiss as they became lost in one another.

As she moved to narrow the gap between them, Tristan pulled himself from her, looking down at her swelling womb pressed against his stomach. Amalya ran her hands down his arms as he shot her a glance laced with uncertainty.

"You are with child," he whispered breathlessly.

"Yes."

His acknowledgment of her condition festered, twisting her lungs so she could not breathe. Looking away from him, she did not know if she could face his disappointment. Guilt riddled her mind as her arms fell away from his.

A few stray tears rolled down her face to saturate her quivering lips. "You are ashamed of me." She rubbed her cheek to cast away her sadness. "I am sorry. I have betrayed you. If you wish to never see me again for what I have done—"

"No." With a gentle hand, Tristan cupped her face, drawing her gaze back to his own. "I could never be ashamed of you."

She placed her hand on his, sniffing to keep her tears at bay.

"You are the air in which I breathe. You have carried my heart since you first laid hands on my flesh. And now. . . " He placed his hand on the crest of her carrying.

A wave of unencumbered warmth consumed her, awakening the growing babe. Every kick, every movement of their form enveloped her, creating a sense of safety and love she only ever knew in Tristan's arms. Now it was part of her, being cared for within her.

"Now you carry my very essence."

His essence.

Not a vial. Not a trinket. But a child.

His child.

Uncontrollable tears poured from her eyes as she struggled to breathe. Tristan ran his thumb across her face, catching every drop of joy that escaped her eyes.

She had always known, but there was a small part of her that continued to believe it was a lie. Now there was nothing left in the dark. She was carrying Tristan's child. A child of the Draughtrìnd. The gift of peace laid down by Marin herself was not what the skald songs conceived it to be, but rather a being created from the flesh of both man and dragon. A Draudkin.

Her muscles became tense as the realization of Fane's threat fell into place. "Fane," she uttered, grasping him tightly. "If he finds me. . . He wants to punish you and—"

"Fane has—"

"Who is he? He wants our child. He wants—"

Tristan held her firmly, his golden eyes emitting strength and security, but the tightness of his jaw betrayed him. "I will come for you, but you mustn't find me again. It is too dangerous."

"Where are you? Why are you not with me?"

"You cannot stay here. If he finds you here—" Tristan drew back, his body doubling over in agony. When he came up, a trickle of blood escaped from the corner of his mouth, dripping down his chin onto her dress.

Reaching for his face, her fingers trembled. "What is happening to you?"

"You need to go. Leave this place *now!*"

He stood, staggering backward as he expelled a bloody cough, splattering crimson across the sand beneath them. Amalya could do nothing but watch as Tristan fell to one knee, clutching his chest as if keeping himself from breaking. Ominous gray clouds swarmed above them, bellowing a thunderous roar as the wind whipped her blonde hair across her face.

"The rune stone," Tristan muttered as his gaze crept to meet her trembling eyes, "keep it with you. Do not move without it."

Amalya rose to her feet, watching with wide eyes as the torrent of clouds crashed down upon him, blanketing him in a terrible storm where only his shadow remained. "Tristan!"

Before she could rush to him, a hand shot out and grabbed her arm. Looking down, the lavender-eyed girl pulled her backward, dragging her away from the growing nightmare.

With a final glance, Amalya followed the cylindrical fire that was about to consume him. The shadow of Tristan's form changed, wings bursting from his back as his body contorted into his true form. With a thunderous cry, he grew to full strength, angling his perpetual snout up to combat the onslaught, expelling flames from deep within the forge of his massive scaled belly.

A wave of impossible heat washed over them. Amalya's vision went dark and soon all sound was sucked dry like water in Sól's light. When she could finally open her eyes, she staggered backward at the force of her vision's immediacy. Her feet touched the pool at the Rau shoreline, the Safír Sea gently rolling up to kiss the sand. Looking around, she saw the girl standing next to the dragon carving, her hand gently falling away from its body.

"What happened?" Amalya asked frantically, her lungs unable to capture enough breath to calm her. Blood coursed through her veins, pounding against her temples, causing her focus to bend in the dull light reflecting from the waves. The salted air caused her lungs to heave. Sickness rolled inside her stomach, shutting her eyes. As she brought her hands to her face, she stopped, feeling a wetness that was too thick to be water. Her gaze fell open to blood, fresh and seeping into the cracks of her hands.

The girl took a few hesitant steps toward her, raising her finger to direct Amalya's attention. "Blood."

Looking down, Amalya could feel warm drips down her legs. Her dress saturated as it fell into the pool, discoloring the water a hazy red. Her hand graced below her, feeling the wet source of life draining from her.

Amalya swayed, her eyelids fluttering as she fought to stay awake. The slow drain clouded her mind, unable to grasp what was happening. As the lavender-eyed girl rushed toward her, she allowed the darkness to take hold, shutting off all awareness as the cool water of the pool splashed against her face.

THIRTY

"Love was what she offered
Resting safe around her neck.
Close to the heart
That had raged, swelled, and wept.
Would Aethelwulf find truth
In the words she had delivered?
Had she rescued his black heart
From this harsh, warring blizzard?
He took her hand,
He touched her hair,
And plunged his sword through the lady fair.
Glaring into her waning eyes,
He raised his voice at her demise.
'There are few things that draw my breath,
And those, my lady, are fear and death.'"

- The Death of Marin and the Mad King -

"That was rather foolish of you."

Amalya's eyes burst open at the sound of Fane's deep, encroaching voice. She struggled against the softness of the bed she found herself in. The walls were familiar. Somehow, she had made it back to Mira and Laird's. There was no light streaming in from the windows, the square openings coated with a dim haze that seeped into the room, causing the air to feel moist as it traveled down her throat.

Fane leaned in the shadows of the door, his red eyes piercing through the fog, left floating ambient and still.

"What have you done with Tristan?" she demanded.

His head tilted to one side, a sly smile etched across his chiseled face. "Nothing he does not deserve."

The memory of Tristan bleeding from his mouth, crippled from internal pain she could not understand, roiled in her mind. Suddenly, she remembered her own turmoil. Blood dripping down her leg, soaking her flesh.

Amalya scrambled to relinquish the blanket covering her legs. As her eyes touched upon them, she noticed they were unblemished. She still carried the child quietly stirring within her.

"You'll live, for now." Fane slowly slipped closer to her with his hands clasped behind him. "Tristan is weak. His attempts to thwart me bring him closer and closer to his ultimate surrender. And now, you have little doubt as to what truths have led me to enact the punishment you both justly deserve."

His lips curled into a conniving smirk laced with power. "But your actions have led me to you."

"What do you mean?"

He stopped, his heels coming together as the dark robes settled upon his frame. "Magic is a pulse, the very lifeblood of the land that spans over countless others. When that pulse is slowed or quickened, those with the ability to wield it can feel the change. A ripple upon the surface.

"Your recent descent into a realm unfit for man to encroach upon has created a wave powerful enough to distinguish—so powerful it was quite easy to find where you've been hiding all this time."

Amalya looked at her hands as they shook. A tightness constricted her chest as the air turned poisonous. The moisture settled on her skin, dripping heavy droplets along her elbow and off the tip of her nose. The need to discover all the answers had kept her from slipping back into the void, but it had also blinded her from heeding Primeveire's words. She had sought magic; accepted it and allowed herself to surrender to it without thinking of the consequences. Now, Fane would have her.

A shadow cast over the curtain of her tangled locks. Amalya brought her eyes upward, widening as Fane appeared before her, his face a mere breath away, eyes burning like hot iron through his sockets to scorch her thoughts.

"Who are you?" Her voice caught with each word spoken.

"I told you. I am a god. The only true god left since man decided they deserved what I possess. But they deserve nothing."

A sinister smile crept across his face as a solitary finger came to rest below her chin. "I know where you are." The corners of his lips twitched in anticipation. "I will find you. And I will rip that bastard from your womb as your heart still beats."

2,200 SÓL SETT | FOURTH SEASON

NÓTT WIND

THIRTY-ONE

"Even as he lay dead in the ground, Aethelwulf still drove the sisters of magic into the dust. Forever to be cast aside to find their way in the darkness. Alone."
-*The Tombs of Andi*, Verse 3, Section 16

L aying down on the soft feathered pillow, Amalya stared outside at the graying sky as the midwife moved her palms against her belly. They met every press with a kick or a movement from the still-growing babe.

"Very strong legs, this one." The midwife pulled her hands away, adjusting the handkerchief holding back her curled locks. "I am not seeing any signs of distress."

"Good. That's good." Mira looked at Amalya, her eyes alight with relief.

"Though it seems odd—you say you came to be with child during Dag Light?"

Coming up on her elbows, Amalya nodded. "Yes."

The midwife tightened her lips, drawing a dark ribbon

from her apron and stretching it around Amalya's midsection. Pressing her fingers against Amalya's side, the midwife pulled back, observing the girth that the ribbon conveyed. "The child is developing rapidly. With Marin's blessing, you may go early. I would say before the Eve of Sól Sett." Stuffing the ribbon back in her belt, she looked at Amalya. "May I examine further?"

With a gentle nod, Amalya laid back down, staring up at the wooden slats of the ceiling as she felt the midwife slip her fingers between her legs. Biting her lip, Amalya stiffened momentarily as the pressure from the touch moved her to discomfort. It only lasted a moment, then the midwife came away to wipe her hands on a pale cloth.

"The head has not descended. You still have time." With a sigh, she waited for Amalya to sit up before she continued speaking. "I suggest you stay in the city until you give birth. If that's possible." She looked to Mira, who nodded profusely in response.

"She may stay for as long as she needs."

"Good. I am still unsure what caused you to bleed so distressingly, but it seems to have stopped. You should rest as long as you can. Do not exert yourself too much. The physical toll could cause another incident, and if that happens, you may not be so fortunate."

Collecting her things, the midwife stood, wiping her hands on her apron. "I will come see you again soon. If anything were to happen, please send for me immediately."

Mira stood as she left. "Thank you."

Amalya watched her pass Laird, who leaned in the room's entry, a slow heaviness quietly pooling in through the doorway.

Mira clenched her fists, her chin dropping to her chest as she turned. "Amalya," she whispered with subtle authority, "this has to stop."

"Mira—"

"No!" The shrill urgency of her voice shook deep within Amalya's ears. "You almost died! Whatever this is, it is killing you."

"It does not matter."

"Are you so selfish that you do not think of your family? Elra, Arthur. . . Wesley. He loves you! Do you even care if they are harmed because of your actions?"

Amalya pressed her lips together. "*I do*." She met her friend's critical stare. "I do."

Crossing the room, Mira brought her hands to her forehead, pressing her palms against her skull as she twisted on her feet.

Laird came away from the doorframe, dropping his arms to his sides. "I understand your need for answers, Amalya. But Mira is right. If something worse were to happen," he reached Mira, taking her arm to quiet her frustrations, "we must be reasonable. As delicate as this is."

Mira's glare pierced Amalya like a threatening blade. "You do not realize how fortunate your life is, and you cast it away like it is nothing." She heaved a heavy sigh. "You have so little care for what you cause. You are not the Amalya I once knew."

Amalya sat up, pinning her hands against the bed to provide her leverage. "How could I be? After everything that's happened, how do you expect me to be that girl ever again?" She grasped the linen of her nightdress at her chest, balling the cloth in her hand. "I can no longer believe in that life. The life Wesley wants for us so strongly that he willingly refuses to listen."

Laird dropped Mira's arm. "He is trying to make things right for both of you."

"It is too late. I can't. . . "

Mira rushed to kneel before her, placing her hands in Amalya's lap, looking into her eyes with weak hope. "Wesley loves you."

"I know. And he deserves far better than I. One whose mind is not stained from the darkness that has soaked deep into her bones."

"Elra will remember everything that's happened."

"She is strong. Stubborn, but strong. Just as I was as a girl."

A small tear escaped Mira's sullen green eyes. Turning away from Amalya, she took a deep breath. "You are trying to convince yourself of this. You are trying to justify abandoning them. Do you know how terrible that sounds?"

Taking her hands, Amalya pulled Mira closer, catching her gaze yet again. "Maybe I am trying to weave my words so I do not crumble from the weight of them. But you cannot tell me you did not feel different after magic gave you life. You cannot say it did not change you."

The child moved, pressing against the walls of her protection with vigor and grace.

Any hope that lingered in Mira's eyes had faded. "It has." She watched Amalya closely. "But I will not let it cloud me from what matters most. To put those I love in danger. I would never let it pull the strings of my life."

The truth of her words stung Amalya like a dagger to the heart. She would be taken away from her children, her old life of comfort, and the rolling hills kissed by Sól's light. It would take her from Wesley, a man whose devotion and love for her was drenched in a frail trust that she could no longer believe in. It would take her from her father, her dearest friends, and the city she had grown to know and love for much of her young life.

She was living in a skald's song now, a life she once dreamed of having. One to take pride in and be admired for. But what would it do to those forced to be its victims? What was at the heart of a life that others would sing of in taverns and around roaring hearths with friends?

So much sacrifice for such a life, so much risk. It frightened her, stepping into the trap so willingly that she could not deny it as a misstep. Even though her heart had become consumed by Tristan, she could not help but feel it pine for those she would willingly sacrifice. Innocence and ignorance stripped away with a single word. For she was the cause of it all. A terrible curse on their suffering.

Mira breathed a sigh. "I do not know if I can help you anymore."

Silence lingered between them for a few strained moments. Amalya gazed down at her still-growing babe, caressing her mound as if to soothe herself. She felt herself surrender to sadness as it streamed down her pale cheeks. "I tried, with Wesley. But I am porous. I wish I was not. I wish I could."

"You always have a choice, Amalya." Mira swallowed harshly, her throat tensing.

Laird took a step toward them, his jaw tensing. "What will you do now?"

Amalya let the sadness drag her down into the looming

threat that still possessed her life. No matter which way fate guided her to step, Fane was still an obstacle. He not only threatened her life and Tristan's, but the lives of her friends and her children. He could not be left to linger in the shadows.

"I must know who Fane is. I will not sit here and wait for him to find me like a mouse in a hole. If I find the answers, perhaps I can discover a way to save. . . "

The uncertainty of her mind erupted in favor of each thought that scrambled to draw her focus. A life with Wesley and her children or a life with Tristan.

"How will you do that?" Mira asked.

Holding her breath, Amalya squinted, her heart beating uncontrollably. "I must find Primeveire."

"Then I will go with you." Mira hardened her jaw despite her tears never ceasing.

"Mira," Laird came to stand behind her, "you cannot do this."

She looked to her husband, standing up to face him. "She will do it with or without me. I cannot let her go alone."

"Then I will go with her."

"No." Mira reached to cradle his bearded face. "You are Wesley's most trusted friend. You cannot be partial to this any more than you already are."

They kissed with such tenderness; Amalya's heart ached knowing they would not be so troubled if not for her.

Laird brushed his finger behind Mira's ear. "Please be safe." He glanced at Amalya. "Both of you." He left, leaving Mira and Amalya alone in the room.

With a slow turn, Mira faced her friend again, sitting beside her on the bed. "Perhaps you are right not to run away, and perhaps I am wrong for wanting this to stop." She took Amalya's hand. "But this is all I can do for you. After it is done, I will not stand by you again in this."

Amalya squeezed Mira's hand tightly, a grateful smile caressing her face. "Thank you."

THIRTY-TWO

"In the stoking fires of Enda, the last of the great walls fell. In its wake, a cry so shrill that any who stood along the outskirts of the dying city could not be damaged by it. It was there. In the heart of this once-grand place, a Draughtrind fell. The fourth child of Dag and Nótt turned to ash in the wakes of war."

-The Tombs of Andí, Verse 1, Section 47

Rain pattered on the overhang as Amalya stared out into the waning days of Sólsun. Nótt Wind was brimming with wetness to make the days long and dreary, changing the colors of the grass and trees that speckled the countryside to prepare for their long, white sleep during Rókkur. Why Sól repeated his cycle during the coldest, darkest of seasons, Amalya did not know. Perhaps to inspire those who were forced to live through those dreary days, waiting with bated breath for Sól to crest the horizon and melt all the stale sorrow of their lives from sight.

Wesley approached, kneeling beside her with a calm yet worried sigh.

Casting a smile, Amalya touched the top of his dark red hair, which was longer each time he visited. It was slicked back, barely keeping hold after a long day toiling in the day's dreariness.

"Are you sure you do not wish me to stay with you?" he asked.

"I'll be fine. My father is taking the children for the night and will let me rest peacefully, without disruption. And Mira will be with me."

"After what happened at the shore. . . "

Amalya clasped his hands between hers. "You need to breathe just as much as I. Laird will not let you forget it if you choose to ignore his request."

"He can get sloshed just fine without me."

"But with you, it is even more enjoyable." Amalya caught his smirk and was unable to stifle a slight giggle herself. "You'll come home and lie beside me once you return. I will be fine."

Wesley reached up and touched her face, dragging his thumb across her cheek with a charming smile. "Try not to wander off."

Amalya's eyelids fluttered, if only to keep from closing. Every word he spoke of her person drove the sword of deception deeper. The moment he understood the truth, she could not imagine the hatred he would hold. It would be too great, greater even than the depths of the Safír Sea. And yet, she deceived him and accepted the anger before it passed. At moments such as this, she didn't even know who she was.

How could she covet this man's hope?

Taking his hand from her face, Amalya squeezed it gently. "Go. You mustn't keep him waiting."

Wesley swooped down and pressed a kiss to her forehead before he walked back toward the house. The smile she held for him sank gradually into her cheeks until there was nothing left of the false joy she maintained for him. To be cruel was a damaging thing, and she did not think she could continue without coming to despise herself.

Puddles of water formed and sank in the streets. Hardly anyone was walking about in the inclement weather, only the ones who desperately had somewhere to be.

Amalya tightened the hold on her dark brown dress, knowing in her heart what warnings she was about to demoralize and disgrace. A small lump sat in her pocket. She gingerly slid her fingers in to grasp it, pulling out the stone Tristan had given Arthur the day they first met. How distant that day seemed now. She rubbed her fingers over the points and curves of the triangles etched upon its surface, wondering why Tristan wished for her to keep it with her.

"Amalya."

Mira came to sit beside her and Amalya slid the stone back into the safety of her dress. Laird and Wesley exited the house, wrapping themselves in light cloaks to shield them from the rain. Mira smiled and waved as they made their way toward the market to enjoy a night of skald songs and ale at one of the local taverns.

As they disappeared into the haze of the heavy night, Amalya met Mira's gaze. She did not know what to say, if there were even words to convey what they were about to do and how much Mira's friendship had meant to her these last few seasons.

"We should not linger too long," Mira said softly, "or I may convince myself not to help you."

"Then let's go. Together." Pressing her lips together, Amalya held her breath for a moment. "Mira—"

"Don't thank me yet, my dear." Mira sat up, helping Amalya to her feet. "Thank me when it's done."

AMALYA AND MIRA's feet sank into the street as they made their way toward the docks, where Stéinia's Keep buzzed with life. Amalya stood in the wake of the flickering lights as laughter escaped through the open windows onto the wooden porch before the road.

Holding the cloak over her blonde crown, a sudden heaviness settled in her bones as the child jumped to life. Wincing as her sides tensed, Amalya took a step back to displace the pressure. A seasoned mother in her own right, she was familiar with the trials before birth. This was the first; that familiar discomfort that she could not dispel no matter what remedy they gave her. It was just a matter of time now. All she could do was wait and see what would come.

Mira appeared from the alley leading behind the tavern, ushering Amalya to follow. Neither of them knew if Primeveire would indeed be here. Witches rarely stayed in one place for very long, but Amalya could sense a pulse vibrating off the many drops of rain as they touched down on her skin. It was something unexpected, how she could feel such a change in the air.

They approached the foreboding house of her first

293

meeting with the witch. As they came to the door, Mira rapped it with her fist, hearing the forceful echo within the dark halls of the rooms beyond. They waited, letting the drops from the sky dictate the passing of time. The door finally opened to reveal the same crooked man as before. He looked at them, his mouth upturned, creasing his scruffed cheeks.

"*Lykt af rósinni,*" Mira intoned in a strong voice.

The man licked his lips, smacking them together loudly as he bared his teeth. "She's not in."

Before he could move to close the door, Mira thrust her foot between the gap. "Please. We have an urgent matter."

"Aren't they all, sweetheart?" the man scoffed, snorting as the rain tickled his nose. "She ain't hea'. I can't help ya."

Hardening her stare, Amalya reached for him, gripping him by the arm to catch the attention of his disgruntled, dark eyes. "Sir," she said abruptly, unblinking and without faltering, "please."

His unbridled expression slowly softened as they stood together in the rain. After a breathable moment, he gestured with his head. "'Round back. If you can catch 'er."

Amalya whisked herself from the stairs and around the building. She could hear Mira breathe a thank-you to the man before her soggy footsteps fell in behind her. There was a wooden gate, half-detached from its post, swaying in the night's dampness. Amalya pushed her hand against it, making her way down the small pathway until she reached the wide-open view of the mouth of the sea.

The clouds hung over the water like a dense army, waiting for the order to rain fire and destruction upon the surface. A large winch was being moved toward the edge of the cliff where the land ended, harboring a small boat in which someone was making ready to launch. It creaked as the water loosened the metal. The one moving to escape had no means of protecting themselves from the rain.

"Primeveire," Amalya called, causing the figure to whip around, her hair snapping across her narrowed face.

Primeveire stood, hesitantly aware of their purpose. "You should not have come here." She returned to packing up the boat, making haste to leave.

Mira looked from the boat to Primeveire, pulling her cloak tighter against her head. "You're leaving? But where will you go?"

"Wherever the waves deem to carry me. It has grown too dangerous here."

"We need your guidance. Please."

"There is nothing I can do for you."

"Who is Fane?"

Amalya's question froze Primeveire where she stood.

Taking a few steps closer, Amalya stopped beside the witch, keeping her composure as the tightness in her loins pressed against her ribs. "Why does he threaten me?"

With careful poise, Primeveire moved, unblinking, to face her. She straightened her posture against the wind, carrying herself with precision and strength. "You are familiar with the children of Dag and Nótt."

"Yes." Amalya swallowed. "The five children of Dag and Nótt were the first of the Draughtrìnd. They spread their wings across the many lands of Jöro to oversee and protect all life that dwelled within it."

Primeveire took a step forward. "Jöro, divided into the five regions the Draughtrìnd swore to protect. Each of them ruled for thousands upon thousands of Sól Setts. Nurturing and cultivating life and passing on their knowledge to those worthy of it.

"As time crept forward, other Draughtrìnd took their place. One by one, the children of Dag and Nótt fell, by the fires of death or by the younger generations feasting on their hearts and taking the magic that dwelled within. All but one."

Amalya felt Mira's hand clutch her arm as the truths spilled forth.

"Fane is the last surviving child of Dag and Nótt, the oldest and strongest of the four Draughtrìnd lords. None could best him. Not Draughtrìnd nor man. Fane led his kind in the onslaught of the Dragon Wars, witnessing the death of his kin, Marin and the Mad King. He was the first to bear peace with a woman, creating the Draudkin."

Primeveire's palm met Amalya's shoulder, lifting the shock festering in her lungs. "If Fane wants you, he will have you. There is no escaping his fiery gaze."

Amalya could not escape Primeveire's absolution. The heaviness that settled in her bones only grew as the hope of ever relieving herself from this nightmare was quickly extinguished. If there was no hope, then Tristan would be lost. Her unborn child, lost. She was lost.

"There must be something we can do," Mira whispered.

The witch's eyes did not waver from Amalya's fragile stance. "The essence you carry was passed to you without the consent of the council of lords. You are a stain on the Draughtrìnd. Unconsummated and impure. A stain that must be washed out."

Primeveire's jaw went rigid, nostrils flaring. "There is

nothing I can do for you. Farewell, *Adgerdaleysi*." She grabbed the edge of the swaying boat to steady it, but not before Amalya lunged forward to take hold of her. The witch's head whipped to attention, like a snake waiting to strike.

"You told me I would know what was to be done," Amalya protested. "You said it was my destiny!" The pang in her voice echoed across the open sea.

Watching her closely, the corner of Primeveire's lips twitched ever so slightly. Her narrow eyes, darting once as if to avoid her, softened the skin stretched tight across her prominent cheekbones. The rain dripped from the edges of her nose, soaking her dark hair flat against the curves of her silhouette. Primeveire lowered her brow for one final fruition. "I was wrong."

Pulling her arm from Amalya's grasp, she pushed herself over the edge of the boat, falling into its belly. The rope that hung just above her swayed in the rain as Primeveire grasped it in her hands and pulled herself out to sea.

THIRTY-THREE

"There was a boy. A lost boy. All had been stripped from him. Left lying in the darkness of decay so his life could move ever forward. But those sacrifices made him bitter. Filled him with hate. For he deemed himself undeserving of life."

-*The Tombs of Andí*, Verse 4, Section 1

T he dampness soaked into Amalya's leather boots as she hastily exited the alley. Flashes of Fane's fiery rage pierced her mind, muffled by the silent pangs of Tristan's desperate attempt to free himself from whatever sorcery had caged him. Primeveire only aided her in divulging more of the truth, but to say there was nothing she could do to stop it made the final decision for her.

"Amalya!" As she reached the alley alongside the tavern, Mira grabbed her by the shoulders and turned to face her. "What will you do?"

"I cannot stay here," Amalya said through gritted teeth to

dispel the rising strain within her. "I must go back to where I found Tristan and seek a way to stop this."

Mira's eyes grew wide, her mouth agape. "For Marin's sake, Amalya. This is madness! Get as far away from here as you can and do not look back."

"If I run, he will find me. If I hide, he will still find me. I would rather die with his poison breath in my lungs and claws through my chest than let myself, once again, be ruled by fear."

Mira stood before her in the rain, lips quivering, unable to speak or move. Amalya did not expect her to understand, not entirely. Anyone sane enough to run would do just that—run for as long and as far as they could before reaching the end.

"I am tired of being lost, always looking for a way to break free. Fumbling in the dark, waiting to be saved." Amalya felt her boots sink into the muddied road. "If that means I must give all that I have, all that I am, so that the ones I love can live without fear, then let Sól deem me worthy enough to beget such a fate."

As the rain continued to fall, she spun on her heels and continued forward. The lights from the tavern grew as the windows came into view. All the simple pleasures being had within had not ceased.

She had to rest. If only for a minute. The gravity of what she must do weighed her down like a stone being swallowed up by the mud. Before she could breach the wooden stairs leading into the establishment, though, a sharp twinge of pressure ceased her movement. Drawing down, Amalya winced as she leaned against the damp planks, her legs barely able to hold her as they shook at the knees.

Mira hurried to her side, grasping her arm to support her. "You need to rest. Let's head inside for a bit."

"No, I'll be fine out here."

"Amalya, please."

Amalya could see there was no disputing with her. With a small nod, Mira helped her onto the bottom step. "I will go inside and see if someone can draw a place for us. Just for a little while."

As Mira fled into the tavern, Amalya slowed her breathing, taking deep gulps of air. Looking up into the darkened sky, she noticed the rain had diminished to a light drizzle, moving like mist in the dull lamplight.

"Excuse me, miss. Are you all right?"

She looked up to see a woman with long red hair and dark skin. She was bundled against the rain, but her hands remained unseen under her sullen garb.

"Yes, thank you. I'm—"

Before she could finish her words, the woman bore down on her. Gritting her teeth, she lunged forward and caught Amalya by the wrist, a sharp dagger glistening mere hairs from Amalya's throat.

The woman was strong beyond any strength Amalya could hope to muster. Another onslaught of discomfort squeezed at her sides, causing her to slip backward against the stairs.

The woman was still bearing down, a smirk flashing across her face. "*Eldur eydir pér.*"

Amalya felt the moments of her life slip away with each drop of rain that fell upon the blade's edge. As it drew to touch her skin, a deep burning heated the side of her thigh.

Tightening her jaw, she pressed her head into the post behind her to create as much space between her and the blade as she could. She slipped a hand into her pocket. The heat of the stone numbed her fingers as she grasped it firmly in her palm.

The arm that blocked the bearing weight of the woman began to falter. As the blade grazed the surface of her skin, Amalya pulled the stone free and pressed it into the woman's face.

A wicked cry escaped her attacker's lips as she fell to the side, clutching her face that now glowed with unnatural light where the stone had touched.

Amalya scurried back across the stairs, falling to the ground with the stone still clutched in her hand. A small trail of blood trickled from where the knife pressed into her throat. She tried to get to her feet, but the steady tightening of her loins caused her to stumble, sinking her hands into the mud. She dragged herself forward, her belly being pulled through the muck, mud burying into the cracks of her skin.

She heard a growl from behind her and turned to look. The assailant was walking toward her with the blade, but this time it glowed with a bluish light, as if infused with some sort of spell.

Explanation blanketed the fear that had grown from the woman's attempts to slay her. This was a witch, sent by Fane to end her life.

Amalya turned onto her back, holding the stone up again with brutal force. An unseen wave pulsed from the stone, sending the girl stumbling to her knees with the blade still raised in her hand.

The stone throbbed in Amalya's grip, becoming so unbearably hot that she could no longer force her fingers to grasp it. It fell into the mud, glowing with a deep orange light as Amalya found the strength to stand, falling against the railing of the porch beside her.

With labored breath, her attacker staggered to her feet again. She glared at Amalya, teeth bared as if driven by madness. *"Eldur eydir pér,"* she snarled, closing the gap between them.

As the words leaked from her mouth, another came from behind her, slipping arms underneath the girl's armpits and pulling her back into the mud. Falling to her knees against the soaked ground, Amalya watched as the perpetrator struggled to free herself from the stranger's hold. It was then she saw a flash of her rescuer's violet orbs and light russet skin.

They struggled in the mud, but it was clear to Amalya that the purple-eyed girl was no match for this fire-haired raven. Finally gaining the upper hand, the assailant threw the girl over her shoulders, tossing her flat onto her back. With a single draw of her wielded arm, she plunged the dagger into the girl's chest, expelling a satisfying growl.

"No!" Amalya stumbled forward as she tried to reach them.

"Amalya!" Mira's voice rang into the night, catching the attention of her attacker as she pulled the dagger slowly from the purple-eyed girl's chest.

Tears overflowed from Amalya's eyes, shadowing the pressure that rose and fell as angry waves did on a stormy tide. She fumbled through the soaked mud to find the stone, her fingers finally capturing it as Mira collapsed by her side.

The sounds of shuffling feet and stifled yelling spilled from the tavern door.

"*Fyrir eld!*" Raising her now-bloodied blade, the attacker lunged forward to free Amalya from this darkened world. But just as she was about to take an irrevocable step, an angry flash of yellow light bolted from the alley, piercing the woman in the chest. Her body slid across the damp road like a stone skipping on the surface of the water.

Both Mira and Amalya held their breath, watching the red-haired woman flail uncontrollably. Bubbling seafoam escaped from her lips and billowed from her eyes before she went limp and lifeless.

Despite all the troubled voices erupting around them, Amalya did not waver from the death before them. Turning her head slightly, she saw the figure of Primeveire glide forth from the alley, wielding a long, twisted staff proudly in her hands.

The sounds of stifled breathing sounded like thunder in her ears as Amalya stumbled toward her purple-eyed rescuer. The girl's chest rose and fell with sudden desperation. Blood poured from her chest and mouth, coating the ground beneath her.

"No. . . " Amalya pressed her hands to the girl's chest to keep the red life from escaping, even though she knew it was already too late.

Mira rushed to her side, placing a calm hand on the girl's leg, looking down on her with bated breath. "She's dying," she murmured, choking on her words.

The girl coughed loudly, a jumble of words barely discernible escaping from her crimson mouth.

"You saved my life," Amalya whispered, clutching the girl's bloodied hand in her own.

Looking at her with glassy eyes, the girl squeezed Amalya's fingers tightly. "Friora." Her mouth trembled as she pounded Amalya's hand to her heaving chest. With her final breath, she sank into the ground, the brightness of her eyes fading as Sól relinquished her essence from where she lay.

"*Witch!*" a voice shouted.

"She's a witch!"

Looking up, Amalya caught Primeveire's gaze as men swarmed her. She dropped her staff without protest, gaze unwavering from where Amalya and Mira sat on the sullied ground.

"Call the guard! *A witch! A witch!*"

The crowd forced Primeveire to her knees, pulling her arms to tie them crudely behind her back. Amalya's pulse quickened, her cheeks ablaze. She wanted to scream in protest at her capture, but Primeveire's eyes shone with apparent conviction as words she did not need to speak entered Amalya's mind.

Be still. This is what must be.

Amalya could only watch as they dragged her away, pulling a sack over her head as the guard came to collect her, her fate taken into the hands of mirth-hungry men.

Every pillar of feeling Amalya harbored stretched thin, leaving her numb to all else. The only sense of her consciousness was the sound of her name echoing in the far corners of her mind and the stone still clutched in her hand, burning its mark permanently into her skin.

Through the darkness of faceless bodies and undecipherable words, she saw him. He stood in the fade that polluted the rain-filled air, his red eyes glowing in the purest form of hatred she had ever witnessed.

Fane kept her there, both of them unblinking, one in sorrowful defeat and the other in an ascension of fire fed by her attempt to thwart him.

Amalya swallowed the sand coating her mouth. She may have slipped through his fingers this time. But never again.

THIRTY-FOUR

*"Magic is the blood that pulses through the land and sea. It is
what we have been created from. What has granted us our
very nature. But it is also a stain that no amount of rain could
wash away. A curse left in the wake of Sól for us to surrender
to, forever cowering in its presence."*
-*The Tombs of Andí*, Verse 1, Section 3

Amalya sat in a wooden chair back in Mira's home,
the guard standing over her. The remaining light
reflected into her sea-cast eyes like a gnat
consumed by the promise of rotting fruit. Amalya focused on
the tips of her knees, barely visible as they crested the
horizon of her womb. The continuing pressure had subsided,
but a lingering discomfort remained with every stir.

"For clarity, again," the dark-bearded guard said, the firelight glinting off his iron armor, "what was your business in
the trade district?"

"I told you." Mira swooped in to keep Amalya from

having to relive the telling once more. "We were just out for a stroll. Amalya wanted to walk down to the bridge."

"Rather a long walk for someone in her condition. And on a rainy night such as this."

"There is no crime in wanting to walk through the city."

"To end up by Stéinia's Keep, no doubt," the guard huffed. "Not the safest area for two women to be milling about."

"We have done nothing wrong." Mira's voice raised as Laird grabbed her arm to calm her.

The guard looked from her back to Amalya, his light eyes studying her with quiet deliberation. "And you do not know the witch who tried to harm you? Nor the one who executed her?"

"I told you." Amalya held her breath as she looked up to meet his glare. "I do not know why she tried to harm me."

"Witches do inexcusable things." Wesley stepped forward beside her. "Does it matter?"

The guard glanced at him, extinguishing a breath as he adjusted the sword fixed to his belt. "Witches do not act without a reason."

"Maybe you are wrong about witches." Amalya's words caught the guard's attention. He eyed her cautiously as she tightened her jaw, digging her fingers into her palms to keep her muddled anger at bay.

The violet-eyed girl and Primeveire had saved her life. It was man who placed the mark of distaste on them, not their own actions and deeds. She was naive to it before, but now she knew how selfless they were.

The guard took another step toward her and folded his arms against the etching of the Vandermarchen River over his chest, glaring down at her with considerable poise. "What do you know of the nature of witches?"

"She knows nothing." Wesley placed a hand on her shoulder. "Can't you see she is shaken by what has happened? She needs rest."

The guard eyed him cautiously, his mouth twisting as a deep sigh echoed in the chambers of his throat. "Two dead witches and one in our possession," he mused, stepping away from them cautiously. "Do not stray from the city." The guard bowed. "Rest well."

As the door slowly closed behind him, the room fell silent save for the deep, winded breaths of Wesley as he came around to stand before them. Amalya could feel the tension rippling through the air as he ran his hand down his face and through his beard. Looking at him, she waited for the accusations riddling his gaze to dispel in force. Quietly, she straightened in the seat, watching him as he bit his lip and tightened his fists.

"You will tell me what is going on." His words were harsh and sullied with disappointment.

Mira took a step toward him. "I brought her there, Wesley. I am to blame—"

"Mira." Amalya looked at her friend, seeing the cast of worry stretching across her face. "Thank you, but there is no need. If I could speak with my husband alone. Please."

Watching her carefully, Mira nodded, letting Laird lead her toward the back of the house. Laird's eyes did not leave them until they stepped through the back door. Amalya watched them go, turning back to face Wesley alone.

"They knew, then? Both of them? This was your plan all along?"

"Wesley—"

"What were you doing there, Amalya? And do not lie to me." Wesley raised a shaking finger in accusation. "I am so tired of your lies."

"I have not lied to you. Never have I lied."

"But you kept it from me! The reason. . . whatever it was you planned to do. Putting you and Mira at risk. Our child, for Marin's sake!" Casting his gaze to the ceiling, he paced, pivoting on his heels as he ran his hands through his hair. "Has anything you've said been true? Any of it? The chance, the hope, the dreams of a better life for us. Has any of that come from your heart?"

Amalya closed her eyes, taking in the heavy air through her nose. "I never wished to hurt you."

"Hurt me?" he scoffed, letting his tense laughter escape. "Well, you've failed to protect me from your self-ishness."

"You do not understand."

"Again, you believe I am so ignorant that I cannot decipher that which drives you to such conclusions." He came to a stop in front of her again, raising his hands in desperate surrender. "Why were you there, Amalya? Tell me your secret!"

She watched him, eyes unblinking, ready for the ax to fall. Amalya gritted her teeth, unsure if she should dispel everything—all that had planted itself at her feet since that fateful knock on the door of their farm. Pushing her hair from her face, she tensed and raised her chin. "I was seeking a witch."

"A witch?" Wesley's brow furrowed. "Why were you seeking a witch?" He waited a moment before a flash of realization eased the wrinkles in his forehead. "The one who was taken?"

"Yes."

"Why?"

"I needed answers. . . " Panic twisted her stomach and pressed against her temples. The controlled rise and fall of her chest pulsed in short, gasping breaths, quickening the beating of her heart and the rush of blood through her veins. "Something is coming. Something has found me."

"What are you talking about?"

"Remember, the night I woke, screaming and stumbling to the floor? You held me and told me I was safe. But I am not safe. I am plagued each day with the threat that has set its gaze on me."

Wesley came to kneel before her, grasping her shaking hands to calm her. "Amalya, this is all in your mind."

"It is. And it has escaped. It is here now, lying in the shadows, waiting to slit my throat. He almost did, had it not been for her." The image of Friora, lying in a pool of crimson blood, left riddled footprints in her memory—her eyes, so vibrant and full of light, falling into eternal darkness, all to save Amalya. It was too much to bear.

"He?" A sigh of uncertainty escaped Wesley's lips. "Who is he?"

Her mouth fell open. "Fane. . . "

Wesley pressed his fingers into his eyes. "Amalya. . . this is—"

"Mad? I sound mad? I sound unbelievable. This could not be true, not for you. You never believed me about Tristan and you never will believe me about this."

His jaw tightened. "Tristan is *not* real."

"*He is real.*" Amalya pulled him closer to her. "You carry so much hope for a life we will never have. Hope that is more a dream than Tristan ever was. How could I tell you if you do not wish to hear me? How can I lead you to the truth if you believe it to be false?"

He searched her face for something to hold on to, but there was nothing she could give him that would make him understand. Her blood boiled to the surface, heating in her throat and her eyes. She would hold nothing back, and if he believed her, it was his doing. If he chose not to, it was also his.

"This child," she said quietly, unsure if she could breathe the words, "belongs to someone else."

Wesley let go of her hands. He stood, backing away. "You are saying this to hurt me."

"Whether you choose to believe me or not, it is for you to decide. You wanted the truth and now you have it. What you think of me because of it does not hold sway." A sudden onset of sadness streamed down her cheeks, falling into the evidence of the night's struggle. "Mira was helping me. She believes me. Laird believes me. You. . . you could never believe me."

Wesley flexed his fists at his sides as tears surfaced in his eyes. "How could I. . . " His jaw clenched as he drew in a sharp breath. "Do you even love me?"

She swallowed, willing herself to lay everything bare. "That girl grows quieter each day."

"I am done being patient." He puffed out his chest before collecting himself and his words. "That child is mine. We will return to the farm. In three days' time, I will come and collect you and the children."

As he turned toward the door, Amalya rose to her feet. "Are you even listening?"

He stopped with his back to her. "I am listening, Amalya. To every word." He looked over his shoulder. "*Three days.*"

As he stepped through the door, Amalya lowered herself to the chair with a thump.

Wesley was lying to himself, trying to convince himself she was false. She could see it in his eyes, no matter how hard and controlled he tried to appear. They shifted and wept for the truth she dispelled onto him. Her words flickered like a firefly, unrelenting in its nightly dance, leaving him in awe and unable to breathe. What would happen when he deciphered the message it carried in the light?

Her tears ceased as her hands caressed the sanctuary of her child. "My dear one," she whispered, "I ask Marin that she grant you the strength to recover from a broken heart. And the strength to know when you must be the one to break one."

How much longer would she continue to chip away at the pieces that remained? How it would shatter him. The very thought stung her heart. It was unfathomable, even though she still pined for Tristan. It begged her not to destroy another soul; to witness the cause of her love for a lord of the Draughtrìnd—and not turn into the red-eyed fiend who wished to end her life.

THIRTY-FIVE

*"It is hard to trust when a mother casts her child into the
endless green of the forest, the snowcapped mountains of the
north, or along the sands of the sea. Like you were nothing but
a speck of dirt staining their sight."*
-The Tombs of Andi, Verse 5, Section 19

A new day brought unexpected threats. As Amalya
walked with Mira to her father's home, she could
sense the silent unrest stirring between them. Not
even the lightheartedness in the streets during this bright,
cool day could shake what ailed them. Wesley would return
in two days, intending to take his family with him. As much
as she did not want to run from her fear, she realized she
feared the life that Wesley offered her just as much as she
feared Fane.

"It is good you will go home," Mira voiced. "Fane knows
you. It is only a matter of time before he sends another, or
comes himself."

"And you? You are in danger as well." Amalya clutched her friend's hand tightly. "The guard suspects something."

"I know." Mira squeezed her hand. "We. . . just need to act as though we know nothing."

"What does Laird think?"

Mira remained quiet as they approached the first line of houses before entering the trade district. "We are here." She let go of Amalya's hand and walked up to the fence encircling the yard of Horace's small home.

"Mama's back!" one of the girls shouted from within the house, coming to the door and prying it open.

"Hold off, Polli!" Horace called as he walked in from the narrow hall with Arthur in his arms.

The girls had already welcomed them with arms opened wide, Elra leaping at Amalya's legs with glee. "We baked some bread, Mama. You must try a piece!"

"I would love to." Amalya followed the girls inside.

Horace's eyes dropped slightly at the sight of Amalya as she stepped into the kitchen.

"It was so good of you to watch them for us." Mira smiled, watching Polliann and Elra clamor toward the table to grab a piece of the bread they had so dutifully aided in baking.

Polli pulled a piece of bread from the host, carrying it over proudly to her mother. "This is for you. Try it!"

Mira knelt and took the piece excitedly. "I cannot wait to taste it."

Elra soon joined them, holding her offering to Amalya, stretching up high on her tiptoes. "For you and the baby."

"Thank you—it smells delicious." Amalya bit into the soft, white belly of the bread. It simply melted in her mouth, coating her tongue with the warm comfort her father's bread always imbued. "Why, this is the most scrumptious bread I have ever had the pleasure of tasting. You girls did a marvelous job helping Grandfather make this."

"Does the baby like it too?" Elra twirled in wait.

"Of course he does." Amalya placed a hand atop her daughter's head.

With a quick smile, Elra danced away, simply overjoyed at the success of her baking abilities.

"Very well done," Mira added, swallowing her piece. She looked at Horace, who placed Arthur on the floor, where he wobbled over to catch his sister. "I was wondering if you could watch Polliann for another day."

"Why, yes. No trouble." Horace looked from her to Amalya. "Will you be leavin' them as well?"

Amalya squinted at her friend, unsure of what she was requesting.

"No," Mira clarified, "Amalya will stay with you."

"Mira—"

"Is anythin' the matter?" Horace asked, seeing how Amalya was taken aback by Mira's suggestion.

"No, there are just a few things I need to do. And Laird is so busy." Mira looked at Amalya. "I would love it if you stayed as well. Just. . . for one day." She fiddled with her braided hair cautiously. "You have much to tell your father. Please."

"I enjoy staying with Grandfather," Elra said.

"Mrs. Amalya! You can tell us stories if you stay too!" Polliann jumped up and down with lighthearted excitement, the springs of her hair bouncing at her shoulders and her light blue dress fluttering, its hem brushing against the wooden floor.

"Then it's settled. You cannot deny the girls' request." Mira forced a smile and wrapped her arms around Amalya, hugging her close as her lips fell on her ear. "Do not worry. You are safer here. Everything will be fine."

"What is it you are not telling me?" Amalya whispered.

Mira kissed her cheek and drew away, scooping Polli into her arms for an embrace. "Be good now. No misbehaving."

"I never misbehave, right, Mr. Horace?"

"She's a well-mannered young lady." He smiled as Mira placed a hand on his arm.

"Thank you. I will return tomorrow evening to fetch her."

Amalya reached for her, but Mira rushed out the door. No amount of breathing could untangle the knots forming in her throat. She didn't know what to do. Her heart told her to follow Mira and help in whatever was causing her so much unrest. But she asked her to stay, and stay she would, if only out of trust and respect for her friend. Whatever she was about to face alone, she prayed Marin was watching over her.

"All right, you lot!" Horace shouted. "Let's go in the yard."

"We can have a tea party!" Elra squealed with glee, grabbing Polli's hand and racing toward the back of the house.

Horace picked up Arthur, who meagerly tried to catch up with the girls, but his small, round legs hindered his balance. "Come on, then." Horace looked at Amalya. "I'm sure ya have much on yer mind."

Polli and Elra sat at a small wooden stool pressed against a gray stone well. Each held a wooden cup in their hands, stirring an imaginary brew and serving it to their straw-filled dolls. Amalya watched them quietly. A faint smile drew into her cheeks at their innocent play. Horace sat comfortably next to her with Arthur in his lap, the boy busily chewing on a handful of leather.

The yard was small, with patches of green against an overgrown path, barely visible, leading to the edge of an alley where more yards met. There were no trees here, just a big, open area for Sól to gaze down upon on the brightest of days and to settle his sleeping eyes at night. Amalya recalled when her father first purchased the property for himself. She insisted he could do better, but he was quite happy to settle here. A quaint little house with four rooms on the outskirts of the trade district.

"So," Horace breathed, "I heard what happened at Stéinia's Keep." Amalya turned to him. His eyes were soft with understanding. "A woman with hair of wheat 'n' with child, they said. Couldn't be anyone but my Amalya, now, could it?"

"You may not work a field, but still have your wits about you, I see," Amalya observed.

The jovialness of the mystery solved was short-lived. Her memory flashed to the murderous glint in her attacker's eyes, the failed heroics of the violet-eyed Friora, and the quiet acceptance of Primeveire as they bagged and carted her away like a murderous renegade. And then there was Fane, breathing fire with his stare and coating her with fear.

Amalya closed her eyes, feeling the swell of despair fill her lungs and threaten to burst. It all happened so quickly.

Surely her father would question her just as Wesley had. Another chance to dispel the truth only to fall on deaf ears. Her father would never understand or accept what was happening and why.

"Ya don't need ta tell me what happened."

Amalya's eyes flashed open, turning to her father with a flutter in her chest. "You do not wish to know?"

The corners of his mouth rose into his wrinkled cheeks. "It doesn't matter the reason now, does it? Yer safe, unharmed." He bounced Arthur on his lap, who giggled in response. "Besides, what good would knowin' tha truth do an ol' weathered fella like me? I can't do nothin'. I can't stop ya. Yer stubborn, like yer ma. I could never convince her out o' anythin' that was driven by 'er heart."

The heaviness in her lungs drained, bringing relief as she exhaled. Amalya had forgotten how wonderful her father was. Ever since the truth behind her mother's death was exposed, she had thought little of him or of why he had kept it from her. The reason was obvious to her now, so clear she did not know how she overlooked it from the start.

Horace did not want her mother's death to define her. A tragedy so shrouded in despair could rattle a child's essence, never to be put right again. By keeping her from it, he had allowed her to become what she was without burdens or undefinable pain. He let her experience joy and sorrow according to her, never to be led by someone other than herself.

"I understand why you kept it from me." Amalya smiled. "About Mother." She calmly placed her hand on her father's shoulder as Horace's chin trembled. "Forgive me. I have been nothing but cold to you."

Reaching up, he grasped her hand. "No. There's nothin' ya need ta be forgiven. I should be the one askin' ya."

"You're my father. Nothing you say or do will ever keep me from loving you. I will always love you, despite the faults you carry."

A single tear escaped his eye with a smile so wide Amalya did not think it would ever cease.

Elra approached them with a quizzical expression. "Why are you crying, Grandfather?"

Creasing his forehead, Horace sat up, releasing Amalya to wipe the relief from his cheeks. "Nothin', dear. Just happy is all."

"You cry when you're happy?"

"Sometimes." He saw she was carrying a cup in her hand. "That fer me?"

"No." Elra pulled it away and leaned toward Amalya. "This is for Mama and the baby." She presented the empty cup to her. "We made you something that will make the baby strong. So he won't cry so much."

"How kind of you." Amalya took the cup and brought it to her lips, tilting it to mimic taking a drink. "Mmmm. It is very sweet."

Elra's eyes brightened as she placed a careful hand on Amalya's belly. After a moment, a swift kick met her palm from within. Elra's mouth popped open in sweet surprise. "He kicked me! It's working!"

"You better make me some more, then." Amalya handed the cup back to her.

Elra skipped back to Polli, who was jumping up and down in excitement at the success of their brew. It was a welcome change to bask in the innocence of her children. So much was still new to them, filled as they were with wonder and excitement. Being with them, in the yard's safety, Amalya could allow herself to let go of the frantic nature of her life, if only for a time.

What tomorrow would bring? She did not wish to dwell on it. The only moments that carried any true meaning were the ones fussing over wooden cups and straw-stuffed dolls.

THIRTY-SIX

"Stories give us lessons to behold. Morals to obey. And a song in our hearts."
-*The Tombs of Andí*, Verse 20, Section 1

"Dag watched Nótt trail her long, dark form across the sky, awakening the sparks of Sól as they glinted on blankets of purple and blue. Her snout breathed out the slumbering smoke that put the kingdom to rest and her long, flowing tail would sweep the last dustings of day from the now-perfect night."

Elra and Polli sat together with their legs folded in their nightdresses, looking up at Amalya as she weaved the story for them. Splintering cracks from the small fire kept the cold at bay. The last remaining warmth of Sól cast the sky in red and violet hues.

A day had passed, and Mira had still not arrived as she said she would. Amalya could only quell her anxious mind with a story and a pair of wanderlusting girls to enjoy the tale.

"*What a wonder,* Dag thought," Amalya continued, "*a dream of dreams to deliver the night sky.* He admired Nótt and believed her to be the most beautiful creature he had ever seen.

"*I must give her a gift,* he thought, *to show my admiration and love for her.* So as she painted the darkness across the sky, Dag thought and thought of what he could give her. Something she would treasure as much as she treasured the night, as much as he treasured her."

"He loved her!" Polli swooned, clutching her chest and sighing deeply as her eyes fluttered.

"What happened, Mama?" Elra asked, wide-eyed with wonder.

"Be patient," Amalya hushed them, looking at the sleeping form of Arthur in his cradle by her side. She raised her hands, spreading her fingers wide and cascading them down like an arch. "*I will give her what my light can give her,* he thought. *I will grow the most precious and beautiful flowers, a meadow of colors and scents that will make her eyes sing and her nostrils dance.*

"So when Nótt went to rest and Dag's day had begun, he shined his brilliant light on the Southern Plains, more furiously than he ever had before. Blooms of red, pink, white, and gold erupted onto the carpet of green, stretching from the feet of Andí to the edges of the sea. The scents from the flowers affected all who smelled them, inciting love and compassion across the Southern Plains.

"Dag was pleased and could not wait for Nótt to gaze upon the gift he had made for her. As Nótt stirred to usher in the night, Dag approached her. 'I have made you a gift,' he said."

Both girls giggled to themselves, anticipating the disappointment Dag was about to endure.

"'A gift?' she asked.

"'Yes, to show my love and admiration for you, deliverer of the night, I have made you a meadow of blooms, with colors as brilliant and wonderful as Sól himself, sweet scents that will warm you and fill you with comfort and love.'

"Nótt looked upon the meadow but she did not smile. 'It is too dark to see such brilliant colors as you say and the scents I smell leave me tired and wanting to rest. What good is a gift that I cannot see or one that makes me wish to slumber when I must deliver the night across the sky?'

"And with that, she went on her way to awaken the night."

"Dag is simple-minded." Elra shook her head.

"Where in Marin's name did that come from?" Amalya asked, raising a brow in accusation.

Elra wearily pointed toward the table, where Horace was enjoying his nightly pipe with his feet up.

"What?" He shrugged, making the girls giggle again.

"I might have known." Amalya smiled before settling back into the story.

"Dag thought and thought until it was time to awaken Sól into the morning sky. *The flowers did not work. What gift can I give her that she can see in the night?*"

It was then that a heavy knock erupted against the door. Amalya looked up, unblinking as she stared at the door, the frantic beating in tune with her heart. Both girls rose to their feet, and Amalya took their hands and dragged them to her as she stood.

Horace moved from his chair, lowering his pipe as he came to stand behind the door. "Who's there?"

"It's Laird! Please, let us in."

Glancing at his daughter, Horace unlatched the door. As he pulled it away, Laird and Mira fell into the home, each wearing a heavy cloak to combat the cold.

"Mama!" Polliann shouted as Mira's frantic eyes fell upon her. Polli ran to her with open arms, greeted with a fell swoop as Mira clutched her to her chest.

Horace closed the door behind them, eyeing Laird's pack, which was filled to the brim. He dropped it to the floor. "We need to leave the city."

"What?" Amalya's stomach sank, not even realizing Elra had let go of her hand.

"Go grab your things, Polli. Quickly now," Mira urged breathlessly.

"But why?"

"Do as your mother says, Polliann!" Laird's words were heavy, and Polli whimpered.

"Help her, Elra." The request fell from Amalya's lips as she closed the gap between her and Mira.

Elra grabbed Polli's hand and led her to one of the back rooms in which they slept.

Grasping Amalya's hand, Mira squeezed as she tried to quiet the shakiness in her voice. "We're leaving Rau. Tonight."

"What in Marin's name happened?" Horace asked.

"We saw the guard dragging a child away from their

family. A family Primeveire gave a child just as she did for us," Laird said.

"It was dreadful." Mira closed her eyes. "He was screaming for them, the guard taking him in one direction while his parents were dragged in another." Wetness rolled down her cheek. "They burned the house. And then went to another. It will only be a matter of time before they come for us. For Polli."

Amalya opened her mouth to speak, but her throat was as parched as scorching sand. Terror rose to the surface, turning her skin to ice and setting her mind ablaze with insufferable flames.

"How ya gettin' out?" Horace caught their attention briefly as Polli and Elra returned with Polli's things.

"We need to cross the river, but the south gate is surely guarded." Laird grabbed his daughter's things, attaching them to his swollen pack.

"Then go under it. There's a way." Horace grabbed his cloak from a hook beside the door. "I'll take ya."

"No." Laird approached to block his way. "We cannot put you in danger."

"Yer not. Trust me. You'll get across wit' no notice at all."

"I don't want to go, Mama!" Polli whimpered, her chin trembling.

It was becoming harder to breathe as Amalya held onto Mira's arms, trying to steady herself to keep from collapsing. "Where will you go?"

"I don't know. I don't know what's going to happen." Mira brought her hands to Amalya's face, sadness leaking from her green eyes. "Do not break. Be strong. For them. And you."

Amalya's lips quivered as she pulled Mira into her arms, letting the fear for her dearest friend fall from her eyes. They stayed together, each unwilling to relinquish the other. Amalya could hear both Polli and Elra crying, realizing that they may never see each other again.

"Come on now," Horace grunted. "We need ta go if ya hope ta make it befer Nótt Fall."

"Mira." Laird placed a comforting hand on his wife's shoulder and the other on Amalya's back. "We need to leave."

As the two friends drew apart, Amalya's breath caught in her throat, breathing the last words she could think to speak. "I love you, Mira." She turned her teary gaze upon Laird. "Laird, I. . . I'm sorry. . . "

Laird brought Amalya tight against his chest, kissing the top of her head. "Tell Wesley I'm sorry. And if Sól is kind, we will see each other again."

Elra and Polli hugged each other in their sadness, both inconsolable as Mira pried them apart with remorseful hands. "Come now, dear."

"No!" Polli reached for Elra's outstretched hands. "Elra!" She wrapped her arms around Mira's neck, crying in the crux of her shoulder.

"Be safe, please. Let nothing happen to them." Amalya touched Laird's darkened beard, extending herself on her toes to kiss his cheek.

"I won't." Laird took Mira's hand. "Come now."

"Farewell, Amalya." Mira touched her dampened cheek.

Amalya kissed her hand, holding onto her wrist for the last few moments she would have with the most beautiful friend. She never thought she would be without her for the rest of her days. "Farewell, dear sister."

Taking their pack from the floor, Horace breathed a hearty sigh. "I'll be back. Lock tha door behind me."

Drawing the door closed, Amalya pressed against it, lifting the latch to secure them safely inside. As the aftermath of the chaos fell to silence, her legs finally gave out, bringing her to the floor in a heap of sadness. Her hands trembled as the sobs shook her entire body. This was all her doing. She was to blame.

"Mama."

Elra's quiet voice forced her from her wallowing. Seeing her daughter's reddened eyes and soaked face, Amalya clutched her to her chest, letting her sorrows stain the fabric of her light cotton dress. It took all her strength to control the shaking in her hands as she stroked her daughter's hair to calm her.

Each beat of her heart felt weaker as it knocked against its cage, pieces of it falling into the unknown depths of the forgotten darkness.

What have I done? Amalya thought as she steadily sank deeper into the chasm of unfathomable despair. *Oh blessed Marin, what have I done?*

THIRTY-SEVEN

"One must overcome all else. Pain. Hopelessness. The need
for sacrifice. They must look beyond the horizon; away from
all that distracted their mind, if only to discover the true
magic that Sól has beseeched to us."
-*The Tombs of Andí*, Verse 2, Section 5

malya could not find rest as she tried to settle in her father's house, no matter how weary her body. Clutching her daughter to her in the small bed was the only comfort she could find, knowing that she was once again alone. Mira and Laird were the only ones who knew all that she knew. Amalya had overlooked their safety so callously. The thought of them being in danger because of her actions had rarely crossed her mind and, if so, seemed so insignificant in the moment that it left her almost fleetingly.

I am cruel. I am selfish. I am guilty.

Closing her eyes, she could not unsee the fear in Mira's eyes, and yet she had still tried to be strong for Amalya, despite all that she had done to them. She had never regretted her love for Tristan more than in this moment. How could she let such a thing as love completely overrule everything she cherished? Mira, Laird, her children.

"I can smell your fear."

The sound of Fane's voice burned her ears. She could not see him as her eyes remained closed. Heaviness encased her arms and legs, her chest heaving as she strained to breathe. The air thickened as the pulse of his vengeance bubbled across her skin, leaving her unable to move or speak.

Then, Amalya opened her eyes and he stepped into view like a king in his own right, back straight, hands poised and folded against his darkly clad chest. A cape mimicking the powerful wings of the Draughtrind swept a cold wind against her face as he moved to stand in front of her. Amalya could only watch his eyes flare in the darkness, drawing his mouth into that wicked smile he carried with him.

"Your allies have been diminished." He closed his eyes, tilting his head as if to expel discomfort from his neck. "I may have failed in my first attempt to end you. But I will not fail again. Even with the stone you carry. It will not save you from what is to come."

Amalya could feel the deep-rooted satisfaction he had gained from her demise. She was weak. There was no one to hold on to but herself and she was wavering in the harsh winds of degradation.

"How does it feel," he continued, taking a step toward her stricken frame, "to be truly alone as you wait for me to pluck you into the sky?"

In the blink of an eye, he was before her, breathing his harsh breath into her sullen eyes. "You are exposed. Defeated." The lines of his lips stretched into a full-fledged grin, shining the white of his fang-like teeth. "You are mine."

It took all her strength to open her eyes and break free from her nightmare. Amalya pushed herself up with her arms as the air flowed freely into her lungs once more. The beaded sweat from her brow traced her profile before disappearing down the notch of her neck and beneath her nightdress. She looked down, frantically searching for something to steady her heart. Elra was still sleeping beside her, untouched by Fane's ill intentions.

"It would be so easy to take you as you are."

Her hair whipped across her face as she turned toward the space behind her. Fane was there, standing as he was in her dreams. Only this was not a dream. Not anymore. His back peeled from the wall as he leaned down toward her. Amalya clutched onto Elra, drawing her close as her heart slowly ascended in her throat.

Fane's blazing eyes shifted from her daughter and settled back on her. The scent of flames, so dangerous that they burned the tip of her nose, pulsed from him like a coming storm. One she could not escape.

"It would satisfy me greatly to kill you now," he breathed, dragging a gloved hand through the strands of her limp blonde hair, "but even I possess something of a heart."

Amalya could feel her bones begin to quake. She could not move from him, completely stricken by the fear that she harbored for him. Mira had said to stay strong, but without her, Amalya was nothing.

His fingers moved to her face. Amalya flinched as he cupped her cheek. Even with covered hands, her face burned from his touch. She could feel the blood beneath her skin begin to rise, stewing and threatening to melt into the leather of his gloves.

"The next time you see my face," he took her chin between his fingers, squeezing, "it will be the last thing you ever see."

Her lungs caught in a final breath as he drew away from her, becoming nothing but a shimmer of smoke in the waking light of Sól.

Amalya's eyes fluttered as she searched the corners of the room, but Fane was gone, the threat of his last words striking unavoidable fear into her heart.

He would not take her because she was with her daughter. Elra had saved her by merely existing. By only being what she was. How ever could Amalya not wish to covet her? This small, innocent child who only wished to love her mother.

Bringing her nose to Elra's long brown hair, she inhaled the dull scent of Dag's first dew upon her soft, wavy locks. This child deserved to be cherished and loved unconditionally. And while Amalya told herself she did indeed love her children, she also convinced herself how much better they would be without her presence. To willingly rip herself away from their lives seemed unfathomable. How could a mother ever think of doing such a thing?

She placed a weary hand on her shifting belly, feeling her smooth, stretched skin that kept the new life safely wrapped within her. This child was Tristan's and yet for the first time she wished it was not. Lying next to her firstborn, she begged Marin to change the fate of it all. She could not bear the thought of what had become of her Draughtrìnd lord, but she also could not bear to leave her children, now more than ever.

"Mama." Elra's soft voice trembled. "I miss Polli."

Amalya pushed strands of her daughter's hair away from her face. "I know, I miss her too."

"Will we ever see them again?" Elra's chin began to tremble, the soft brown of her eyes pooling with sadness.

Amalya forced her own grief to stay in her throat, causing her to choke on her words. She gathered Elra in her arms, kissing the top of her head as she snuggled against her chest. "We will, my dear."

"I love you, Mama."

Dampness tickled the corners of Amalya's eyes. Her teeth pierced her bottom lip as she breathed words she had not spoken to her daughter since last Sett. "I love you too, Elra. With all my heart."

It was time to stop running—to stop looking for answers that did not wish to be found. Perhaps Fane would forget her if she stopped seeking, stopped trying to find things, and left them hidden. How foolish she was to believe the most renowned and powerful lord of the Draughtrìnd would carelessly let her be—but if she would try to forget, perhaps it was enough.

Wesley would love this child as his own. And she could love him again. She could.

"Amalya." Her father's whisper traveled into the room as Dag Light crept in through the small window of the room. "Wesley's hea'."

Carefully, she stirred from the bed, reluctantly slipping from her daughter. "Go back to sleep, little one." After pulling the blanket over Elra's weary shoulders, she crept from the room, following Horace to the front of the house.

Wesley was pacing back and forth, his usual slicked-back hair all disheveled. His boots were caked in mud, the muck almost reaching to where the leather met his dark trousers. The moment he saw her approach, Wesley rushed over to her. Concern and doubt clouded his eyes. Amalya was unsure what to do, feeling the panic rise from her belly and into her throat.

"Thank Marin you're safe. I've just come from Laird's shop. It's in complete disarray. Guards searching the house like mad."

"Did they say anythin' to ya?" Horace asked him.

Wesley glanced at him. "They asked if I knew them. I only said I was a regular patron, and that Laird was working on a sword for me."

"A sword?" Horace grunted. "What'd ya needin' a sword fer?"

"It was the first thing that came to mind. They handed me one and sent me on my way. Said they wanted the blacksmith and his family for associating with witches."

Amalya could feel her sadness overflowing from her eyes. Chin trembling, she grabbed Wesley's hands and sobbed. "It's all my fault! If I just. . . I've been so selfish and I put them in danger! I should be taken, not them!" Heaviness overtook her mind, and she sank to the floor. If not for Wesley holding her, she would have surely collapsed from the weight of sorrow building up inside of her.

Wesley's arm came to her side, wrapping around her waist and pulling her up. "Look at me." His rough fingers touched her chin, briefly pulling her away from the guilt. "Look at me, Amalya."

Amalya clutched his arm like a hook, looking into his soft, earth-shaded gaze.

His muscles pulsed beneath his beard, unblinking as he waited for her to focus on just him. "This is not your fault. None of this is your fault."

"But it is—"

"No. It's not."

Amalya let the flood escape her, clutching his strong farmer's build with trembling hands.

He stroked her hair, leaning atop her head as a sigh escaped him. "Are they safe?"

"I led 'em out of the city. They crossed the river without bein' seen. As fer if they met any resistance once they entered the plains, I can't rightfully say." Horace stroked Amalya's back as he continued, "Ya should get them out of the city. They've seen 'er and the children wit' them. An' you. If a guard were to recognize ya, they'll take ya in."

"I know. We'll leave as soon as we can for the farm. I'll send another to do the market runs until things settle."

Amalya turned abruptly to her father, her eyes sunken and swollen from crying. "You'll come with us? Please."

Horace's sullen frown flattened into a momentary grin, too fragile to hold weight but enough to satisfy her. "If ya want me ta come wit' ya, I will."

She turned back to Wesley desperately. "He can come with us."

"Of course." Wesley glanced at Horace. "You're always welcome."

"Right then." Horace sighed. "Best get packin' befer the

334

children wake. Then we'll eat quickly and be on our way. Ya brought the cart?"

"Yes."

"Good then. Water's hot if ya lookin' to fix some tea for yerself." Horace disappeared down the hall to his quarters, leaving Amalya and Wesley alone as Sól awakened to the new day.

It was becoming easier to breathe and Amalya could quiet the quaking in her body. Wesley continued to stroke her hair, drawing his fingers through the tangles without meaning to free them. "Laird asked me to tell you he's sorry."

Her words seemed to move him, and he averted his gaze to the floor briefly before looking at her again. "Sorry for what?"

"I don't know. Perhaps he wished to say goodbye to you, his oldest friend." She choked on her words, swallowing them like an unchewed piece of stale bread.

"We'll see them again. One day. Perhaps in our travels. They'll be safe."

Amalya could sense the harshness in his voice, not out of malice but to mask the sadness in his eyes. Bringing her hand to rest carefully on his neck, Amalya quieted her breathing as her heart leapt from her chest. "Forgive me for being so harsh with you. I acted out of fear and misguidance, stumbling for so long."

His hand cupped her soaked cheek. "I, too, acted out of fear. You are everything to me, Amalya. Our family is all I live for. I cannot bear to lose you."

"You will not lose me." She nodded. "I must stop this selfishness. I can no longer be selfish. I will be true to you and the children. This child," she placed his hand atop her belly, "we will be happy again. We will be free. Together."

"Is that truly what you want?"

Licking her lips, Amalya searched his shifting eyes. Her heart ached, longing to tame her mind into submission to the love she was abandoning, hoping the pulsing waters would eventually cease. Perhaps she would forever be a fool, always lying and never letting what was truly laced into the fine weavings of her essence come to pass without disruption. Mira was right; she must do what was right for her children. Who she was could never become canon. Her dreams were frivolous. They should not hold sway over what was best for them.

She could forget—perhaps not now, but soon. She would make herself forget. His long coal-dusted hair, his smooth, curved muscles, his copper-cast skin and deep Sól-kissed eyes.

"Yes." The last remaining tear rolled from her cheek. "That is my wish."

THIRTY-EIGHT

"He flashed his gold-forged eyes. She would never be rid of them. They would always be lurking in the shadows, awaiting her chanced gaze. And when her sea-cast orbs fell upon them, she dared not look away again."
-The Song of the Lost Dragon Lord of Jöro

"Is this everything?" Wesley scanned the back of the caravan, visually surveying if anything of value had been left behind.

"Aye, it's everythin' I have fer them and meself." Horace lifted Elra into the back of the caravan before climbing in.

It was already midday, the busiest time, as they prepared to head into the market district. If they wanted to reach the farm quickly, heading out from the north gate was the most direct route, but also the most dangerous. Where there may be a guard or two that recognized either Wesley or Amalya as suspects in the incident at Stéinia's Keep, they would be stopped. But Wesley was confident that the city guard had more pressing matters to attend to than to keep a victim of magical unrest under their thumb.

Amalya climbed into the seat beside Wesley, Arthur sitting between them in a long shirt and trousers. He was holding some rolled leather, attempting to chew it with his gums. Placing her hand in her apron pocket, Amalya pulled out the stone Tristan had given her and placed it in her son's hand. She no longer wished to be protected. Whatever it was that would come for her was her own doing. Perhaps nothing would come—though she thought it foolish to think such things.

Amalya pulled a knitted shawl around her head, pushing her braided hair beneath it to keep her from being recognized. Placing thick folded blankets on her lap, she took a deep breath, closing her eyes.

A strange tightness pulled in her chest as Wesley whipped the ox into motion. Keeping her hand on Arthur's lap to steady him, Amalya could not help but think she was abandoning Tristan to whatever fate he was served. It pained her to dwell on the thought of his imprisonment, or worse. Fane could very well be torturing him as she rode away from the city to safety.

The longer they rocked against the bumps and divots of the street, the more difficult it was for her to breathe. Why it had been almost seamless for her to think of abandoning her family for the Draughtrìnd lord, she did not understand. Knowing she had willingly left him to his fate stole the air from her lungs.

"We're going home now?" Elra asked.

Amalya forced her eyes open to turn back to her daughter. "Yes, my dear. Back to the farm."

"I wish Polli was here." Her lips puffed and Amalya could see a single tear shining in the corner of her light brown eyes.

Horace gathered her up and plopped her on his lap. "Aye, I know ya do, love."

Elra leaned against his chest, the sadness never leaving her eyes. It made it impossible for Amalya to stay with her, turning away to distract herself with the bustling crowd dispersing like water on stone before them.

"It'll be all right." Wesley spoke softly, reaching over to grasp her arm, garnering a gentle squeeze of support.

Amalya offered him a weak smile, allowing the guilt of their friends' fate to fall down her cheek. As they made their way through the rows of merchant stalls and caravans, a worsening sight came into focus. The remains of Laird's blacksmith shop, burned and broken, lay amongst the colorful city. Men and women were picking through the rubble, grabbing any smithed metal, armor, or weapons that others had not already taken. A guard stood cautiously in front, eyeing the rabble that sifted through the ash like scavengers.

Amalya turned away, suppressing the need to weep at what Laird's life had been reduced to. She wondered where they were now; if they were safe. *Marin, please watch over them.* The thought of her friends in peril because of her actions would forever leave a scar on her heart. But it was too late to take it back, too late to beg for forgiveness.

The tightness in her arms and legs traveled to her womb, causing her to brace in unrelenting strain. Concentration squeezed her brows together, keeping herself steady as the caravan moved on through the market.

"Yer all right, Amalya?" Her father placed a hand on her back, causing her to buckle.

"Yes, I'm fine," she gasped. Placing a hand over the swell of her belly, she waited for the moment to pass. Relief soon came, enough for her to open her eyes and see that they were approaching the gate.

Four guards manned their posts, addressing travelers both entering and exiting the city. An icy chill ran down Amalya's spine as her heartbeat quickened. As they approached, Arthur stirred beside her, holding the stone up for Amalya to see. She welcomed the distraction, smiling at her son's bright, round face.

"Good day to you." Wesley tipped his head as they passed through the gate.

The guard returned a nod in greeting. Amalya glanced briefly and smiled, but as they were about to cross under the gate, another tense pull forced her hands around her growing child, forcing her to lean forward and keep her eyelids pressed shut.

"Anything the matter?" one of the guards inquired, taking a step toward them. "You look unwell."

Wesley leaned forward to shield Amalya from view as Horace's hand came to rest on her back. "Breathe through it, Amalya," he whispered.

She held her breath, forcing her body to straighten as she opened her eyes to the concerned guard. "Oh, I'm fine, thank you for your concern."

He studied her, his gaze passing from her to Wesley and then back again. He focused on her ripening belly before his eyes narrowed and returned to her face. "What's your—"

A sudden commotion sounded behind them, drawing his attention.

His fellow guard sprang from his post and passed their cart. "Oy," he shouted, "stop that this instant!"

The guard addressing them stepped back, now clearly distracted. "Come on then," he gestured, "carry on."

Wesley did not hesitate to usher their ox forward. They soon passed over the threshold into the countryside beyond the city. He looked at her, raising an eyebrow with a relieved grin. "See, nothing to worry your head about."

As soon as the sight of faded grass came into view, the line that kept her tethered to this place snapped, severing the tie that had left Amalya bereft of air. A chilled breeze caught in the wavering branches of the trees, their colorful leaves lying in a blanket beneath the bark. The dirt road stretched on, following the river seamlessly in quiet unison. The smell alone left Amalya feeling refreshed, almost reborn. Perhaps there was nothing to fear now. Fane, Tristan, and all the magic that had ensnared her would fall away, leaving her weightless and free.

Just as the thought came, another strain pierced her womb, this one more intense than the last. Leaning forward, Amalya clenched her teeth, playing a song in her mind to try to give her relief.

With careful steps across the fade,
Crimson tides will come away.
Sól to rise and then to fall,
The Lady Marin to carry all.
Let her dance through the skies left bright,
Dag to fall to Nótt's great night.

Draughtrind to take man by the hand,
And lead with love across the land.
Draughtrind to take man by the hand,
And lead with love across the land.

As the sudden discomfort waned, Amalya opened her eyes to the dirt road ahead. They were far from the city now, in the open countryside of Rau. Very few were left wandering the road so late in the day. They would not make it to the farm before Nótt Fall.

A band of travelers and their carts passed to the left of them, smiling and waving in polite greeting. There was one that walked behind, cloaked in ragged, dirty black garments. His long, dark hair kept his appearance hidden.

Amalya's gaze locked on to him, almost as if instinct had taken hold. She did not blink as he walked toward them. When he was within arm's reach of the wooden wheels that shook and stirred beneath Amalya, a flash of Sól light escaped from the darkness surrounding him. His head rose, drawing the curtain of hair from his face.

As soon as his golden orbs consumed her sea-gray eyes, her legs buckled, and all relief ceased. Wetness traveled down her legs to the wooden floor where her feet rested. Every fiber of her being twisted in unison, sending her throat ablaze as her hands braced her body for what was about to take hold of her.

"*Amalya!*"

Horace's voice was but a whisper to the waning focus of her gaze. All she could focus on were the Sól-kissed eyes still trained on her as she faded into darkness.

THIRTY-NINE

"Men will aim their arrows to the skies to pierce our flesh and all authority over those deemed inferior will fade with the blood cast from our wounds."
-The Holdeldur Prophecy

"Wake up, *Amma*. Wake up."

A sharp ray of light penetrated Amalya's eyes. It was painful at first, but once she settled her gaze, it calmed and fell like a pulsing tide. A boy knelt beside her on a green carpet of grass.

Amalya sat up, frantically scanning the endless horizon that lay before her. There was no sign of Tristan, Wesley, her father. No one was there. Just her and this boy in a meadow that stretched so vast and wide, it looked as if it drew upward into the clear, blue sky.

"You're awake." The boy's innocent voice drew her to look at him. He was young, perhaps a few Setts more than

Elra, his hair a golden-brown with shimmering streaks of white woven within the strands that brushed against his round cheeks. His eyes radiated a familiar soft shade of red. They reminded her of Fane and sent shivers through her bones. But this boy did not look at her as Fane did. His gaze was full of admiration and love.

"Who are you?" Amalya whispered in a single breath.

"I am part of you," the boy said. "Part of this." He looked down at where her unborn child would rest, but there was nothing. Just a flat stomach under her dark dress.

Amalya grasped at her abdomen, her lungs unable to capture the air as panic rose in her gut.

"Don't worry," the boy said. "The child has not come to harm. You are both safe."

Amalya looked at him, searching for an answer within the swirling wells of his gaze. "Where am I?"

"She instructed me not to see you, but I could not keep myself from telling you." The boy leaned in closer to her. "You must follow your heart. It is the only way. Do not stray from it or all will be lost."

"What?" Amalya searched his features, which seemed more familiar as each moment passed. "I do not understand."

"That is where you are wrong." The boy's face shone with exhilarating brilliance. "You have always known the truth. Even when others moved to thwart you. To strike fear in you. You have always known." He threw his arms around her, hugging her in a tight embrace that eradicated all sense of fear and uncertainty. "I love you. With all my heart. I love you, *Amma*."

Amalya trembled as she brought her arms up to cradle the boy. Resting her chin atop his golden crown, she breathed in the honeycomb scent of him as tears breached the horizons of her eyes. A deep sense of pride filled her, sending a warm wind to envelop them as they sat quietly in their embrace. He felt familiar in her arms, as if she were holding Arthur or Elra. Unconditional love filled her heart, and she never wanted to let him go, as if he would forever be erased from her memory if she dared loosen her hold.

"I love you too, my child."

After a few moments more, the boy slipped away, maintaining a smile of hope. "You must wake up now."

"No." Amalya shook her head. "I do not wish to leave you."

"I will always be with you." The boy giggled softly. "But you must wake up now." He stood, backing away from her. "Wake up, Amalya. Wake up. Please, wake up."

His voice faded, melting into their surroundings. Amalya could feel her body grow heavy. She sank down into the darkness, closing her eyes once again as the boy's last words echoed with every beat of her heart.

"Wake up, Amalya. Please, wake up."

Rising from sweat-soaked sheets, Amalya's vision returned to the familiar wooden walls of the farmhouse—her desk pressed against the wall, the small cradle where Arthur had slept as a babe, and the looming wardrobe that brought everything together.

Wesley grasped her shoulders before pulling her to him. "Thank Marin."

"What happened? What—" Pressure mounted in her loins, crushing against her with such force that Amalya tasted blood as her teeth clashed with her bottom lip. Pressing her hand to her womb, she felt the strands of her cradle tear at the seams. Her eyes clenched in tandem with her naked toes curling as she held onto the pain coursing through her body.

Wesley gently bore down on her shoulders, leaning into her ear to whisper softly, "It will pass. Breathe, Amalya. Breathe."

Grasping his arm, Amalya dug her fingernails into his bare skin, holding on for dear life. Every shaken breath barely escaped her lips as fresh perspiration beaded across her forehead and down the tip of her nose. Soon, the pressure dissipated. Amalya relinquished her hold, drawing her fingers away to reveal deep red welts where her nails had penetrated his skin.

He came to sit beside her, patting her head with a cool, damp cloth. "You're doing wonderfully, dear. The midwife should be here before Dag breaks."

Horace came into view, offering her a cup of cool liquid. "Take this down if ya can."

Amalya brought it to her lips, relishing the water's freshness as it quenched her cracked throat. Wiping her brow, she noticed the flickering candlelight dancing around the room, the sky outside blanketed in Nótt's voided tail. Despite this moment to refresh, Amalya's heart would not stop its relentless attack against her ribs. It gained strength with each passing moment, dulling her senses and tiring her eyes.

But before she could sink back into the pillow, the wave came again, striking with such strength that Amalya could not keep herself from screaming. All she could hear was the rapid drumming against her temples. Sweat mixed with tears of uncertain pain cascaded down her cheeks, falling helplessly atop that which was struggling to break free.

Horace's voice trickled in. "I do not know if she can hold out much longer."

"Grab a washbasin, clean linens. Make sure that Elra and Arthur—"

Nothing else was clear to her, their conversation lost amidst the heat slowly incinerating her mind. Clenching her sides, she sank into the bed, surrendering to the only relief left for her to take.

"Amalya," Wesley lowered himself beside her, "it will be all right."

She braced herself against the stained sheets. "Will it?"

"Try to rest."

She did not think she could, but as soon as she shut her eyes, all went black.

CONSCIOUSNESS CAME SUDDENLY. Her gaze fell upon the window, where a dull haze of fresh Sól light penetrated the waning night. Wesley sat in a chair in the room's corner, asleep.

Amalya floated up from her pillow, swinging her legs over the side of the bed. She did not know why she felt so light, like a feather drawing in a breeze. No evidence of the grueling pain lived within her. It was as if she were dreaming. Perhaps she was.

Again, her gaze came to the window. Something was calling her without words. It skipped like a pebble through the air. Beckoning her to find it. Pressing her feet into the floor, Amalya swayed ever so slightly as she took her first step forward.

She sailed across the bedroom into the main room. Horace snored loudly in a chair by the fire. His chest rose and fell with Elra peacefully aboard in a restful sleep. This room was brighter and airier, with the windows left open to catch the morning air as it blew the night away.

Arthur slept in his crib beside the chair. He was getting too big for it, his little pudgy feet hanging over the sides along with one arm that escaped the folds of his blanket. Amalya approached him, seeing the rune stone tucked protectively beside his dark brown curls. Her heart swelled as if this were the first time she had ever truly seen her son.

"Arthur," she whispered as she touched his soft cheeks, "what I believed you had taken from me, I offer it to you willingly. For you will carry it better than I. You will become greater than I could ever hope to become. My little king."

She ran her fingers through his curls with a sad, adoring smile. A great pain twisted the strands of her heart, as if this would be the last time she would ever see him. "My strong, noble boy. Know that I love you. And I always will."

With one last caress, she drew away from him. Amalya placed a hand on the front door, pressing it open without a single creak. Fresh crispness washed over her. She closed her eyes, basking in the day's newness. A whisper tickled her ears, drawing her gaze to the side of the house. She placed her hand on its wooden face, dragging her fingers along its surface as she neared the window to the bedroom.

Something lay bare in the dew-coated grass, like a babe tucked away from the cold. Amalya approached, sliding down and coming to rest on her knees beside it. As she leaned forward to part the grass, a dull pinch twisted at her sides. She pressed her lips together, not allowing anything to distract her.

The grass gave way to her fingers, revealing a shimmer of white. Amalya's breath caught in her throat. As she touched its pure surface, feeling its long, smooth stem, absent of any disruptions, she closed her eyes.

It was a rose, as pure and as white as any she had yet to possess. She was unsure if this was part of the same dream that had held her prisoner since leaving the city. But this felt different. Bringing the rose to rest under her nose, she inhaled its rich scent, letting it envelop her like a cool spring.

A shadow moved over her, shifting her heart into a frenzy. Her lips quivered as she watched its stoic form. The scent of ash and earth clouded her mind. With a slow turn, she closed her eyes in fear of who she would find standing before her. Careful fingertips ghosted over her face. Amalya lifted her gaze.

Tristan.

FORTY

*"It came as a wave broke upon the staggered cliffs. All that
had been left to burn had quickly been laid to rest with the
hiss of dying flames. He was her salvation. The water to
quench her undying thirst."*
-The Song of the Lost Dragon Lord of Jöro

Tristan stood firm in his unwavering stance as she
rose. Amalya could feel the pressure building
inside her, causing her to strain. Before she lost all
sense of herself in the grass, his arms came around her,
catching her in her fall.

She dared not look at him for fear that he would fade
once again. Curling up in his arms, she released all her
sorrow; for Mira and Laird, for Primeveire, for Friora. So
many lives disrupted because of her. Because of him. This
conjured dream that was nothing but a dream for so long
now stood with her, holding her in his arms.

"You have come too late," she cried. "It is too late. . . for so many—"

"Not for us."

His voice brought her teary stare upon him. Fingers graced her cheek, wiping away the sadness and uncertainty they had fed her for so long. Extending his hand, he pressed his thumb upon her forehead, bringing his face down to hers, looking into her eyes. "You cannot cast yourself to blame. What has passed has passed. Everything is how it was meant to be."

Amalya swallowed. "How can you believe that?"

"That is all that is left to believe." His arms settled around her. "Fane may sever my limbs or pluck the sight from my eyes. But he can never bleed me of my reason for being. You are the air in my lungs. The vigor of my beating heart. Since the day you refused to allow men's fractured vision of what I am keep you from healing more than my flesh."

Amalya closed her eyes, pressing her forehead to his.

Follow your heart.

The boy's words echoed through the chamber of her mind. Her heart had never beat so strong, never felt so free, except for when she was in Tristan's arms. This God of Old, this curse among men, the vessel in which magic was created to wreak havoc through the kingdom of Jöro and beyond. This is where her heart truly belonged. She had surrendered to it the first moment she graced his armor-scaled skin.

And it would always belong to him. Always.

"And you are mine."

Relief paired their lips together. Sensual elation ravaged her senses, down to the very tips of her toes. She would indeed abandon everything she had ever known and loved for him.

Another twist of pain bent her spine and loosened her lungs in agony. Tristan's hands fell to her womb as miraculous warmth emanated from his palm, coating her like honey.

"You must come with me." He lifted her, keeping his arms around her so she would not fall in her weakened state. "If you deliver here, Fane will find you. There is no protection for you here."

"Fane has—" Another wave of pressure squeezed at her sides, causing her knees to shake and her eyes to clamp shut.

Tristan tightened his hold, letting her nails dig into his arms. Even through the knitting of his leather tunic, Amalya could feel the natural heat of his body through the tips of her fingernails.

"We cannot linger," he said, and she finally allowed herself to look at him. His eyes shone with the radiance of Sól himself. "Will you come with me?"

A long breath gave her poise enough to respond without shaking. "I will come with you."

"Amalya?"

Both she and Tristan whipped around to see the disheveled form of Wesley standing just off the corner of their home, his eyes wide with both wonder and despair. He took a few hasty steps toward them.

Amalya could feel Tristan's hands contort into claws against her back. His skin grew dark as his teeth flashed a warning growl from his half-transformed being.

The sight of this developing creature before him stopped Wesley from advancing any further. Amalya could see his gaze darting to her, wondering how he could relinquish her from Tristan's terrible clutches.

Scales broke free. Long, pointed quills broke from Tristan's tunic, flowing up his arms and snaking around his neck as massive horns burst from his skull.

With her breath caught in her throat, Amalya cupped her hands around his scaled flesh. "Please, do not hurt him." Her words were soft and true. Looking back at Wesley, she felt a tear catch the corner of her eye as it fell for him. Pressing her lips together, she placed her hand on Tristan's now-monstrous forearm. "I must go, Wesley."

"Amalya. No—"

She wrapped her arms around Tristan's neck as he scooped her up. Wings pulled upward from his back. With one last sneering growl, he leapt into the sky. Burying her face in the crux of his shoulder, Amalya closed her eyes as fresh air swirled around her, eradicating her fallen tears in an instant.

"*Amalya!*"

Wesley's voice rose like a desperate plea. She dared not open her eyes to gain a last glance. She was sorry, so unimaginably sorry for the fragile promises and false hope she had given him. The only comforting thought that could combat the shock of strangling her innocence was the hope that he would despise her and never wish to think of her again.

WESLEY WATCHED them sail through the air, a torrent of wind whipping around him as they disappeared into the sky. He squinted his eyes as Sól peeked over the East Eldur

Mountains, lighting a path as if beckoning him to save Amalya.

With bated breath, he ran back into the house, barreling toward the fireplace where a trapdoor dwelt. Horace snorted awake, disoriented and puzzled as Wesley drew open the hatch and pulled forth the sword the guard had handed him just the day before.

"What's happened?" Horace eased Elra from his body, settling her on the chair before standing.

"She was taken."

"Taken? Who?"

"Amalya! A Draughtrind has taken her." Wesley tied the sword around his waist hastily. Returning to the door, he pulled on his dark brown boots and rushed out of the house toward the barn.

Horace soon followed, keeping up with Wesley's quickening pace like a hound on the heels of a hunt. "Call the guard. Ya can't go after 'er yerself."

"I cannot wait. I must go." Wesley threw open the barn door, heading toward Bard's stable.

The weary horse chewed his morning hay quietly, twitching his ears as he sensed the tension of the moment. Wesley grabbed the saddle and threw open the paddock. Troubling thoughts riddled his mind. Everything Amalya had said now seemed undeniably true.

This was what she had been trying to tell him all this time—that Tristan, *her* Tristan, was indeed real. That he had stolen her heart, and she had willingly given herself to the winged beast without question. Why had he refused to believe her for so long? As if denying it would make it false. But only he was false.

He shook it from his mind as he drew the bit under Bard's tongue.

No. She did not wish to go. She was only trying to protect him.

"Wesley!" Horace grunted, gripping his son-in-law's shoulder with a heavy hand. "Stop this! Ya can't do it alone."

"*I will not wait!*" Wesley's gaze whipped around to meet the man who had taken him in all those Setts ago. Who had given him a job, food, and shelter. Whose daughter captivated him the moment he saw her standing by the barn, put off by an orphan boy joining their family. Horace had done everything right, everything a man could do for another. And yet, Wesley failed him. He failed the man who filled the role of father.

"Send for the guard. Watch over the children." Wesley pushed past Horace, dragging an unwilling Bard from his stall and out of the barn.

The horse bucked and snorted, trying to pull away as Wesley readied to mount him. As the steed's massive head rose and fell, Wesley pulled him down, keeping his body firm and his eyes fixed on the horse's shifting gaze.

Wesley took a deep breath, trying to control the panic collecting in his gut. "Bard. You will help me find her. Amalya. She needs us. Please. Help me save her."

Bard shook his head, whinnying quietly as his front hooves lifted from the ground. Wesley held onto the reins, waiting for a sign that Bard understood his plight. It wasn't until the horse nudged his arm that a moment of relief punctured his lungs and loosened the binds in his shoulders.

Wesley pulled himself up onto Bard's weathered back.

Positioning his feet in the stirrups, he looked down as Horace came into view. "I won't return without her."

Horace breathed a sigh, running his hand down his face. "I'll send fer tha guard. May Marin protect you."

With the last words spoken, Wesley kicked Bard in his sides, sending the steed into a gallop. Leaning down in the saddle, he fixed his eyes on the light Sól had cast before him, never losing focus as jaded determination leaked from his eyes.

FORTY-ONE

"The smoldering life of our fire will ignite the loins of a
woman's flesh, into the form of a mother."
-The Holdeldur Prophecy

The surge of air pushed down by Tristan's wings was the only warmth Amalya felt as she listened to the rush of their escape. She kept her eyes closed, the hair on her arms shivering in the thinning air of the skies of Jöro. Her nightdress became part of her in the chaos of flight, hugging her body, unwilling to loosen its hold. But the comforting scent of Tristan's oaken skin and the strength with which he held her to him kept the fear from swarming the deep reaches of her mind.

A sudden break in speed caused her to open her eyes. Clutching his arms, she fixed her gaze upon the approaching mountain face before them. She could feel the tension in Tristan's hands begin to fade as the beast he became to deliver them slowly began to fall away, molding back into the man she had met on her doorstep a few short seasons ago.

They landed on the mountain face. Amalya could hear water dripping in the faint winds. The mountain was so vast and cold, she feared leaving the comfort of Tristan's arms. With great care, he set her down on the dampened rock beneath their feet. Leaving her side, he approached the cracked lips of the mountain, waving his hands across their surface. Wafts of flame ignited within its edge, brightening the nothingness with a dim, flickering light.

Amalya's eyes grew wide as the pointed edges of the symbol carved from the protective trinket breathed to life across the stone. It sat ablaze for only a moment before fanning outward, revealing an endless hall with smooth, curved walls and deep, rounded pillars etched along its face. Amalya had never seen such magic before and it stirred at the consequences of her actions, bringing her to tears.

Tristan took her by the hand. "You are weeping." He pulled her closer. "If you wish it, I will return you from whence you came."

"No. It is just. . . " she cast her gaze downward, "I cannot be forgiven for what I have done."

Tristan lifted her chin to look into her eyes. "No choice is immune to consequence." He placed his hand on their unborn child, his touch carrying an immediate warmth that soothed her sorrow. "You will never be alone to face that consequence."

She smiled at him, genuinely comforted by his words.

"How did you escape?"

"With patience. Fane may be relentless, but such strong determination can also leave you blind." Tristan found her hand once more to lead her down the lit passageway into the belly of the mountain. "Come."

Despite the emptiness of the hall, their footsteps did not echo off the walls. Amalya stared at the pillars as they passed. Each depicted the Draughtrìnd, fine specimens of their kind. Symbols were etched from the tips of their stone-cut teeth to the points of their tails. All had their own unique qualities. Some had horns as tall as trees, others had shorter tails or a void of razored spikes along their backs. One Draughtrìnd's wings were small, his body snaking through the waves of a choppy stone sea.

"Draughtrìnd of Stéinia," Tristan said calmly. "The most renowned are honored in this mountain fortress. Their legacies are forever cast in stone."

They reached the far side of the hall, blocked by a wall with two pillars on either side. Tristan placed his hand against its surface, scraping against the stone first to the left, then to the right. Each pass seemed to weave a pattern of some sort. Amalya stepped back as the wall shifted and fell away, almost in a mirage of light, stepping out of the bare and into the beauty.

Her eyes grew wide at the brilliance that lay before her. There were intricate patterns and images carved into the smooth, beveled walls that gleamed with a golden light. Everything shone like precious stones. Large pits of fire hung from the far-reaching ceiling. Domed arches created entrances into countless halls, each with a path of fire running along the red- and gold-polished floors. Intricately decorated walls, spanned with scenes of beautiful imagery and artistic skill, separated each section. Men, Sól, Draughtrìnd, and their creators. Some in peace, some in war, some trying to rectify the balance.

Amalya ran her hands over the beautiful work as she passed. The paintings beveled and flowed beneath her fingertips. It was almost as if they came alive from her touch. A skald tale brought to life. She had seen nothing like it and doubted she ever would again.

"Does this please you?"

She glanced at Tristan, his brow raised and the corner of his lips curved. "It's beautiful."

"It is the work of thousands of generations." He took a step toward her as her hand fell from the wall.

"What is this place?"

"It is the Fortress of Stéinia. My home. And now yours."

A few women approached them, jewelry and trinkets decorating their crowns with colorful articles of nature. Some had long hair while others kept theirs short. Their faces were each painted with a unique symbol and they all brandished heavy and intricately carved wooden staffs. There was little doubt in Amalya's mind—they were witches.

"*Þú ert kominn aftur, herra minn í steini,*" one woman stated as she bowed to them, the others following suit.

Tristan raised his hand, speaking to them too quickly for Amalya to comprehend the words. Each acknowledged whatever he had instructed them to do and a few dispersed to attend to their given duties. Two stayed, ready to lead them to wherever they were to go.

"They have prepared a room suitable for the birth of our son." Tristan extended his arm to her. "My lady."

Amalya was so lost in all that was happening, she had

barely the chance to notice the discomforts of her current state. Her focus drew back to the tightening of her loins, creating an unsteadiness that plagued her knees and feet. She took his arm as the witches led them down the intricate hallway.

"How do you know we will have a son?" she asked curiously.

"Draughtrìnd lords only father sons."

"I've dreamed of him."

Tristan glanced at her.

"I've dreamed of our son."

He smiled softly. "That is a comfort to me."

"He called me *Amma*. He told me to be strong."

"He called you. . . *Amma*?"

"Yes." Amalya blinked abruptly. "What does that—"

A wave, like burning coals thrown into a chilling stream, singed the walls of her womb, flexing and bearing down on her so forcibly, she could no longer stand. Tristan gathered her up as a sharp scream escaped from deep inside the well of her chest. Clenching her teeth, Amalya shut her eyes as the fire intensified, her lungs bereft of air.

Scooping her off the floor, Tristan carried her, his pace quickening. The witches spewed words from their mouths, but Amalya could no longer focus.

IT WAS pain like no other. It waited like a taunting predator making its prey believe it would not strike. When it did, it was all she could see, feel, and hear. Nothing else could be determined. Her body was moving but had yet to claim a destination. Her muscles were tight and weary, despite the softness she had been laid upon.

Others were there, talking and chanting in muffled tones. She could feel hands caressing her body, sliding up her legs to position her for the birth of their child. Gritting her teeth, Amalya held on to whatever she could reach for. Soft, silken fabric pooled into her sweaty palms. Screams of pain overwhelmed her, shaking the very tendrils of her essence.

Tristan's voice surfaced, causing her to open her eyes. Everything was a blur. Bodies moved so quickly, she had no chance of knowing them. Looking down, she recognized the dark locks of her love, standing between her straddled legs with his arms beneath her, ready to deliver a new life from her very being.

Amalya's head snapped back with the urge to bear everything that was left of her downward. Her screams silenced the light chanting as she pushed with all her strength. Every heave that her body commanded of her, she consented, leaning into each unrelenting strain. The air smelled like burning rosemary and lavender, piercing her lungs as the scent seeped deep within her skin.

The chanting grew louder as she continued to push, leaving little time to catch her breath. Wisps of fragrance fell upon her. She could feel her heart breaking against the bones of her chest. The taste of her sweat tickled her lips and the sights and smells both confused and comforted her as they surrounded her.

With one final push, Amalya dug her chin into her chest, allowing the last of her efforts to leak from her eyes and mouth. A smooth ease came over her, as if all the weight trying to force itself from her had ceased. Falling back against the sheets, Amalya finally caught a taste of air as she panted. There was a moment of eerie silence, not a sound to be heard.

Then, like a cricket in the night, the first sounds of life pierced the veil. Not a voice dared to carry over the desperate cries of a newborn child.

Amalya gazed up as all those surrounding her stood fixed in awe at the tiny, wriggling form in Tristan's arms. His eyes were ablaze with pride at the presence of his child.

Amalya reached for them. "Give me our child. Let me see our son."

"We do not have a son." Tristan looked at her with a fire she had never seen in his gaze before. "We have a daughter."

FORTY-TWO

"The rose that he offered was a tempting poison. A sign of a
love that would never wither, left to haunt all she had left
behind."
-The Song of the Lost Dragon Lord of Jöro

Wesley pushed onward vigorously. The old
horse had not ridden so hard and so fast in
many Sól Setts. Hearing the grunts breaking the
silence of the morning did not warrant a reason to slow
their pace.

The tops of the jagged mountains grew with each stride.
Farms had become scarce this close to its rocky feet. The
knowledge alone that this place harbored magic beyond
man's ability to harness was deterrent enough to stay away. It
was only those with purpose that dared creep so close into
the forbidden realms of witches and Draughtrìnd.

As Sól rose above the peaks, a pulse radiated from the

body of the mountains. It rolled and broke over Bard's graying hide, causing him to stifle his stride. His ears rolled as a startled whinny escaped him, backing up a few hand lengths, casting Wesley from his blind vigil on the mountain.

"Woah, boy. Easy now." He drew his hand along the horse's neck. Twitching at his touch, Bard shook his head, clearing out his nostrils before settling quietly.

A rumble escaped from the sky. Wesley glanced upward, watching as dark, hedonistic clouds rolled in from the north. They moved and billowed like an angry flood, sucking in the newness of the blue sky as if it were barely an obstacle to thwart. The anger of the storm soon overtook Sól. Shards of flashing light pulsed within the clouds, casting a dark blanket over the tops of the mountains.

Wesley narrowed his eyes as the storm grew to encompass the entire sky. A shadow moved, protected by the haze, flashing its faded silhouette as light pulsed from its depths. Clutching the reins, he waited as it flowed toward one of the many peaks and came to rest, brooding in its form. The lightning within its bowels became more frantic and, as it came to touch the very tip of the mountain's rocky head, voided smoke billowed from beneath the chaos. It smothered every inch of slick, jagged stone along the mountain face like a fire, waiting out its last moments before being smothered from existence.

Wesley's eyes pulsed wide as a face emerged. Fire-caught lungs breathed flame down upon it, the creature's head the very mass of the mountain itself, a spiraling gnarl of horns sitting atop its massive crown. Wings spread and forced away the darkness. Giant taloned feet hooked and ripped at the rock, diminishing the natural wonder as if it were barely a challenge. Its body glistened like obsidian as the menacing fires parted from its bared snout, black smoke reaching toward the storm.

A red-eyed Draughtrìnd, as mighty as the very storm that encompassed it, destroying the East Eldur Mountains. Its reason did not need to be explained. Reason did not seem to merit the actions of the Draughtrìnd.

Holding his breath, Wesley ignored the excessive shaking in his hands and the rapid torrent of his heart as he spurred Bard toward the mountain that would soon be destroyed.

Words Amalya did not understand filled the room. All were in disbelief, as if they felt unworthy of being in the presence of this small, innocent being. As Tristan reached her side, he stood erect and diligent. His words of authority carried above all others and those remaining left quietly. Soon it was just them, together in the silence.

He laid their daughter in Amalya's arms. Her eyes were as brilliant as her father's, shining with the eternal light of Sól. Amalya was in awe of her—she was the most beautiful thing she had ever seen. Not a crease or blemish tainted her smooth fawny skin. Faint sprouts of dark hair tickled her small, rounded head as she wiggled to settle within her mother's arms.

Amalya did not think she would ever possess a love like this again. The birth of Arthur had stripped it from her life, never to be found again. But it swelled now, encompassing her in an elated glow more real than anything this livable dream could muster into existence.

"She's perfect."

"She is more than that." Tristan rested a hand on the child's head. "You cannot imagine what she is."

Watching the little one nuzzle against her, Amalya determined there was only one name worthy of their child. Memories brought her back to that fateful night when a shy, purple-eyed girl gave her life to save her. It was a name she would never forget. There was a reason she gave it to her then, and that reason was now lying in her arms.

"Friora." Amalya glanced at Tristan, who settled down beside her. "She is Friora."

He looked at her with love and pride. "She is. And forever will be."

Taking his thumb, he pressed it to Friora's forehead, dragging over her crown and downward to where the neck met the spine. A heated glow trailed his touch, spreading in all directions across the child's back. As Tristan drew away, a bright red symbol remained ablaze on her skin. The angled peaks Amalya first came to know from the protective stone, encompassed inside an endless circle, pulsed with a colorless light, swimming with the humbling scent of ash and pine. When the glow dissipated, it intensified the symbol's sharp edges and towering mast.

"Friora, daughter of Stéinia."

Tristan then took her hand and slipped it behind Amalya. Helping her sit up, he pressed his thumb just behind her ear. A tingling sensation traveled from the tip of his finger down to the base of her spine. "I am now forever yours. I will never sway from you, nor will I ever seek to abandon you."

As he drew away, Amalya looked into his eyes, holding their daughter in her arms. She thought this level of bliss to be unattainable. As much as life changed around her, he was the one thing she was never uncertain of. "What is your true name?"

His gaze did not stray from her. "I am the Draughtrìnd Lord of Stéinia, *Dreki Herra Eldri Steini, Herra Brynjaður Vog*. But it matters not what name I have earned. Tristan is the name you have given me and it is who I prefer to be."

Her love for him overwhelmed her at that moment. It swelled like a rich, bubbling stew, frothing over its fiery cauldron, unable to contain the flavor it desperately sought to be tasted. "I love you, Tristan. Lord of Stéinia."

"And I you, Amalya. Mother of Stéinia. In this life and the next." His face drew close, but before their lips could collide, the door swung open and thudded against the mountain wall.

Tristan looked up, voicing his anger at the interruption. The witch was frantic, and her words seemed wrought with foreboding. Before she could finish, the ground shook beneath them and small billows of rock and dust escaped from the corners of the room.

Amalya clutched their daughter to her chest. "What is happening?"

"It is as I feared."

"What is it?"

Looking down at her, Tristan tightened his fists at his sides, his mouth contorting as his brow furrowed with determination. "Fane."

The walls shook again, emitting a roar that would have stripped her ears of sound had they not been tucked beneath the belly of the mountain. Amalya clutched Friora to her chest, a terrible fear creeping into the pit of her stomach.

Fane had come for her, for Friora.

She gritted her teeth together as her eyes narrowed, letting the fear fester if only to feed the determination in her heart.

He will never take her.

Tristan gathered them up, sliding Amalya off the table on wobbly legs. The witch rushed toward them, wrapping Amalya up in her arms as Tristan led them to one of the far walls. Lifting his hand, he pressed his palm into the stone. It came away at his touch, swinging soundlessly into an endless darkness. Small flames came to life along the walls, leading down a faded tunnel.

"Go. Through the tunnel. It will lead you deeper into the mountains." Tristan pulled the cloak from his back, taking Friora into his arms and swaddling her against Amalya's chest. "Do not look back." He glanced at the witch. *"Verndaðu hana með lífi þínu."*

"What will you do?" Amalya frantically grabbed his arm. "I do not wish to leave you."

"You must." Another quake and he cast his gaze to the ceiling above. "I will do what I have failed to do from the beginning. I will fight."

"No!" Amalya pulled at him, but Tristan held her firm.

"I must do this. You are all I wish to protect. I will not fail. I will save us. And we will be free."

He pressed his lips against hers, the bees stinging her skin until she was numb to all else. She could not bring herself to draw away, knowing that this may be the last time she would ever be with him. Through the brief and tasteful passion, Tristan finally broke, looking deeply into her eyes.

With a gentle hand, he placed a soft kiss atop Friora's head. "I will find you."

Reaching into her belt, Amalya pulled free the rose, still pristine despite the ordeal that it had endured on their journey. "Give me this when you find us again." She thrust it against his chest. "Go. Let it be finished."

Tristan turned from her sight and Amalya dropped her arm, a single tear cascading down her cheek and cresting her chin to fall onto their daughter's sleeping frame.

"Come, Mother." The witch ushered her into the tunnel, her staff held firmly in her grasp.

Closing her eyes, Amalya took a step into the shifting light as the stone door closed behind them, swallowing them up as they entered the mountain's rocky vein.

FORTY-THREE

"Let the voice guide and the sword protect, for only under the wings of the lost son will life beget life. Giving birth to all our futures. And death to all our past."
-The Holdeldur Prophecy

Wesley climbed higher and higher. Rock and stone fell away, skipping across the mountain's face. A path was forged, snaking up toward an unknown destination. Wesley could only hope it would lead him to Amalya. Wind barraged his face. No manner of cloth nor strength of his arm could stop it from stinging his eyes and whipping his hair into a frenzy. He looked down, seeing that Bard was nowhere to be found. Hopefully, the steed sought to find shelter or fled to safety.

The path was narrow and his feet could barely find holds. Pressing his body against the mountain, he steadied himself with each careful step. Sweat dripped down his face and back. His palms struggled to grasp any notch that would offer support. Wiping them against his tunic did nothing to aid him.

A great chasm split the path as he neared a landing. Deep breaths suspended the fear growing within him. As he held the last one, Wesley leapt across. His hands grasped the jagged rock, legs smashing against its fallen face. Pulling himself up, his skin broke to leak small trickles of blood against his ripped trousers. There was no time to assess the damage as a heavy thunder nearly broke his ears. Pressing his hands against the sides of his head, Wesley cowered as he waited for the ringing to stop. The sound was so tremendous; it shook his bones and rattled his teeth. Even the ground beneath him vibrated and cracked from the pressure omitted from the Draughtrind's heavy jaws.

No amount of waiting would cease the aftershock, but as rapidly as it fell upon him, it ended. A tremendous impact shook the mountain to its roots. Wesley looked up, his eyes flashing open as a sizable chunk of rubble moved toward him. Launching himself off his knees, he reached forward, barely escaping a quick demise as he tumbled from the landing. He came to a stop, sliding down into a small alcove of dancing trees along its face. Wesley's back ached and his muscles throbbed where he stood. Another roar broke out, this one a different frequency than the first. Training his gaze upward, he spotted another form soaring through the sky, heading straight for the large, dark Draughtrind storm.

It was another winged God of Old, sleeker and trimmer compared to the might of the other. Its horns tapered and the sharp daggers along its back drew a familiar shock. It was all too familiar, a sight Wesley wished to never see again if it meant remembering how much it had splintered the course of his life.

The dragon of his youth—the one he had dragged Amalya to see so many Setts ago—was charging toward the cacophony of dismal terror that was slowly destroying the mountain. It opened its jagged jaws, breathing fire toward its enemy as it wrapped around its throat, loosening the stormed Draughtrìnd from its clouded chariot, plunging them both into the mountain range.

Turning back around, Wesley ran through the small alcove of trees, sliding down a narrow passageway between the mountains. He kept his hand on the hilt of his sword as heat waves billowed above him, the two Draughtrìnd continuing to scrape and claw against each other. The air filled with black smoke, forcing its suffocating stench into his lungs. He had to stay focused. Fear could not take hold of him. He had to keep going.

He felt the rocks shift beneath his feet, causing him to stumble. The draw toward its source could not be avoided as Wesley pressed himself against the mountain once again to watch the carnage between the dragons unfold before his very eyes. The smoky air swirled into a storm of calamity. The red-eyed dragon swept its tremendous wings against the mountain peak. His treacherous talons extended, driving upward into the crux of his opponent's limbs. Amalya's dragon snapped its head back before twisting its neck like a coiled snake, pushing its horns forward.

Their weapons hooked together, breathing blackened flames into the torrential smoke surrounding them. The waves of scalding heat caused Wesley to cower, attempting to shield his skin from the burn. He covered his mouth as his throat was scraped raw from the stifling heat. As quickly as it came, it was expelled from the air by a rush of wind that kept him frozen to the mountain wall. A thunderous crack pushed Wesley to his feet, and he sprang upward as the sharp tip of the red-eyed dragon's tail scarred the face of the mountain.

He raced onward, guided by the frantic beating of his heart. The path continued to rise and fall as he kept his legs moving and his mind focused. Amalya was here, somewhere. He had to find her or die trying.

FORTY-FOUR

"How one could find forgiveness in the eyes of the ones they dare to love. She did not know why he chose to love her still. Or why she felt overwhelmed by that love as they stood together on the mountain."
-The Song of the Lost Dragon Lord of Jöro

ust rained, filling the tunnel. Amalya kept a steady hand on Friora's body, doing her best to shield the babe from the plumes that threatened to poison the little one's lungs. The witch accompanying her never offered a name, but her skin was dark, speckled with bright, starlit markings, making it easy for Amalya to find her through the dust.

"Stay close." The starlit witch led her up and down the winding tunnel. "We are almost there."

Amalya was not sure how long they had been running through this mountain vein. Many twists and turns left her mind and feet disoriented, barely able to make sense of what

375

direction they had come from. Blood inched slowly down her legs with every effort she put forward. Most women who had just given birth were not forced to flee from a crumbling mountain. Her body needed rest, but she could not stop. With no time to recover, Amalya tried to keep herself focused on their escape. Deep bellows vibrated the jagged walls, flickering the firelight that still ignited as they made their way through the mountain.

"Just beyond this bend." The witch held her arm across her face, shielding her brilliant green eyes from another terrible freeing of rubble and stone.

A breath of relief helped keep Amalya from falling over with fatigue. As they rounded the bend, a tremendous force shuddered the walls, releasing a hailstorm of sharp rocks and stone from above. The starlit witch grabbed Amalya's arm, pulling her in as she lifted her staff. A pulse echoed through the passageway as she held back the rubble, keeping it suspended in the air above them.

With teeth clenched and arms rippling with powerful tension, the witch gritted her teeth. "Run, *Móðir Stéinia!*"

Amalya watched in awe, almost too frightened to abandon her sworn protector. "I will not leave you—"

"You must. *Go. Now!*"

There was nothing she could do. As much as she did not want to abandon the witch to an uncertain fate, she could not choose to perish. Friora had to live. Turning on her heels, Amalya hastily rounded the bend. She did not look back. Even when she heard the rubble finally meet the ground, she did not look. She could not bear it.

Light, muffled and welcoming, shone in the distance. Though her muscles were aching and her feet burning with every step, Amalya pushed herself through the poison of the dying mountain. Fresh air met her face as she burst through the opening.

She immediately cast her gaze upward, eyes widening in trembling horror. Tristan was there, in all his magnificence, his wings pointed and flailing as a larger, more powerful dragon dragged him across the sky. Their bodies crashed into the impenetrable rock, crumbling away its face like a child crushing dried bread between his fingers. Tristan roared as the mountain crunched beneath him with Fane's bloodred gaze commanding his demise.

"Tristan," Amalya whispered, taking a hasty step forward. She wished she could run to his aid. But there was nothing she could do but heed his words and pray that Marin would protect him.

Looking at her surroundings, she found herself in a small alcove of trees and grass, sitting undisturbed—until now, it would seem. Amalya hadn't the faintest wondering of where she needed to go. All she knew was that Tristan sent her this way, so wherever it took her, he must know how to find her again.

Friora stirred against her chest. Amalya looked at her, pushing the cloak gingerly from her head to gaze upon her. "Don't worry, little one. I will keep you safe."

Breaking into the trees, Amalya found a small path that wound through what appeared to be a gap in the mountain. Not knowing from where she harnessed the strength, she followed it. Branches whipped her face and large stones threatened to trip her, but Amalya kept her eyes focused and her mind alert. Fatigue would not win. Not now.

The passage turned sharply to the left upon exiting

the grove. She twisted her neck to witness the monstrous bellows echoing from the fire-drenched sky. Tristan beat his wings with tremendous ferocity, deterring Fane's forceful hold. His massive body twisted beneath him, snaking his neck to strike the cushy flesh under Fane's forearm. As his pearled fangs sank into his flesh, a tornado of fire erupted from Fane's mouth, showering Tristan in a blaze of his own making. Amalya cupped her hand over her mouth, a stray tear escaping the corner of her eye. Tristan was entirely consumed in the flames, but what seemed like a fated demise soon turned into jaded hope.

Tristan launched his body forward, crashing into Fane and forcing him into the air. Fane's wingbeats snuffed the fire from his belly, revealing Tristan's sizzling scales in the faint light. Blood curled through his teeth as he again brought them to meet the armored flesh of Fane, wrapping around his neck as they disappeared into the rising smoke above the mountain.

A rush of elation urged Amalya a few small steps backward, clearing her vision of the spots of light trapped within her eyes. Fane was a tremendous force, but Tristan was leaner, quicker. He would find a way to best him. And then they would be free.

"Amalya?"

Amalya's hair whipped across her cheeks as she turned sharply toward her addresser. A cool wash of relief cascaded across Wesley's face as her eyes met his. He stepped toward her, not hesitating to wrap her in a warm embrace. Amalya barely had time to question his presence here, shielding Friora from this unexpected reunion.

"Thank Marin I've found you," Wesley said. "I did not think—"

A gurgle escaped Friora's clumsy mouth as she wiggled from the sudden pressure of Wesley's body pressed against her. He fell back immediately, looking down at the small form nestled close to Amalya's bosom.

Fear crept over her like spiders to a fly. Amalya tightened her protective hold on her daughter, afraid of what Wesley might do. He would never harm a child, Amalya knew, but that did not stop her motherly nature from taking hold.

Wesley's mouth gaped as if he were trying to speak. No words left him. His gaze remained fixed on her, searching for an answer to the question she was sure he had kept buried in the far reaches of his essence. Amalya would not keep him in the dark. There was nothing left to hide, though she knew in her heart that seeing him look upon a child that was not his would only bury her deeper.

She held her breath as her muscles tightened, her fingers drawing away the veil protecting Friora from the outside world. The shine from Friora's golden eyes squinted at the strange, bearded man she had yet to meet.

WESLEY DID NOT KNOW what he was looking at, only that it did not seem to be anything he had ever seen before. The child was bright, radiating her own light just by drawing breath. Her skin was that of a fawn's, soft and glistening as if drenched in the finest oils. Light tufts of dark hair adorned her small crown and her eyes were brilliant and unwavering, as if Sól himself were staring back at him after a restful sleep.

Looking from the child to Amalya, Wesley could feel his heart sink into the soles of his boots. Dread filled him like an angry sea, drowning him in the sudden urge to disappear for all time.

Amalya's gaze wavered. There was fear in them; fear of what he would do or from what she had done. He was uncertain. The only certain thing was the small, precious child she had carefully pressed against her. A child with both Amalya's and Draughtrìnd blood pulsing through her veins.

"Wesley." His name pierced his heart like a sword as Amalya spoke.

Wesley placed a hand on his chest, driving his palm against his heart's relentless beating. "Do not speak." He shook his head. "Do not try to make me understand why." His mind swam toward what truth lay within arm's reach. Everything he had feared, everything he had denied was there. Innocence from infidelity.

"Please," she whimpered like an injured hound, "I tried to—"

"It does not matter!" Wesley's hand fell like a chipped boulder from the mountain, crashing to his side, leaving a dent that would forever remain.

He did not want her to explain. It happened. It was done, despite how terrible it was to be near her, to feel her presence so close, knowing what lies he had told himself to keep him safe from all this.

He kept his eyes trained on the ground, holding back tears of disappointment. "I should have listened," he muttered, clasping his eyes shut. "I should have understood."

He did not need to convince himself anymore nor draw

lies from the truth. There was nothing he could have done. What could have prevented this?

His hand raised to press into his creasing forehead. "I should have never brought you there." His brow furrowed as he attempted to steady his quivering voice. "I should have shielded your eyes and left that dragon to rot in the lake."

It was he who had first infected her with the notion of the dragon. The fault was his own. Every shred of it.

"Wesley, I—"

He fisted his hand, driving it to his side once again. The other strained against the grip of his sword lying dormant on his belt. "*Son or daughter?*"

The child stirred, drawing his attention. Curiosity had brought her eyes upon him, but there was something else he did not fully understand. A hint of awareness no child in their first few breaths of life could possess.

"A daughter." The words passed through Amalya's trembling lips. "Her name is—"

Thunder struck above them. Gazing upward at the now-blackened sky, Wesley watched as the two dragons crashed against the mountains, breaking through the peaks and scattering their remains into the air.

The despair had been stricken from his bones, bringing forth the heroism that drove him from the beginning. Grabbing her wrist, Wesley pulled Amalya back through the gap in the trees, running with such ferocity so as to escape the torrential downpour of stone.

The ground began to fall away beneath them. Rock and stone broke free from the mountain's eternal rest. Amalya held Friora close to her chest. Everything shook with the pulse of fire. Wesley's hand dug into her wrist like a heavy iron chain from which she could not escape.

FORTY-FIVE

"She could not outrun the fires that rained from the sky. The flames coating her skin. Burning the air and poisoning her with each breath taken."
-The Song of the Lost Dragon Lord of Jöro

Fire beckoned, so close Amalya could feel the invisible waves break against her face. The noise of the battling beasts was deafening. How Friora could remain so calm, only Marin knew. It beat against Amalya's ears so harshly that she was convinced she would never hear again.

Finding a chance, Amalya looked at Wesley. He was determined and focused in his stride. Out of the corner of her eye, she saw the two dark forms of Fane and Tristan twist in the air like serpents navigating in the wind. If she did not know they were hoping to rid the land of the other, she would think they were dancing.

Fane's terrible jaws came down on Tristan's front leg,

twisting him with his powerful head. The momentum forced Tristan's wings to flail over Fane's entire being, crashing into the side of the mountain. But his tail constricted around Fane's neck as he forced him into the rock before the once-impenetrable landmass folded around him, blanketing him in dark rubble, hiding him from any eyes that cared to wander.

"Look out!"

Wesley's words cracked her neck forward as the mountain came down in front of them. Pulling her to the right, Wesley dragged her against a strong standing wall of stone. Pressing against it, they watched the mountain chip and crack beneath them, buckling and raising the ground to unfathomable heights. Holding her breath, Amalya and Wesley waited for a sign that it was safe to continue their escape. What that sign was, she did not know.

Her eyes wandered downward. Dark streams of blood still pooled inside her slippers, staining their pale cream color crimson. She should not have stopped. The wind had been ripped from her sails. Round circles of light danced in her vision as she struggled to keep her body erect.

Wesley took her arm again. "This way. We must climb." He pulled forward, but Amalya stumbled, barely able to catch herself. She was so tired. The strain on her body was becoming too great.

"I don't know if... I can."

"You must!" Wesley turned to face her. His gaze tracked down to the blood still trickling from between her legs. "I will help you."

"You cannot carry me."

Not waiting for permission, Wesley reached across her

back, taking hold of the sling that carried Friora. Careful to not disturb the child, he pulled her free. Amalya cradled her daughter as Wesley brought the sling across him, nestling Friora against his chest.

There was no fear in letting him take her. Though his eyes grew sullen and his beard sank as he held her, his arms were careful. Watching him look at the child drove the stake deeper through Amalya's heart.

"Wesley. . . " Her eyes closed, knowing all the heartache and pain she had brought upon him. He deserved nothing but love and devotion, a family to cherish and a wife to age with as Sól came to set upon their lives together.

He held her chin up as though to pass his strength to her. "Now is not the time for words."

Her lips spread into a faint smile, which Wesley matched through the settling dust. He loved her eternally and a small part of her loved him just as endlessly.

"We need to climb."

Wesley took her hand and they stepped around the wall together, slipping against the loose gravel toward a viable escape.

THE AIR WAS GRAY, like a dense fog. Breath drew in the land itself, reduced to dust on the dragon-fed wind. Wesley held on to Amalya's arm as he helped support her in their climb. The babe settled against his chest, unfazed by her new carrier. Wesley could feel her pulse absorb into his skin and the warmth of her little frame. It was like sitting by a fire, mere inches from the flame.

As they breached the edge, he straightened to look down upon what was once a green and open canopy of plain, now a last resting place for the disembodied mountain. A gasp came from Amalya's lips as she gazed down.

"It is broken." Her voice carried all the sadness one could harbor at seeing such grandness reduced to nothing. Her hand squeezed Wesley's arm as she looked up at him.

"Come. We must descend."

Carefully, he eased Amalya in front of him, holding her at the elbows as they leaned into the slope, carefully sliding down. Gravel loosened under their weight. They were almost on solid ground, then they would flee. Escape Rau forever. Never again dare to look back. He would be with Amalya and their children—even the one that was not his own. The thought stung momentarily, but he whiffed it free, biting on his lip as he continued to concentrate on keeping them steady.

Despite how this child came to be, she was innocent. He would not judge her for what she was, but protect her for it. Though it may pain him for a long time, Amalya would be with him. She would make it impossible to see the child as anything but his own.

"Wesley!"

Amalya's voice ripped him from his daydream. They trained their eyes on the sky, where the enormous dragon was still circling above. A terrible roar escaped the Draughtrìnd's long, spiked snout as he dove straight down. His wings pressed against his magnificent body like an arrow loosened from its quiver.

Grabbing Amalya by the waist, Wesley held her to him as she leaned into the slope. The momentum of their descent whipped dust and stone into his eyes, stinging his skin. Amalya slipped from his grasp, and he felt her fingers lace around his forearm, her head tucking into the crook of his elbow.

We'll make it. We have to make it.

A tremendous stirring of wind swirled around them. Wesley squinted as golden eyes that matched the babe's flashed across the sky, the beast plunging his jaws across the face of the other. A horrible screeching roar shook Wesley down to his very bones as the momentum from their bodies soared off the edge of a jutting vein.

They sailed through the air. Wesley kept one arm around the child as the other desperately tried to hang on to Amalya. Fire raged beneath them, rolling upward, kissing his backside as he continued to rise. Heat enveloped him, so strong he had to shield his gaze.

It was at that moment he felt Amalya slip away.

FORTY-SIX

"Upon this new age cast from the sparks of Marin, eternal rest will find us. To weave the final threads of our essence into the soils of Jöro. Where peace and prosperity will stand as one."
-The Holdeldur Prophecy

Wesley tried to sit up, his back cracking and pain shooting through his spine. He squinted, grinding his teeth together as he came to rest on the tampered ground. His arms draped over the moving form at his chest.

He looked down to find the child was unharmed. Her eyes narrowed, perturbed by the sudden disruption. Wesley squeezed her through her protective sling, checking her legs and arms. Nothing he did granted him a reaction, except that of sudden surprise from the pressure.

Fog found homage in the air. A low tremor still shook the ground every few moments. Wesley pressed his hands to the ground, forcing himself to stand. The pain from his back traveled down his legs, but it was not enough to render him useless. Taking a moment to let the dull ache subside, he cast his gaze down to where the air was less polluted. Long, drawn-out breaths refreshed his body, though still tampered with dust and rubble.

The gentle quakes became steady, almost like something was walking, its mass too large to be silent. Standing erect, Wesley tightened the sling and made his way forward. He dared not call Amalya's name for fear one of the Draughtrìnd would discover him. He would find her and then they would escape this place forever.

AMALYA'S EYES FLASHED OPEN. She was on solid ground, decorated with jagged pieces of the mountain. The rush of awareness brought her to her feet. Her hair whipped around as she tried to get her bearings. The mountain had been reduced to mere rubble. An overhang hovered above her. It was too high for her to reach, though she doubted she had the strength to pull herself up.

She took a few weary steps forward before catching herself on a boulder. Hands splayed across its surface, she glanced down at her nightdress. It was caked with dirt and blood, which still dripped from beneath. Shutting her eyes, she consumed heavy amounts of air to gain control of her failing body. Her head was spinning, her eyes unable to focus. She had to rest. But she could not.

The ground quaked under her feet, but only subtly. It played a rhythm like that of a steady drum, inching closer and closer to where she stood. The sound of cascading rubble turned her attention to the fallen mountain. The form of a Draughtrìnd forcibly breached from beneath a tomb of stone. For a moment, her heart caught in her throat, believing it to be Fane. But when he opened his Sól-kissed eyes, she settled in mild relief. Tristan's long, slender head shook itself free. His body was tainted with crimson.

He was alive.

Her eyes widened, and she clutched onto the boulder as a shadow moved toward where Tristan was still attempting to free himself. Fane, in all his terrible glory, dragged his legs as he plodded harshly along the ground. His head hung low, curving his neck, ready to strike. The red of his eyes glowed menacingly, reflecting off his blood-tinted scales and sharp-tipped horns.

He was fixated on Tristan. His intentions were clear. Tristan struggled to free himself from his rocky prison. His tail was next to surface, swinging toward Fane to defend himself from the inevitable onslaught. A tattered wing extended from the rocks, but only one. The other was still buried, along with his left front leg. Tristan wrenched and pulled as he roared at Fane's steady approach.

He would not free himself in time. Fane would kill him.

Amalya closed her eyes as she forced herself to rise from the boulder. Licking her cracked lips, she tightened her muscles, digging her dampened feet into the disrupted ground. A low rumble pulsed inside of her. Heat wafted in waves too quick to bask in their embrace.

"Amalya." A voice, almost a whisper, trickled down to her ears.

Glancing up, she saw Wesley looking down at her from

atop the overhang, his hand outstretched toward her. "Take my hand."

Deep snarls and snapping jaws drew her attention back to the scene about to unfold before them. Fane was almost on top of Tristan, who was still struggling to free himself. A plume of fire and smoke erupted from Tristan's jaws, breaking over Fane's impenetrable form.

Follow your heart. It is the only way to save us.

The boy's words echoed in her mind as she stood there, wavering and without direction. Tears pushed the dirt and debris from her face, falling against her sullied gown and meeting the blood that mixed at her feet. She did not blink as smoke stung her sea-cast eyes.

"He will never stop," she said, "as long as I remain, he will never stop."

"What. . . what are you saying?"

Looking back at Wesley, she settled on his desperate form. Sweat dripped from the tip of his nose as he waited with bated breath for her to reach for him. "Fane. He is my consequence." Her eyes traveled to the sharpened poise of the red-eyed Draughtrind lord. "I cannot run anymore. I must face my consequence."

"Amalya," Wesley reached further for her, "please. We can flee this place and never look back."

With a graceful stride, she lifted her hand to barely grasp his fingers. As he moved to get a better hold, Amalya focused on the blinking form of Friora. She watched her quietly, settled and calm. Her eyes matched those of her father, and her presence lent a reassurance that whatever was to unfold was what must be.

Biting her lip, Amalya trembled as a flood of emotion

poured from her eyes. Why she believed she could ask anything of Wesley, she did not know. But she had nothing left to lose.

You are strong. I believe in you.

"I was afraid," she uttered, "even when I professed I was not. It is I who have failed you, Wesley. Failed our children and our friends. I did not see. . . " The heat in the air singed the dampness from her face. ". . .I did not see what was right in front of me. I crumbled without trying to stand. I disregarded everything. Without compassion. Without care of what became of the song we had sung from the very moment our lips touched beneath Nótt's tail."

Wesley stopped, watching her surrender to the sadness. "I do not care what you've done. It doesn't matter. Just. . . please. Come with me. Let us put everything that has stained our lives behind us. I just. . . I need you with me."

"She is all I have left to give. Please." She squeezed his hand, waiting for him to realize what was about to happen.

Wesley's eyes searched for an answer he would never find. He shut his mouth, the edge of his beard shuddering as he managed to speak. "I will love her. As my own. I promise."

A rush of relief filled her lungs as his devotion brought a smile to her lips. "Thank you." She looked back at the approaching threat of Fane. "I do not regret our life together. Our children. Every moment. Each one." Amalya turned back to Wesley. "I love you, farm boy."

"I. . . " His hand trembled beneath her fingers.

She let go and faced her impending fate. Amalya bundled the long, dirtied train of her nightdress into her arms, holding it against her stomach. With an arm cradled underneath, Amalya sprinted forward as an unseeable force compelled her to lengthen her stride with each passing moment.

"*Amalya!*" Wesley's voice pierced her hearing, fading into the distance. "Amalya! *No!*"

The smoke broke as long tresses of blonde flowed behind her like a sail in the wind. Heat weighed down on her shoulders the closer she approached. It wasn't until she felt the fire in the air that she parted her eyelids.

"*Fane!*"

Her voice carried as harsh as a Draughtrìnd's roar. Both Fane and Tristan looked at her small, approaching form. A deep snarl escaped through Fane's dripping fangs. He turned without hesitation, lifting his head and moving toward her, the tips of his wings trained to guide him.

Follow your heart.

The faint silhouette of Tristan battling against his prison faded from her gaze as her feet came closer and closer to her demise. "*I am sorry, Tristan,*" she intoned in her mind, praying that he would hear her. "*I cannot be with you here. But I will wait for countless Setts beyond Sól's horizon for you to find me again.*"

No fear was left to riddle her bones. No shred of uncertainty or guilt disrupted her mind. She was tired of being afraid. Now she would face what had shrouded her in despair for so long. For her children; for Mira and Laird; for the violet-eyed Friora; for Primeveire. She would face it all for them. Never again would she be the cause. She would be the solution. Willingly and without protest.

You are strong.

Fane's angry snout began to smoke. All her senses

carried her forward, leaving remnants of her pain in the narrow footprints she left behind.

I believe in you.

A hurricane of fire erupted from the deep chasms of the Draughtrìnd's furnace, buried within his armored frame. As she came to meet his cleansing breath, her clothes melted from her body. The shades of her essence burst forth from her eyes, creating a dull blue storm that twisted and collided with the ashy sky. It blinded all as it whisked her away with fiery determination.

It was her truth, brought forth by dragon flame. The light was taken from her for a reason. The darkness was a mask for her to wield so she would be brave enough to face her fate.

As the blood boiled under her skin, the scent of ash and turned earth overtook her into the arms of a gentle willow tree surrounded by a deep purple haze.

I believe in you.

The flames parted to a sea of stars, flickering with the brilliance that Sól had granted them. And then there was nothing. No fire. No light.

Only peace.

FORTY-SEVEN

"Fear and death hold hands in the eyes of man. But death is
peace. Death is salvation. Death is the eternal light we all
seek."
-The Song of the Lost Dragon Lord of Jöro

"**A**malya!"

The inferno consumed her as the dark
Draughtrìnd kept the fires trained on where she
disappeared into the tongues of death. Smoke boiled and
bubbled around the dragon, coating him in a blanket of his
own making.

Wesley clutched the babe to his chest, angry tears falling
into his dusty beard. It was impossible to watch as the jaded
slivers of hope cut his heart into a thousand pieces. Nothing
but his own desperate will was keeping him from falling to
his knees. It was over, every shred of hope he carried snuffed
out by the dragon's flame.

Blood curdled and pressed against his temples, unable to

keep his gaze from the creature who had eradicated his love. Screaming, Wesley coiled his hand around the hilt of his sword. Another scream responded, this one deeper and more violent.

The fallen Draughtrìnd, biting down on his trapped forearm, ripped himself free from his captured appendage, now left to rot in the wreckage. Broken from its mountainous cage, he sprang with jaws fully extended. Dagger-like fangs broke against the larger dragon's face, cutting deep through one of his crimson eyes. A cry like no other broke the fall of fire from his mouth, as the now one-armed dragon pulled the other into the sky, driving his skull down with such force that the ground opened and wept in an onslaught of stone tears.

Wesley jumped down, his legs buckling as they clashed with the jagged stone. Wincing from the sudden pain, he dragged himself to his feet. The child stirred and wailed as he ran to avoid being crushed by the sky, with only the grace of Marin to protect them.

As he threw himself on his side, Wesley curled into a ball, allowing himself to tumble. He came to a stop at the base of a disembodied tree. With a swift turn, he rolled into the bark as a wall of rock fell around them. The hurried rush of chaos surrendered to silence in their burial.

<hr>

THE EERIE NOTHINGNESS crept over the once-majestic range. There was a haze in the air, floating on stillness he was almost afraid to disrupt. A large tomb of rocks surrounded the broken tree it pressed him against. Though his muscles were sore and aching, he kicked down the wall with little effort. Stepping out into the fog, Wesley spun around to take in his surroundings.

He did not know how long he remained hidden, but it was long enough to eradicate everything the East Eldur Mountains once portrayed. There was nothing left. No grass, tree, or semblance of what once was. A void, almost like a bite taken from a round of freshly baked bread, gave way to a sky that had never looked upon the land of Jöro before this day. Pieces of the mountain, as long and as tall as the trade ships that sailed up the Vandermarchen River, lay lifeless and still.

Looking up the slope, Wesley's heart thundered to life. "Amalya."

He propelled himself forward, ignoring all probable reasons for what he had borne witness to. The effort toward the top left him panting and breathless. As he came to the overhang, he fell to his knees, holding his arms out at his sides.

Gone. Everything tainted black. It was said, once a Draughtrìnd drew its fiery breath, all that it touched would die. This land would forever be cursed.

Tears fell from his face. He could not save Amalya. A deep, gaping hole collapsed his chest. What would he do? How could he go on without her? He did not care if she hated him, though she said that she loved him. If he knew she was happy, that was all that mattered. If she were alive, he would have recovered.

Small hands reached up to his face. He opened his eyes to see this child of the Draughtrìnd staring at him. He should have hated this child, hated how she came to be and why. But he could not. He had forgiven Amalya because he loved her. This child, with eyes kissed by Sól himself, held the final piece of her that he would ever hope to hold. He had promised he would love her and he would. He would love her and allow no hand to strike against her.

A deep-throated groan emanated from underneath the overhang. Wesley swallowed, clutching the child close to him as he reached for the edge. He peered down.

There he was—the Draughtrìnd who had ripped off his own arm, sat against the rock in human form. He held his stump with his right hand as dark blood pooled from him. His long, ashen hair was matted and his strong cheekbones rubbed raw. The sight of his copper-toned skin pulled Wesley's heart tight in his chest, winding it up like a spool of thread.

He was the one Amalya called Tristan. The one who bewitched her all those Setts ago.

Wesley's body pulsed with anger. Everything screamed inside him to drive his sword through the God of Old's heart. He was the reason for all of this. Everything that had befallen them was because of him.

It erased all semblance of pain from his body as blood surged with the currents of revenge. Clutching onto the child safely, Wesley jumped down from the ledge, his feet planted only a few feet from the fallen Draughtrìnd. He wasted little time and quickly brandished his sword, placing the tip against the betrayer's throat. It would be so easy to cut him down where he sat. He was injured, losing blood and not at full strength. His wounds may not kill him, but a swift blow to the heart would.

The Draughtrìnd did not blink nor flinch at Wesley's swift advance. His golden gaze was unwavering as he watched Wesley with poise and conviction. Though his hands were shaking with anticipation, Wesley held him there. Deep, labored breath escaped him as his heart pommeled viciously against his chest. Every bit of time that trickled by led Wesley ever closer to finishing the deed. But something was still there, pulling at him, begging him to understand the truth.

The apple of Tristan's throat rose and fell as he glanced at the blade. His hand moved away from cradling his missing arm, but Wesley pressed the blade deeper, breaking the skin of the already broken god.

"She is gone." His deep, calm voice rattled the cage of Wesley's heart.

"*Don't!*" Wesley squeezed his eyes closed, dampness seeping from between their lids. "You. You are to blame. My Amalya. You poisoned her mind with your magic and you *took her from me!*"

A seamless tilt brought Tristan's head away from his stone pillow. The tip of the blade ran down his neck, allowing his blood to drain along its edge. "Love. . . " He blinked. "It is blameless."

"No. She was *good*. You are *wrong!*"

"Was I wrong to fall in love?" Tristan's words stifled the rage building within Wesley. "A woman who did not see what man has painted me to be. She was not afraid to stand beside me, to touch me, to heal me, to look me in my eyes and accept everything Sól has granted me, and not just the vessel I am forced to dwell within."

Lacing his fingers around the blade, Tristan clutched it in his hand. "Tell me I am wrong, and I will aid you in ending my life."

ONIKA HOWDYN

For all he had taken from Wesley, Tristan deserved to die. It was only a small, fragile knot that kept Wesley from taking the irrevocable step. Could he really fault him for falling in love? He could see it as clear as a cloudless day. Not an ounce of deceit filled the Draughtrìnd's words. And Amalya. She had protected him, sought to find him, bore his child. . . his undeniably beautiful child.

How could Wesley fault them for following their hearts, even if it meant he would be forever broken? As much as he wanted to lay all the blame on another, it seemed to only fall on himself. If he never took her to the lake that day, none of this would have happened.

"What are you waiting for?" Tristan barked impatiently. "*Kill me if you must!*"

Wesley was thrown from his thoughts. "Hold your tongue!"

Tristan's weathered, broken face mustered a smile. "You are afraid."

"No." He placed the blade under Tristan's chin, fighting to keep his hands steady. "It could have been anyone—anyone else in the entire kingdom—and you chose her. She had a family. Children. She had a life."

Golden eyes remained unblinking. Tristan did not break nor falter, staring at a man who would be an enemy, but now, only a desperate soul searching for an answer. A reason Wesley was sure he would not receive. "I have fallen into the warmth and comfort of love's embrace. Just as you did. Now, we have both been left in the ashes of it. Alone. 'Til the end."

A coo escaped the tight cloth of Wesley's chest and Tristan's determined stare immediately softened, cast directly to the wriggling form Wesley kept barred from him. "She is alive."

Wesley dropped his sword, letting the iron hit the ground beside him. An immediate sense of security fell over him as he cradled the child in his arms, turning his body away.

Tristan watched him, his hand falling over the fresh blood dripping down his neck. His face grew stern, his gaze sharp. With his only hand, he reached out in front of him, mustering all his strength to appear unwavering. "Give her to me."

The child stirred, looking rather disgruntled, as if she sensed her true father was near. Wesley watched with caution. He could not deny a man his child, but he promised Amalya he would love her and care for her as his own.

Holding his breath, he carefully lowered the babe and slipped her into Tristan's arm. Cradling her close to his heaving body, Tristan seemed calm, despite the blood still pooling beneath him.

Wesley watched them. If he did not already know, he would think Tristan to be a mortal man. His face was that of any who had just become a father, happy and afraid. Magic may course through his veins, but, for a single glance, he was not the heartless monster of which the skald tales had sung. He could be like any other, if not more.

The child looked up at her father with awe, reaching for his face with fisted hands. A small arch of the Draughtrìnd's lip sent chills through Wesley's entire body.

Would he take her from him? Would he let her go? A promise eradicated by the child's true blood. Does that make it worth breaking?

As his mind raced with the notion, Tristan drew a deep breath. "I cannot take her," he said solemnly, his gaze lifting to appraise Wesley. "She will not be safe with me."

"She's your daughter."

"That is why I must do what is right."

Holding his breath, Wesley waited for the pain to wash away from Tristan's eyes. The thought of being parted from his child caved in the impenetrable demeanor of this God of Old. Choosing to give up a child—Wesley could not imagine how much it would break him if Elra or Arthur were taken from him.

With a careful step, Wesley approached, bending down to meet them. "I will keep her, but know I am not doing it for you."

The corners of Tristan's eyes pulsed. "Place your hand on her head."

Wesley did not question Tristan's motives as he placed his palm gently atop the child's crown. As his fingers touched her forehead, her fawny skin dissipated, dripping away to uncover smooth ivory. It slowly overtook her tiny form, spreading over her neck, chest, and down to the tips of her little toes. The dark strands of her hair lightened to an almost reddish hue. Wesley watched her stunning transformation in awe. The only parts of her untouched were her intense Sól-kissed eyes.

"What have you done?"

"I have cast a spell on her, one that cannot be broken unless by me. She will grow in your image, and her mother's." Tristan looked into Wesley's eyes. "She must never know what she is. Not yet."

Wesley moved his hand off the child's head. "I will not

dictate her life based on your agenda. But if she lives knowing none of this, I will be happier for it."

"The truth can only remain hidden for so long."

"I promised to protect her. And I will. Especially from *you and your kind!*"

The elevation of his voice forced the child's lips to purse. She scrunched her face, grimacing in discomfort, moving her hands and feet in tandem, as if denying the mask Tristan had forced her to wear.

Tristan drew his face down to her, keeping her safe in the cradle of his arm. Soft words Wesley could not understand floated from his lips on a whisper. The tune carried a calmness one could only compare to that of a warm hug, a feeling of safety and endless comfort. The child looked at her father as her arms settled. Melodies filled her eyes and slowly they closed as she nestled quietly against him. Soon she was in a deep sleep, the only signs of life being the steady rise and fall of her chest under the blanket.

"She is part of me, despite your adversity." Tristan leaned forward to present the child to Wesley. "She will sleep now until you arrive home. The guard will be here soon to pick up the pieces left behind and claim it as victory. You must leave."

"I will never make it unseen on foot."

A shrill whistle flew from Tristan's teeth.

Whipping his head around, Wesley heard the far-off whinny of a horse. Soon, Bard came running toward them, unscathed and ready to receive their weight.

"Bard." The horse nudged his shoulder as Wesley touched the steed's wide nose.

"He will get you home safely."

Wesley rubbed his neck. "What will happen to you?"

"I must go into hiding. Recover my strength if I am to see this come to fruition."

"What do you speak of?"

The question silenced any motion to respond from Tristan's eyes. They did nothing but watch each other in the few delicate moments left between them. Wesley could feel his gut twist. Perhaps he did not mean to speak it aloud, but now it was too late. The seed was planted, and it would only keep growing every moment Wesley looked upon the child he had willingly accepted as his own. To believe this small, innocent new life could shake the lands of Jöro was far-fetched. But nothing was certain. Especially now. Wesley knew that truth far too well.

Tristan laid a gentle kiss upon the child's forehead, leaving his lips to linger on her skin before pulling away. "Take her."

Not needing to be told again, Wesley gathered her up in his arms and strapped her to his chest. Tristan reached forth before she was completely settled, tucking something long and white into her blanket. She did not stir once from her restful sleep.

As he returned his sword to his belt, Wesley took Bard by the bridle and moved to mount him.

"Thank you."

Staring at the saddle, Wesley clenched his teeth as he turned to face the Draughtrìnd for the final time. "Do not think all is forgiven. I will find you again. And when I do, I will drive my sword through your heart and cut off your head."

Tristan smiled as a cough escaped him. "Until then."

Placing his foot in the stirrup, Wesley pulled himself into the saddle. He tapped the steed's sides gently, casting them into a gallop through the untainted countryside.

Revenge had been planted in his heart—though not because he promised to be the keeper of a Draudkin. He knew he would grow to love her, but he would never not see the eyes of Tristan staring back at him, a constant reminder of how he had failed the only woman he would ever love.

The destruction of the mountain would soon be behind them, and Wesley had no intention of ever looking back.

FORTY-EIGHT

"Sleep. Sleep. Dream as you awake. Rise. Rise. Sól will guide
your feet."
-A Draughtrìnd Lullaby

Wesley reached the fields of his home as Sól climbed in the bluish sky. A fire was dimly lit inside the home. He had seen the guard stampeding toward the broken mountain, laid bare and dying against the horizon. They did not look at him. It was as if he did not exist in their eyes. Tristan's promise of a safe return rang true.

Wesley dismounted and walked up to the door. He did not know what he would say. It would not be easy for him to admit Amalya's disloyalty to her father or anything regarding all that had happened. The child still slept soundly against him. No amount of disruption could wake her.

Before he laid a hand on the handle, Horace opened the door. He looked frantic and tired, eyes heavy and face drawn. "Yer back. What's happened? Where is she?"

Wesley stood in silence, not knowing what to say. Perhaps nothing needed to be said.

"Where is Amalya?"

The child stirred in her hiding place. She drew all attention away from the hanging question. Wesley gathered her up, pulling her free from the safety of her swaddle. "She is here." He pulled away her coverings, letting her open her eyes to take in the early light of Sól. "Here is all that is left of her."

Horace peered at the golden-eyed child of the Draughtrìnd. His mouth hung open, eyes flickering with both uncertainty and wonder.

Wesley took a deep breath, trying to swallow the knot of despair forming in his throat. "No one can know what she is."

Horace made no reply. He only looked at her, as if drawing his own conclusions from her presence.

"I promised Am—" Wesley stopped as Horace looked at him. "I promised I would keep her safe, but I need your help."

"You will have it." Horace raised his hands. "Give 'er to me."

Wesley relinquished her.

As soon as Horace held her in his arms, a shaken smile drew upon his troubled face. "She'll look just like 'er mother." A tear trickled down into the wrinkles of his cheek. He looked at Wesley. "What should we call 'er?"

Letting go of the intense pain building behind his eyes, Wesley sighed. "There is only one name left to give."

Drawing her close, Wesley pressed his nose against her little face. The child's tongue flicked from her mouth as a delightful coo escaped her curled lips.

"Amalya, my little Sól-fire. Welcome home."

2,201 SÓL SETT | FIRST SEASON

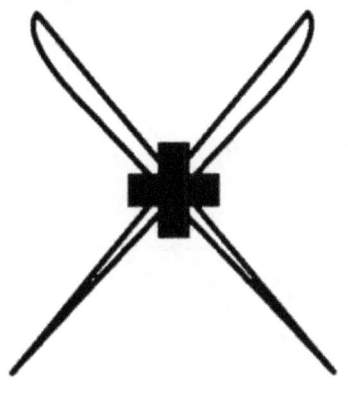

RÖKKUR

AWAKENING

"You've done it, *Amma*. I knew you could do it."

The familiar voice lifted Amalya's eyelids. Bright light streamed forth, causing her to squint and lift her arm for protection. The silhouette of a small person sat beside her and, as she adjusted to the blankness of where she lay, she realized who it was.

"You," she said as the boy with crimson eyes smiled at her.

He nodded excitedly and wrapped his arms around her neck. Amalya lost her breath as she felt his warm body pressed against her chest.

"You were so brave," he whispered in her ear.

"Indeed, she was," said another voice, this one smooth and carrying all the weight of authority without fear.

Amalya turned her gaze. A woman, her skin as dark as deep mahogany, wrapped in layers of white, stood a few arm lengths away. She was tall, with no hair escaping her crown.

Her round, painted eyes shone brilliantly as they smiled at Amalya with deep satisfaction.

The boy giggled as he drew away, standing to join the shrouded woman. She took his hand as they stood before Amalya. There was nothing in the foreground of them. Blank, empty land stretched on for an eternity. Even the ground she lay on was empty. It was as if she were lying amongst the clouds, completely consumed by them.

Amalya looked at herself. There was no blood, no sullied garb draping her body. Her hands traced the smooth curves of her head, void of her blonde tendrils. No burns or remnants of where she had come from were left behind. Her body was pure, as if she had never carried and never bled.

"What is this?" She looked back to her hosts. "Have I died?"

"Not quite." The woman glided toward her. The little boy followed, bouncing joyfully in his steps. "There is still something you must do." She bent down to meet Amalya's gaze. Her presence was astounding.

Suddenly Amalya was young again, stumbling upon a dragon injured in the lake. The brilliance and awe, her heart beating while her voice sang to comfort her love, it all came back anew.

"Who are you?" Amalya whispered.

With a steady hand, the woman found Amalya's cheek and cupped it gently. "It is time for you to go." Leaning toward her, the woman kissed Amalya's forehead, flooding her with the deep comforts that only magic could offer. "I will be watching over you."

As she drew away, Amalya's vision blurred. She reached

forward, unable to grasp anything but the frail, colorless air surrounding her.

"Remember me!" the boy's voice urged as her eyes fell back to darkness. "I love you, *Amma*! Go!"

Go.

Go.

"*Go.*"

With a desperate breath, Amalya arched up from where she lay. Wood and cloth blanketed the hard surface beneath her. Large barrels and bunches of colorful linens crowded her eyes. She was on a cart of some sort, sitting in the middle of a treeless plain. Men with painted faces and sand-swept skin scurried and yelled words she did not understand. She tried to move her body, but it was sluggish. She was wearing nothing, just a few cast linens draped over her lap and shoulders. She was clean, unblemished, just as she was when she first awoke to the beautiful crimson-eyed child.

The sky was cast into darkness. Not a single flicker of Sól sparked in Nótt's night. She could hear only the sounds of rustling echoing against the long chambers of stone that surrounded them.

"Go."

The voice came again, but it was not the voice of a man. Looking around desperately, her gaze fell upon four women standing before her. The one who spoke looked at her and all the demands of her person melted into a comforting smile. "Good evening, Mother of Stéinia."

"What?" Amalya's hands ran over her rounded head, smooth and unencumbered. "What. . . what happened?"

"My lady."

Amalya turned to see the pointed face and tear-shaped eyes of Primeveire.

"Primeveire." Amalya willed herself forward, wrapping the witch in a tight embrace. Primeveire's body went rigid before softening to accept her greeting. "You're alive."

"Yes. And so are you."

Amalya pulled away as small trails of tears escaped down her face. "I never meant for you to be discovered. Please, can you ever forgive me for what I have done?"

Primeveire pulled forth a simple blue dress, fixing it around Amalya's shoulders. "You have done nothing that swayed me from my destiny. Or your own."

Amalya slipped her arms through the sleeves as Primeveire pressed the buttons into the holes to adorn her slender frame. As she fitted the last of them, Amalya raised her chin, looking toward the woman who first greeted her.

She was tall, taller than any woman Amalya had ever seen. Her hair was woven like thick, gnarled branches. Flowers and leaves adorned her crown and grew into her olive skin. Her eyes shone a brilliant green, as if she had stolen the colors of the trees on the cusp of Dag Light.

The woman watched them in quiet satisfaction before stepping forward and lowering her chin. "My name is Teru." She spoke calmly. "Mother to the Forest of Andi."

A witch mother. Amalya had heard many skald tales of witch mothers, those deemed the most precious and powerful wielders of magic. She had thought none remained.

A man approached from the wagon, yelling. Teru

quickly glared at him, matching whatever language he spoke. The man was silenced, glancing at Amalya before stepping out of view.

"You must go with these men. They will take you to Alnaar."

"What? No." Amalya straightened, still unsure if she could stand.

Alnaar was the land beyond the North Eldur Mountains, an endless and desolate sea of golden sand that bred hungry warlords and death. Wicked winds carried their scent through the veins of the mountains, hindering any who thought to breach them.

"I cannot leave. I must find my daughter and Wesley. Tristan—I must know that they are safe."

"You must leave Jöro until it is time for you to return."

"No! I will not. You cannot make me—"

"*Módir Stéinia.*" Teru approached her, grasping her hands as she stared at Amalya with blazing eyes. "If you do not leave, they will die. Wesley. Tristan. Your children. They will all die."

The truth of her words sank into Amalya's skin. She did not know how she survived the dragon fire or how she ended up in the back of a cart surrounded by painted men and witches. She recalled her dream of the child and shrouded woman, who had said there was something she must do. Perhaps this Mother of Andí knew what that something was.

"Please, my lady," Primeveire intoned. "You must hear her. Mother Teru will not lead you astray."

Licking her lips, Amalya inhaled deeply, ready to confess what her heart could not interpret. "I saw a woman.

Skin as dark as Nótt's scales. Shrouded in white. Her eyes were not one hue, but many."

Teru's face softened. "Marin, Mother of All. She has blessed you with the child who has come from you. If you trust her, then you know what I say is true."

Swallowing the last tastes of doubt, Amalya nodded. "Then I will go."

Teru grinned and squeezed her arm. "Good. These men will take you and not taint you. You are to be a gift for the Great Unkulu. He will grant you safe passage across the Safír Sea. There, you will find refuge until it is time for you to return to Jöro."

"How will I know when to return?" Amalya asked.

"When your name is whispered in the deepest corners of the land and the Draudkin are untethered. Then you will know it is time."

There were so many questions she wished to ask, though she knew time was not meant to hold the answers. "Who is this Unkulu?"

The men grew silent at the second mention of the name. They stood together, watching the women intently as they waited for Teru's response. She did nothing but draw herself away, sliding her hand from Amalya's.

"He is the Lost Son. One of the Draudkin. He must return to Jöro. Only your presence will sway him to do so."

Amalya tried to concentrate on this title, but nothing could be pulled from the countless tales she had been told. The name was unfamiliar to her, but perhaps not unfamiliar to the Draughtrìnd. This must be what Marin had meant for her. To find this Lost Son and return him to Jöro. "What will I say to him?"

"What your heart tells you." Teru looked at the men and commanded them in their tongue before looking back at Amalya. "May Marin keep you, Mother of Stéinia."

"Goodbye, my lady." Primeveire laid a gentle kiss on Amalya's cheek. "Your children. They will be safe. I will watch over them from the shadows."

"And Mira? Her family, they—"

"They will be safe. You have my word."

Amalya smiled and drew her into one last embrace. "Thank you."

A sharp whip echoed through the crisp night air as the cart lurched forward, breaking the bond between them. Amalya let Primeveire slip away, watching the witches until they, too, disappeared from sight.

She sat alone, bringing the blanket around her shoulders to combat the cold. One man came down to her, offering her a bowl of steaming liquid. Amalya took it graciously. The fresh smell of mushrooms and herbs filled her lungs and made her stomach rumble. Bringing it to her mouth, she took a savory sip of its warm contents. The taste filled her belly and warmed her from within.

Her mind wandered to what had become of her family. Wesley—how she hoped he survived, and that Friora was safe. Tristan—she could still sense his pulse, faint as it was. He had somehow bested Fane, but at what cost? One day she would see them again, but not today.

Alnaar was her destination now and countless other lands thereafter. This Lost Son, Unkulu, whoever he was, she would find him. To keep her children safe. Elra, Arthur, and Friora. To keep Tristan and Wesley safe. If this was what she must do, then she would.

She had eluded death so they could live.

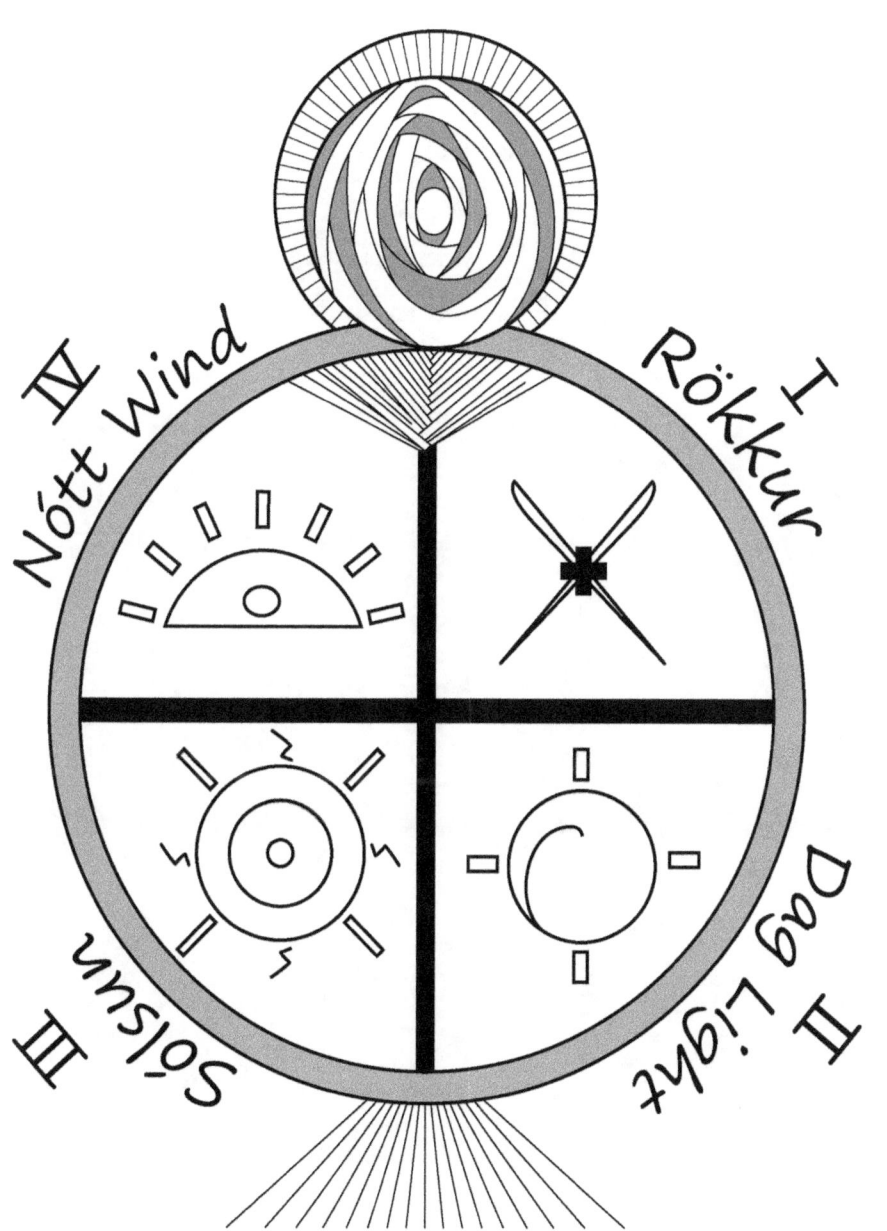

I Rökkur

II Dag Light

III Sólsun

IV Nótt Wind

NAMES & TERMS

This is a list of names, terms and pronunciations in alphabetical order that appear in the novel.

Character Names

Aethelwulf (*A-TH-EL-WOLF*) - The mad king, during the time of The Dragon Wars set over 100 years before this novel takes place

Amalya (*A-MAL-YAH*) - The main character

Arthur (*AR-THER*) - Amalya and Wesley's son

Baldir (*BALD-EER*) - A guardsman referenced by Mira

Bard (*BAR-D*) - Amalya's horse

Earfinn (*AIR-FIN*) - The general who slayed Athelwulf during The Dragon Wars

Elra (*EL-RA*) - Amalya and Wesley's daughter

Fane (*F-AIN*) - Antagonist, A dragon lord of Jöro

Great Unkulu (*OO-N-COO-LOU*) - The Lost Son, a Draudkin

Horace (*HOR-AS*) - Amalya's father

Ivy (*I-V*) - Mira's sister

Laird (*L-AIR-D*) - Blacksmith, Mira's husband

Lorrigan (*LOR-I-GAN*) - Blacksmith

Marin (*MARE-IN*) - Peace maker during the Dragon Wars

Mira (*MEER-A*) - Amalya's best friend

Polliann (*POLL-E-ANN*) - Mira and Laird's daughter

Primeveire (*PRIM-A-VERE*) - A witch, Mira's friend

Teru (*TE-ROO*) - Witch mother to the Forest of Andí

Tristan (*TR-IS-TAN*) - Farmhand, A dragon lord of Jöro

Ulfrick (*UL-FRICK*) - The king, during the time of this novel

Wesley (*WES-LEE*) - Amalya's husband

Worldly Names & Places

Adgerdaleysi (AD-GER-DA-LACE-EE) - a term to represent Amalya

Alnaar (ALL-NAAR) - a desert kingdom, north of Jöro

Andí (AN-DEE) - a vast forest that spans across the lands of Jöro

Berge (BUR-GE) - a northwest city of Jöro

Dag / Light - The light dragon, the second season, of sun

Dragon Guard - army of the king, to hunt down dragons and their followers

Draudkin (DRAW-D-KIN) - a child born of dragon and man

Draughtrìnd (DRAW-T-RIN-D) - the dragon race of Jöro, guardians of the land

East Eldur Mountains (EL-DOOR) - the eastern stretch of the vast mountain range

Enda (END-AH) - a city that fell during the Great Dragon Wars

Fortress of Stéinia (ST-EN-E-AH) - the home of the Draughtrìnd lord of Steinia

God of Old - a term to represent the Draughtrìnd

Great Dragon Wars - a period of time when war waged between King Athelwulf and the Draughtrìnd

Holdedur Prophecy (HOL-DE-DOOR) - a prophecy laid down during the Dragon Wars

Honey Milk - A delicious, sweet drink

Hugafar (WHO-GA-FAR) - the realm of dreams

Jar - a northeast city of Jöro

Jöro (JO-ROW) - The kingdom the story resides

Mare (M-AIR) - a western coast city of Jöro

Nótt / Wind (NOT) - the night dragon, the fourth season, of snow

Rau (RA-OW) - a south eastern city by the sea and river, the setting of the novel

Rökkur (ROW-KER) - the first season, of life

Safír Sea (SA-FEAR) - A sea that surrounds the peninsula of Jöro

Sea of Sands - a term to represent Alnaar

Skarpur's Teeth (SCAR-PURR) - a horseshoe mountain range to the west

Skuldabréf (SKOOL-DE-BREF) - a sacred ritual between a woman and Draughtrìnd

Sól / Sett - creator deity, the passing of the seasons

Sólsun - the third season, of decay

Southern Plains - a southernmost plains of Jöro where Enda resided

Stéinia / Keep (ST-EN-EE-AH) - The eastern-most province of the Draughtrìnd, an inn in the fishing district of Rau

Vandermarchen River - a river that runs through the city of Rau to the Safír Sea

Willow's Lake - a lake northwest of Amalya's family farm

ACKNOWLEDGMENTS

It has been a long road. This novel wasn't a one and done kind of book. It took over twelve years for it to become what it is today. Twelve years of scrapping draft after draft. Of shelving for years at a time without so much as a second glance.

It has taken so many life experiences for it to cross the threshold into publication. And no one has been there, more for me during those long years, than my smizmar.

It was he who gave me the coffee table book on dragons that inspired the idea for this novel, back when we were dating in college. He who never told me that my dreams of being an author weren't worth it. That I should keep writing. That I should try new things, even when it scared me to get started.

As much as he could, he has supported me through thick and thin, helping me with the language and world-building. Letting me talk his ear off about the story and how I could move it forward.

There would be no Jöro without him. So thank you, hun. For all the years of ups and downs. For sharing a life with me that would help the pages unfold.

Until our next adventure

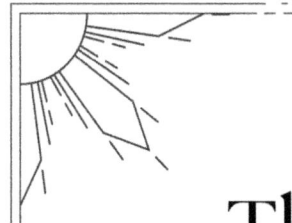

Thank You

to all our backers on Kickstarter for making this
book a reality:

Nicholas Paynter
Nikki T
Bela Flores
David DeHaan
Ashley Hagood
Glori Medina
Tirzah Veale
Katie Judy
Gorilla Games
McKenna Hubbard
Samantha Newberry
Hayden Moore
Erin
Amanda Sloothaak
Arashi (Danny Ride)
JD Estrada

Billye Herndon
Heidi Hacsi
Rosum
Joey Wojtowicz
EJB
Ashley Binder
Bree Moore
Madge Watson
Jasmine C
Neil Bullock
Nicole Birk
Sarolta
Kacey Thiele
Shiloh I Reeves
Tara Rolstad
Amanda

May Magin Protect You & Keep You

ABOUT THE AUTHOR

Onika Howdyn has been a weaver of tales in the deepest realms of Jöro for a decade or more. Besides being an author, she is a wifey, a mother of two, and a backyard chicken enthusiast.

Growing up, she adored films with a hint of darkness such as *The Dark Crystal*, *Watership Down*, and *The Last Unicorn*.

This is her first fantasy novel.

instagram.com/oahowdyn

goodreads.com/onika-howdyn

threads.net/@oahowdyn

pinterest.com/oahowdyn